CW01509109

DUKE WITH A SECRET

WICKED DUKES SOCIETY

BOOK THREE

SCARLETT SCOTT

Happily Ever After Books

Duke with a Secret

Wicked Dukes Society Book 3

All rights reserved.

Copyright © 2025 by Scarlett Scott™

Published by Happily Ever After Books, LLC

Edited by Grace Bradley and Lisa Hollett, Silently Correcting Your Grammar

Cover Design by Wicked Smart Designs

This book or any portion thereof may not be reproduced or used in any manner whatsoever without the express written permission of the publisher except for the use of brief quotations in a book review.

The unauthorized reproduction or distribution of this copyrighted work is illegal. No part of this book may be scanned, uploaded, or distributed via the Internet or any other means, electronic or print, without the publisher's permission. Criminal copyright infringement, including infringement without monetary gain, is punishable by law.

This book is a work of fiction and any resemblance to persons, living or dead, or places, events, or locales, is purely coincidental. The characters are productions of the author's imagination and used fictitiously.

Scarlett Scott™ is a registered trademark of Happily Ever After Books, LLC.

For more information, contact author Scarlett Scott™.

https://scarlettscottauthor.com/

DUKE WITH A SECRET

Rhys Northwick, Duke of Whitby, has unabashedly devoted himself to a life of debauchery and hedonism. With his friends falling prey to the despicable institution of marriage, the responsibility of hosting the sinful Wicked Dukes Society house parties has fallen largely on his shoulders. Rhys doesn't mind. He'll happily seduce bored widows and wives out of their drawers any day. Until an encounter with a tempting divorcée leaves him longing for the only woman in London who is immune to his rakish charms…

After a scandalous divorce from a coldhearted earl, Lady Miranda Lenox is finally free to pursue her dreams of operating a school of cookery. If she wants to continue attracting a polite clientele, however, Miranda needs her reputation to remain above reproach. What she doesn't need is a rakish duke determined to lure her into further disgrace.

But Rhys will stop at nothing to get what he wants—the delicious Miranda in his bed. He's so assured of his success that he offers her a wager. If she can resist his seduction for the duration of the next house party he's hosting, he will abandon his pursuit of her. But if she succumbs, she'll be his mistress in secret for a month.

It's the perfect bargain. Except that once Rhys wins, he realizes one month with Miranda will never be enough. Nothing less than forever will do. But Miranda refuses to marry again, even as each clandestine encounter with Rhys leaves her one perilous step closer to ruin.

For my Aunt Julia, again. Words are insufficient to describe all you mean to me. I hope you know how very loved you are.

CHAPTER 1

There was only one thing Rhys Northwick, Duke of Whitby, enjoyed more than a luscious pair of naked, bountiful bubbies and a wet, inviting cunny.

And that was why his carriage was presently parked outside a Marylebone school of cookery. And also why he was peering out the Venetian blinds like a house cracksman watching a street of homes to decide where it would be most opportune to strike first and where he might find the most silver.

Rhys wasn't planning to rob the cookery school, of course. Rather, he was planning to cozen its owner into allowing him to hire a student for the house party he would be hosting in a week's time.

Ordinarily, he wouldn't give a damn about something as bourgeois and feminine as a school of cookery. Hell, he wouldn't even be awake at this ungodly hour, for he was firmly of the opinion that mornings were either for fucking or for sleeping and sometimes both, but absolutely never for anything as taxing as being awake and—ye gods—*fully clothed* at half past eight.

His valet had been astonished and confused. But Lavenue had dutifully shaved and dressed him, and now Rhys was awaiting the blasted owner of the cookery school who had so maddeningly refused his request. Not just once, but thrice.

"Bloody fool," Rhys muttered, reaching into his waistcoat and extracting his pocket watch to consult the time.

He wasn't certain of whom he spoke—himself or the cookery school's stubborn owner. The bastard hadn't even possessed the courtesy to respond to Rhys's perfectly polite and more-than-generous request himself. Instead, he'd had a secretary dash off one insulting refusal after the next. No matter how hard Rhys tried to persuade the fellow and regardless of how much money he offered, a meeting between the school's owner and the Duke of Whitby would not occur. *On account of His Grace's reputation*, the final missive had so damningly said.

Rhys had ripped that particular epistle in two, and then he had thrown both halves into the fire, delighting in watching them catch flame and curl into gray ash. He had also decided that enough was enough. The arrogant arse would see him today. And he would also give Rhys exactly what he wanted.

Or else.

A carriage drew up to the cookery school, coming to a halt before Rhys's equipage. Hastily, he stuffed his pocket watch back into his waistcoat. Drumming his fingers on his thigh, he waited. Watched. Yesterday, he had arrived in the afternoon—at a decent time—only to be turned away because the owner had left for the day. He had demanded to know from the stammering lackey who had attended him just when the owner deigned to arrive each morning. Nine o'clock, he had been told.

He had been here for one quarter hour already. Biding his

time. And now, his patience was about to pay him dividends. He would not give up until he had what he wanted.

The carriage door swung open. Rhys held his breath and watched as the owner of the cookery school emerged. A pair of dainty, embroidered boots first, a flash of stockings, and then the hems of a pale-gray day gown, a wrap draped over small shoulders, a bonnet atop her head.

What was this? An early student? He knew well enough that classes did not begin until ten o'clock. What was the woman doing here now?

Realization descended.

Surely, the owner of the school of cookery couldn't be a woman.

Her profile was proud, head held high as she descended from her carriage. She cast a frowning look in the direction of his conveyance before she hastily walked up the front steps with the self-assured posture of a woman who knew her place in the world. And despite himself, he was intrigued.

Perhaps the owner *could* be a woman. A vexing, maddening woman who was about to be stunningly routed in this little war of theirs.

He slid off the Moroccan leather squabs and flung open his carriage door, leaping to the pavements and ignoring the steps. She was almost inside now, and he wasn't about to let her escape him.

"Madam," he called.

She stopped, glancing over her shoulder, too far away for him to see the details of her countenance. Her hair was a sleek ebony, confined at her nape beneath her millinery. From here, she looked vaguely familiar to him, but then he had met—and bedded—more than his fair share of women. It wasn't impossible that their paths had crossed somewhere along the way.

She cocked her head at him, rather in the fashion of a curious bird. "Sir?"

He approached her, his long-limbed strides closing the distance between them easily. She was lovely, he realized, taking her in: high, elegant cheekbones, dark brows arched over eyes that were a vibrant emerald, full lips that were made to be kissed, a retroussé nose, and a stubborn chin. But he hadn't come here to admire her.

"Allow me to introduce myself," he offered. "I am the Duke of Whitby."

Her eyes widened, those sensuous lips parting before she gave her head a vehement shake. "No."

With that one, lone word, she spun about and hastened into the building.

What the devil? He watched her skirts bustling away for a moment before gathering his wits and following in her wake. Gray silk disappeared inside the door in the second before it slammed closed.

Well, *almost* closed because Rhys had braced his forearm against it and wedged his boot over the threshold just in time.

"You are not welcome here," she told him frostily, pushing on the door as if she truly believed she possessed the strength to overwhelm him and snap it closed.

He hated to tell her, but she didn't. He would play along for now, however.

"Madam," he tried politely, "I insist you let me in. I need to speak with the owner of this establishment."

"You are looking at her," she snapped, "and I've already told you that my school of cookery will have nothing to do with a man of your reputation. Now, please leave."

Tenacious wench.

He pushed against the door, overpowering her with ease, and stepped inside, closing it at his back. "There we are.

4

This is a much better way to conduct business, do you not agree?"

Her lips thinned to a firm, grim line that made him think about kissing them to restore their fullness. "You cannot be here."

Rhys grinned, immensely entertained by her icy disdain. "And yet, here I am."

Footsteps sounded then, scurrying into the entry. A bespectacled woman with white hair surged into view. "My lady, forgive me. I sent Mr. Lucas for more ice, or he would have been at the door."

My lady? The luscious termagant before him grew more intriguing by the moment. This bit of information could certainly be used to his advantage.

"Don't fret, Mrs. Kirkeland," his reluctant hostess told the older woman. "You may return to your duties. I shall see to my guest."

"Of course, my lady." The woman bobbed, her dark skirts fluttering, before she disappeared again.

He turned back to the beautiful woman who was glaring at him as if he had just flung horse dung all over her entryway.

"Please leave, Your Grace," she said sternly.

"After you give me an audience, I'll do as you like," he said reasonably.

Rationally.

Because he had come here to offer the silly woman a fortune. And she was attempting to toss him out on his ear.

"I have already informed you that I have no wish for an association between yourself and my cookery school," she said primly.

"And I have a thousand pounds that says you will change your mind after you hear what I have to say," he countered.

She stared at him, her mouth still compressed, unsmiling

and unspeaking. Until finally, she relented, nodding with the regal air of a queen. "Very well. Follow me, Your Grace."

Without waiting for his response, she turned and swept from the entryway in a glide of dove-gray skirts. He prowled after her, a predator intent upon his prey. It was a testament to her culinary prowess that he was here, but he wouldn't allow her the upper hand. Not for a second.

Even if her prowess was the stuff of legends. He knew because he'd tasted it.

He had made the startling discovery purely by coincidence. A fortnight ago, he had been to a small, private dinner gathering where his hostess had proudly served a confection called *cornets à la crème* for dessert. The apple and ginger cream ice had been a decadent delight when paired with a crunchy cornet decorated with chopped pistachios and royal icing. He'd never had anything quite like it, and neither had the rest of his fellow guests.

Rhys had politely inquired after the origin of the course, unique in addition to being delicious. The dish was a novelty that he had instantly known would be perfect for the indecent house party he would be hosting soon. His hostess had been annoyingly tight-lipped about the cornets until she had finally admitted their origin: a cookery school in Marylebone.

Finding the school had been easy. Finding its elusive owner had not. Time was running low, however, and so was Rhys's patience. He was bloody well going to have the *cornets à la crème*, and she was going to have to accept it.

Because once the Duke of Whitby settled his mind on something he wanted, he didn't stop until it was his.

LADY MIRANDA LENOX, formerly the Countess of Ammondale, present owner of the Lenox School of Cookery, had made a great many mistakes in her life. But she had risen from the ashes of her failed marriage, and she was determined not to make another. Which was why she intended to chase the scandalous Duke of Whitby from her precious school by any means, fair or foul.

There was the rather unfortunate matter of the thousand pounds he had dangled before her, a tidy sum she could put to excellent use if it were hers. But she would not allow monetary concerns to sway her. She would instead permit him to have the audience with her he had been so set upon having. And then when he had concluded his arrogant demand, she would tell him, unflinchingly, no.

No, no, no. Never. Absolutely not.

That must be her answer for this man. For *all* men. For the rest of her life.

She skirted the small, chipped desk she had commandeered for her personal use in her office—a place of private magic and infinite rejoicing, a space that was finally *hers* alone—and forced her countenance to remain serene as she faced the Duke of Whitby.

He was infernally handsome. Golden-haired, with an angular jaw and high cheekbones, a strong blade of a nose and a divot in his chin. He had lips that were too full for a man, tipped with a slight hint of smugness, as if he were infinitely entertained by the plebians surrounding him or perhaps privy to some deliciously witty secret. His shoulders were broad, his waist lean, and he was taller than Miranda, which was impressive since she had forever mourned her unladylike height.

But she mustn't spend too much time inspecting him. She needed to entertain his whims and then send him on his way, never to return and plague her with his scandalous presence.

Miranda clasped her hands at her waist and refused to sit, not wanting him to make himself comfortable for this interview. "Please, Your Grace. Relay whatever message you are intent upon delivering."

His gaze was a striking, dark shade of blue that reminded her of a summer sky after a storm had passed, and it was settled upon her now, inspecting her in a way that felt far too familiar.

"You are a lady," he said, ignoring her request.

Not truly. She had surrendered her titles, her marriage, and most of her respectability. All for the chance to escape Ammondale and begin anew.

"I am the owner of this establishment," she said primly instead of directly answering the unspoken question in his observation.

"And a lady," he pressed. "The servant woman in the entry called you my lady just now."

She exhaled, holding his stare. "Does it matter?"

"Hmm." He stroked his jaw with ungloved fingers, drawing her attention to how nicely formed his hands were. Masculine, large, long-fingered. They weren't the pale, thin, elegant fingers of so many gentlemen in her old life. "I suspect it does. I know of no other ladies in my acquaintance who are owners of cookery schools."

Why was there somehow an implication of intimacy in his words?

She clenched her jaw. "We are not acquainted, Your Grace."

"Not well acquainted," he said agreeably, his lips turning farther upward, into a sinful smile. "I'm happy to rectify that problem, however."

His silken words were like a caress.

She forced herself to think of something dreadful. A snake, slithering around her ankles, poised to strike and end her life. There. That banished the unwanted, peculiar feeling rising within her.

"I, however, am not, Your Grace," she informed him coolly. "Please, tell me what it is you have come here for, and I will do my best to answer."

His regard warmed considerably, his smile deepening, and good heavens, why was her office so dratted overheated? Her palms were sweating. The look he gave her was nothing short of smoldering, a blatant invitation.

"I begin to think I came here for more than I realized, madam," he said, arching a brow. "Please, won't you have a seat? It isn't done for a gentleman to sit in the presence of a lady, but I do so hate to conduct a private conversation whilst standing."

She didn't mistake the sensual intent in his deep, pleasant voice. He was a wickedly handsome man, and his reputation preceded him. The Duke of Whitby was a voluptuary. But of course he was. One need only take one look at him to know he could charm a lady out of her petticoats with nothing more than a promise and a coaxing smile.

Fortunately, she was immune to his charms.

Snake, she thought. *Hissing, vile snake. Venomous, poisonous, dangerous serpent.*

"I would prefer to stand," she told him, forcing a tight smile in an effort to show him just how unaffected she was by his masculine beauty and rakish wiles.

He shrugged with an elegant ease, his gaze still burning into hers. "As you wish. But before we continue, perhaps you would deign to tell me your name, lovely."

He had called her lovely.

How achingly embarrassing it was that his compliment— meaningless and likely the same he had given to many before her—should make her feel such a deep and abiding sense of longing. Should bring warmth to her cheeks and a tingle in her belly, as if a spark had settled there just waiting to burst into flame.

"You may address me as Miss Lenox," she said frostily, banishing those unworthy thoughts and feelings.

"Miss Lenox," he repeated, the *l* in her surname lingering on his tongue as if it were something to be savored. "If you are a mere miss, why did your servant address you as *my lady?*"

Oh, why was he here, prying into her affairs, taking all the air from the room, making her drown in his eyes?

"I hardly think the vagaries of the proprietress of a cookery school should so concern you," she pointed out tartly. "Now, kindly tell me what it is you require so that I may attend to the many matters awaiting me today."

He chuckled, as if her daring amused him. "Prickly as a rosebush. How delightful."

She had come too far to become a duke's source of diversion.

Miranda stiffened her spine. "If you have come with no purpose other than to make light of me, you may go, Your Grace."

"Ah, and now she dismisses me." He caught his lower lip between irritatingly even white teeth, considering her with his head cocked to the side. "You are an intriguing woman, Miss Lenox. My lady. Do you know what occurs to me? I seem to recall some recent scandal broth concerning a Lady Miranda Lenox, formerly the Countess of Ammondale. But surely the prim Miss Lenox of this cookery school and the Fallen Countess couldn't be the same. Could they?"

The Fallen Countess was what the newspapers had begun calling her during her humiliatingly public divorce from the earl. The sobriquet still stung.

"Please leave, Your Grace," she urged, moving around the

desk to escape his unsettling presence, the room itself, and the specter of her past.

"Forgive me," he said instantly, his expression sobering. "I meant no insult."

"Then you should not have repeated idle gossip."

"It was badly done of me."

"Yes," she agreed through clenched teeth. "It was."

Bearing the mockery and scorn she had faced had been worthwhile in her estimation. Anything to escape her unhappy union. But that didn't mean the wagging tongues, the caricatures, the salacious tales bandied about, didn't hurt. If her heart had been sufficiently hardened to weather such storms, she wouldn't have needed to leave Ammondale in the first place.

Whitby startled her by closing the gap between them and taking one of her hands in his. The contact of his bare skin on hers sent a jolt of awareness through her she did not like. The undeniable knowledge hit her that this man was far more dangerous to her than any snake could ever be.

She was attracted to him. Deeply drawn to him in a way she'd never experienced before. And it alarmed her. Because if there was ever a time in her life when she couldn't afford to make a mistake, it was now.

She tugged at her hand, but he refused to relinquish his grip, and before she knew what he was about, his touch slid to her wrist. Gently but firmly encircling it with his fingers, he startled her by jerking her open hand against his cheek, making her slap him.

She gasped, not just at the sudden motion, but the warmth of his skin, stubbled with the texture of golden whiskers that caught the light and glinted. He hadn't shaved this morning. Somehow that intimate knowledge didn't belong to her, and yet she relished it anyway.

"There," he said, eyes dancing with merriment. "I earned that slap. Please consider it my most sincere apology."

Miranda couldn't find her voice. She was shocked, and not just from the blow he'd forced her to give him, but because of the way it had felt to touch his face. Because now she was thinking about other things she ought not. Such as what it would feel like to have his lips on hers. And because he was still holding her wrist in the same masterful grasp.

She could escape his hold and she knew it, but some foolish part of her liked the way his long fingers wrapped around the delicate bones of her wrist. Liked his hold on her, even in this small way.

"Two thousand pounds," he said into the silence as he stroked the underside of her wrist with his thumb, tracing over her veins as if they would reveal all her secrets to him.

She blinked, confused. "I don't understand."

His touch ventured higher, finding the base of her palm. "I am doubling my initial offer to you. I'll give you two thousand pounds."

"For heaven's sake, Your Grace, why would you pay me two thousand pounds?" Her voice was irritatingly breathless, and her wits were vexingly scattered, her heart thumping madly at his nearness and touch both.

"I am hosting a country house party in Hertfordshire in a week," he explained. "I wish to have your *cornets à la crème* there, along with any other confections you find suitable. The house party lasts a sennight. After its conclusion, you are free to return to London two thousand pounds wealthier."

This was not what she had expected. And Miranda had to admit that it was difficult indeed to concentrate when his thumb was gently, patiently stroking her palm as if he had all the time in the world to touch her.

"How do you know about my *cornets à la crème?*" she asked, frowning at him.

She had been perfecting the cornets, to be accompanied by cream ice, for weeks now, and although she had allowed several members of her small, inner circle to try them and even serve them at a dinner party, she had yet to settle upon a recipe to include in the book of cookery she was assembling. Few people, in other words, knew of their existence.

"A hostess served them to me," he explained, his voice low and melodious, almost as if he were casting a spell over her. "They were the most delicious morsel I've ever had on my tongue, and I can assure you that I've had many wonderful delights on my tongue over the years."

Sinful. There was something sinful about the way he said that. She should be horrified, and yet Miranda couldn't summon even a modicum of outrage.

"You wish me to provide your house party guests with desserts," she repeated, trying to keep her wits about her.

It was deuced difficult when he was looking at her as he was, keeping her pinned in his dark-blue stare. When he was saying such wicked things.

"Yes." He smiled again, the corners of his eyes crinkling in a way she found alarmingly attractive. "Your decadent desserts in exchange for two thousand pounds."

Her heart pounded faster. Such a feat could be accomplished with ease, and two thousand pounds could solve a host of problems currently facing her. Miranda was tempted.

"I can send two of my most promising students to your house party," she suggested.

His wandering thumb had found the center of her palm now, and he lingered there, asserting just enough delicate pressure to give her a gentle massage. "That won't do, I'm afraid."

"Why not?" Belatedly, she pulled her hand from his grasp.

"Because I want you, Miss Lenox," he said, his smile fading. "No replacements shall be suitable."

I want you.

Her stomach flipped.

Her response was instant. "No."

But the Duke of Whitby simply shook his golden head slowly, unperturbed by her refusal. "Don't give me your answer now, lovely. Think upon it. I'll return in a day or two for your response."

He sketched an elegant bow and, without awaiting her reply, took his leave from her office.

She gaped at his retreating form, utterly stunned. The Duke of Whitby was a madman. A beautiful one, but a madman, nonetheless. And whenever he returned to her school of cookery, her answer would remain unchanged.

CHAPTER 2

"*D*amn it all," Rhys grumbled to himself as he soaked in his bath.

Ordinarily, the tub was a place of relaxation. If he was submerged in hot water, he was a happy man. He could easily spend an hour or more within, contemplating life with a glass of good French wine. Or fucking.

Tubs were *made* for fucking.

But presently, his wine remained untouched, and the gorgeous woman awaiting him in the adjoining chamber held precious little interest to him. Because he was a man possessed.

Why couldn't the owner of the bloody Lenox School of Cookery have been a disagreeable, bald old chap with stains on his shirt? Or a crone with a wart-speckled face and a mustache? It would have made Rhys's life so much easier.

But no.

She had to be exquisite. It was a sin her raven hair had been swept into an unforgiving knot at her nape. A woman as lushly beautiful as Lady Miranda Lenox—or Miss Lenox, as she oddly preferred to be styled—should always wear her long locks cascading down her back. Preferably naked. Naturally, she'd been anything but, demurely covered in her unadorned gray gown, buttoned up to her creamy throat. But Rhys had a discerning eye, and there was no denying the lush, full breasts and curved waist hiding beneath her silk.

The Fallen Countess who'd had an affair with the Marquess of Waring, leading to a scandalous divorce that had been the talk of Town for some time, no longer appeared to be particularly wicked or indecent. Instead, she was hiding herself away in a cookery school, of all places, creating confections that tasted as if they had been ripped from the heavens themselves. And masquerading as a lowly miss.

Mystery surrounded Miranda Lenox, and Rhys couldn't deny he found it intriguing. But he was also drawn to her. Her skin had been soft and smooth and warm. She smelled of roses and orange blossoms, and he had no doubt that the woman herself was every bit as decadent and delicious as one of her culinary creations.

Now he didn't just want those blasted coronets of hers. No, he wanted *her*.

He wanted her naked and beneath him. Moaning and riding him. He wanted her in this tub, bare-breasted, her hard nipples above the water so he could see if they matched her berry-pink lips before he sucked them. He wanted the water sloshing around them as he fucked her.

Rhys groaned and allowed his eyes to close as his head fell back against the rim of the tub, the scene he had been inventing in his mind ever since their morning meeting returning. His cock, already hard, stirred and lengthened beneath the warm water. He grasped himself at the base then stroked firmly, pretending it was her dainty hand on his prick instead of his own.

Speaking of scandalous, he was almost ready to come. He'd scarcely even touched himself, and yet the memory of

Miranda Lenox's fluttering pulse and wide eyes, the heat of her skin burning into him, was enough. His hand moved faster, his hips undulating in mindless thrusts as he imagined her hot pussy gliding down on his cock, tightening and welcoming him deep. As he imagined suckling her breasts and licking those pretty nipples and nibbling on her shoulders, threading his fingers through her long, dark hair and filling her with his spend.

If he breathed deeply enough, he could almost discern her scent. His breaths were faster now, ragged. His need was boiling, an ache deep in his ballocks telling him he was close. But then the scent grew stronger, and it wasn't his imagination, but it was all wrong. It was roses and amber-gris instead of orange blossom, and a throaty chuckle cut through the silence as a feminine hand closed over his beneath the water.

Rhys's eyes shot open, his head jerking up. The naked woman smiling down at him with sensual promise wasn't Miranda Lenox. She wasn't a black-haired beauty, but an ethereal blonde whose long curls had been draped artfully over her full breasts so that only her nipples peeked through.

"Beatrice," he said, trying to keep the disappointment from his voice.

The scene in his mind was effectively broken, like a fine piece of Sèvres hurled from the top of a staircase to smash below.

"Why are you in this tub alone, handling your big, delicious cock, when I am here to do it for you?" she asked, pouting as she caressed his hand.

The Marchioness of Levenwood had been his lover for the past few weeks. She was insatiable and pretty and bored of her elderly husband. Rhys was also insatiable and pretty and bored of his previous lover. The arrangement had suited them both. But his cock was wilting by the moment, strangely uninterested in the enthusiastic attentions of the woman at his side.

He released his softening shaft and gently drew her hand above water, bringing it to his lips for a kiss. "I was washing," he lied. "Why don't you wait for me? I'll be finished with my bath soon."

What he truly meant was that he would be finished taking himself in hand to thoughts of the sharp-tongued beauty he had clashed with earlier that day. The notion of bedding Beatrice when all he wanted was Miranda left him feeling cold. He couldn't do it.

And that was a problem in itself. When had the Duke of Whitby ever turned down a beautiful woman who wanted him? Never.

"Let me bathe you," Beatrice invited, undeterred as she dangled her bountiful bubbies in his face.

Rhys adored breasts. The bigger, the better. He loved women with rounded rumps and curved waists and soft bellies. He could write odes to sweetly seductive feminine forms. Beatrice would put any Venus to shame. And yet, as he stared at the creamy flesh offered to him, he felt…

Nothing.

Not even a stirring of desire.

His raging cockstand had gone utterly soft.

"Perhaps another evening, my dear," he denied smoothly. "The day has been a long one."

But Beatrice was determined.

She licked her lips. "Do you want my mouth?"

He thoroughly enjoyed a woman sucking his cock. And yet, again, his stubborn prick refused to so much as twitch. This was damned out of the ordinary.

"Not tonight, sweeting."

She plumped up her breasts, cupping them in her hands, and shook her head so that her hair fell enticingly down her back, baring herself to him entirely. "Do you want to fuck my bubbies?"

He glanced at her ripe breasts, pressed together just as he liked. But all he could think about was the enigmatic former countess in her tepid gown, those dainty hands capable of crafting such divine delights. That pretty pink mouth firmed into a disapproving line. What he wouldn't give to kiss the condemnation from her lips.

Unfortunately, it wasn't Miranda Lenox offering herself to him just now, however. It was Beatrice, awaiting his response, her sultry gaze assured that his answer would be yes.

"I'm afraid that I'm quite tiresome and poor company tonight. As tempting as your offer is, all I want is a bath and some sleep," he told her gently, the same feeling of finality settling in his chest that he inevitably reached when he had tired of his lover of the moment.

As beautiful as Beatrice was, as enjoyable as he found her company, and as talented as she was in the bedchamber, she had become a shadow in the face of a blazing, burning sun.

She frowned, her expression stunned. "You don't want to bed me?"

He couldn't blame her. Their time together had been enthusiastically passionate. But he did not keep two lovers at the same time. Rhys was a rake, but he did have compunction, and whilst he was with one woman, he was loyal to her.

"It isn't that," he reassured her gently. "Of course I want to bed you. You're unutterably lovely."

Her eyes narrowed. "It's someone else, isn't it? Who is she?"

He wasn't going to answer those questions. A pang of guilt sliced through him. It wasn't his intention to hurt Beatrice's feelings. But every association ran its course. This one was done. He felt it in his bones.

"Tomorrow, pay a call to Edwards & Co.," he told her softly. "I'll inform them in the morning that you will be visiting their establishment. Choose whatever piece of jewelry pleases you."

Understanding dawned on her face, joining the shock. Beatrice had always been calm. He had enjoyed that quality in her; not all his lovers had been so composed. He bore a scar on his collarbone from where an opera singer had hurled a glass at him in a fit of rage.

"That is it, then?" Beatrice demanded, her voice vibrating with outrage. "Why did you not tell me so when I arrived? I could have spared myself some humiliation."

"Because I didn't know when you arrived," he answered honestly. "But I do now."

"Bastard," she hissed. "I should have known better."

With that parting verbal parry, Beatrice spun about and flounced from the chamber in his St John's Wood house. The door slammed in her wake.

Rhys waited a few moments for the cloud of Beatrice's scent to disperse before allowing his head to fall against the lip of the tub again. With a heavy sigh, he closed his eyes and saw emerald eyes fringed with long, sooty lashes, a mouth he couldn't wait to possess, and the promise of full, heavy breasts hidden beneath her modest bodice.

His cock stirred, as if on cue.

He wrapped his fingers around his stiffening prick and stroked beneath the cooling waters of his bath. Faster and faster, gripping hard as he thought about opening that maddening line of buttons on her gown and tugging down her corset. About his hand gliding up her inner thigh until he found the slick, plump, hot lips of her sex. He would part her folds and seek her pearl, play with her until she cried out his name. Lift her skirts and sink deep inside her pussy while he sucked her sweet nipples.

It was too much. Not enough. Need roared through him, and he held his breath, working his cock until he came with a low groan, his seed jetting into the water to thoughts of making her his. His breathing was ragged, his heart thundering in his chest, and he'd just had one of the best orgasms in recent memory, but he hadn't even touched her yet.

There was no denying it. He wanted Miranda Lenox. And he was damned well going to have her—and her cornets and cream ice too.

SHE WASN'T GOING to surrender to temptation.

Miranda inwardly reminded herself with stern determination for at least the tenth time that morning as she pored over the ledgers for the school. One thing was becoming increasingly apparent. The funds she had managed to scrape together to begin the Lenox School of Cookery were thinning with more haste than she had supposed they would.

She needed more pupils. With each day, her advertisements appeared in every daily newspaper she could find, from *The Morning Post* to *The Times*. She needed that two thousand pounds.

"No," she muttered to herself as she finished a column of sums and settled her pen back in its glass holder. "I do not need his two thousand pounds."

That was a lie, however, and the glaring obviousness on the ledger page before her told her so. Yesterday, they had lost more fish and other ingredients that were unable to be kept for more than a day to a lack of pupils present to prepare the dishes. This pattern could not continue, or her fledgling school would be at an end before it had even completed its first three months.

Ammondale would no doubt revel in her abject failure.

Securing the building had been her greatest expense. But then, there were the men and women in her employ, the supplies, the endless need to pay for placements in newspapers. So much was reliant upon her success and her ability not just to attract new pupils and income for the school, but to publish her cookbooks, and to grow her employment agency. All of it in the name of giving women the means of securing their own futures instead of relying upon the men in their lives.

Freedom.

It was what Miranda had now, finally, at long last for the first time in her life. She hadn't realized just how costly that liberation would prove—and in every way.

A subtle knock at her office door interrupted Miranda's frustrated musings.

"Come," she called, straightening her spine and pinning a sunny smile to her lips.

Mrs. Kirkeland appeared at the threshold, frowning. "My lady, forgive me for interrupting, but His Grace, the Duke of Whitby is demanding to see you."

He was here.

Warmth coursed through her, something deep within her fluttering to life.

She swallowed hard. "I must see to the lesson on savories today. Please tell His Grace that he may call another day."

"Of course, my lady." Mrs. Kirkeland dipped into a curtsy in a show of deference Miranda had already told the older woman she didn't require.

But she had been one of the few members of her old life whose loyalty had been strong. Mrs. Kirkeland continued to observe the strict societal deference that had existed upon their first meeting six years ago when Miranda had been a shy young bride terrified of ruling over her husband's household.

Miranda couldn't lie. There had been something inherently satisfying about taking Ammondale's prized housekeeper with her. She had been able to offer a more appealing situation—overseeing the school—to Mrs. Kirkeland. And now she was relying upon Miranda just like so many others.

"How disappointing."

The deep, masculine drawl had her jolting in her seat as she glanced up to find a familiar, elegant gentleman hovering just behind the unsuspecting Mrs. Kirkeland.

"Your Grace," she greeted grimly. "I am afraid I haven't the time to speak with you just now. I have a lesson to teach and pupils awaiting me."

In truth, the classes were not set to begin for another hour. But Whitby didn't need to know that. What he needed to do was take his handsome self back to wherever he had come from. To stay away from her. To no longer tempt her with either his presence or the impressive sum he had offered for her services.

"I promise not to keep you for long," he said, unmoved by her plea.

It was clear he was a man who was accustomed to having his way in all matters. His kingly air of potent command was overwhelming.

Mrs. Kirkeland cast a fretful look in Miranda's direction. What could she do? Have a row with him before the faithful retainer who had followed her from Ammondale's employ? No. She must remain circumspect.

Miranda smiled at the former housekeeper. "Thank you, Mrs. Kirkeland. I shall see to His Grace's concerns and then proceed to today's lesson."

"Of course, my lady." Mrs. Kirkeland dipped into a curtsy and hastened from Miranda's office.

Leaving her alone with the duke, who prowled into the

chamber with leonine grace and a complete lack of contrition for his interruption to the serenity of her day.

"What is today's lesson?" he asked as he seated himself in a chair opposite her desk.

"Hot and cold savories," she answered, taken aback by his question and his familiarity, settling in as if he belonged here.

He grinned. "Are your lessons open to gentlemen?"

And dear heavens, but something inside her was melting faster than cream ice in the sun. The Duke of Whitby was far too handsome. And when those summer-storm eyes of his twinkled with devilish merriment, she couldn't help but want to smile back at him.

But she wouldn't.

Because his reputation was notorious. And because if she caused even the slightest hint of further scandal, the fledgling business she had managed to build would disintegrate into the ethers, and she would be left with nothing.

"No," she blurted, then straightened her spine. "The school of cookery is not for gentlemen. I am afraid you would be most unwelcome."

"Pity." Idly, he drummed his long fingers on the arm of his chair. "How many pupils do you have, *Miss* Lenox?"

She didn't miss the emphasis he placed on miss, as if it were dubious. But although she had been born the daughter of an earl and the honorific Lady Miranda was her due, she had chosen to shed it just as she had the hollow title of countess. Her family had disowned her, and she would be damned if she continued to acknowledge that familial connection. She was Miss Lenox now. Most importantly, she was independent, beholden to no one.

"I have a large number of pupils," she lied. "Indeed, I don't dare keep them waiting, which is why I must disappoint you, Your Grace. My students need me. I must refuse your generous offer."

Proud of her control in issuing the pronouncement, she rose with as much stateliness as she could muster, given her present discomfiture. The Duke of Whitby left her flustered and hot and uncomfortably aware of his blazing masculinity. He made her feel vulnerable in a way she hadn't in some time.

"Sit," he instructed, his tone languorous, as if they had all day to conduct a tête-à-tête and suit his whims.

"I am not a dog, Your Grace, nor am I your servant," she informed him with icy reserve. "You cannot command me."

"Of course you are neither." He gestured implacably. "Do sit down, lovely Miss Lenox."

It was the second time he had referred to her as lovely, and whilst she had once felt quite pretty, her bitter marriage had left her without vanity. She hadn't even thought about her appearance, other than to make certain she was properly dressed. The weakest part of her could not help but to warm to his praise.

To long for more of it.

Ruthlessly, she banished such ridiculous feelings.

"As I said, my pupils await me," she countered, refusing to obey him and seat herself again.

The less time she spent in this magnetic duke's presence, the better.

"If you shall not sit, then I reckon I must rise," he said, standing. "Pupils, you say."

"Yes." She held his gaze, hoping he couldn't read the desperation in her eyes. "They are the reason my school can continue to exist."

He stroked his jaw, his expression turning thoughtful. "It is interesting indeed to me that a handful of pupils are able to keep such an establishment flush in funds."

She stiffened. "I have more than a handful, Your Grace."

He sauntered around her desk, drawing dangerously

near, invading her personal territory. "That is not what I've heard from your neighbors."

"My neighbors?"

She was astonished. Had he been conducting interviews? The sheer nerve.

"Those whom I was fortunate to speak with," he said, propping his hip on the end of her desk in an indolent pose and trapping her neatly where she was.

She could not flee this corner of her office without moving past him. And she could not bear to do so, lest she touch any part of his person.

Miranda crossed her arms over her chest. "And what tales have my neighbors been telling?"

"Only that the trail of students into your still relatively new Lenox School of Cookery has been a trickle at best." He paused, his gaze dipping to her folded arms, and curse him if she didn't feel the heat of his gaze to her toes. If it didn't make her breasts tingle and her nipples tighten to hard points. "Some think you shall fail within the next few months, given the expense of upkeep. Fresh ingredients daily that are never used. Fish, butter, eggs, to say nothing of the fruits and all that ice." He shook his head. "A terrible shame, according to the fellow across the street."

Her pride forced her to carry on, even if what Whitby said was not entirely wrong. "Any excess is sent to the orphanages, who welcome it. Nothing goes to waste."

"Generous of you to be sure, madam, but can your coffers withstand such largesse?" he asked with far too much perception.

"The school attracts new pupils every day," she insisted— also a terrible hyperbole. "We continue to grow."

"Mmm," he hummed, as if deep in thought, tapping on the divot in his chin with his forefinger. "Do you know what I suspect, Miss Lenox?"

"I am certain I should not want to know."

But he was going to tell her anyway. Of that, she was equally sure.

"I suspect that you have a few more weeks before you begin needing to take drastic actions to keep this cookery school of yours solvent."

He was not wrong. And blast it, she had just reached a similar conclusion before his unwanted appearance in her office. It was as if he had somehow bored into her mind to see its contents laid before him. Either that, or her dire straits were painfully plain for everyone to see. Her last, futile hope was about to be ruthlessly dashed.

"How amusing, Your Grace," she said tightly. "I do so hate to disappoint you, but your suppositions are all wrong."

"Prove it to me, then."

He was unrelenting. And nettlesome.

Her chin went up. "I need not prove anything to you."

"So, I am correct."

"You are not correct." She glared at him, huffing with indignation she had no right to feel. "You are decidedly wrong."

"Is it your pride that stops you from accepting my offer, Miss Lenox?" He cocked his head, studying her with an intensity that made her long to shield herself from him.

What did this glorious rake see when he looked upon her? Some foolish part of Miranda was desperate to know and terrified at the prospect of what she would discover just the same.

"Accepting your offer would be disastrous," she told him firmly. "My reputation has sustained enough damage, and I cannot afford to place myself in an unseemly position at a house party hosted by a notorious rake."

"Am I notorious? I confess, I didn't know." He smiled, looking amused again. "You assume anyone would know you were present at the house party. I can assure you that every guest in attendance adheres to a strict policy of secrecy."

"You may wish to believe so, Your Grace, but no one knows better than I do how swiftly, eagerly, and viciously tongues wag."

His levity faded, his countenance turning serious. "My guests do not dare breathe a word of what happens at my house parties or who is present. When I tell you that your reputation will be unblemished by attending, it is not an empty promise."

"I have been promised a great many things before, and all of them were lies. You must forgive me my reticence." Miranda couldn't keep the bitterness from her voice.

Some old wounds were slow to heal.

Perhaps they never would.

"Not by me, however." He straightened, his pose no longer languid but instead alert as he loomed over her. "I pride myself upon being a man of my word."

She wanted to believe him. He seemed earnest enough. But the past had taught her to trust almost no one. And anyway, it did not signify. She couldn't accept his offer. Didn't dare.

Miranda forced a polite smile, trying not to note his proximity or the way his scent—amber, musk, and forest— curled around her like a loving embrace. "Nonetheless, I am afraid that my answer must be no."

"If two thousand pounds does not persuade you, then perhaps three thousand will," he said, shocking her.

Three thousand pounds. It was a veritable fortune in terms of what it could do to support her school. It would give her the ability to publish her cookbook on her own. It would grant her the means to do so much, without the crushing dread that her debts would forever outweigh her ability to pay them.

"Just think of how three thousand pounds could comfortably keep you and your school of cookery afloat," Whitby added in his low, melodic voice.

His voice was an invitation to sin.

So was his face.

Everything about him.

She should refuse his offer yet again.

"When is this house party of yours again?" she found herself asking instead. "I do believe you mentioned it yesterday, but it has flitted from my mind."

"In six days."

Ah yes. He had told her a week yesterday. Scarcely any time to prepare herself.

Oh, what was she thinking? Surely she was not truly entertaining this outrageous proposal of his. Was she?

"You must be mad to spend three thousand pounds for dessert courses," she said, which was decidedly not the denial she needed.

And would scarcely further her cause if she were indeed considering his proposition. Which of course she wasn't.

His sensual lips curved upward again. "I've spent far more on considerably less."

There had been a period of Miranda's life where money had not concerned her. She had been cosseted as an earl's daughter. And then she had been a countess. Not cosseted, certainly, but Ammondale had been wealthy. Gowns, jewels, a carriage, and a house filled with domestics had all been without price. Her life had altered considerably.

Now, she could not fathom anyone spending three thousand pounds for a week's worth of cream and ices. But if he was willing to outlay that great a sum, then why should she not ask for more?

"Taking a week away from my pupils would cost the school lost revenue," she countered.

He chuckled, the sound low and decadent. "The business-woman emerges. You and I both know that you haven't enough pupils to earn one hundred pounds in a week, let alone three thousand. However, I have a further proposition for you."

He was all silken persuasion. Miranda longed to press her back into the corner, to put some distance between herself and the tempting duke. However, she knew that doing so would only show her vulnerability. So she remained where she was, near enough to touch him, to breathe him in, to find herself yearning, impossibly, for more than she could ever dare.

She swallowed against an insidious rush of longing. "What is your further proposition?"

"It involves something more than dessert." His stormy blue gaze swept down her form, making her feel as if he could see beneath her modest gown.

Danger, warned a voice within her. *Nothing but danger lurks ahead. Save yourself before it is too late.*

But she had already ventured this far.

She raised a brow. "Oh?"

"And something more than three thousand pounds," he added. "Ten thousand additional pounds, to be more specific."

She barely contained her gasp. "Your Grace, if you are suggesting something depraved—"

"Hardly depraved," he interrupted smoothly, his gaze burning into hers. "What I propose is a bargain, Miss Lenox. For three thousand pounds, come to Hertfordshire and provide my guests with your unparalleled creations. By the week's end, you will be free to return to your school and your pupils. If, however, you are amenable at the end of the week, I will give you an additional ten thousand pounds for a full month of your time."

Her eyes narrowed. "A full month's worth of desserts in exchange for ten thousand pounds?"

No one would make such an extravagant and ludicrous bargain. Not unless he wanted something more. And whilst Whitby had not explicitly stated what he expected of her, she was no innocent miss.

He reached for her then, nothing more than a lone brush of his forefinger along her jaw, as if he drew a line there on her bare skin. The touch was so fleeting, she might have believed she had imagined it if not for the trail of fire he left in his wake and the accompanying burst of desire.

Stupid desire.

Fruitless desire.

Dangerous desire.

"A month of your time," he repeated.

Outrage warred with something else. Interest.

She pinned him with a glare. "You said you weren't suggesting something depraved."

But Whitby only smiled. A devilish smile. A knowing one.

"I suppose that depends upon your definition of depraved. I promise you that it would be a very enjoyable month, Miss Lenox. Or may I call you Miranda?"

"You may call me Miss Lenox," she said crisply, her fingers clenching in her skirts.

"I'll be honest with you, *Miss Lenox*," he said, taking his time on her name and drawing it out. "I desire you. But I want you to desire me as well. If, at the week's end, you find yourself uninterested in pursuing an association between the two of us, you will be free to leave three thousand pounds wealthier. However, if you should desire to continue, in a discreet fashion, of course, you will receive ten thousand pounds in return for one month."

Carte blanche.

The Duke of Whitby was asking her to be his mistress.

Was offering her money to share his bed. What would that make her? A kept woman?

"No," she bit out. "I will not be paid to be your...your strumpet."

"You would hardly be that," he said with a small smile. "But either way, I don't want your answer to the latter portion of my offer now. Save it for the house party's end. For today, all I require is your answer concerning the three thousand pounds and your heavenly cream ices and cornets."

He thought her cream ice and cornets heavenly?

Miranda couldn't deny the notion pleased her. For all her life, her true passions and aspirations had been repressed. Ladies did not toil in kitchens. Countesses did not work closely with their cooks and create their own recipes for ices. Nor did they dream of writing recipe books and giving other women the means of seizing their own independence.

A flush stole over her cheeks as he continued to regard her in that thorough, frankly sensual way. "If I were to agree to the first portion of your offer only, what promise do I have that you would honor my decision?"

He took one step closer, bringing their bodies nearly flush, and leaned down to murmur in her ear, "I only bed willing women."

Her knees trembled. His breath was hot and sweetly scented of mint. Her body's reaction was instant, longing unfurling deep within her. Her marriage with Ammondale had been a cold one, but that didn't mean she didn't remember what longing had felt like. Nor did it make her incapable of feeling now.

She jerked her head back, nearly cracking her skull on the plaster behind her. "Then I need not fear you will go back on your word."

"Do you agree to delight the guests of my house party

with your exceptional ices and desserts?" he asked, clasping his hands behind his back.

Her common sense told her to cry out a denial and charge out of the room. To run far and run fast. But there was another part of her—the practical businesswoman—who knew she could not afford to turn down such a sum. She needed it. The school needed it.

Miranda bit her lower lip, then huffed out a sigh. "In exchange for three thousand pounds?"

He nodded, his gaze slipping to her mouth. "For the first week, yes."

Why did his stare feel as intimate as a kiss?

"I'll need half the funds at once, in order to keep the school running in my absence," she demanded.

"Of course. You may have the other half at the completion of the house party. Or, you may have the full thirteen thousand at the month's end."

"Three thousand shall be sufficient, Your Grace."

He grinned. "You seem so sure of yourself, lovely."

Her lips thinned. "Because I am."

"Excellent. I like nothing so much as a challenge. Half the funds will be delivered to you today, with the other half awaiting the party's end. As for the rest—" here he paused, a wicked glint entering his eyes— "we shall revisit it when the time arrives."

She gave a jerky nod, wondering what she had just consented to.

"You agree to my terms?"

Miranda swallowed hard. "Yes."

He took a step back, leaving her feeling oddly bereft as he swept into a courtly bow that would have been far more at home in a ballroom than in her small office. "I will send the remainder of the information you require along with the payment. If you should need anything, only ask it of me. Otherwise, I shall see you in Hertfordshire."

He straightened, turned, and began striding from the chamber with the same casual elegance he had used to enter it. She watched him go, fraught with a worrying sense of foreboding.

Just as he reached the door, he stopped, glancing over his shoulder at her with a look that could have sent her silk gown up in flames. "Oh, and Miss Lenox? I fully intend to do everything in my power during that week to persuade you to change your mind."

Without awaiting her response, he left, the door clicking closed behind him.

"I won't change my mind," Miranda declared to the paneled mahogany.

If only she felt as certain of those words as she sounded.

CHAPTER 3

*M*iss Miranda Lenox.
        Countess of Ammondale.
Lady Miranda Lenox.
The Fallen Countess.

So many names for just one woman. But regardless of what one called her, Rhys had one more to add as he drummed his fingers on his knee and glared at the door to the Lenox School of Cookery.

Late.

He reached into his waistcoat and extracted his pocket watch to consult the time. Ten minutes late, to be exact. Rhys slid the watch back into its pocket. He had told her when his carriage would arrive for her. He had already overseen the collection of every ingredient and utensil she had required of him in the lengthy, enumerated lists she had sent his way since they had parted last.

And now, here he was, sitting in his bloody carriage, getting a sore arse before their journey had even begun—and despite the relative comfort of the leather squabs—all because the lofty proprietress whose services he had employed had not deigned to appear. Had she changed her mind? If so, she might have sent round word to him—and far sooner than the day they were embarking to the country.

He had done everything she required of him, even using an unmarked conveyance to meet her at her place of business so as to maintain strict secrecy and professionalism. Of course, she couldn't know, and she didn't need to know, that this little display of decorum for her benefit would end the moment she entered this carriage. For if he had his way, she'd be bouncing on his cock by the time they reached the outskirts of Town.

As Rhys was no fool, he very much doubted he would have his way. His Miranda was quite firm in her belief she could remain impervious to his rakish charm. He would happily prove her wrong. But doing so would require patience. Effort. What better way to shake the ennui he had been suffering since well before Beatrice?

He was about to throw open the carriage door and storm the damned school himself when at last Miranda emerged, dressed in a travel gown of muted gray that was every bit as demure as everything else he had seen her wear, a handsome matching hat covering much of her inky tresses.

Two sins, in Rhys's opinion. A woman as beautiful as Miranda Lenox should not be swathed in the same subtle shade as a plump little dove. She ought to wear bold emerald to heighten her eyes, deep red to bring out her lush lips, brilliant blues and purples and pinks. Anything but gray.

Also, in a perfect world, she would be naked. Not on the street for the *hoi polloi* to see. But in his presence alone, her curves would be on full display, his to admire instead of swathed in too much fabric and boning, a veritable sea of undergarments to hide her glorious body from him.

The carriage door swung open, emitting light and a burst of air that smelled of impending rain. Also, the faintest hint of orange blossom. She was handed up into the carriage, head down to watch her step, her hat obscuring his presence from her until the last moment when she was already within and the groom was snapping the door smartly closed.

A gasp tore from her parted lips, and she collapsed onto the bench seat opposite his. "You!"

Not precisely the reaction he'd hoped for, but he *had* deliberately misled her about the carriage arriving to take her to Wingfield Hall. He had known, of course, that she would flatly refuse if she knew she was meant to share the confined space with him.

"Me." Rhys grinned at her now, feeling like the dangerous cat who had chased the saucy mouse into a corner from which there was no escape. "Good day to you as well, my dear Miranda."

Her dark brows snapped together, and she clutched her reticule before her as if it were a shield. "I have not given you leave to be so familiar, Your Grace. What are you doing in this carriage?"

He shrugged. "What wouldn't I be doing in this carriage? It is mine after all."

"You promised me an unmarked carriage to take me to Hertfordshire," she reminded him sharply.

"Yes," he agreed, quite pleased with himself for his cunning. "But I did not say I would not be in it. Now, did I?"

"Oh! You...you...scoundrel!" she sputtered, twin patches of color rising on her cheeks.

Fuck, she was delectable.

He rapped on the roof, and the carriage jolted into motion before she could attempt to fling open the door and throw herself to the pavements in flight. "If you had wished for a personal carriage, you had only to request it."

"I assumed this was to be a personal carriage," she said, her voice cross.

"Just as I assumed you would expect to find me within," he lied smoothly. "I am heartily sorry for the confusion, but now that we are on our way, the journey shan't last long."

"I cannot travel to the countryside in this carriage with you," she protested. "It would be nothing short of scandalous."

"The carriage is unmarked," he pointed out. "The hour is early. No one knows you entered any conveyance other than your own."

"I don't have a carriage."

"A hired coach, then."

"This is far too fine to be a hired coach."

She was a bloody stubborn woman. "It is the most modest conveyance I possess."

She gave him an arch look. "Of that, I have no doubt."

His Miranda had a rapier tongue. And he loved it.

Rhys laughed. "You wound me. Do you mean to imply I am a vainglorious gentleman?"

"I mean to imply that you lied to me about the carriage that would take me to the house party," she said pointedly, apparently not about to be distracted from her original source of displeasure with him.

"*Lied* is a strong and ugly word. As we already agreed, the travel arrangements were a mere misunderstanding," he said magnanimously.

"One that is in your favor."

He allowed his gaze to slip to her tempting, pouting lips for a moment before meeting her disapproving stare once more. "It could be in yours as well, if you but allow it, my dear Miranda."

"Miss Lenox," she corrected icily.

"No, I do think it shall be Miranda when we are alone," Rhys decided.

Which will be as often as I can possibly manage, he kept to himself.

"This was a mistake," she pronounced, sliding to the edge of her seat. "Please, take me back to the school. I have changed my mind."

His sweet purveyor of decadent cream ices. She wasn't so naïve that she believed he was going to turn the carriage around and deliver her back to the haven of her school, was she?

"You cannot change your mind," he reminded her. "I have already furnished you with one thousand five hundred pounds."

The color fled her cheeks. "You also said that you prefer women who are willing, Your Grace."

Well, sweet God, what did she think he was going to do, tear her gown off and fuck her on the Moroccan leather?

"That hasn't changed."

And she *would* be more than willing. If there was anything Rhys knew, it was how to seduce a woman. Judging from the palpable attraction crackling between them like roaring flames, said conquest would prove easy, despite her determination to cling to her prim façade. There was a passionate woman hiding in the depths of her eyes, and he would find her.

"Then you cannot insist upon seducing me in this carriage," Miranda bit out, looking flustered.

"What an imagination you have. I'm planning nothing of the sort, I promise."

Her eyes narrowed. "You aren't?"

"Of course not." He beamed at her. "Since you required two carriages of provisions to be sent ahead, this was the only vehicle remaining in my stables. Short of having the two of us travel with the cookery, fruits, and ice, this is the best I can provide."

A lie. Rhys had more carriages at his disposal. But he hadn't been about to lose this opportunity to be alone with her for the duration of the journey to Wingfield Hall.

"You did manage to find everything I requested?" she asked, her agile mind now going to the task awaiting her.

A suitable distraction for the moment. At least until it was truly too late to turn around and deliver her back to safety.

"My servants are unparalleled," he told her. "I cannot accept the praise that is due them. All I did was provide them with your intricately detailed list."

She nodded. "Yes, that is quite good. And as for the items I needed from my school? My ice caves?"

Rhys still didn't know what the bloody hell an ice cave was, but he didn't want to ask. "Naturally."

Another nod. "Thank you, Your Grace." She paused, frowning. "But you must see how inappropriate it is for me to travel anywhere with you."

"If it is up to me, you shall be doing far more interesting things with me than traveling in a boring carriage to Hertfordshire before our association is done," he said.

Her raven eyebrows winged upward, her emerald eyes widening. "I have already told you, anything improper is out of the question."

"On the contrary. Nothing is out of the question." He decided to relent, not wanting to push her too far. They had time aplenty. "However, I will accept your refusal of my suit."

Her shoulders stiffened, the pose of a warrior goddess going into battle. "I would hardly call making me your mistress pressing your suit. You are not courting me. There is nothing proper about this set of circumstances."

"I don't court, my dear Miranda. I fuck."

She gasped. "Your Grace!"

Well, blast. There went his attempt at trying not to push her too far. And so soon. Still, it was worth it to watch the color creeping back into her cheeks, the flush traveling up her creamy throat beyond the maddening set of buttons bisecting her bodice. Her allure was so potent, he could practically taste it on his tongue. He couldn't recall ever wanting a woman more.

"Forgive me." He winked at her. "I am sometimes too forthright for my own good, I'm told."

Her gloved fingers were twisting on her reticule, worrying it, her lush lips tightened. "I will not... I have no intention of... You may do whatever it is you like with someone else. This is a business arrangement. I am providing your guests with desserts for a week. That is all."

Watching her attempt to avoid repeating what he had just said made his cock twitch. If only she knew how tempting she was, she would likely pitch herself from the conveyance here and now, the danger to herself be damned.

"Of course," he agreed. "Unless you change your mind, that is."

"I shan't."

Rhys smiled. "As you wish."

"You say that in a tone of disbelief or perhaps mockery, as if I could not possibly refuse you."

"To be fair, no woman has."

Her nostrils flared as she sucked in air. "Then I shall be the first."

Rhys said nothing, merely continued smiling.

She could keep telling herself that all she liked. They both knew it wouldn't be true.

SHE WAS TRAPPED in a hell of her own foolish making.

Trapped in a carriage with the Duke of Whitby, who was unfairly dashing this morning, his hat settled on the squabs at his side to reveal his blond hair. Sunlight was presently streaming through the slats of the Venetian blinds, making his wavy locks glint as if they were fashioned of spun gold. His long legs were stretched out, his ankles crossed, his trousers brushing her skirts with each sway of the carriage over the roads carrying them farther from London.

Farther from sanity as well, it seemed.

This was her fault.

She need not have agreed to the rogue's scandalous invitation. She could have turned away from the three thousand pounds he had offered, particularly after he'd made his true intentions known. And yet, she had not. She had believed herself capable of remaining unaffected by his handsome face, his charm, and his every heated, rakish look that suggested they ought to adjourn to a bedroom at once.

Digging into her reticule, she fished out a fan. Heavens, she was overheating. With a snap of her wrist, it opened, and she proceeded to wave the stagnant air in an attempt to cool herself. But that was all wrong, because the air smelled of him. And he smelled despicably inviting. Like a forbidden forest tinged with musk and sin. It didn't help that he was so elegant, so sure of himself, so quick-witted and confident, everything she could not resist.

And then, there were his words. His wicked, wicked words. *I don't court, my dear Miranda. I fuck.*

She went even hotter just thinking about them again. How would she survive the week? How would she resist him? He was like the sun, burning hot and bright, dangerous to look upon for too long.

At the moment, resistance was not her problem, at least. Because the Duke of Whitby was sound asleep. Head tipped back to reveal the sturdy column of his throat, his Adam's apple a prominent bulge, his lips parted, his breathing even, those storm-filled eyes thankfully closed.

How could he sleep in a time like this?

He had cozened her into sharing a carriage with him, said all manner of sinful, wrong things, had scorched her with his words, with his stare, with his blatant intent to seduce her. And her body had a mind of its own, still reeling. Still filled with unbearable, unwanted desire. She was not meant to be a creature of passion. She was meant to remain stoic. To cling to her honor. She needed her reputation.

She was beyond discomfited. She was…bothered. She was *overheated*.

Miranda shifted on her seat, pressing her thighs together to stave off the unsettling ache between them. But it was no use. The longing just persisted—if anything, growing stronger. And meanwhile, her fellow passenger was blissfully asleep.

Why couldn't he snore?

Or drool?

Why did he have to be so unfairly breathtaking and elegant and handsome, even in slumber? She huffed an irritated sigh and fussed with her skirts to distract herself.

"Are you uncomfortable, Miranda?"

The velvet-soft question had her gaze jolting back to Whitby, whose eyes were still closed.

"I thought you were asleep."

His lips curved upward in a slight smile. "Merely resting. Do you know I had to wake despicably early today? Ye gods, I daresay it was even before the sun rose. A terrible travesty, really. Travel can be so tiresome."

"I have been awake for hours already," she told him pointedly. "Rising with the sun is good for one's constitution."

He opened his eyes, nary a hint of drowsiness in their glittering depths. "I would beg to differ."

Of course, it would not be done for a duke to rise early. Waking at dawn was for lower classes. But Miranda now found herself in a curious world where she no longer belonged anywhere. She had been born a lady, but the scandal of her divorce had stripped her of everything, save a few treasured, loyal friends. Even her own family had disavowed her.

But she mustn't dwell on such unpleasantness, for the Duke of Whitby was watching her again. Seeing too much, she feared.

"On this matter, we shall have to agree to disagree," she told him, attempting a politic air she scarcely felt.

"I might be persuaded of the merits of rising early, given the right reason," he drawled.

There was no mistaking the underlying implications in his smooth baritone. Or in his frank gaze. He was challenging her.

She whipped her fan back and forth, thinking she would need to gird herself for his full assault over the coming days. The Duke of Whitby was like a cavalry brigade charging determinedly across an open field, and she wasn't certain she possessed the defenses to stay the enemy racing toward her.

"A dog," she ventured.

His golden brows drew together. "I beg your pardon. What did you say?"

"I said that if you require early-morning persuasion, you ought to get a dog. I had one as a girl, and she was remarkably adept at urging me from slumber each day."

He chuckled. "Somehow, I find the notion of a little Miranda being awakened by a hound ridiculously endearing."

There was an open warmth in his smile, in his voice, that had been absent from her life in the wake of the scandal. But even before her divorce from Ammondale, it had been far too long since a gentleman had looked at her or spoken to her with such intense regard. Perhaps not ever. Her debut and the beaux who had gallantly courted her seemed a life-time ago now. The closest she had come to male affection had been her dear friend the Marquess of Waring, but their relationship had been strictly platonic.

Either way, she mustn't be charmed, just as she must not lower her guard.

"Miss Lenox," she reminded the duke primly.

"Yes, but you were not Miss Lenox then, were you? Rather, you were Lady Miranda. You still are, despite your insistence to the contrary."

"I have chosen to eschew all honorifics," she said, plucking at the fall of her skirt as the familiar knife's edge of sorrow burrowed itself between her ribs.

"Why?"

No one had questioned her on the matter before, and Mrs. Kirkeland had chosen to continue referring to her as *my lady* out of habit, one Miranda had not bothered to correct. Her friends had accepted her decision, not wanting, she expected, to pry.

She decided to answer him honestly. "I am no longer the Countess of Ammondale, and I have no wish to hold on to that courtesy title any more than I desired to remain married to the earl. And when my family refused to acknowledge our connection following my scandalous divorce, I decided to follow suit."

His jaw tightened. "Your family has disavowed you?"

"Are they to be blamed? The scandal was tremendous." Secretly, she did blame them. Their defection cut deeply.

But she could understand. Divorce was exceedingly rare for good reason, and she had been forced to obtain hers by resorting to extreme, disgraceful measures. With the aid of Waring, she had feigned adultery, a sin that only the two of them knew had never been committed. In the wake of the scandal, Waring had left for America. Miranda would be forever grateful to him for the sacrifice he had made to his own reputation so she could secure her freedom.

"Yes, I do think they are to be blamed," Whitby said, surprising her. "You are family, are you not? Blood ought to be thick enough to weather any gossip."

She had thought so as well. How wrong she had been.

She could still recall Mother's countenance when she had informed Miranda that she was no longer welcome. *On account of your sisters*, Mother had added. *You cannot expect Daisy and Elizabeth to suffer because of your actions.*

Her actions.

As if she were solely to blame for the misery of the marriage her parents had selected for her. She had never wanted to wed Ammondale. It had been Father who had arranged the match with the earl's sire. Father who had urged her to marry in such haste, when she had been naïve and young and eager to please.

"It proved considerably thin," she said at last, her voice irritatingly thick with old emotion.

Miranda did her best to keep her thoughts from straying to hurtful happenings she was incapable of changing.

"Is that why you started your school?" Whitby asked softly. "Have you no other means of sustaining yourself?"

Her cheeks went hot. "That is none of your concern, Your Grace."

"Rhys."

She was lost. "I beg your pardon?"

He smiled, and this time, there was far less of the suave rake in his countenance than genuine tenderness, taking her aback. "My given name. It is Rhys. When we are alone, I hope you might call me by it. *Your Grace* is so dreadfully formal. Do you not agree?"

Formality was what she must cling to where he was

concerned. Much to her dismay, she found herself wanting to try his name. Wanting that familiarity between them.

She stiffened, casting such treacherous notions away. "No, Your Grace, I very much do not agree. In this situation, you are my employer. We are not equals. Nor are we even friends."

"But of course we are equals. You are the daughter of an earl. I am the son of a duke."

And a duke in his own right. A gorgeous temptation. Sin incarnate. A peril to her future in every way, lest she surrender to her attraction to him as he wished. He held all the power in this game of theirs. If he took her as his mistress for a month, he would walk away with his reputation intact. Whereas Miranda's future would be destroyed. It was difficult enough trying to lure pupils to lessons being taught by a notorious former countess. If she were a kept woman, it would be the end of the Lenox School of Cookery forever.

Miranda fanned herself with increasing vigor, nettled with him. "You know what I mean."

He tsked. "I think this silly society of ours has left you suffering from the misconception that you are somehow lesser because you are a divorcée."

"Because I am." She snapped her fan against her palm, closing it with one frustrated motion. "You may call society silly, but I haven't the same luxury. As a man—and a duke, at that—you have no need to adhere to propriety. As a woman, I am treated with scorn for every mistake I make, perceived or otherwise. All the blame is heaped upon me."

He stared at her, his expression pensive. She wondered if it was the first occasion in his life where he had been made to confront the disparity between men and women, a gaping chasm that only grew with scandal.

"I am sorry, Miranda."

These were not the words she had expected from him. More subtle suggestions, more practiced wooing, yes. True understanding, perhaps even contrition, however? Decidedly not.

She shifted again, uncomfortable on the squabs for a new reason entirely. His kindness—seemingly genuine—made a rush of longing sweep over her before she could help it.

Summoning her bravado, she forced a smile. "You need not pity me, Your Grace. I have found that I would rather know the truth of the world around me. It's far preferable to mistakenly believing in a falsehood."

"It isn't pity I feel for you," Whitby said, his voice low. "Not at all."

Miranda swallowed hard. Part of the ice inside her was melting already, and she didn't like it. Couldn't allow it.

Before she could say anything more, the carriage slowed to a halt.

Whitby leaned forward, peering through the slats of the blinds. "It looks as if we're to have a little break in our travels. Just in time. I'm ravenous."

The look he sent in her direction made molten heat pool between her thighs, pulsing like an echo in her sex. Miranda had a feeling he wasn't merely speaking about food.

But that was too bad. He wouldn't be getting anything from her during her time in Hertfordshire other than her desserts.

CHAPTER 4

"*H*ere we are."

Rhys stopped at the door that would be Miranda's bedchamber for the duration of the house party. He had intentionally chosen one that adjoined his, in a wing where none of the other guests would be in residence. Naturally, she didn't yet know that his room was connected. She also didn't know the manner of house party he was hosting.

He could only imagine the tongue-lashing he would receive when both discoveries were made.

"This is where I am to stay?" she asked, a frown furrowing her brow.

"Yes."

The efficient servants were at work with the unpacking, and because the domestics at Wingfield Hall were charged with their discretion—and the Wicked Dukes Society paid them a pretty penny for it too—the housekeeper kept her distance unless specifically called for. In her place, Rhys had escorted the delectable woman at his side to her room.

"But I expected to be situated belowstairs," she said. "This is wholly unnecessary."

"You are a lady," he countered, angry on her behalf for the way everyone in her life had apparently abandoned her. "You are not accustomed to such accommodations."

"I am a lady no longer," she countered briskly. "It would better serve me to be amongst the servants if they are to respect my presence in the kitchens."

"They will respect you because I command it of them. Because they are paid well. And you'll not be staying below-stairs. It's out of the question."

Not just because doing so meant she would effectively be beyond his reach. Though, there was that consideration as well. But because he was concerned for her comfort and welfare also. He didn't want any of the guests lusting over her, nor did he want her to be treated as a servant. She was here as his guest, damn it, even if he was paying her for the creation of her cream ices.

Miranda shook her head. "I cannot stay here. Surely your guests will be alarmed by my presence."

Her divorce from Ammondale had left her little more than a shadow in polite society, he realized. Neither seen nor heard. She was simply there.

He didn't like it.

"The guests will not be in this wing," he reassured her. "And even if they were, if they objected to your presence, I would be pleased to bid them farewell. I'll not tolerate anyone paying you insult. Neither servant nor guest. You are to tell me at once if anything is amiss. Is that clear?"

Her lips parted, and she stared at him for a moment, as if his concern surprised her. And he did not like that either, for it suggested that in the wake of her divorce from Ammondale, few others had been concerned for her at all, if indeed anyone had.

Had she no one to whom she could turn for aid? Had she no other recourse, save teaching cookery lessons to undeserving pupils? He wondered, but now was not the time to ask, not when he had to persuade her to settle into this chamber.

"Is that clear?" he repeated when she continued to maintain her silence, and he feared she would argue with him.

"I… Yes, Your Grace," she said. "Thank you."

"The footmen are seeing that everything you required is delivered to the kitchens," he informed her. "Your cases will be brought here to you soon."

"I should go belowstairs now, then. The sooner I am able to begin, the better."

"No guests are arriving today," he reassured her. "They won't begin to arrive until tomorrow."

Meaning the two of them were well and truly alone for the evening. Because of the six friends who ran the Wicked Dukes Society, presently two—the Duke of Brandon and the Duke of Camden—were tied up in matrimony and unable to attend. Dreadful stuff. Riverdale, Kingham, and Richford were not set to arrive until tomorrow either since it was Rhys's turn to play host. Rather convenient, that.

Miranda's eyebrows rose. "Not until tomorrow?"

Yes, that had been a truly brilliant plan of his, bringing her here before anyone else was in residence. He had her all to himself tonight. And Rhys couldn't be more pleased about the prospect. An additional evening to persuade her to spend a month as his lover.

"I reasoned that a bit of time for preparation would not be unwise," he lied smoothly.

In truth, he and his chums had perfected the highly secret, sought-after house parties that they had been hosting at Wingfield Hall, an estate that had once belonged to the Duke of Brandon's grandmother but was now his. There was no need for preparation. There had, however, been a dire need for Rhys to have as many hours alone with Miranda as he could.

Her eyes had narrowed upon him, as if she were privy to his thoughts. "You wished to prepare?"

"Of course." He grinned. "Would you care to see your chamber, or do you intend to remain here in the hall, frowning at me?"

"I'm certain it is lovely," she said, making no move to enter. "And I am not frowning at you, Your Grace. I am merely wondering at the timing and means of our arrival."

Her gaze was pointed, as was her tone. She was an intelligent woman. He'd made no secret of the fact that he wanted her. Undoubtedly, his ruse was as obvious as the Axminster at their feet. But he was unapologetic.

"Can you blame me for selfishly wanting you to myself for an evening?" he countered.

Her stubborn chin went up, and damn but she was glorious in her dudgeon. "I have told you already, my answer to your other proposition is no. Absolutely, unequivocally, no."

"Of course it is," he agreed. "Until it is not. For now, you may as well get yourself situated, my dear. Dinner shall be here before we know it, and you will be eating with me."

She huffed a nettled sigh. "It wouldn't be proper for me to have dinner alone with you."

He had guessed that might be her protest. "No one will know."

"The servants will know, and I must work by their sides for the next week, creating desserts for your guests. I would not be able to bear it if they were all looking upon me in scorn, thinking me your kept woman."

"As I have already assured you, no one will look upon you in scorn. Your presence here will remain unknown. And if you should prefer it, you may take a pseudonym for the duration of your stay at Wingfield Hall. I've already thought of a few surnames that might suffice."

"A pseudonym?"

"Of course. You are not so notorious that the servants shall recognize you. Thus far, no introductions have been performed, and by design. Choose the name you wish to be called, and no one will ever be the wiser." He cocked his head at her, wishing he had the freedom to reach out and brush a stray tendril of hair from her cheek and restraining himself just the same. "Do you want to hear my suggestions?"

She eyed him as dubiously as he imagined she might a snake that had just slithered into her path. "I'm not sure I dare."

"You must be a married woman, of course," he carried on, despite her suspicion. "Mrs. Lovely is an excellent option. There is also Mrs. Lovejoy, Mrs. Love, Mrs. Loveless, Mrs. Lovett… Shall I go on?"

"No," she denied, giving him a shrewd look. "I begin to sense a certain theme. Perhaps I shall be Mrs. Loveless, then, if I must assume a surname containing love at all. It seems far more apropos."

He didn't like it, but he reckoned it would have to do. The name was only necessary for the week anyway.

Rhys inclined his head. "Mrs. Loveless, then."

"However, that does not solve the problem of your domestics believing there is something inappropriate between us," she pointed out.

He had to admit he hadn't considered as much, but he was determined to get what he wanted. "We will dine *à la Francaise*. I'll have the servants place all the dishes on the table and then leave the room before we go inside."

"Do you not think some of them will see me?" she persisted. "Or wonder why I am staying in this chamber?"

He moved past her, opening the door to her chamber.

"They are paid handsomely not to think or wonder and to hold their tongues. The only servant who will be attending to you personally is a lady's maid I'm paying an extortionate fee, and I can assure you she won't carry so much as a hint of a tale to another soul. Now, have a look inside, if you please. Tell me whether it shall be sufficient for your comfort."

If she intended to argue with him, she would only lose. This was not a battle in which Rhys was about to concede defeat. And besides, he was the one with the upper hand here.

Instead of crossing the threshold, she peered around his shoulder. "It looks lovely, thank you."

"I won't go inside with you," he said on a sigh. "I promise."

Not unless you issue an invitation, he added silently.

Giving him a stern look of spinsterish admonishment that was at odds with the passionate woman he sensed hiding beneath her prim exterior, she swept over the threshold and into the room.

"There," he murmured, leaning his hip into the doorjamb and unapologetically watching her as she skirted the chamber, taking interest in the *bric-à-brac* scattered about. "That wasn't so difficult, was it?"

She paused and cast a suspicious glance over her shoulder, making certain he had kept his word. "Not terribly." Clever as ever, she pointed to the door adjoining her chamber to his. "Where does that lead?"

"To the chamber next door," he answered smoothly. "Never fear. It locks on both sides."

With purposeful strides, she moved to the door, testing it in a blatant show of distrust. And, well, he could scarcely blame her, could he? Rhys was not exactly trustworthy where she was concerned. But he hadn't lied about the locking mechanism. Her test proved the door to be sturdy and soundly locked from his side. Not that she knew whose chamber was on the other side of hers.

Yet.

"Good." She nodded, turning back to him, all business. "Who has the bedchamber next door?"

Blast. He was going to have to deceive her. He didn't dare reveal the truth just yet.

"At present, no one." He flashed her a grin, deciding it was time they parted ways until dinner. "Now, I should allow you to freshen yourself after an arduous day of travel. Your cases will be brought round, and the maid assigned to you will see to the unpacking. The bellpull is in the corner should you require anything at all, and if you need me before the dinner gong, any of the servants will direct you to me."

"Oh." She fussed with her skirts, looking suddenly like the sails of a ship bereft of wind. "Yes, of course."

"Never say you miss me already, Miranda," he teased, secretly pleased at the notion.

"Certainly not," she denied hastily.

Too hastily.

She'd been caught.

Rhys pressed a hand over his heart in dramatic fashion. "O lovely maiden, how you wound me so. My vanity shall never recover from this mortal blow."

She laughed then, the sound clear and gorgeous, as sacred as a church bell calling the faithful. As quickly as her mirth emerged, it was gone. She pressed a gloved hand to her mouth to stifle it, looking horrified with herself for deigning to find him amusing.

"Your vanity appears to be quite omnipotent, Your Grace," she said, sobering.

She wasn't wrong. Women adored him, and he knew it. He was handsome. He was wealthy. He was a duke. He had a big cock. Life had blessed him immeasurably in most ways.

Except the ones that mattered most.

He banished that stupid thought at once.

"Do you hear that sound?" he asked theatrically, cupping a hand to his ear.

"No." Her inky brows knitted together in an expression he recognized. "What is it?"

"Come here," he urged her.

She moved nearer with a hesitant air, just as he imagined she might approach a strange mongrel who she was not certain would either kiss her hand or lick it. "What sound, Your Grace?"

He waited until she had drawn almost close enough to touch, before answering. "The shattering sound of my pride cracking and disintegrating before you."

Miranda stopped, still clutching the worn reticule that he knew from their carriage ride contained a similarly shabby fan. "You bounder. I believed you."

"And there is a very important lesson for you to learn, Miranda." He flashed another grin. "You ought to never trust me. Not completely."

Her eyes widened. "You promised—"

"Oh, not about something as boring as money," he inter-rupted, waggling his fingers at her. "You will have the other half of your funds at the week's end. And more, I hope, later."

"Just the three thousand pounds," she insisted.

"For now," he agreed, pushing away from the doorjamb and straightening. "But I truly dare not tarry a moment longer here. The hour grows late, and soon, we will meet again for dinner. Until then, my dear Miranda."

He offered her a bow and then turned on his heel and strode back down the hall from whence they had come.

"Miss Lenox," she called after him sharply, sounding vexed.

As always, her ire was an aphrodisiac. Rhys couldn't recall the last time he'd ever had this much bloody fun.

MIRANDA STARED at her reflection in the looking glass, unable to shake the feeling that had been chasing her from the moment her host had left her to explore her room earlier.

The Duke of Whitby was the spider.

And Miranda?

She was the hapless fly. Ingloriously trapped. Awaiting the spider's leisure.

"Are you certain you don't wish to wear the blue silk, Mrs. Loveless?"

The query drove Miranda from her musings. She turned to the lady's maid who had been assigned her for an extortionate fee, if Whitby was to be believed, a girl with a round, friendly visage and the seemingly endless cheer of the young and unjaded. Along with Miranda's cases, a particularly suspicious trunk of gowns had arrived. Gowns that did not belong to her.

Which meant that the Duke of Whitby had somehow procured a small wardrobe for Miranda during the last week. Naturally, she had decided to eschew the dubious gift, opting instead to don another of her no-nonsense gray gowns. She may be the fly, but she still had wings.

"This gown shall suffice, Green," she reassured the younger woman.

The lady's maid gave Miranda's *toilette* a somber look over her shoulder. "Of course, madam. The gray does complement your eyes well."

They both knew that was a lie. Gray was not a becoming hue on Miranda. With her black hair and pale skin, she looked like an apparition risen from a grave. But she didn't wish to look her finest this evening. Far from it. Moreover, the gown also buttoned to the throat, unlike the daring bodice on the blue silk evening gown.

Yes, it would suit admirably for her purpose.

"Thank you," she told the lady's maid. "Do you know when the other guests will be arriving?"

"Tomorrow, Mrs. Loveless." Green frowned at Miranda. "Are you certain I can't help with your hair? I know a lovely Grecian braid."

At least Whitby had not been deceiving her about a house party, then. From the moment they had arrived to an empty estate, with no other guests set to arrive that day, Miranda had been suspicious.

Miranda's hair was scraped into a severe chignon, wound so tightly at her nape that it was already beginning to give her a headache. "Thank you, Green, but that won't be necessary."

"Of course, Mrs. Loveless. Will you require anything else from me?"

The name felt strange. Miranda only hoped she could remind herself to continue answering to it for the duration of her time in Hertfordshire.

She forced a smile she didn't feel, a liquid sense of anticipation settling in her stomach. "That will be all."

The lady's maid dipped into a curtsy, but before she could leave, a muffled sound from the chamber next door cut through the quiet of the room.

"Green," she called, spinning away from the mirror.

The younger woman halted. "Yes, madam?"

"Is someone staying in the chamber adjoining mine?"

Fresh pink suffused the girl's cheeks and throat. "Yes, Mrs. Loveless."

It would seem Miranda would have to pry any information she wanted from the lady's maid. "May I ask who?"

Green cleared her throat, casting her eyes to the Axminster. "It is His Grace, of course, madam."

The scoundrel.

He had settled her into the bedchamber beside his, as if he were already anticipating her capitulation. As if she were his mistress, joining him for the week's revelries. As if they were as familiar with each other as man and woman could be.

Green's ill-concealed embarrassment made sudden, awful sense. She believed Miranda was a woman of ill repute.

"I see," she forced out, struggling to keep her expression unconcerned. "Tell me, Green, is this sort of arrangement customary for the duke?"

The lady's maid squirmed. "I couldn't say, Mrs. Loveless. I'm new to Wingfield Hall, I am. Was brought on to be a lady's maid just three days ago. It doesn't show, does it? I was happy to take this situation, I was."

That also explained the girl's desire to please.

It would seem that the Duke of Whitby had hired Green specifically to be her lady's maid. Just as he had procured a small yet costly wardrobe for Miranda. Just as he had cleverly maneuvered himself into the chamber next door to hers.

"Of course not, Green," she reassured the younger woman. "I would have suspected you had years of experience."

Green beamed, dipping into another curtsy. "Oh, thank you, madam. Please know I'll have discretion in…all that transpires. I will bid you good evening."

With that, she disappeared, leaving Miranda alone with her thoughts. *All that transpires indeed*, she thought with a nettled sigh.

Whitby's earlier words returned, echoing in her mind. *You ought to never trust me. Not completely.*

Well, he certainly hadn't been wrong about that. She was fast learning she had underestimated her opponent. Like any good chess player, the duke had swiftly and cunningly maneuvered her into a position of great danger. But this would not be checkmate, she vowed.

She would simply have to prove to him she was not a woman who could easily be wooed. Because she wasn't. Her disastrous marriage and the scandal of her divorce had left her without choice. She could not indulge in an affair with the seductively handsome Duke of Whitby. The unwise urges that boiled to the surface whenever she was in his presence could and would be controlled.

Her tenuous future depended upon it.

CHAPTER 5

*W*ith a deep breath, Miranda emerged from her room, half expecting Whitby to be awaiting her there. But the hall was empty. Not even a servant in sight. Which made Miranda painfully aware of the fact that she didn't know her way around Wingfield Hall. Good heavens, she wasn't even certain she could find her way to the dining room.

At least she knew how to reach the staircase. She made haste in moving in that direction, but a familiar voice at her back had her halting.

"Going somewhere?"

She turned to find the duke sauntering toward her in a leisurely prowl that was at once both smug and elegant. He had the unhurried gait of a man who knew he commanded the attention of every eye in a room.

In this case, hers, and not just because he had called out, staying her progress. But because he was the most compelling man she had ever beheld. He was dressed in evening black, interrupted only by the slash of a crisp white shirt and matching necktie. His golden hair shone in the lamplight, looking soft, the waves falling naturally over his brow, as if he had run his fingers through the strands.

Oddly, her own fingers itched to run through his hair too.

"Your Grace," she forced herself to greet him, clinging to formality in sheer desperation. "Good evening to you. I was attempting to find dinner."

"I see my timing is excellent, then." He executed a bow that felt somehow like the prelude to something far more intimate than what next ensued as the duke strode forward, offering her his arm. "I shall be pleased to escort you there."

She eyed his proffered elbow dubiously. "You need not squire me about as if I'm a lady."

He raised a brow at that. "You *are* a lady."

"I am a businesswoman," Miranda countered sternly. "One you hired to please your guests."

The duke took her hand and settled it on his arm. "I'm far too selfish and greedy for that. I hired you to please me."

She stiffened.

"With your cream ices and those delicious cornets of yours," he added, chuckling. "Pray, don't grow vexed with me before we've even had the chance to sup. I'm ravenous."

For some odd reason she didn't care to investigate, the way he said the word ravenous sent a frisson down her spine.

She gritted her teeth and smiled. "Then by all means, Your Grace, let us descend to dinner without tarrying another moment longer."

"I do think I would happily starve if it meant lingering anywhere with you for but a moment." His voice was low and deep and pleasant. Intimate.

Here was the rakehell, the charmer, she reminded herself. The man she must at all costs resist.

"What a fanciful notion," she said, willing herself to remain unmoved. "I hardly think one moment of anyone's time would be worth forgoing dinner."

"How wrong you are, Miranda dear." His blue eyes flicked down over her, and a sudden frown drew his brows together. "Why are you still dressed like a spinsterly governess?"

She moved to release her hold on his arm, but he clamped a hand over hers, keeping her from withdrawing. "I am dressed like a woman who has a care for her reputation. And I am wearing my own gown because that is what is proper. You cannot buy me gowns, Your Grace."

"I didn't buy them. I borrowed them."

Jealousy seared her, the thought of him borrowing the castoffs of a former lover making her stomach tip. "I will not wear gowns you've loaned from a mistress."

"Oh, they don't belong to Beatrice."

She had begun walking with him, but now she nearly stumbled at the mentioning of another woman by name. The envy flared into a roaring fire. "You *do* have a mistress, then?"

"Of course not. I did have an understanding with Beatrice, but she was married, and quite respectable, believe it or not." He shrugged. "We have parted ways, but rest assured that the gowns do not hail from Beatrice's wardrobe. Such an arrangement would be wholly inappropriate. For one thing, your breasts are much larger."

She gasped in outrage. "Your Grace, I must demand that you cease such unnecessary crudeness."

"It's nothing to be ashamed of, Miranda dear. Your bubbies are nothing short of luscious. I can see that quite plainly despite your every effort to hide them in restrictive corsets and bodices more suited to a nun."

Miranda almost tripped over her hems as they descended the staircase. "Your Grace!"

He sighed. "I do so wish I could persuade you to call me Rhys."

"Who did you borrow the gowns from?" she asked, even though she didn't want the answer.

"A friend."

His enigmatic response left her feeling no better.

"A female friend," she repeated.

"My dear Miss Lenox," he drawled, "I do believe I hear just a hint of jealousy souring your dulcet voice."

He was baiting her. There was no other explanation for what the Machiavellian man was doing.

"Don't be silly," she snapped, irritated with him as much as with herself. "Why should I care if you have a bevy of women from whom you may borrow gowns on a whim?"

"She truly is a friend and nothing more." The fingers over hers tightened ever so slightly as they reached the foot of the staircase. "You need not fret. Ever since I made the acquaintance of one particular lady, I find myself decidedly uninterested in all the rest."

He was speaking of her.

Was he not?

And why did a weak part of her secretly rejoice at the notion that he was?

"Hmm," was all she said in response, because she was incapable of coherent speech just now.

Everything about this man had her at sixes and sevens. His nearness, his scent—this time with the added allure of shaving soap and the fresh, musky notes of his bath—his voice, his hold on her, his teasing words. Every part of him.

"Did the gowns not fit properly?" he asked quietly as he guided her through the great hall and an assorted collection of statues and antlers.

"I wouldn't know," she answered primly, taking care to keep a proper distance between their persons.

So proper that her body was held at an awkward angle, almost as if she feared her own arm and sought to remove herself from it. The result left her with a cramp in her shoulder, but she refused to so much as frown and allow him to see her further weakness.

"Never mind. There is something irresistible about that infernal line of buttons," he told her *sotto voce* as they reached another hall and approached a room where the doors had been left open and the savory smell of food wafted outward, along with the inviting glow of lamps. "A man cannot help but think about undoing them, one by one." They crossed the threshold to find a table dressed in snowy linens and gleaming cutlery, an epergne laden with fresh flowers at its center, domed platters and twin tureens neatly laid, awaiting their delectation. "With his teeth," Whitby added, his lips so close to her ear as he spoke those final, sinful words that Miranda swore she felt the graze of them, like hot velvet, brushing over her.

She shivered, but not from cold. "I have already given you my answer, Your Grace."

"Ah, but your hungry emerald eyes give me one answer, whilst your honeyed lips tell me another." Gallantly, he escorted her to a chair and held it out for her as she seated herself.

"I do believe you are being intentionally ridiculous, Your Grace," she said coolly, trying to tamp down the stupid thrill his words somehow sent through her.

"What part of what I say is ridiculous, Miranda dear?" he asked smoothly.

"I have neither emerald eyes nor honeyed lips." She kept her tone soft and curt, despite their lack of audience.

True to his words, the room was bereft of servants, as if the entire affair had been arranged with one courtly wave of his hand. She knew he could not have timed their arrival with such perfection. Perhaps the food awaiting them had been standing for several minutes already, but the silver domes, etched with engraving and placed neatly over each dish, served to keep them warm.

"On that, we agree." He seated himself at the place setting opposite her. "Your eyes are bolder and more brilliant than emeralds. Likewise, your lips, one must imagine, are sweeter than any honey."

Miranda was determined to remain unaffected by his effusive charm. "How do you utter such claptrap with a bland expression?"

"Wine?" he asked, holding up a bottle. "It's *une grande année*, *Chateau Margaux* 1864."

She eyed the bottle, then the duke. "I cannot think it wise."

He tipped the bottle and poured a handsome amount into her glass. "Wisdom is boring."

She swallowed, watching as he filled his own glass, trying not to admire the strength of his jaw or the way his hair curled under his ears, too unruly to be tamed, just like the rest of him. "Having been the recipient of far too much upheaval, I can assure you that there is nothing wrong at all with boring. Boring is safe."

He raised his glass to her, regarding Miranda with a solemnity she found disconcerting. "May you always feel safe with me, but never bored."

Her inbred sense of politeness stirred, forcing her to raise her glass in kind, despite her inclination to avoid drinking so much as a drop of the wine it contained. "As we won't be spending much time in each other's presence this week, I cannot think it shall matter either way."

Whitby took a slow, considering sip of his wine, never ceasing watching her as he did so. And she found herself stupidly entranced by a drop of wine lingering at the seam of his lips until his tongue darted out to catch it. His Adam's apple dipped as he swallowed.

"I do hope to make a liar of you. I'll have duties as host which will require my time and attention, and naturally, you shall have your cream ices and cornets to make. However, there is no reason why we cannot see each other often."

Seeing him often sounded akin to torture. Acute, sensual torture. Miranda was sure her resistance couldn't possibly withstand it.

"The cornets and cream will take up a large portion of my day," she said, before taking a sip of her own wine.

"Delegate duties to the kitchens," he told her, reaching forward to lift the lid on one of the tureens. "They are at your disposal and have likewise been instructed to aid you in all matters. You have *carte blanche* over them. Would you care for some duck soup, my dear?"

"Of course," she murmured, trying not to be distracted by the underlying implications of the phrase *carte blanche*.

He ladled some of the richly scented soup into her waiting bowl. Orange, herbs, and savory broth made her stomach rumble. It had been some time since they had partaken of a modest meal *en route* to Hertfordshire, and she couldn't deny she was hungry.

"But I still shan't be spending any time with you, Your Grace," she added frostily as he added soup to his own bowl next.

"But we will have to plan the menu," he protested, a small smile pulling at the corners of his lips.

"The housekeeper can attend to that."

"No," he countered swiftly. "She cannot. I don't wish to speak with Mrs. Gilliebrand. As kindly and efficient as she is at running this household, she is old enough to be my mother, and she jingles when she walks."

"That would be her chatelaine," Miranda protested, amused in spite of herself.

"A dreadful cacophony." He shuddered.

"A point of great pride for any housekeeper," she argued stoically. "I will be pleased to consult Mrs. Gilliebrand myself so that I may arrange the cream ices and cornets to best pair with the menu each day."

He nodded. "Only promise me that you will provide apple and ginger cream ice one of the days, if you please. I've been consumed by thoughts of having it upon my tongue again ever since I tasted it last."

There was something potent and sensual about the way he uttered those words, as if he were speaking of more than mere cream ice. His gaze was inscrutable and deep blue, piercing hers as he brought the soup spoon to his mouth. She caught her wine goblet in trembling fingers and raised it to her lips, needing the fortification.

When she had all but drained the glass, she replaced it upon the table linens, aware of the amused smile he sent in her direction. He knew the effect he had upon her, the wicked rake, and he was well pleased by it. But what did he expect? She would have had to be fashioned of stone to be unaffected by the potent lure of the Duke of Whitby.

"I will make certain to find a meal best suited to the apple and ginger cream ice," she forced herself to say.

As if her heart weren't racing. And as if her nipples hadn't tightened into aching buds beneath the punishing constriction of her corset. Green had tight-laced her with far more vigor than Miranda was accustomed to, particularly since she ordinarily did for herself. Now that she was seated, the boning was pinching her sides. Neither the slight biting pain, however, nor the tightness detracted from the reaction her body had to the sensual rake opposite her.

"Thank you." He nodded toward her as-yet-untouched bowl. "Now I must exhort you to eat your soup. It is a delight, though it pales in comparison to the marriage of flavors you created in your dessert."

Yes, she ought to eat, and for no better reason than she was famished and consuming her soup would provide an excellent distraction. She spooned some of the broth and brought it to her lips, reminded of the etiquette that had been sternly embossed upon her soul by a demanding governess years before. Here was a reminder of how it felt to eat in company. To cling to manners and societal niceties, neither of which had the slightest thing to do with hunger.

The soup was excellent, laced with sherry and fresh herbs, but it may as well have been gruel. She couldn't seem to enjoy it when she was seated at the table with the Duke of Whitby. He stole all the air from the room. His golden, seductive presence denied her the simple pleasure of enjoying the fine meal laid before her.

She consumed her bowl, trying not to look at him.

But it was no use.

"More soup?" he asked.

"I shouldn't indulge."

"Whyever not?"

"There are a great many other dishes upon the table," she reasoned.

He ignored her and served her another ladle of the delicious dish. "But you want more," he pointed out, and quite correctly too. "Why deny yourself?"

The decadent scent of the soup teased her nostrils. She was close—so close—to bringing the spoon to her lips and draining her bowl a second time. But there seemed to be a more important point to be made, one that superseded all else.

"Miranda," he prodded gently. "Go on. Eat the bloody soup."

Her gaze jolted to his. They engaged in a battle of wills that finally saw him sighing and lifting the dome over one of the other dishes. "Sirloin of beef *à la Pompadour*. Would you care for a slice?"

"Please."

He carved into the roast and produced a perfectly proportioned slice for her. The rest of the domes were lifted to reveal *haricots verts*, potatoes, asparagus *à la Princesse*, braised lettuce, and a salad of carrots.

Her plate was filled, the duck soup still calling to her longingly from her bowl. Determined, Miranda turned her attention to the various foods on her plate, cutting dainty, judicious bites.

"Your soup is growing cold," he remarked knowingly.

She ignored him, sawing at her beef with more vigor than the tenderized loin required.

"Stubborn to the last, I see."

Again, she said nothing.

"Tell me about yourself, Miranda. Do you have any siblings?"

It didn't surprise her that Whitby was more aware of her divorce and the scandal it had caused than he was of her family's makeup.

"I have two younger sisters and one brother who is my junior by a year as well."

"You are the eldest." He didn't sound surprised.

She glanced up at him, distracted from the act of slicing her beef into infinitesimal pieces. "Yes."

The duke took a contemplative sip of his wine, his stare never leaving hers. "I cannot say I'm shocked to learn so. I take it that your younger siblings have something to do with your family's decision to disavow you?"

Miranda loved her siblings. Her heart squeezed at the reminder that they must forever be lost to her.

It was her turn to nod, the lump in her throat growing larger. "My sisters have yet to find marriageable husbands.

Our parents feared an association with me, following the divorce, would leave them tainted."

Whitby swore beneath his breath. "They ought to have welcomed you. You're hardly the first divorced woman in England. Instead, they threw you to the goddamned wolves."

He was furious on her behalf, she realized. His anger was not feigned. And his ever-ready charm had swiftly died in the face of his vehemence.

"It is done now," she said, struggling for a lighter tone and the pretense that her family's abandonment hadn't cut her to the very marrow, for it most assuredly had. "I cannot change what has happened. Tell me, do you have any siblings, Your Grace?"

Although Whitby's reputation was notorious, she couldn't recall any mentioning of brothers or sisters in relation to him. And Miranda found herself genuinely curious to know more about him. Still, she turned her gaze to her plate, not wanting him to see the tears pooling in her eyes, blurring her vision. Far safer to look at her beef and *haricots verts*.

"You may seek to change the subject all you like, but it shan't make what they've done to you right."

She blinked, holding her eyes closed for a moment. To her humiliation, a hot tear rolled free of her lashes, coasting down her cheek. "Please. Let us speak of something else. You didn't answer my question. Have you any brothers or sisters of your own?"

There was a lengthy pause, during which she blinked furiously, trying to clear the tears from her eyes and restore her composure.

"I have one sister," he said at last. "Rhiannon is a hellion."

His voice was tender, a smile lingering in it. It was plain he doted upon his sibling. Miranda drained the remainder of her wineglass, continuing to avoid his gaze. "Tell me about her."

"She is ten years younger than I, and she's bold and fearless and is forever finding herself in one scrape after the next. Woe be to the man who one day takes her to wife. Rhiannon is a bit like fireworks—bright, loud, and unpredictable."

At last, Miranda ventured a glance in his direction again, finding that his expression had softened, taking on an almost boyish air as he spoke of his sister with unrepentant fondness.

"The two of you are close, then?" she surmised, unable to quell the pang of envy deep in her heart.

She missed her siblings. Missed her family and the seemingly unbreakable bonds that had once tied them.

"We are." He smiled. "I would protect her with everything I have. And I would never forsake her, not even if she caused the biggest scandal in all England."

His words were a pointed barb aimed at her family, and she knew it. But she was also grateful he had heeded her plea and hadn't directly spoken of the rift with her siblings and parents again.

"You are a good brother to her."

"I try to be." His smile turned self-deprecating. "Our father was a horse's arse and ignored her because she was a daughter instead of the spare he so desperately wanted."

Miranda took note of the bitterness that had suddenly entered his voice. "How dreadful for Lady Rhiannon."

"It was by far not the worst of our sire's cruelties, but yet another for which I'll never forgive him." Whitby refilled his wineglass and added a bit more to hers. "But enough of all such unpleasant subjects. Let's leave the past where it belongs, shall we?"

Miranda had her own healing wounds from the past, so she didn't argue. "Yes, let's."

She took another sip of her wine, thinking she would

need it for fortification if she had a prayer of continuing to remain unmoved by the duke's dashing charm.

THE FIRE WAS CRACKLING low in the grate of the library at Wingfield Hall. Rhys's left arm had fallen asleep approximately half an hour ago and was presently numb. Despite this, he hesitated to move the sleeping woman at his side.

She was soft and warm, all the starch and stiffness leeched from her, her head leaning against his shoulder, the gentle gusts of her sleep breathing a pleasant rhythm only occasionally interrupted by a small, feminine snore.

No doubt about it, Miranda Lenox was foxed. Adorably, utterly soused. Too much French wine at dinner, he reckoned. Getting her drunk had certainly not been his intent. No, the rake in him had been determined to press his suit.

To woo her.

Win her.

To seduce her.

But as they had decamped from the dining room and she had accepted his offer of a cordial in the library, it had become increasingly apparent to him that his Miranda was not in any state for wooing.

Instead, they had sat together before the ornate marble fireplace, chatting about everything from cream ices to poetry to art until she had gone abruptly silent. She had fallen asleep sitting up, her head tilted back and her lips parted.

"Poor lamb," he had murmured, settling her into a more comfortable position against his side.

And there she had remained, not even waking when he had shifted her so she might use his person as a pillow. There was presently a fine patch of drool darkening the black of his coat, and he didn't even care. From the little she had shared with him about her divorce and the ensuing scandal and her family's severing of ties with her, he could glean that she had been through the fiery flames of hell.

Somehow, she had emerged from it all a businesswoman determined to see her school of cookery thrive and succeed. She had earned this rest. And he couldn't deny there was something pleasing about the way she had trustingly melted against him. The way she had burrowed into his shoulder and slumbered.

He had never, in all his days, dreamt that the act of a woman falling asleep upon him would make him feel as he did now—strangely warm in the darkest cockles of his heart he had believed long dead and cold, a searing sense of rightness lodged behind his collarbone. That last was most concerning of all.

Hell, perhaps he was in his cups as well, and he just didn't know it. Surely that was the reason a seasoned, jaded rake such as himself would remain as he was, listening to Miranda's sleep breathing, her perfume coiling around him like a rope. His cock wasn't even hard. He had simply been sitting here for Christ knew how long, enjoying her presence and proximity.

Liking the way she felt against him.

He sighed. Yes, likely he was soused as well. He'd never even shared a bed with one of his lovers after fucking. The act of sleeping with another, of the expectations that might accompany such an intimacy, had always made him flee. Strangely, he had no urge to run now. Instead, he was plagued by a persistent, protective urge where she was concerned.

Her bloody family had disowned her. He wasn't sure which bothered him the most, her family's lack of loyalty where she was concerned or the upset they had caused her. There had been tears shimmering in her eyes earlier when she had spoken of them, and after that lone tear had spilled down her cheek, he had been overtaken by the simultaneous urge to slam his fist into her father's jaw and to hold her in his arms and soothe her.

He couldn't shake the all-consuming notion that she was *his*, damn it. That he ought to tear off to London at once and give her arsehole family the dressing down they so richly deserved for abandoning Miranda to whatever fate awaited her. He had no right to feel that way, and he knew it. He had hired her ostensibly for her culinary expertise for the next week, and perhaps even to warm his bed for the next month if he had his way. But he wasn't meant to have feelings for her.

This was all wrong. That didn't mean he didn't savor these remaining moments he had her all to himself. Tomorrow would inevitably arrive, and with it, an influx of guests he would be expected to entertain.

Moving slowly, he extricated his pocket watch from his waistcoat to consult the time. Half past one. Damn it all, he regretted volunteering to host this house party. The lack of anticipation was deuced odd. Ordinarily, he looked forward to the debauchery that inevitably happened at the Wicked Dukes Society house parties. The members of their club paid a small fortune to be assured of both secrecy and carnal abandon in equal measure. Rhys had always enjoyed the revelries. But now in the shadows of the night, the glow of the fire dancing on the walls, he wished he had spirited Miranda to his own country seat instead.

They wouldn't have been interrupted. He would have been free to seduce her at leisure. To allow her to sleep in his arms in the library. To savor her. But tomorrow would come far too soon, and he also needed to warn her about the true nature of the house party. She was going to be furious with him when she discovered it.

But her outrage would be too late, just as he had planned. She was already in Hertfordshire where he wanted her, the fifteen hundred pounds he had paid her having been applied to her cookery school's debts.

Rhys swiftly banished an accompanying pang of conscience at the thought of how thoroughly he had deceived her. He had merely done whatever was necessary to persuade Miranda to join him here. And he would compensate her handsomely, both in pleasure and monetary gain.

He allowed a few more minutes to tick by on his pocket watch before reluctantly pocketing it once again. He knew he could not continue delaying the inevitable.

Gently, Rhys stroked a wisp of hair from her cheek that had worked itself free of the unforgiving knot at her nape. "Miranda, sweeting."

She mumbled something he couldn't identify and then nestled closer, like a kitten seeking solace from its mother. Only, Miranda was no kitten, and he was decidedly not her mother.

"Miranda," he tried again, his voice a bit louder this time.

"Mmm," she murmured, eyes still closed. "Better than my favorite cream ice."

"What is?" he asked, curious, even though he knew she was still half asleep.

She gave an indelicate snort and smacked her lips.

Rhys stifled a chuckle. Dear God, she was nothing short of delectable. A fresh wave of something built in his chest, strong and forceful. Something that felt remarkably like tenderness.

But no, surely that was wrong.

He scarcely knew this woman. And he, Rhys Northwick, Duke of Whitby, did not develop tender feelings for the women he fucked. Not that he had bedded Miranda yet, of course, but it was inevitable that he would. Their attraction was palpable, and the only present obstacle to having her naked and beneath him was her damnable sense of pride.

"Miranda, sweeting," he tried again, giving her shoulder a gentle shake. "The hour is late, and we should both find our way to our beds so that we can get some sleep tonight."

With a throaty sound, she awoke, making soft noises that made his stupid cock twitch back to life. Excellent. Now he would have to go to bed alone, and with a cockstand. Apparently he was just as depraved as he'd always been after all.

Her eyes fluttered open, her long, dark lashes parting to reveal the brilliance of that shocking verdant gaze. "Whitby?"

"Rhys," he reminded her, hoping that her sleep-and-wine-dazed mind may be persuaded to eschew her infernal insistence upon adhering to formality.

A vee had formed between her brows. "Wh-where am I?"

"In the library," he reminded her, tamping down the rising, raging urge to kiss her. "You accompanied me here after dinner, and I fear the journey left you wearier than I had realized. You fell asleep."

"Oh dear." Pink crept up her throat, and he longed to undo some of her buttons to see just where her flush began. "I fell asleep?"

"Indeed." He grinned down at her. "You snore adorably, you know."

"I snored?" Her frown deepened, lucidity returning to her eyes and her voice now as sleep rapidly fled. "And I fell asleep on you. Good heavens. *On* you."

As if he were fashioned of flame, she jolted away from him on the Grecian couch, sliding hastily to the opposite end.

"You also drooled on me," he added, amused by her reaction.

Clearly, her body felt more at home with him than her mind did.

Her face flamed. "I am certain I did no such thing."

Still grinning, he tapped on the damp spot on his left lapel. "Right here."

"I must beg your pardon."

"You must, indeed," he said with mock levity. "You see, it isn't every day that a woman falls asleep on me. My pride is unutterably destroyed."

"I thought it had already cracked and disintegrated earlier," she pointed out, that rapier-sharp wit and tongue of hers returning.

"It is remarkably adept at restoring itself," he quipped, enjoying himself far too much.

He would happily stay here with her all night, trading barbs and nothing more. The realization was both astonishing and alarming.

"Of course it is. You are a duke after all."

"What does that have to do with pride?"

A small, sad smile tipped the corners of her lips upward. "You are important. A well-titled, wealthy, handsome gentleman. I have no doubt that legions of women chase after you daily."

His mind caught on only a fraction of what she had said, because her lips were glistening and full, and he very much wanted to feel them against his, but he wouldn't kiss her now because she had drunk too much wine and he was trying to be a gentleman, damn it.

"You think me handsome?" he asked, pleased.

"You own a mirror, do you not? Of course you must know that you are."

"Yes, but hearing you grudgingly say it after you've spent the last two hours curled up to me like a kitten is more gratifying than I can possibly convey."

His teasing words had their intended effect.

Her lips parted, her mouth forming a perfect *o* of indignation. "Curled up to you like a kitten?"

"A sweet kitten who has awakened and unsheathed her claws," he drawled.

"I haven't claws."

"I beg to differ."

They stared at each other, another errant strand of hair clinging to her cheek that he could not resist. Rhys slid across the couch in one swift motion, then reached out and tucked the curling tendril behind her ear. As he did so, his fingertips brushed her cheek ever so slightly.

She trembled, her eyes widening, her pupils going black in her brilliant green eyes. "What are you doing, Your Grace?"

He was far too close for propriety's sake, but it didn't bloody well matter. They were alone, no one would happen upon them, and he intended to be far closer to her than this soon. So he lingered where he was.

"Your coiffure is coming undone," he murmured. "Did not your lady's maid assist you this evening?"

He would admit, he had hoped to see her in one of the gowns he had brought for her, all borrowed from the dressmaker he often used to buy gowns for his lovers should they wish it. Mrs. Williams had an entire wardrobe available that no longer fit the intended lady because she was increasing. The timing had proven excellent. Likewise, he had chosen a lady's maid to assist Miranda in the hope she might take at least the week to attend to herself. He had underestimated her determination.

"I coiled it into a chignon myself," she said, her voice still a trifle breathless. "I don't need your gowns, Your Grace, any more than I need a lady's maid."

"There is a vast difference between needing something

and wanting it," he pointed out, remaining where he was, deliciously near to her on the couch.

If she had a hint of self-preservation, she would leap from the furniture and flee at once. Because now that she had awakened, it was plain to see she was no longer in her cups as deeply as she had been before her little nap.

"Wanting something does not mean you should have it," she countered, ever practical, rather like a martyr, willing to sacrifice herself for the good of her cause.

"Nor does it mean that you should not have it, and everything else you want, too," he cajoled.

"Are you saying you do not deny yourself anything that you want?" she asked softly.

His grin faded, utter seriousness overtaking him as he propped his forearm on the back of the couch and held her gaze. "Of course not. I want you very much, Miranda. More, I think, than I have ever wanted anyone or anything. And yet, I must deny myself until you reach the inevitable conclusion."

Her chin went up, her lips parting. "Which is?"

Her voice had gone husky. Her eyes settled on his mouth. And holy God, it was the most erotic moment he had known in as long as he could recall, her gaze on him, tempted and curious and hungry too.

"That you and I are meant to be lovers," he answered.

Her swift inhalation of breath cut through the silence, followed by the pop of a log in the fireplace. Sparks shot over the grate in his peripheral vision, and he couldn't help but to think it a metaphor for what was happening now.

If only she hadn't consumed too much wine. He cursed himself for refilling her goblet with too liberal a hand. For tonight, all they would have was flirting. He had to know that she was not otherwise influenced. That she wouldn't regret what passed between them.

"I have already given you your answer," she reminded him.

"And I will accept it when you mean it." He winked. "For now, we both ought to retire. The morning will come soon enough."

He reluctantly rose and offered her his hand, which she eyed dubiously.

"I cannot accompany you to your bedchamber."

He would have laughed had he not feared she might misconstrue his lightheartedness. "Nor did I invite you. As I said, I want you very much. But you will come to me of your own volition, or not at all."

"Then I am afraid you are doomed to be disappointed."

This time, he did chuckle, just as she laid her hand in his and his fingers closed around hers. "My sweet Miranda, how wrong you are. Before this week is over, you will be begging me."

And that was a promise he intended to keep.

CHAPTER 6

"*O*h, Mrs. Loveless, you're awake!"

Green's cheerful voice interrupted Miranda's perusal of her recipe collection. It took a moment for her to realize she was the one being spoken to and to recall that she, in fact, was currently "Mrs. Loveless."

She looked up from her task, seated at the writing desk that was situated by an eastern-facing window. She had been awake as soon as the fingers of daylight slowly stretched across the dawn sky. Ever since leaving the town house she had occupied during her marriage to Ammondale, Miranda had been rising early. There was so much to accomplish in her days and never sufficient hours.

"Good morning, Green," she greeted with a smile.

The girl was ruddy-cheeked and beaming, fairly vibrating with the enthusiasm and optimism that was the hallmark of the unjaded and truly young. Miranda wondered if she had ever been as filled with joyful cheer. If she had, she could no longer recall that time or what it had felt like. The misery of her marriage and divorce had eclipsed all else.

"You're already dressed," Green observed, her smile

faltering as she bustled across the room. "And your hair, madam. I was hoping I might try to dress it for you today."

Miranda had performed her morning ablutions and dressed herself in another of her serviceable gray gowns. Likewise, she had coiled her heavy hair into a tight knot at her nape. Her hair was parted severely down the middle.

The style was unbecoming, and she knew it. But particularly after the Duke of Whitby's silken warning the night before, she had decided that she must make herself as unattractive as possible.

Before this week is over, you will be begging me.

A shiver passed through her, and she couldn't fight the vexing ache that pulsed to life between her thighs.

"Are you cold, Mrs. Loveless?" Green asked, hastening to the banked fire in the grate. "Last night got quite cool, it did. I'll fix this in a trice, and you'll be warm in no time."

She wasn't cold. Not at all. Rather, she was overly warm. Overly warm thinking about the Duke of Whitby. And not for the first time since she had awakened to regret and a dry mouth this morning either. No, she had been thinking of almost nothing *but* Whitby.

She had fallen asleep on him. Had committed the sin of drinking too much wine in his captivating presence and then had promptly gone alone with him to the library. She remembered enjoying the pleasant timbre of his low voice. Remembered staring at the fire. And then she remembered slowly waking to the scent of musk and forbidden forest with a hint of citrus. Recalled feeling warm and safe and utterly at ease until the moment she had truly jolted awake and realized where she was and whose side she had been intimately pressed against.

Worse, there had been a wild, foolish moment when her gaze had somehow strayed to his lap as they had been speaking, directly to the thick ridge straining against the fall of his trousers. The most inane, inappropriate thought had occurred to her in that moment. *The Duke of Whitby has an immense cock!*

Shame filled her anew now as her mind played over that realization, the wicked words, the memory of that long, large member making a tent of his trousers. With a groan, Miranda braced her elbows on the writing desk and sank her head into her waiting hands. Another ache had begun throbbing, this time in her temples. She was never drinking French wine again. And certainly not with the Duke of Whitby. No, she was never going to find herself alone with him again. Not for the remainder of the week.

"Is something amiss, Mrs. Loveless?" Green asked, fussing with the coals in the grate. "You're not ill, are you?"

Yes, she was ill. But her sickness was all her own making. She was to blame for her throbbing head. Just as she was to blame for lowering her guard and falling asleep on Whitby last night. Good heavens, she had even snored and drooled upon him. Meanwhile, the peculiar man hadn't seemed to even mind.

His stormy eyes had been glittering with mirth, as if he had enjoyed the way they had spent the evening. But that wasn't right. He was a rake. Surely he would have been disappointed he had been denied the opportunity to ply his charm.

"Mrs. Loveless?" Green prodded.

Miranda blinked, realizing she hadn't answered. "I'm well, thank you, Green. Merely caught up in the tangled web of my own thoughts this morning, I suppose."

"Ah yes, that I can understand, madam," Green said, working the fire back into a tidy little blaze that had further warmth washing over Miranda. "My dear mother has always told me that she can tell the moment I begin gathering wool. Never listened well as a girl, I must say. Of course, I didn't mean to suggest that you weren't a nice, biddable lass as a young woman, Mrs. Loveless. I'm certain you were."

She dusted her hands off on her skirts as she spoke, looking worried now.

"Fear not," Miranda reassured the younger woman. "I was not offended in the slightest."

"Oh, good." Green gusted out a sigh of relief and grinned. "The fire's settled now, madam. Mightn't I take a look at your hair?"

Miranda reached up, her fingers smoothing over the tightly bound strands that were all but pasted to her scalp. "That won't be necessary. I have already finished it."

"I can see that, madam. But your hair is so beautiful, and I have a style in mind that I think would serve you ever so much better, if you don't mind my saying so."

It was apparent that the girl was new to her position. No seasoned lady's maid would dare to gainsay the woman she attended. Miranda wanted to deny Green's request, but her hopeful countenance of unfettered friendliness and sanguinity had her sighing.

"Very well, if you insist, Green."

"Oh, Mrs. Loveless, I can promise you that you won't regret it," Green gushed, before gathering up the tools of her trade and bustling across the room to the writing desk.

She was a whirlwind of energy and vigor, and Miranda couldn't deny she found the girl's enthusiasm catching. With smooth, efficient motions, Green plucked the pins from Miranda's hair. Some brushing and separating, and then her hair was plaited into elaborate braids on either side of her head, leaving a smattering of curls free at her temples, the heavy fullness of the remaining braid coiled into a high, looser chignon.

"Your hair has such a lovely curl to it," Green praised, examining Miranda from the front as she wound a few strands of hair around her finger for good measure. "There. Perfection, if I do say so, madam. Although, a day gown with a spot of color might prove even more appealing."

"My curls are the bane of my existence," Miranda said without bite. "They never do what I wish them to do."

Which was also why she smoothed them into tight chignons. It had been quite some time since she'd last had a lady's maid of her own or cared what happened to her hair. Hair had simply become a task instead of another part of her *toilette*.

"I have two younger sisters with curls," Green told her, beaming as she inspected her work. "I've had ample time practicing taming their hair into whatever I wish. There. Now, and don't you just look impossibly lovely, madam? Come and have a look in the mirror."

Solely to pacify the excited lady's maid, Miranda rose and crossed the chamber to inspect her new coiffure. She couldn't deny that Green was a dab hand at dressing hair. She had fashioned Miranda's stubborn curls into an elegant and feminine style that was quite becoming.

"What do you think?" Green asked, fairly bouncing on her toes in her eagerness.

"I think you have worked wonders upon my hair," she said, turning back to the lady's maid with a smile. "Thank you."

"It was my pleasure, it was." Green grinned. "Is there aught else you'll be needing from me this morning, madam?"

"That will be all," she said, before rethinking mid-sentence. "Unless you might ring for a tray of breakfast? I am famished, and I have some work awaiting me this morning."

She gestured back to her recipes, still laid out neatly on the writing desk and in need of review. Perhaps with some food to fortify her constitution, she would be able to concentrate upon the task at hand instead of dwelling on the maddening Duke of Whitby.

Green's countenance suddenly turned sheepish. "I'm sorry, Mrs. Loveless. I almost forgot to tell you that His Grace is wanting your presence in the breakfast room this morning."

Anticipation coiled in her belly, along with something else. Something she refused to acknowledge for how perilous it was.

"Have any of the guests begun to arrive yet?" she asked her lady's maid hopefully.

"Not until this afternoon, I believe, madam," Green informed her.

Miranda forced a tight smile. "I suppose I shall descend to the breakfast room, then. Until later, Green."

Abandoning the recipes she had scarcely been able to concentrate upon and the safe haven of her room, Miranda descended to the dining room. The absence of servants was once again notable. Not a hint of a maid or footman to be seen. Not even a flurry of movement out of the corner of her eye. It was as if Wingfield Hall had been left empty.

Had Whitby truly kept the servants from view specifically for her?

It hardly mattered, Miranda told herself as she hastened toward the room where they had dined the night before.

"There you are."

The all-too-familiar voice had her breaking her stride and turning to find the duke approaching her, dressed this morning in country tweed that made his golden mane even more pronounced, his blue eyes twinkling with their customary mischief as he sauntered toward her.

She remembered herself, dipping into a hasty curtsy. "Good morning, Your Grace."

"Good morning to you as well, my dear." He offered her

an elegant bow in return. "I was beginning to fear you were avoiding me."

Mortification made heat climb up her throat. "I must apologize again for my lack of restraint yesterday."

For falling asleep on him, for snoring, for drooling upon his coat. *Heavens!* By day, her shame was not any less stinging than it had been the night before.

But he just grinned, as gorgeous and unperturbed as ever. "You needn't apologize. I'm pleased that you feel comfortable enough with me to lower your guard, Miranda."

That wasn't what she felt. Was it?

"I was soused," she pointed out, her voice sharper than she had intended.

"My fault, no doubt. Too much *Chateau Margaux*." He offered her his arm. "May I escort you to breakfast?"

"When are your guests arriving?" she asked, eyeing his arm dubiously. "When am I to consult the menu with your housekeeper? I need to prepare."

"Later today," he said smoothly, his gaze lingering on her lips in a hot look she felt like a touch. "And you may consult the menu at your leisure. I was selfishly hoping you might conjure your cream ices for dinner. I would also be honored if you joined us there."

How tempted she was to accept his invitation. To forget who she was and what she must be.

Miranda shook her head. "You know I cannot."

"As I said, my guests are sworn to secrecy. Nothing that happens within these walls leaves Wingfield Hall."

"That sounds rather ominous," she observed as she at last settled her hand in the crook of his elbow.

He began guiding her from the main hall. Curtains had been pulled aside to allow sunlight to stream in windows, and although the day was overcast, the multitude of panes meant the cavernous room was bathed in a cheerful, natural glow. She couldn't help but to admire the way it brought out the glints of gold and copper in his hair.

"Hardly ominous," he said. "The ladies and gentlemen who gather at this assemblage are a part of a secret, highly exclusive club. They pay a more-than-generous sum so that they may be assured of privacy."

His words hardly allayed the creeping concern that something rather out of the ordinary was about to take place at Whitby's house party. "Why should they require privacy?"

"Because the happenings at a Wicked Dukes Society house party can be a bit…debauched."

The deep rumble of his voice sent a frisson through her. "Wicked Dukes Society?"

She was unfamiliar with such a club.

"Yes." They reached the dining room where breakfast had been laid out in the same fashion as dinner the previous evening, *à la Francaise*, no hint of servants about.

"I'm beginning to think all the domestics here are wraiths," she quipped as they stopped before her chair.

"Not wraiths, I assure you." He offered her a dashing smile as he pulled the chair out for her. "Merely well trained and amply paid to do whatever is asked of them."

She seated herself as he courteously pushed the chair in at her back. She settled her napkin in her lap and turned back to him. "What is the Wicked Dukes Society?"

"It is a club that was begun several years ago as a drunken jest," he answered, skirting the table to sit opposite her. "Brandon, Camden, Riverdale, Richford, Kingham, and I all came up together at Eton. We've been like brothers ever since. One night, we were engaging in a bout of Bacchanalian revelries, and the notion came upon us that we might gather like-minded individuals in the name of a singular pursuit."

"And what pursuit is that?"

His gaze seared hers. "Pleasure, of course."

Something naughty unfurled in her belly. Was it the word? The way he said it? His voice, his eyes, his nearness? She ought to be appalled. She *was* appalled.

"Pleasure?" she repeated.

He nodded. "Indeed. Being venal souls, we also decided that membership in our society should come with a substantial fee. The members pay a small fortune, their secrets are secured, and they are free to do whatever it is they wish, within reason of course."

"Do you mean to tell me that you have lured me to some…some manner of orgy?" she demanded.

His grin deepened, making crinkles edge his sparkling eyes. Oh, he was almost too beautiful when he smiled like that. Her breath caught in spite of herself.

"Miranda dear," he drawled, "you quite astound me. Speaking of orgies, and we have yet to break our fast. Do you mind if I take my eggs and a bit of coffee before we reach such a prodigious part of the morning's conversation?"

The urge to box his ears rose within her.

"I wasn't speaking of orgies," she snapped. "You were."

"I'm afraid I wasn't. I was speaking of house parties. It was you who mentioned orgies. I must confess, I'm rather shocked a lady such as yourself is even aware of that word, let alone its definition." He paused in the act of removing a silver dome from one of the dishes awaiting them on the table. "You *do* know what an orgy is, don't you, kitten?"

Heat rose to her cheeks. "Of course I know what an orgy is."

"Oh, good. For a moment there, I feared you were confusing it with orgeat." He removed three poached eggs and laid them upon his plate. "A similar sound with two greatly different meanings, of course."

Her face was flaming; she was sure of it. "And do not call me kitten," she added as a frosty afterthought.

He was toying with her, and she knew it.

"But I do like to think of the way you were nestled so trustingly against me last evening."

She ground her molars, not even certain how to respond, if at all.

"Perhaps you would prefer cat? Is it the diminutive size which causes your objection or the general naïveté of a kitten as opposed to a cat fully grown?"

Miranda glared at him.

He arched an eyebrow, feigning a look of innocence. "Would you care for some poached eggs?"

Her stomach growled, answering rudely for her. Curse the devil, she was going to have to endure more of his teasing if she was to have any sustenance.

"Please," she bit out.

He served her two eggs without asking how many she would like. "Bacon?"

"Yes."

This, too, was placed upon her gleaming plate, followed by hothouse pineapple and strawberries. Miranda had been served many times before. By servants, by other gentlemen. But there was something decidedly intimate about being served by the Duke of Whitby. He somehow managed to make even the smallest of gestures sensual, as if every mundane move had its purpose, each gesture, look, and act a part of the seduction campaign he waged.

"Kippers?" he inquired mildly, as if he hadn't just been discussing orgies.

"Thank you, but no," she demurred.

"Do you care for coffee?"

"I prefer tea. Coffee is far too bitter for my liking."

"As I am a host most considerate, you have both at your disposal," he said, gesturing to the tea tray, which had been partially obscured by the massive epergne and its spray of fresh flowers. "Cream and sugar?"

"Yes."

"I thought so."

He sounded smug, and she didn't like it. Not the tone of his voice or the implication that he could somehow anticipate what she would want.

She accepted the dish of tea he prepared her, and he filled his demitasse with richly scented coffee.

"Now, then, I expect you are wondering about the nature of this house party," he said without even a hint of concern.

"You know I am. If I had known for a moment that there was something sordid about this house party, I would have refused you." Although she tried valiantly, Miranda could not keep the ire from her voice.

"Would you have, though?" His gaze, like his question, was direct. "As I recall, you needed the three thousand pounds."

Curse him for pointing that out.

"I could have managed without it," she said, clinging to her pride.

"And a man can also bail water from a leaking boat, but only for so long before the whole affair sinks with him in it," Whitby pointed out.

He was not wrong. Her cookery school had been in dire need of pupils and funds. The expenditures had been outpacing the income she received by far. Too many more months of such a predicament would have spelled failure. Which was why accepting his money had been so alluring.

She frowned at him. "I surmise that in this little analogy of yours, my school is the leaking boat. But my pupils are growing with each day. The establishment will be profitable, particularly when I can begin the situation placement portion of the school and start selling my recipe book."

"I can assure you that nothing of mine is little," he purred.

And she knew what he was insinuating. Of course she did. He was speaking of his cock, the scoundrel.

"For heaven's sake," she burst out, tea sloshing from her cup and onto its saucer in her agitation. "Are you trying to make me go mad? Has that been your plot all along?"

"If I did want you to go mad, it would only be with longing." He winked. "Is it working?"

That was *it*.

The Duke of Whitby, that handsome cad goading her to her wit's end from across the table, that beautiful, evil rake, that wicked sybarite, had lured her to Hertfordshire so that she could provide cream ices for an *orgy*.

And he was grinning and plying his charm and looking so unfairly glorious that he might have been a Greek god descended to toil amongst mortals for the sennight, having grown bored of all the beauteous goddesses attending him in Mount Olympus.

"You utter rogue," she charged, forgetting about her breakfast entirely. "You know how important it is for me to avoid even the slightest hint of scandal. As a ruined woman, I have naught but my present reputation to commend me, along with the meager skills I can offer my pupils. And yet you have brought me here to this den of sin, knowing the grave peril it would place me in."

He frowned at her, his teasing air vanishing. "There is nothing meager about your talent. I've never eaten anything as refined and delicious as your cornets and cream."

His praise sailed past her ire and tickled her pride. But she would not allow him to scale her walls of defense so easily.

"I thank you for your compliment," she managed, her voice trembling from the force of the emotions coursing through her. "However, it does nothing to assuage my fury for your selfish recklessness with my reputation and my school."

Whitby stared at her, silence descending after her outraged pronouncement.

"I promise that no harm will come to your reputation by your presence here," he said softly.

His countenance was so earnest, his stare holding hers, that she wanted to believe him. But she was also a practical-minded woman. One who had scrabbled and clawed to regain her freedom, despite the tremendous cost.

"That is something you cannot promise me," she countered. "Tongues wag. I am not unknown amongst polite society. All I need is one person to see me and carry the tale."

"No one will recognize you because most guests in attendance for the next week will be masked," he said. "I can see that several are delivered to your chamber for your use as well."

His assertion quelled some of the fear roiling within her, though not all. "You have ladies' masks lying about?"

The notion of him collecting masks from his various paramours made her stomach tighten into a jealous knot, and she didn't know why. She had no claims upon him. Heavens, she could not dally with him even if she wished to, which she decidedly did not.

"I always make certain to bring extra sundries to our revelries." He took a sip of his coffee, and she couldn't help but to watch the movement of his lips, the dip of his Adam's apple. "It is the host's duty to make certain that all his guests are well entertained and provided for."

There was something about his assertion she didn't like any more than his previous admission.

"And how do you entertain and provide for your guests, Your Grace?" she asked with just a trace too much bitterness.

"I'll not lie to you, Miranda. In the past, I have enjoyed

partaking in any number of revelries." He settled his demi-tasse back upon the table linens.

Of course he had enjoyed participating in his orgies, she thought grimly. Why else would he host them?

She stood abruptly, the notion of remaining here whilst he cavorted with any number of ladies who would be in attendance making her stomach twist violently. She didn't think she could bear it.

He was on his feet, his long legs taking him around the table before she could flee. Strong hands grasped her waist and he spun her about, pinning her against the breakfast table with his lean, muscled strength.

"Not this time, however," he rasped, his gaze hot and hard on hers. "This time, all I want is you."

The charm had been stripped from his voice, his face. Here was the cunning seducer in the raw, the practiced rake free of his smooth drawls and effortlessly unaffected mien. It was as if a wall had fallen away, and she was seeing him—the true Duke of Whitby—for the first time.

Her breath caught in her throat. "I didn't come here for a dalliance."

He tightened his fingers on her waist and dipped his head. "You may tell yourself so, but deep inside, you know the truth."

She stared at him, shock making her go completely still, making her incapable of doing anything. She could not even move. Because in this wild moment, all pretenses were gone. They were man and woman, their heated bodies pressed together, their breaths melding. And she recognized the veracity of his words to her very marrow. She had told herself that she had accepted his offer because she needed the funds. That was not wrong. But there was another reason as well. A reason that was glaring and dangerous.

The wickedest part of her wanted the Duke of Whitby as her lover.

Wanted to strip him of his tweed, to feed her hands the sensation of his broad shoulders bereft of fabric, to explore the taut bands of his abdomen, to rake her nails along the strong plane of his back. And then to move lower. To find the waistband of his trousers. To undo the tempting buttons at his falls. To reach inside the slit of his drawers and pull his big, hard cock free of all polite restraints.

The animal in her wanted to lie on the breakfast table and lift her skirts. To urge him between her spread thighs and to beg him, just as he had warned her she would do. She wanted him to mount her, to thrust himself inside her so deep that it felt as if he would never leave. She wanted the taste of him on her tongue, the pounding of his heart against her bare breast.

"You know it," he repeated softly, almost triumphantly, one of the hands at her waist lifting to cup her cheek. "Go on and say that you don't. Lie to me."

His thumb stroked lightly along her jaw as he spoke, the touch so exquisite she almost moaned aloud. His hand opened, his other fingers splaying hot and possessive against her throat, curling around to her nape.

Try as she might, she couldn't say it. Couldn't mean it. Couldn't feel it.

"Whitby," she protested weakly instead, her voice annoyingly breathless.

"You can't, can you?" He smiled slowly. Not a practiced smile and not a rakish grin, but something else entirely.

A smile that felt as if it were meant for her alone.

"I…"

She wanted to deny him, but the words would not come.

"I'm a man of my word," he murmured, his head dipping nearer, their lips perilously close. "Your presence here will have no bearing upon your reputation or your school. I vow it upon my life. Do you believe me? Do you trust me?"

No.

It was on the tip of her tongue. She knew better than to trust a man like him. Better than to trust any man.

But as she searched his stormy eyes, she read what felt like sincerity there. And she heard it in his voice, in his promise. He had already paid her half the sum. She owed him the week. She had already promised to uphold her end of their bargain.

"I'll do everything in my power to protect you," he added. "Nod your head, darling."

She nodded, obeying like a fool. It would seem she had misplaced both her wits and her pride. The Duke of Whitby had, quite impossibly, thieved them.

"Good." He closed the distance, but it wasn't her mouth that received his kiss.

Instead, his hot, smooth lips pressed to her forehead.

She swallowed hard, realizing that her hands had been trapped between them, her fingers curled against his shirt and waistcoat. She moved them now tentatively, gliding them up his muscled chest to linger on his shoulders. Miranda clutched at his tweed, feeling as if the world had tilted and she needed to cling to him for purchase.

Somehow, over the course of the breakfast they had failed to consume, everything had changed. He kissed her temples next, first one, then the other. Her lips parted. Surely he would lay his mouth upon hers next.

"I'll have the masks sent to your chamber," he murmured against her ear, his lips finding her earlobe next. "Anything you want shall be yours. You need only but ask. For the next week, I am at your disposal." He paused and pressed another kiss to her throat, just above the demure collar of her gown. "Do with me as you like."

She couldn't. Her heart was galloping, her breath coming faster. She had never been so attuned to a man in her life.

"I shan't be doing anything with you," she managed.

"No?" He kissed the very edge of her jaw, the farthest point from her mouth. "That would be a travesty, darling. Be warned. Just as I'll do everything I can to protect you, I'll also do everything I can to change your mind. And I do mean *everything*."

One more heated kiss to her cheek, and then he withdrew from her as suddenly as he had pressed her to the table, the loss of him leaving her aching for more. He hadn't kissed her. Hadn't settled his lips over hers, and now she was desperate to know what that would feel like.

"Now, let's eat our breakfast, shall we?" he asked, his façade firmly in place again. "The day promises to be a long one, and I have a feeling we'll both require all the sustenance we can get."

Miranda watched as the Duke of Whitby sauntered back to his side of the table. She was badly shaken and all too aware that she had just proven herself infinitely vulnerable to his seduction. Not just to herself this time, but to the both of them.

CHAPTER 7

*A*fter what had seemed a lifetime of overseeing the arrival of the weeklong house party's guests—during which time he had not seen Miranda at all, curse it—Rhys at last sat at the head of the Wingfield Hall dining room table, flanked on both sides by his good chums Riverdale, Kingham, and Richford. The final course was laid before them by the efficient domestics. Perfectly molded cream ices served on golden cornets with edges that had been dipped in red royal icing and chopped pistachios.

All around the table, exclamations of delight went up, as if on cue.

"Ye gods, this is damned delicious," said one chap in a scarlet mask.

"I've never had cream ice in anything other than a mold before. How clever," praised a lady in a mask trimmed with peacock feathers and encrusted in gemstones.

"How delightful," exclaimed a sultry brunette in a purple satin mask. "What is this crispy bit?"

"I have a crispy bit for you, love," her male companion suggested with a chortle.

She curled her lip. "I don't think that particular appendage ought to be crispy, my lord."

"It was a figure of speech," the chastised chap mumbled into his dessert course, before shoveling another spoonful of cream ice into his mouth.

"What has you so bloody happy, Whit?" the Duke of Richford grumbled darkly.

Rhys realized he was grinning with pride. Grinning like a witless idiot. Because he was proud. He was proud of Miranda and her accomplishments. But he wasn't about to share that with his friends. Not before an audience of club guests. Perhaps not at all. He was struck by the odd, possessive need to keep her to himself like a priceless jewel.

"Dessert," he said succinctly. "It's glorious, isn't it?"

"Passable," Richford decreed, his countenance grim beneath his black mask.

He was clearly in one of his moods.

That was just as well.

"What's the matter with him?" he asked Riverdale.

Riverdale shrugged, mouth full of cream ice. "He's in a foul mood."

"I'm not in a foul mood," Richford snapped.

"Rather proving the point, old chap," Kingham drawled. "Perhaps it's on account of that wretched waistcoat. I know I would be bilious as well if I had chosen to wear such a monstrosity in public."

King was notoriously pedantic when it came to fashion. Mostly, their circle ignored his icy quips where their choices in waistcoats or hats or even neck ties were concerned.

In this instance, however, Rhys found himself agreeing. "The gold damask does look a bit like paper hangings, now that you mention it, King."

Richford scowled. "He didn't mention it, and it doesn't

look like paper hangings. There's not a single goddamned thing wrong with my waistcoat."

"Is the chest padded as well?" King asked, grinning like the devil he was, unmoved by Richford's sullen response.

"Looks more like the middle is padded, if you ask me," Riverdale interjected, having already eaten his cream ice and cornet.

"No one did ask you," Richford pointed out acidly.

"Perhaps it was implied," Riverdale offered mildly. "I say, you don't pad your waistcoats, do you?"

"I have no need to pad them," Richford growled. "Except I am perhaps too lean in the waist, unlike certain cream ice vultures I might name."

Their insults were not heated any more than they were accurate. Riverdale was built like a prizefighter, muscled and massive, and Richford had a smaller though similarly brawny build.

Riverdale only chuckled, amused. "Richford needs one of your potions, King. No doubt that will improve his spirits."

Richford did appear to be remarkably cantankerous, even by his standards. Rhys found himself wondering at the reason.

"Does this have something to do with a woman?" he asked gently.

"No," Richford bit out quickly.

Too quickly.

Rhys, King, and Riverdale exchanged knowing looks. The reason for their friend's mood was obvious.

"Who is she?" King asked.

"Stubble it," Richford snapped with a glare.

"Has she thrown you over?" Riverdale wanted to know.

"Judging from the thunderous expression on his face, the lady has," Rhys offered.

"No, she hasn't," Richford snarled. "Because there is no woman."

His glare was that of a wounded wild animal, cornered and prepared to fight to the death.

Rhys sighed. Apparently their friend's mood was even worse than any of them had supposed.

"Perhaps you ought to get some rest, old chap," he suggested, taking pity on Richford. "You look weary."

"Tell me, Richford, did you commission that waistcoat out of one of your grandmother's dresses?" King asked slyly.

Richford's only response was to bare his teeth, rather in the fashion of a dog hell-bent upon protecting his bone.

"Christ," King muttered, shaking his head. "You need a drink, old chum."

"I need four drinks," Richford said. "Enough to render me insensate."

"That bad, is it?" Riverdale shook his head in commiseration.

Rhys scraped up the last bite of cream ice and cornet, savoring the creamy delicacy on his tongue. Damn, but it was glorious, and he was momentarily distracted by the wicked thought of smearing it all over Miranda's nipples and then licking it off. Not the cornets, of course. No need for crumbs. But the cream ice. The cold would make her nipples stiffen into taut pink buds. He'd swirl his tongue over the peaks, lick up the ginger and apple and then suck…

Fuck.

He had to stop himself, for his cock was growing hard and insistent in his trousers, and he was surrounded by his friends and the club members.

"Are you well, Whit?"

Riverdale's voice interrupted Rhys's sordid musings.

He flashed a smile. "Perfectly. Why do you ask?"

"You look like my sister did when she was taken with fever."

"How should you know what your sister looked like when she was feverish?" King jeered lightly. "Never tell us you were playing nursemaid."

"She's my sister, and I love her," Riverdale defended, frowning. "You know what it's like, don't you, Whit? You dote upon Lady Rhiannon."

"Enough about sisters," Richford retorted with far too much speed and bite.

Curious, that. Richford didn't have a sister. His objection to the subject was either an extension of his mood, or something else. Something damned perplexing.

"You object to speaking about sisters now too?" Riverdale demanded. "Is there anything you've deemed a suitable topic of conversation this evening, sire?"

"Don't be an arse." Richford scowled.

King sighed. "Fortunately, I've brought several of my potions along with me. It looks like a restorative will be just the thing."

"Let's play a game of naughty charades," announced the woman in the peacock mask, her voice loud enough to carry through the cavernous dining room.

A chorus of agreement rose up. He thought of Miranda's assertion that he was hosting an orgy. He wasn't. Not strictly. But naughty charades could often lead to a lack of clothes and all manner of sin. Ultimately, the revelers would find their way to bed—their own or each other's. The prospect only left him feeling hollow. He had no interest in playing games that once might have amused him.

All he wanted now was her.

"What say you?" Riverdale asked Rhys, King, and Richford.

"The drawing room would do nicely for such a purpose," Rhys suggested.

Dishes were being removed by the assiduous domestics. The hour was growing late. The wine had been flowing freely enough that, coupled with King's potions, Rhys was beginning to hope no one would notice if he were to slip away from the festivities and go off in search of Miranda.

"I bloody hate charades," King complained, taking care to keep his voice from carrying.

"Bring your potions," Riverdale said, grinning. "I have no doubt they'll make anything interesting."

"I'll join you there soon enough," Richford said, his lip curling in distaste. "There is something I must do first, however."

Rhys cleared his throat. "I fear I'm too tired for such festivities. Preparing for this house party was exhausting. I'll see you all in the morning. Don't drink too much of King's potions, and if you do, stay away from rooftops, swords, and fireplaces."

They all chuckled, but the warning was only partly a sally. With that, he excused himself and escaped from the dining room, his mission clear. An idea had occurred to him over the course of dinner earlier, one he hoped Miranda might approve of. Either way, it would prove an excellent excuse to speak with her again tonight.

Because he missed her.

It had been hours since they had parted ways at breakfast, damn it. The intervening time may as well have been an eternity. He hoped he had left her as desperately wanting as he felt. Hoped that those taunting, teasing kisses he had delivered everywhere but to her lips had made her ache for more. He had vowed he would make her beg, but he had also come to the grim realization that his restraint would only last for so long.

If she didn't ask him to kiss her soon, *he* would be the one begging.

Miranda's lower back ached and her feet were sore, but she was also happily bathed and clad in a dressing gown when the knock sounded at the door connecting her bedroom to the Duke of Whitby's. For a moment, she simply stared, pausing mid-stroke of her brush through damp hair. Surely she had imagined the sound, she thought. Perhaps it had been a thump somewhere else in the manor house that she had mistaken for a knock.

After all, the house was fairly crawling with guests by now. She had seen the arrival of carriages heralding the true beginning of the house party earlier. And she could not lie, she had taken in the presence of others with half relief, half dismay, all for the same reason. She would no longer have the duke to herself.

It would be good for her ability to resist him. However, another part of her, one she was determined to ignore, loathed the notion of him carrying on with an untold number of women below. Giving them his heated glances, his sultry teasing. His lips ghosting over feminine faces and forms, leaving behind a heady path of fire.

No, these were foolish, dangerous, sinful thoughts she couldn't bear to entertain. Doing so would be nothing short of ruinous.

She resumed brushing, trying to ignore the hint of disappointment that came with the realization she hadn't heard anyone at the door after all. And truly, what had she believed, that Whitby would abandon his lascivious house party below to spend time with her? Undoubtedly, the feminine companionship to be found was far more alluring.

Likely, he had already forgotten her existence, in favor of seeking women more amenable to his ample charms. But that was for the best. She had come here for one reason and one reason only. She needed the small fortune the Duke of Whitby had offered her for her services. For her cream ice and desserts, not for anything else.

Knock-knock-knock.

Her breath caught.

The knock was definitely real this time. Firmer, more assertive. And she knew who it was. Knew she ought to ignore it. Ignore *him*. Instead, she strode hastily across the room and glanced at herself in the mirror. Her dressing gown was perfectly modest. She had on a night rail beneath it. But her feet were bare. Her hair was unbound, curls falling down her back and spilling over her shoulders.

It felt wrong for him to see her thus, although she was no stranger to the intimacies that inevitably followed a marriage, even one as cold and passionless as hers had been.

"Miranda?"

Whitby's voice reached her, muffled by the closed door, low and decadent and far too alluring.

"Just a moment," she managed, sounding vexingly breathless.

It was too late for her to sweep her hair into a chignon. Coiling and pinning the heavy mass took concerted effort and a great deal of time. With a deep breath, she rushed across the room to the door, hesitating as her hand hovered over the latch.

If she didn't open the door, he would think she didn't trust herself to be alone with him.

At the same time, she very much *didn't* trust herself to be alone with him.

In the end, her pride had her lifting the latch on her side and trying the door. It clicked open, swinging toward her to reveal Whitby standing there, still dressed in his evening finery of stark blacks and whites. His golden hair was tousled as if he had sifted his fingers through it, and his stormy eyes burned into hers.

"Your Grace," she greeted. "Is something amiss?"

"Of course not." His gaze traveled lower, dipping to her dressing gown. "I was wondering if we might take a few minutes to speak."

He was being carefully polite. Sudden worry assailed her. Had there been something wrong with her cream ice even though he'd claimed nothing was amiss?

She stepped back, opening the door fully, for she felt foolish cowering behind it. She was no innocent virginal miss. Besides, it wasn't as if she had any more bare skin on display than she usually did, aside from her toes. And surely he wouldn't find her feet of interest.

"May I come in?" he asked, hesitating at the threshold instead of sauntering inside as she had expected him to do.

He was being unfailingly polite, which also had her at sixes and sevens. It was as if the way he had crowded her against the breakfast table and melted her with those wandering kisses that morning had been nothing but a wild imagining on her part.

"Of course." She stepped back, allowing him entrée, proud of her ability to maintain her composure.

If the circumstances were unusual, they were surely no more lacking in propriety than they had been on any of the other occasions she had been alone with him. Besides, there was no one to witness her ignominy now.

No one, save herself.

He entered the room in purposeful strides, his gaze dipping to her bare feet. "Forgive me. Were you preparing to go to sleep?"

The lamps in her room yet blazed, and her recipes were

spread over the writing desk in piles, all evidence that she was not yet finding her bed. No point in lying. And good heavens, but why did the way his gaze lingered on her toes make her heart beat faster and send heat careening through her?

"I was preparing for tomorrow's dinner," she answered simply, cursing herself for the huskiness in her voice.

For remembering how sinfully good his kisses had felt, finding her everywhere but on her lips. For wanting him as a woman desired a man when she must remain a steadfast businesswoman instead.

"The ice and cornets were nothing short of perfection," he praised. "I wanted to tell you at once and sought you out following the conclusion of dinner. The guests were all well pleased."

Ah, so that explained his dress. He would return to his revelries. What had she expected—for him to go to sleep before midnight and without a bevy of beauties in his bed? Good heavens, what if he brought a lover to his chamber this very eve? And what if she could hear them?

Her stomach flipped.

"I am glad to hear it," she forced herself to say, seeking distraction by moving across the room to the writing desk, putting some necessary distance between them. "It's fortunate that you are here. I did wish to speak with you concerning my idea for tomorrow's ices."

"You needn't run from me," he said behind her, his tone amused.

That had her stopping mid-stride and whirling to face him. "I'm hardly running, Your Grace. I'm merely going to fetch my recipe papers. I have the most darling notion for a basket made of nougat and chocolate ice mushrooms within. The interior of the basket will be filled with chocolate and raspberry cream ice, but the whole of it will be made to look quite realistic, all edible."

She realized she was rambling because she was nervous. Surely the Duke of Whitby need not know the particular details of the cream ices she would be serving at tomorrow's orgy.

Orgy.

Though he had teased her about it, the mere word made her ill. She found her gaze roving over him, wondering if the fingers that had been through his golden mane had been another woman's instead of his. Had he already indulged in the hedonism no doubt to be found downstairs? Why did she hate the notion?

"Your hair is as glorious as I imagined it would be when it is unbound," he said softly, standing far too near for her comfort. "It's a travesty to confine it as you do."

Did he ply other women with such compliments? Did he admire their hair, kiss their temples, hold them close, and make them long to indulge in all the sensual pleasures he could give them? She hated herself for wondering.

Miranda swallowed hard, belatedly realizing she still gripped her brush in her left hand. How silly she must look, standing before him wielding it as if it were a weapon with which she might fend him off.

"My hair gets in my way," she told him, forcing her mind to stay on the subject at hand. "To say nothing of what is fashionable. I daresay no one would come to my school at all if I were to carry on with my hair spilling down my back no better than a common jade."

"No one would ever mistake you for a jade, and I can assure you that there is not one thing about you that is common." He smiled, sincerity sparkling in the depths of his eyes. "I am in awe of your talent, Miranda. Something occurred to me earlier during the course of dinner, and I wanted to take a moment now to see what you thought of it. Shall we sit at the hearth?"

Sitting with him in her bedroom seemed an incredibly bad idea. It implied that he would stay, at least long enough to render standing uncomfortable. And the longer he lingered here in her room, the greater the danger to her ability to resist him. Even so, a sinful part of her whispered that if he were to remain cocooned in her room this evening, there was a diminishing chance of him finding a woman to warm his bed.

"I don't know if that would be wise," she hesitated.

He flashed her a charming half grin. "I promise to behave myself."

"Very well, then," she agreed, moving toward where the fire was burning low in the grate, prepared by Green's expert hand before she had departed for the night.

Two overstuffed chairs flanked each other, a safe enough distance apart. She settled in the farthest one and watched as he folded his tall frame easily into the other, crossing his ankles in a comfortable pose. He looked at home in the cozy privacy of her bedchamber, and she had a wild, fanciful notion of what it would be like to spend each night alone with him just like this.

She cleared her throat, trying to banish all such unwanted thoughts. "What was it that you wanted to discuss, Your Grace?"

His long fingers tapped idly on the armrest. "Your calling me Rhys is an excellent place to begin. I cannot convey how much joy it would bring me to hear my given name on your sweet lips."

She frowned at him. "You promised you would behave not even a minute ago."

"I am behaving. If I weren't, you wouldn't be sitting opposite me in that chair, darling. You'd be in my lap."

The seducer was back, and more potently alluring than ever. Or perhaps it was merely that he had so eroded her ability to resist him. Her defenses were already lying in ruins, crumbled in the face of his rakish determination.

"Yes, well, I do have a brush if I need to defend myself," she pointed out archly, shaking it at him in warning for good measure.

He chuckled. "Beating me with a brush would be the last thing on your mind, but that's a topic for later. For now, let us discuss my reason for seeking you out this evening. I think you will be intrigued by the proposal I have to offer you."

Her eyebrows rose. "Whitby, I've already told you that I'll not be your mistress."

"And you know I don't believe you that your denial will remain steadfast, but sadly, that wasn't the sort of proposal I had in mind this time."

She pinned him with a narrowed stare. "What manner of proposal *did* you have in mind, then?"

He smiled, and her stupid body continued fluttering to life at his proximity, his magnetism, his cheeky grins and handsome face. "You mentioned a desire to begin a situation placement portion of the school, I believe you called it."

She nodded. "Yes. I intend to offer training for women hoping to find situations for themselves as cooks in well-to-do households. Some of them are my pupils already. My plan is to be the means of connecting households in search of reliable, well-trained cooks with women seeking respectable employ in reputable households. I will charge a small fee to both for my efforts, and it will benefit all parties."

As far as Miranda was aware, there was no other such establishment presently in operation that devoted itself to cooks trained in the sophisticated cookery she taught. But like so many of her ideas, both her reputation and her available funds presented a problem.

"A sound plan." He nodded, an undeniable expression of admiration flitting over his features. "You are an astute businesswoman, my dear. Many in your shoes would have cowered rather than starting anew."

Warmth unfurled within her at his praise. "There was no other choice for me. Had I cowered, I would have lost everything. The Lenox School of Cookery is my chance for a future I was once too afraid to claim for my own."

"I admire you for your determination, your intrepidness, and your skill."

His frank words and his gaze held her trapped for a moment. He had said so much. And it wasn't empty, rakish flattery either. He was praising her for her abilities. Abilities she was desperately proud of, because embracing them had meant leaving a life that was familiar and comfortable. She had been raised to be a gently bred lady, to become the wife of a peer one day. To sacrifice her own hopes, wants, and needs for a greater good that had turned out to be neither great nor good.

"Thank you," she managed, inclining her head.

"Allow me to act as a testimonial for your services, if you will. Everyone in attendance at dinner this evening was utterly enthralled with your cream ice and cornets. You should have heard their exclamations. One would have thought they were in the midst of coital delight."

His words made her frown at him anew. "I fail to see what your guests have to do with my intentions of creating a placement service for domestics."

"I will make it known to them—individually, of course—that all of the week's most divine creations hail from your school. I'll let them know you have begun teaching cooks in your methods, but that this service is exclusive and quite naturally comes at a dear price. That they should be the first to hire from your well-trained cooks. Naturally, they would not know you are in residence. I would tell them that one of your students is visiting Wingfield Hall at my behest to avoid any hint of scandal. By the week's end, you'll have dozens of ladies begging you to find them a domestic capable of crafting incredible ices and other marvels."

She bit her lip, tempted by the description of his plan, but it was almost too lovely to be true. "Why would you wish to help me in this way?"

He grinned again, displaying neat, even teeth. "Because I like you, Miranda."

His words should not take her breath. Make her heart stutter. And yet, they did.

She shook herself from his thrall. "Because you want to bed me, you mean."

Whitby winked, unrepentant. "Of course. But that isn't why I want to help you."

"What would you gain from such an arrangement?" she pressed, unconvinced.

"The satisfaction of knowing a woman I admire very much and who deserves to succeed will do so."

It sounded far too noble for a man like him. She eyed him warily. "You cannot expect me to believe that."

"I'm crushed, darling." He pressed a hand over his heart. "Indeed, I am wounded to the very marrow at your poor opinion of me."

A laugh escaped her before she could suppress it. Just one. He was amusing, the Duke of Whitby. And despite all the reasons she should not, she liked him. Liked him very much.

"You cannot blame me for my suspicions," she pointed out, very near to accepting his offer.

"Naturally not. My own reputation is hardly sterling, and I'll admit to being quite greedy and selfish. Think upon it, Miranda." Suddenly, he rose. "Now, I should leave you to your rest. You must be weary, and I have guests awaiting me."

She shot to her feet as well, feeling already strangely bereft when he had not even gone yet.

"Wait," she said before she could hold her tongue. "Don't go just yet."

Because if he left, he would seek someone else. Surely he would. Another woman would know his lips. Would taste him, touch him. She didn't want that. She wanted him all to herself. Had been sitting here, agonizing at the thought of him downstairs, hosting countless other women.

And Miranda could not even blame this mad, wild desire rushing through her upon too much wine. She hadn't consumed a blessed drop when she'd finally taken a tray in her room earlier. No, it was purely the way her body reacted to his. The way the Duke of Whitby made her feel.

She wanted more of that. Wanted him in a way that she had never yearned for another, so much that her hand trembled ever so slightly beneath the force of it as she reached for him, not quite understanding what she intended.

Perhaps it was the lateness of the hour that spurred her.

Or the hushed air of the night.

The loneliness that had never been far since the day she had first left her home and family to become the Earl of Ammondale's wife.

The desperate need she tried so hard to banish.

The jealousy seething within her at the notion of another woman taking her place with Whitby.

Or all of those things. Or maybe even none of them.

Maybe she just desired the duke, and they were alone with no one to witness her folly. Maybe she was taking what

114

she wanted for the first time in her life. Eschewing duty and obligation and flinging caution to the wind.

Miranda closed the distance separating them, her bare feet padding over the thick Axminster, and then she was in his arms, her brush falling, forgotten, to the floor.

CHAPTER 8

*S*he hadn't begged.

But it didn't matter now.

Nothing else did except for Miranda. His beautiful, capable, independent Miranda.

Her hands were on his shoulders, her pale face turned up to his, the lamplight flickering lovingly over her features, dancing in her emerald eyes and glinting off her obsidian hair. The faint, floral scent of her bath clung to her skin, her lush curves were for once not constrained by unforgiving stays and layers of ghastly gray silk and buttons, and her dressing gown had parted ever so slightly at the top to reveal more of her bountiful breasts than she likely realized.

His mouth was dry, his heart hammering harder than a blacksmith on an anvil. He'd never had such a forceful reaction to a woman throwing herself into his arms before. Hell, he'd never had such a forceful reaction to any woman.

Her berry-pink lips parted. "I accept your offer."

For a moment, a keening thrill of elation soared through him. But then she hastened to clarify.

"To help me with my placement services," Miranda elaborated, a flush creeping over her cheekbones. "I don't need further time to think it over. I'll accept your help."

Ah, he should have known. Stubborn woman. Fondness rose, mingling with the desire.

He smiled, his hands still lightly on her waist, where they had landed instinctively when she had rushed toward him. "Good. I'm glad you've decided to accept."

He didn't want to let go of her. Not now, not yet. *Not ever*, whispered something within him.

Miranda stared at him for a moment, seeming to wage an inner battle, before nodding.

"I like you too, you know," she said softly, her countenance strained, as if she were torn between what she wanted to do and what she ought to do. "More than I should, I fear."

His cock, which had been hard the moment she had opened the door to reveal herself, went positively rigid. "You're right about that. You shouldn't like me at all. Because I don't have a shred of honor where you're concerned."

It was decidedly against his best interest in seducing her to warn her away from him. But Rhys knew Miranda Lenox was far better than he was. Far better than he deserved, even. And some small bit of his conscience had loosened his stupid tongue. He'd simply have to bite it from now on.

Or put it to better uses.

She caught the fullness of her lower lip in her teeth. "Is there…are you…do you have a woman awaiting you down-stairs? Or more than one, perchance?"

Dare he hope she was jealous of the lady members of the club below? That the way she had rushed into his arms heralded an easier, swifter capitulation on her part than her steely determination had thus far suggested?

A long, dark curl had spilled over her cheek, and he couldn't resist catching it between his thumb and forefinger, giving the silken strands a teasing tug. "I am the host of this wicked affair, and there are many women in attendance. I suspect any number of them are wondering where I've gone to."

"Not in the capacity of host," she added, further color washing over her cheeks.

He swept the curl from her face, tucking it behind her ear. "Lovers, you mean. You want to know if any of the ladies in attendance are my lovers."

"It's none of my concern, of course. Forgive me, I shouldn't have—"

"No," he interrupted swiftly, holding her gaze. "I haven't any lovers here. It isn't the ladies presently playing naughty charades in the drawing room who interest me."

There was only one woman at Wingfield Hall he wanted. And she was watching him warily, hands still on his shoulders. At least she hadn't flitted away just yet. He liked simply touching her, the potent aphrodisiac of her proximity.

Her next question took him by surprise.

"What is naughty charades?"

A small laugh gusted from him. "It is what you might imagine it to be. Charades, only with a prerequisite that all words being acted out must be sinful in nature. Garments are optional."

Her eyes widened. "Oh."

"Would you care to play?" He couldn't resist teasing. "Everyone is masked this evening. No one will know your name."

"Charades in the nude? I daresay not."

"Or we could play here together," he suggested devilishly. "Just the two of us. I have it on good authority that I'm quite adept at charades. And other sport as well."

Her lips compressed in her best imitation of a scandalized governess. "We will be doing nothing of the sort."

Rhys didn't bother to point out that she was presently in

his arms, clad in nothing more than a dressing gown, in her bedroom. Doing so would only send her from him, and he wanted her close. As close as possible. And preferably without the impediment of her dressing gown and his bloody evening suit in the way.

"Perhaps we might do this instead, then," he suggested, sliding his hand around to cup her nape beneath the heavy curtain of her hair.

Lowering his head, he placed a delicate kiss on her cheekbone.

Her skin was as smooth and warm as he had recalled from that morning. He wanted to kiss every sweet inch of her. To throw her over his shoulder and carry her to the bed and make love to her all night long.

He heard her inhale sharply, felt her fingertips tightening on his coat.

"Or this." He kissed her ear, then the hollow behind her earlobe, unable to keep from flicking his tongue over her.

A low sound emerged from her, but she made no effort to move.

He took that as a sign to continue, dropping his mouth to her throat, absorbing the hasty beat of her pulse. She tipped her head back, giving him better access to the velvet-soft column. It required all the restraint he possessed to keep from devouring her as he longed to do.

But he was determined to make her admit that she wanted him.

That she wanted his lips on hers.

He found the hollow of her throat next as she shivered and stepped into him, her full, round breasts crushing against his chest. And fuck, her nipples were hard little points he could feel through all the layers separating them.

"Whitby," she murmured, a plea in her voice he would be happy to answer.

He needed more from her first, however.

"Rhys, darling." He rasped his teeth along her throat. "Say my name, and I'll give you anything you want. Anything you need."

Still, she was stubborn. The silence was interrupted only by her ragged breaths and dainty inhalations as he flicked his tongue over her pulse. Undaunted, he moved back up her throat to her jaw, stringing hot kisses over the delicate angle. Her hands shifted, fingers sifting through the ends of his hair as she sighed.

He kissed the corners of her mouth, first one and then the other, avoiding settling his lips over hers and giving her the all-consuming kiss he so desperately wanted to give her. She was tenacious, but so was he. And he would have her surrender before he was done.

Rhys kissed the space below her plump lower lip, then kissed her philtrum above it before withdrawing and staring down into her lovely, flushed face.

"Say it, Miranda," he demanded, his voice hoarse with suppressed desire. "Say my name, and I'll give you my mouth like you want."

But she bloody well wouldn't.

Rhys slid the hand at her waist higher, then slipped it over her dressing gown, cupping her luscious, full breast. Her hard nipple studded his palm through the fabric.

"Your Grace," she countered just before stepping away from him as if he had burned her. "You should return to your guests, as you said."

"Of course," he forced out smoothly—no small feat past the roaring lust coursing through his veins. "You're sure I cannot persuade you to don a mask and join us below?"

"Thank you, but no." With queenly elegance, she righted her dressing gown, smoothing the bodice and clutching the twain ends more firmly together. He had been so close to toppling her defenses, so close he could all but taste her surrender.

Rhys's straining cock was proof of that. But Miranda's countenance had turned positively mulish, and tomorrow was another day. Her desire was feverishly matched with his; he had no doubt of it. Before the week was at an end, he would have her exactly where he wanted her.

Naked in his bed.

Rhys bowed. "Until tomorrow."

As he turned and stalked from her chamber, he decided not to bother descending to the drawing room, King's potions, or the revelries again. They held little appeal for him. Instead, he rang for a bath.

There was no cure for what ailed him this night, save one.

He was going to have to take himself in hand to the memory of Miranda's smooth, warm skin beneath his lips.

IN THE SILVERY glow of a full moon, Miranda walked through the gardens of Wingfield Hall, trying—and thus far failing— to purge the restless, reckless longing from her blood. Although the night air was chilled and she had escaped the maddening nearness to the source of her yearning, she remained as overheated as she was overset.

For a long time after the Duke of Whitby had retreated from her chamber, Miranda had simply stood where he had left her, the memory of his heated kisses haunting her. Resisting him had been almost impossible. She had wanted, in the span of those decadent moments when she'd been pressed up against his muscled chest, to strip him free of his formal blacks. To reveal the true man hiding beneath the debonair rake's clothes. She had wanted to set her lips against his and kiss him with all the pent-up desire burning within her.

But she had known that to do so would have been a terrible mistake. After the scandal she had caused in divorcing Ammondale, she needed to remain as circumspect as possible for the sake of her cookery school. And being circumspect whilst taking a notorious rake as a lover was simply impossible. The Duke of Whitby was a risk she couldn't afford to take.

A risk that had haunted her when she had heard the undeniable sound of a bath being prepared next door. He hadn't returned to the game of naughty charades or his guests at all. Instead, Whitby had stripped himself bare and lowered himself into the hot water of his tub.

She had paced the floor, trying not to think about how he would look, naked and glistening in the bath. Oh, how she had attempted to keep herself from imagining how he would use a cloth and soap to lovingly wash each hard masculine angle, every roped ridge of muscle. And she had failed utterly on all counts. With his teasing kisses earlier, he had brought her perilously near to abandoning her good intentions and reputation both. She had been desperate for his mouth on hers.

Instead of doing something incredibly foolish, she had decided to take some air. Painstakingly, she had removed her dressing gown and dressed again in one of her modest gray gowns, before sweeping her hair into a hasty chignon. A wrap and a solid pair of walking boots, and she had made her way carefully downstairs. The raucous laughter and voices echoing from the drawing room had been enough to tell her that most of the house party's guests were otherwise occupied. She slipped out a door and into the gardens, alone with her thoughts.

And yet, though she must have been pacing the gravel

paths for at least the last hour, and despite the cool nip in the air, she hadn't been able to outrun the troubling thoughts whirling in her mind. Perhaps it was the full moon at work, beguiling her and bringing devilry upon them all.

As she rounded a bend in the path, the scent of cigar smoke reached her, warning her she was not alone in the moments before the tall figure of a man emerged from the distant shadows. She froze, heart thudding in her chest as she realized that in her haste to flee her chamber, she had forgotten to don a mask before venturing from the haven of her room. The bright illumination of the full moon made it appear as though a silver lantern had been hung aloft, brightening the nightscape with unnatural intensity.

If she didn't hide, the man approaching her would see her face. She attempted to skirt a massive rosebush, but in her haste, she passed too near and the thorns snagged in her silk, catching her there. It was either rip her dress or remain as she was, a hare trapped neatly, awaiting the hound.

"What have we here?" the man asked, moving toward her with purposeful strides.

Frantically, she tugged at her gown, trying to free herself from the clutches of the roses. The sound of silk tearing made her freeze anew.

"It looks as if we've a little bird caught in the roses," the unfamiliar man drawled.

She gave another frantic jerk at her skirts and finally managed to reclaim them. Too late. The interloper was almost upon her, and there was no denying the damage to her silk. One less gown in her wardrobe now, unless she could somehow manage to wield a needle and repair the destruction without it being noticeable. She very much doubted so; Miranda had never been skilled at embroidery. She hadn't the patience for it. All thumbs, as her mother had often regretfully said.

"I am freed now," she managed with far more cheer than she felt, attempting to keep her face averted so that the man wouldn't see her.

As he approached, she saw that most of his countenance was obscured by a dark mask. She had no notion of who he was or what he might want with her. And foolishly, she had wandered into the gardens without anyone the wiser of her whereabouts.

"So I see." He stopped and offered a formal bow. "Pity. I do so enjoy rescuing damsels in distress, particularly when the risk is more than worth the reward."

Miranda kept her head ducked toward the ground as she dipped into a polite curtsy. If she was lucky, the man would think her an errant servant wandering in the gardens where she didn't belong and simply leave her to return to her room.

"As you can see, there is no need for either rescue or reward, sir," she offered in a quiet voice, her chin tucked firmly to her chest.

"As I said, it's a pity. I do think I would have enjoyed taking you into my arms to pull you free," the man said, before taking a puff of his cigar.

"I fear you've mistaken me for one of the revelers," she began, careful to keep her face in the shadows as best as she was able. "However, I am merely a guest who lost her way and is eager to return to her chamber for the evening."

"I'll offer you my escort," he was quick to say.

"That won't be necessary. Thank you, but I prefer solitude. I'll just be going."

But as she made to skirt round the man, a hand shot out, boldly capturing her elbow.

"Not so quickly, my dear."

Her heart jolted.

"It would seem I've caught my little bird after all," he

crooned, refusing to release her. "What shall I do with her, hmm?"

She didn't like the tone of his voice or the barely veiled suggestion in his words. Perhaps the man thought she was a seasoned member of the wicked club in attendance and that she was playing some manner of game with him. However, she decidedly was not. All she wanted to do was get back to her room and hopefully garner some much-needed slumber without the endless temptation of hearing the Duke of Whitby at his bath. Surely he would be finished by now?

She chose to ignore the pang of disappointment deep within her at the realization, trying to keep her mind firmly upon the situation at hand.

"What you shall do is release me, sir," she said coolly, forgetting herself and tilting up her head to frown at him with displeasure. "I have already told you that I prefer my own company to that of others and that I'm not a part of your club. I haven't come here for the reasons you undoubtedly have. Now, please, let me go."

"I know you," the man said, his voice taking on a contemplative air.

Heavens, what was she thinking, exposing her face to this stranger's scrutiny? She turned her head as fast as a whip, giving him her profile. The brilliant light of the moon rendered remaining in the shadows virtually impossible.

"You do not know me, sir," she denied, a new sense of dread, heavy and sharp, overtaking her.

What if he *did* know her? There was something perhaps vaguely familiar about him, though hidden behind his mask, he remained very much a mystery.

"But that is where you're wrong." He took another lengthy puff of his cigar, his hand still clamped on her elbow, holding her where she didn't wish to be.

The garden seemed suddenly colder than an ice cave.

"Please, sir," she demanded. "Release me at once."

"I do know you." Jerking her arm, he took her by surprise with his brute force and spun her to face him, moonlight spilling over her. "You're the Countess of Ammondale, by God."

Her blood, seemingly boiling ever since the Duke of Whitby had first trespassed in her school, went cold. Her first instinct was to deny the truth, the shock of hearing her former title and the recognition in the man's voice overtaking her.

"You must be mistaken, sir."

"No." He shook his head, eyes an indistinct shade traveling over her slowly in the moonlight. "I know precisely who you are. What a sweet delight to find you here, m'dear. I don't recall seeing you at dinner."

There was no point in continuing to argue the point. The full moon provided sufficient light.

"That is because I wasn't at dinner," she informed him, keeping her voice as frosty as possible, even as fear swept over her.

One foolish mistake, and she may have thrown her school and her future into peril.

"Off with a fellow reveler, were you?" he asked, crude insinuation in his tone. "Can't say I blame you. Dinner was a deadly dull affair. No doubt it would have been much more interesting, however, if the Fallen Countess had been there. Unless... Christ, I should have known. Are the dukes keeping you for themselves, then? Hiding you away so that the rest of us haven't a chance to sample your lovely charms?"

Good heavens, he believed she was dallying with all the dukes, as if she were a Cyprian at their disposal. She didn't know which she longed to do more, stomp on his foot, punch him in the nose, or box his ears.

Miranda settled for yanking her elbow free of him

instead. "No one is keeping me. I keep myself. Now, I must bid you good evening, sir. The hour grows late."

She moved past him, heart in her throat as she waited for him to waylay her again.

"Countess."

She paused, casting a wary glance over her shoulder at him, where he calmly smoked his cigar. "Sir?"

"I don't reckon Ammondale would be pleased to discover you're a member of the Wicked Dukes Society, even if you aren't his wife any longer. I confess, I thought you'd disappeared from London after the ignominy of your divorce, that you'd run off with Waring."

There was an ominous edge to the man's voice now, a threat-wrapped warning. It was not Ammondale's ire that concerned her, however. It was the impact such a scandalous on dit as her presence at a wicked house party would make upon her school.

She didn't dare allow her trepidation to show, however. She recognized the stranger's sort instantly. If he scented blood, he would only become determined to ruin her or otherwise have the upper hand over her.

"I'm sure I don't care what Ammondale thinks of anything I do," she told him coolly.

"I wouldn't be as certain, m'dear," he said, silken menace in his tone. "No doubt my silence is worth something. Perhaps we can arrange for a mutually beneficial exchange. I hold my tongue to Ammondale, and you grant me a favor in return."

Her fingers curled into fists, nails biting into her palms. "Are you threatening me, sir?"

"I wouldn't say that." He moved toward her, bringing the scent of tobacco smoke with him. "I was merely suggesting that we may find some way to entertain each other. A way that ensures an equal bargain for the both of us."

Her stomach lurched. "There will be no such bargain between us."

The sick sense of fear made the knot of dread deep inside her tighten even more. Oh, how thoughtless she had been to run from her bedroom and into the night, unprotected by a mask or anything she might use to defend herself. If the man were to attempt to force his attentions upon her, all she had was her sturdy walking boots to ward him off.

"Why not?" he asked. "I could make it worth your while."

"I think not, sir." Miranda grasped her ruined skirts and lifted them, deciding it was time to retreat before the man in the gardens attempted to do more than blackmail her.

She set off at a brisk pace across the gravel path, retracing her steps.

"Come back, Countess," the man called after her, the crunching of stone behind her a warning that he was in pursuit.

Her heart hammering against her chest, she broke into a run. Miranda raced as fast as she could around the curved, meandering path until she rounded a bend where a boxwood hedge stood and promptly slammed into the unforgiving form of yet another man.

The wind was knocked out of her lungs, and she would have fallen to her rump had it not been for the man's hands clamping on to her waist, holding her steady. But she had no wish to be caught. Her instincts took control, her palms landing on the man's chest, pummeling him.

He grunted. "Dash it, Miranda. It's me."

"Whitby," she breathed, instantly stopping the blows, relief washing over her.

She felt inexplicably safe with him.

"What's wrong, darling?" he demanded, frowning down at her in the moonlight, concern in his voice, etched on his countenance.

"There's a man," she managed, breathless from her flight and the fear gripping her. "I came across him in the gardens, and he recognized me. He…he was trying to blackmail me into keeping my presence here a secret. He implied that he wanted…favors from me."

Whitby stiffened, resembling nothing so much as a guard dog ready to attack.

"Who is he?" he growled. "I'll beat him to a bloody pulp and then banish him from both the club and Wingfield Hall when I'm finished."

She shook her head, still struggling to catch her breath. "I don't know who he is. He's wearing a mask that covers most of his face."

"Where is the scoundrel?"

"He was in the gardens with me. He was following me. Just behind me, I think. Round that bend."

"Stay here," he ordered, his voice grim.

Before she could protest, he broke away from her, storming around the corner down the path, in search of the man who had recognized her. She remained where she was for a few frantic moments, fretting over Whitby putting himself in danger. What if the man hurt him? It would be all her fault.

Grasping her skirts again, Miranda hastened after him. The duke's legs were longer, however, and he had rage on his side. He had already disappeared from view by the time she rushed down the path. Gasping for breath, she rounded another curve in the gardens and was greeted by the dull sound of a fist connecting with flesh, followed by a groan of pain, and then another thud.

Two men tussled at the far end of the pathway, and she recognized Whitby's superior height and strength at once. He shook the other man by his lapels.

"You will tell no one that you saw her here. Do you understand, you arsehole?" Whitby was demanding.

"Forgive me. I was only wanting to—"

Whitby delivered another sound punch to the man's jaw, effectively ending his protest prematurely. "I don't give a damn what you wanted. The rules of this club are clear. Secrecy is paramount, and no one tries to force a woman who doesn't bloody well want him."

"I'm sorry," the man squeaked. "Please, stop. I meant no harm. I won't tell a soul, I swear it upon my life."

"Damned right, you will swear it upon your life," Whitby snarled, giving the man a shake, quite as if he were no more substantial than a child's doll despite his size. "Because if you do anything to hurt her, I will fucking end you."

"I'd never hurt her. Please. It was all a misunderstanding, Your Grace."

"Consider this your first and final warning," Whitby said, releasing the man.

"Thank you. I won't need another."

"Get out of my sight," the duke roared.

The man didn't hesitate in fleeing, the sound of his harried footfalls echoing through the sudden stillness of the night as he raced away.

Whitby turned to where Miranda stood and held out his hand. "Come."

CHAPTER 9

"*Y*ou're bleeding."

In the glowing lamplight of his bedchamber, Rhys flexed the fingers of his right hand. They were stiff and they ached, but they hadn't cracked open. The blood marring his knuckles didn't belong to him.

"It's not mine," he told her, trying to calm the raging swell of fury within him.

Her lips parted. She was even paler than usual, her jet-black hair coming free of its chignon to curl around her face.

"Oh," was all she said, still lingering at the threshold of his chamber, though the door was closed at her back.

And that was when he noticed it. Her skirt was in tatters. Tears had rent the dove silk, revealing the petticoat beneath.

Fury ignited in his blood anew. If Viscount Roberts had torn her skirts, he was going to die this night after all.

"Did he touch you?" he demanded.

"I…yes, but nothing more than his hand on my arm." She glanced down, following his gaze to her ruined gown. "I caught the silk in rosebushes. I was trying to get away from him, and my skirts tore."

"He's damned lucky." He inhaled slowly, trying to force some of the anger roiling within him to abate and failing.

Right now, there was nothing he wanted to do more than break off Lord Roberts's arms and beat him with them for daring to waylay Miranda in the gardens. For presuming to blackmail her. For making her so fearful that she had been running like a spooked mare when she had slammed into his chest rounding that bloody corner on the path. For perhaps doing far worse to her, if given half the chance.

Thank Christ Rhys had found her when he had.

"Thank you for coming to my defense," she murmured, her hands clenched so hard at her waist that her dainty fingers were even whiter than the rest of her pale skin.

A tremor shuddered through her, and he wanted nothing more than to take her in his arms and reassure her she was safe now and that no further harm would come to her. But he was also keenly aware she had just been propositioned and threatened by Roberts in the garden. Also, he still had that bastard's blood on his hand.

"You needn't thank me," he muttered, hating that she had been accosted. Feeling responsible. "It never should have happened."

He stalked across the chamber to a pitcher and bowl. The water within was cold, but he didn't care as he splashed his hand, scrubbing the blood from his knuckles.

"I should not have gone to the gardens in the midst of the night," she said quietly from somewhere behind him.

"No," he bit out, fury burning up within him anew. "This is not your fault. You did nothing wrong. You should have been able to take the night air without some horse's arse threatening to make problems for you and trying to get you into his bed."

He still had no notion of why she'd been wandering in the moonlit gardens. When they had parted ways, she had looked as if she were exhausted and ready for bed, clad in her dressing gown and bare feet. Somewhere along the way, she had donned her familiar armor of sturdy walking boots and gray gown, her hair neatly pinned up once more.

The sad, tattered state of the skirts suggested she was going to have one hideous sack less to hide her ample curves within. Rhys did not mourn its loss, but he despised the source of the damage to her dress.

"I should never have left my room," she protested. "At the very least, I ought to have worn one of the masks you provided. I wouldn't have been so easily recognized if I had, and then I daresay he would have left me alone."

Rhys scrubbed at the last vestiges of scarlet staining the cracks on his fingers. "Only a scoundrel would have all but forced himself upon you, threatening to cause a great deal of scandal. I'm going to speak with Richford, Kingham, and Riverdale about him in the morning and decide what punishment he must face."

"Oh, please don't." She was closer now, her husky voice wrapping around him like an embrace. Her scent too, floral and sweet.

He wanted her so badly.

But he was also furious at himself for bringing her here. For exposing her to a conscienceless rake like Roberts.

Rhys dried his hands and turned to face her, still unprepared for his body's reaction to her, regardless of how beautiful he already knew her to be. Each time he looked at Miranda, a jolt went through him. It was like his soul was made of dry kindling and she was the spark that set him alight.

"He doesn't deserve your mercy," Rhys told her. "Nor do I. I'm as much to blame for what happened as Roberts is."

"It was Viscount Roberts?" she asked.

"Yes." His lip curled with distaste. "Are you acquainted with him?"

"Scarcely." She shook her head. "I believe he is a familiar of Ammondale's. We met on a few occasions in passing, but I doubt whether we ever exchanged more than a paltry number of words. He is married, is he not?"

"Indeed. His lady wife is a member of the club as well. When I saw her last, she was off to join in the charades."

"Of course," Miranda said dully.

"Some husbands and wives are both members of the club, and others keep it a secret from their spouses." Explaining the rules of the Society felt somehow sordid and wrong, particularly in light of what Miranda had just endured. His gut curdled.

"How did you know where to find me?" she asked, sparing him further such explanations.

Rhys had just finished his bath when he thought he'd heard a sound outside. He had gone to the window and noticed movement in the garden below. The full moon had illuminated the entire expansive maze, paths, and roses with almost impossible detail. And he had recognized her figure moving across the path at once.

"I saw you by chance," he said. "I was at the window when I saw you walking along the path, or who I thought was you. To be certain, I knocked at your door. You didn't answer. What were you doing in the gardens at this hour? I thought you were going to rest."

He had meant what he'd said—she had done nothing wrong in venturing out to take the air. But he also wanted her to take caution after what had happened with Roberts. He couldn't shake the feeling that he had brought an inno-cent lamb into a den of wolves. Rhys would be damned if he allowed anyone to make her the sacrifice.

"I…I intended to rest," Miranda said, pink staining her

cheeks. "But I decided to get a bit of fresh air first. I am sorry that my recklessness led to what happened in the gardens. You are not injured, are you?"

He flexed his fingers. "Still in working order."

She frowned, closing the distance between them and reaching for his hand, taking it gently between hers. "But are you in pain? Is anything broken?"

A rush of tenderness swept over him, along with a protective surge he'd never known before. He wanted to gather her into his arms. To shield her from all the evils in the world. To cut down anyone who dared to hurt her.

"I'm fine," he reassured her. "Besides, even if I were injured, I wouldn't care. I'd break every one of my fingers trouncing any man if it meant protecting you."

Her emerald gaze searched his, his hand still held tenderly by her. "No one has ever said anything like that to me before."

He didn't want to ask about Ammondale. To the devil with him. He hadn't known what he had, or else he never would have let Miranda go. But Rhys couldn't shake the impotent rage filling him that a man who had taken her as his wife had not vowed to defend her so.

"It's a damned shame," he began, but he was never able to finish the rest of his words.

Because in the next instant, Miranda's lips were on his, smothering anything else he had been about to say. It didn't matter. At the first touch of her velvet-soft lips, he was lost to all thought anyway. With a groan, he wrapped his arms around her waist, anchoring her to him, and kissed her back with all the frenzied longing that had been pent-up within him ever since the moment she had first pinned him with an icy green glare.

He had been hers then and there, in that instant.

He was hers now.

And as she opened for him to devour her hungrily, the wild notion he might forever belong to this woman drew taut around him, like a manacle on the wrist of a prisoner. That was how bound he was to her. That was how badly he wanted...needed Miranda.

His Miranda.

He showed her with lips and tongue and teeth, a man starved. She made a low, husky sound as he explored the satiny heat of her mouth, and he swore he could spend an eternity here with her just like this, kissing and holding her, her feminine curves crushed into him in all the right places.

She was a woman who deserved lingering kisses, a slow savoring. To be wooed. To be won.

He inhaled her heady scent, never once breaking the kiss, one of his hands leaving her waist to tangle in the silken cloud of hair at her nape. It was cool and sleek, still slightly damp from her earlier bath. He wanted it unbound, falling down her back. Wanted it unfettered and free. His fingers traveled with a will of their own, plucking hairpins until the coil came undone, heavy and fat, and her curls spilled over her shoulders, lush and scented of orange blossom and rose.

Was it her shampoo, then? Her soap? He had imagined the source had been a perfume she applied sparingly to her wrists and throat. But now he wondered if every inch of her skin would be so decadently scented. It was a mystery he was determined to investigate.

Tonight, if she would allow it.

But he was also cognizant of what she had endured in the gardens, of what might have happened. With great effort, he forced his head up, his lips leaving hers. Her skin was flushed, her lips dark and swollen from his kisses, her eyes glazed with desire.

"You're likely overset after everything that transpired earlier," he said gently, ignoring the lust roaring through his veins, the ceaseless need that urged him to kiss her again. To strip her bare. To take her in his arms and lay her on his waiting bed and claim her in every way he could.

"No." Her tone was adamant if breathless, her gaze unwavering. "That has nothing to do with this."

But he was a gentleman. Or, at least, his mother had raised him to be one.

Rhys tried again. "It may seem that way, but in the morning—"

"Oh, do shut up."

She rose on her toes and kissed him again, her mouth hard and determined, silencing his further protest.

Well, then.

The gentleman within him promptly died. In his place was instantly born a marauding scoundrel with a raging cockstand. She had given him her acquiescence, and that was all he wanted. All he required. She was air, she was life, the beat of his heart, the punishing vise of desire. His tongue plundered her mouth, and she sucked, drawing him in, welcoming his invasion.

He groaned, deepening the kiss as he walked them as one toward the bed inhabiting the far wall of the bedchamber. Rhys kissed her with every step, their breaths mingling and their tongues tangling. Their hands roved over each other's bodies in mutual exploration. More hairpins dropped. They kicked away their footwear, leaving it abandoned and jumbled on the floor. She fought with his coat, pulling it down his shoulders and off his arms. His fingers found that interminable line of buttons.

There must have been five hundred of the little mother-of-pearl beggars keeping him from what he wanted. He unhooked two, then fumbled and struggled with a third. Too many of them, to be sure. With a growl, he began tearing.

Buttons rained to the Axminster, joining the scattered hair-pins. Fabric rent.

She jerked her lips from his, breathing hard. "You'll ruin my gown."

"It's already ruined." He kissed her hard before withdrawing. "I'll buy you a dozen more."

She stared at him, flushed and beautiful, a wanton goddess he could not wait to get naked. "Do it."

With great satisfaction, Rhys grasped the twain ends of her modest gray bodice and tore them in two. Buttons popped away. Silk ripped. And then he was treated to the most erotic sight he'd ever beheld.

Her pale-blue corset was revealed, cinched at her waist and pushing her full breasts high. Bits of blonde lace and cream ribbons adorned the feminine confection, which was so at odds with the bland, uninspiring gowns she wore each day. Here was the heart of her, the true Miranda, hidden away from the unforgiving eyes of the world. His alone.

The fanciful thought pleased him as he lifted a trembling hand to trace over the creamy swells just barely contained by a thin chemise. He flattened his palm over her racing heart.

"Beautiful."

The praise fell from his lips as he smoothed his touch higher, over the silken heat of her bare skin, the delicate ridge of her collarbone, then up her throat, watching the dichotomy of his sun-gilded hand on her pale skin. His hand was large, so large he could wrap it halfway around her neck in a tender hold, his thumb sweeping over her jaw as he simply drank in the sight of her.

Her kiss-plumped lips parted on a sigh, her lashes going low. "Help me out of my bodice."

Fuck.

She didn't have to tell him twice. In a blur of leaden desire and blinding need, he worked her from her bodice first, then her ravaged skirts and the petticoats beneath. Her padded bustle fell to the floor with a thump, and then she was there, in stockings, chemise, and corset only, whilst he was still mostly fully clothed.

Miranda seemed to settle upon that problem in the same moment, for her verdant gaze seared his. "Take off your waistcoat and shirt."

Holding her stare, he tore at the buttons on his waistcoat before shrugging it to the floor. His necktie and white evening shirt met the same fate until he was bare-chested. Her hungry eyes traveled over him, and he felt the effect of her womanly curiosity as if it were a touch. He stood still, allowing her to look her fill, his cock hard as marble, straining against the placket of his trousers.

And then her gaze was back on his, and she was reaching behind her back, the action thrusting her breasts forward. Her arms worked, the lacing of her corset slackening and draping down over her bottom. The undergarment thus loosened, Miranda brought her hands forward, her nimble fingers removing each hook from its eye as he watched.

The last hook was freed, and the blue satin fell away. Through the filmy chemise, he could see her hard nipples jutting outward, the perfect pink circles of areolas. He swallowed hard against a violent rush of need, his ballocks already drawn tight. He wanted her so desperately he thought it might be possible he would explode before he was even inside her.

Slowly, he cautioned himself. *Take your time, you randy arsehole.*

But then she spoke again, and all the caution he had been urging splintered like his restraint. "Take off your trousers."

Her boldness took him by surprise, but he liked it. His prick twitched at her command.

Without a word, he unfastened his trousers and smalls

both in one swift move, allowing them to fall. He was naked now. In his haste to rush to the gardens earlier, he had dispensed with stockings. His cock rose, proud and thick and long. Her eyes widened slightly as she took in his size. He was large, and he knew it.

Rhys stroked himself from root to tip, slicking his thumb over the pool of moisture beaded on the slit. "Is this what you wanted, darling?"

She licked her lips. "Yes."

Bloody hell, with that lone word, he was destroyed.

He released himself and reached for her chemise. "Last chance to change your mind."

"I still haven't changed my mind about your proposition," she told him, her voice husky. "But I want this. I want tonight. With you."

"And you will have it." He tugged at the fine fabric. "Take this off and get on the bed."

Miranda grasped twin handfuls of linen and pulled the chemise over her head in one elegant movement, sending it sailing to the floor. By God, she was glorious. For a moment, he could do nothing but stand there and stare. Her inky hair flowed loose down her back, her breasts were round and high, her nipples puckered buds that begged for his mouth, her waist deliciously curved, her hips wide and lush.

Perfection.

That was what she was.

A living, breathing goddess.

"On the bed," he repeated, his voice hoarse with desire.

She turned away, giving him a view of her backside as she took the remaining steps. Her legs were long and feminine, the arches of her calves making his palms itch, and the sweet handfuls of her bottom swaying just beneath her glorious hair.

Miranda turned again, settling herself primly on the edge of the bed, and he remembered to inhale then exhale. To control his wildly raging need for her. He moved to join her, guiding her so that she was at the center of the mattress, and he knelt between her spread legs. The positioning gave him the perfect view of her cunny, all pink and inviting and glistening.

His hands went to her ankles, caressing upward, his fingertips tracing over delicate, feminine flesh. A dip of his head as he pressed a kiss to first one knee, then the other answered his question. The scent was her soap, and she even smelled like orange and roses here. A growl sounded deep in his chest as he dragged his mouth higher, his hands leading the way as they traversed over the smooth, hot skin of her thighs.

He heard her gasp as if it had come from far away, just above the roaring of lust pounding through him. Perhaps it was eagerness, or perhaps this delight was one she was unaccustomed to enjoying. Either way, Rhys couldn't resist kissing along her sensitive inner thigh, to where orange and rose melded with the musky scent of her. He inhaled deeply, his cock thickening as he pressed it into the bed to stave off his rampaging desire.

He kissed higher, planting his hands on her legs and widening them. He was so close now. Close enough to taste her. He kissed the place where her thigh met her mound, cradling her outer hip with a hand. So near now. He nuzzled her humid flesh, finding her sleek and wanting, her dew coating his cheek and jaw.

She jerked, hips pumping not in the frantic rhythm for more but as if she were shying away.

"What are you doing?" She wanted to know, a new tone of almost panic in her voice.

Rhys soothed her with slow caresses, remaining as he

was, even though denying them both his mouth on her was utter torment. "Pleasuring you, darling."

"But…but…how?"

Her befuddlement was evident, not just in her helpless query but her wrinkled brow. Christ. He had his answer, and it didn't surprise him. Ammondale was a frigid prig. But she'd taken other lovers as well, for that had been the source of the acrimonious divorce. Surely one of them would have shown her such pleasures. Unless they were selfish arses.

"By using my mouth and tongue on you," he elaborated. "Until you come."

Her lips parted, but no sound emerged.

"Ah." He tried to ignore the primitive surge of elation within him at the realization that he would be the first man to introduce her to the sensual art. "Your past lovers were inattentive clods, then. You will enjoy it very much, I promise. Just relax and let me demonstrate."

"Are…are you certain?"

In all his years as a devoted sybarite and rake, he had never once had to convince a woman to let him lick her cunny. This was a first, and it made him strangely hard. Not just because he would be the first to make love to her thus, but also because he would glory in making his prim Miranda come thoroughly undone.

He wasn't going to stop until she had spent at least twice on his tongue. Until she was arching her back and crying out his name to the heavens.

He smiled at her in reassurance and kissed the soft patch of skin nearest his lips. "I am certain. I'll go slowly. If you don't like something, you need only tell me, and I'll stop."

She nodded, catching her lower lip in her teeth, her raven hair spilling over his pillow as he had spent every night since he had met her dreaming it would. "And this is… Men and women do this in bed together?"

He kissed closer to her sex, the heady scent of her filling his head with a haze of desire. "And in carriages and on desks and tables and out of doors and wherever else the mood strikes them."

"Oh," was all she said.

He took that as a sign that he should proceed. "Then your lessons shall commence, darling."

That thrilled him, the thought of him as lust-addled teacher and she his proper pupil, legs spread for his lascivious attentions. He pushed at her thighs, the soft whisper of her skin gliding on the sheets the only sound in the hushed silence of the room. She was open to him fully, like a summer flower, his to pleasure, his to claim.

Rhys bent his head and slowly, painstakingly licked the perfect pink bud peeking from her folds, demanding his worship. The taste of her—sweet, musky, and more delicious even than her cream ice and cornets—invaded his senses. She gasped, stiffening beneath him. But she tasted so good, the slick heat of her clitoris pulsing beneath the tip of his tongue, that he couldn't resist suckling despite his intention to ease her into the joy of the pleasure he could bring her.

She cried out, her body bucking beneath him. "Rhys."

His given name.

He sucked harder, drawing on her swollen bud, the taste of her on his lips, his tongue, his cock practically tunneling into the mattress. His fragile grasp on his control shattered, and he was lost to everything but her pleasure. He worried her with his teeth, the light abrasion earning him a lusty moan and another jolt of her hips. This time, it wasn't surprise that moved her, he knew. He burrowed his face deeper into her folds, using his jaw and the prickles of his whiskers, rubbing his face on her sex so that he was coated in her scent, her slick juices, and she was writhing beneath him, legs moving restlessly on the sheets as she angled her body to accept more.

He would wear the perfume of her pussy on his face all night long and wake in the morning to it. By God, he wouldn't allow his valet to shave him. Not until the scent had faded, just in case he would never be able to bury his face in her cunny again. Just in case the icy Miss Lenox made a return, bringing with her regret and a renewed determination to resurrect her defenses against him.

No, he must not let that happen. He couldn't; he wouldn't. He would please her so well tonight that she would have no choice but to agree to another month. Although, now that she was gasping and beneath him, her cunny hot and demanding against his lips, Rhys couldn't possibly fathom one month with Miranda ever being sufficient.

He toyed with her pearl, flicking his tongue over her and then sucking, before licking down her seam to her entrance. Unable to resist, he drove his tongue into her again and again, the silken glide of her hot entrance and the scent of her clouding his mind with pure, animal lust. Still not enough.

He replaced his tongue with his finger. First one, and then another, the hungry grip of her cunny so damned good. She was hot and wet, her grip on his fingers tight, the fluttering of her walls telling him she was almost where he wanted her to be. His lips settled over her swollen nub, and he alternated between sucks and licks, simultaneously sinking his fingers deep and curling them forward, finding a place that he knew would take her over the edge.

With a strangled cry, she came, trembling beneath him as her cunny contracted around his fingers. He stayed with her, continuing to thrust in and out as she drenched him, flicking his tongue over her clitoris in gentle strokes. But he wasn't finished yet. She owed him another spend.

And he intended to have it.

THE DUKE OF WHITBY'S tongue was a revelation.

Miranda was beyond capacity for thought or speech. And so, as the intense sensation that had overcome her gradually ebbed, she remained as she was, naked in his bed, his head pressed between her spread thighs, his tongue tracing hot, wet patterns over her throbbing sex. And his fingers…heaven have mercy.

His long fingers were inside her, moving in a sinuous glide in time to his sinful mouth. He lapped at her, played with her. Teased her. Everything seemed so beautifully heightened, everything golden—his golden head so sinfully lodged between her legs, the golden lamplight playing over their bare skin, the feeling rolling over her, through her. She was limp and sated, and yet somehow, she still wanted. Still needed.

Rhys had shattered all her restraint. She was a creature of pleasure. Receiving all he could give her and still selfishly yearning for more. Her hips were moving of their own accord, chasing the pressure of his mouth. Deep within her core, that same acute ache was building anew. Perhaps it had never truly left. And all the while, he continued to thrust in and out of her, those knowing fingers gliding through so much shocking wetness she ought to be ashamed.

Curiously, she was not. Her reaction to Rhys was natural, elemental. It was something that simply was, and she could not change it. Nor did she wish to. Not now, not in this moment.

And he seemed to revel in it. In her. He groaned into her, licking and sucking as if he could not get enough of her, using his teeth to elicit bursts of bliss so sharp she couldn't keep herself from moaning. It was agony, it was ecstasy, and she was dangerously close to losing control again.

As if he sensed her thoughts, Rhys lifted his head, giving her a smoldering look over the expanse of her bare body. "I want you to come again for me, darling. Give me your cream on my tongue."

Another merciless drive of his fingers, stimulating that excruciatingly sensitive place within her again as he sucked her clitoris. And it was all she could bear. Miranda spent, head arching back into the pillow as a gasp tore from her lips, eyes closing, and everything was golden once more, stars sprinkling her vision as her second pinnacle roared through her. The force of it was so tremendous that there was a ringing in her ears for a moment, and she struggled to come back to herself.

Miranda simply lay there, heart pounding, breathing ragged, body awash in the glow of the attentions he had visited upon her. She hadn't known it was possible, such pleasure. And now that she knew, how could she go on without it? She had been living for others for so long. First for her parents, then for her husband, and now for her school, always driven by the desperate need to please everyone but herself.

But this new knowledge was as much a gift as it was a sword. Because wanting more was perilous, and yet how could she not risk everything in pursuing it? In pursuing *him*? Perhaps she was selfish and wanton and every bit as wicked as the scandalmongers would have everyone believe.

"You're so perfect, so lovely, and you taste so bloody good," Rhys praised, caressing her hips and dropping a wet kiss on her inner thigh.

He was still planted between her legs, as if she were an altar at which he worshipped. She felt like a pagan goddess, on display and ready to collect her due. She felt powerful.

Desirable. She felt things she had never dreamed she could feel.

"Rhys," she murmured, reaching for him, a curious and uncontrollable jolt of tenderness surging through her, more profound somehow, than mere desire.

Her fingertips drifted over his shoulders, then his arms as she instinctively sought to draw him over her, wanting his body on hers, aligned with hers. Wanting him inside her.

"Darling." He trailed reverent kisses over her belly, his storm-tossed eyes burning into hers so potently that she could not look away.

His shoulders were broad and strong, his clavicle a prominent ridge above a muscled chest. Fine, golden hairs stippled skin that was a shade lighter than his sun-kissed hands, face, and throat. But she was fascinated to realize he was not nearly as pale beneath his clothes as she might have expected, suggesting that he had spent some time out of doors bereft of a shirt.

What had he been doing? There was so much she didn't know about him at all, and yet they were naked in his bed, and his mouth had been on her most intimate place. Indeed, his lips were glistening still as he trailed kisses along the underside of her breast before taking the peak into his mouth.

At the hot, wet suction, an answering ache renewed deep within her. Further ruminations died a swift little death, supplanted by the need to feel. Her fingers threaded through his thick hair, the strands silken and cool. His touch dipped between her legs, and her back bowed from the bed.

He strummed lazily over her already sensitized bud as he sucked her nipple at the same time. She was thoroughly soaked, the wet sounds of him stroking up and down her heated flesh almost obscene. And somehow, it made her even wetter. Rhys moved to her left breast, cupping the right in his big hand, his thumb working over the slick point of her nipple as he licked a lazy circle around the tip of the left. Her nails dug into the firm, smooth skin of his shoulder, and she writhed beneath him, wrapping a leg around his hip.

Another sound stole from her, husky and wanting.

He mouthed the peak of her breast, his tongue flicking over her. "Sweet Miranda. Tell me what you want. What you need."

"You," she managed, the urgency building, growing.

She felt as if she were a different person. Congress with Ammondale had been an unpleasant, pleasureless duty. But now she understood the sentiments in the bawdy books she had secretly read in private, the feverish yearnings she had so sternly repressed for so many years. Now, she wanted her body to be joined with this man's in the oldest and most primitive sense.

Rhys kissed his way to her throat, burying his face there as he nipped her with his teeth and teased her pearl. "How do you need me?"

His voice was a tantalizing whisper against her skin, making her shiver, making her stir restlessly against him, her hips chasing his touch.

She wetted her lips. "I need you inside me."

She wanted him more than she wanted her next breath. Wanted the reassuring weight of him atop her, the brand of his bare skin on hers, the fullness of his cock entering her.

Rhys strung a line of kisses along her jaw, and then his mouth was on hers, firm and possessive and insistent as he fed her the taste of herself. He deepened the kiss, his tongue tangling with hers, as he settled himself more firmly between her thighs. She moaned as he slicked the blunt head of his cock up and down her seam, before notching himself at her entrance.

He broke the kiss, propping himself up on a lone forearm as his gaze seared hers. "Are you ready for me, darling?"

No, she wasn't, and yes, she was, all at once. It was tonight or never. Here was her chance to seize what she wanted, even though it would have to be fleeting. Tonight and never again. No one need ever know but the two of them.

"Yes," she told him, bringing his lips back down to hers and kissing him with all the desire raging inside her.

With a hum of approval, he slanted his mouth over hers, deepening the kiss. His movements between their bodies were hasty, almost jerky. Decidedly lacking in the smooth elegance he ordinarily displayed, and she savored the evidence that he, the experienced rakehell, was every bit as affected as she was.

The blunt tip of his cock pressed, seeking. She tensed, preparing herself for what would come. He seemed to sense her reticence, breaking the kiss to murmur reassuring words to her. Soft words. Sweet words.

He kissed the corner of her mouth. "Relax for me, darling. Let me in."

She inhaled slowly, the scent of him, masculine and decadent, flooding her senses, her hard nipples grazing his chest. Yes, she thought, reminding herself it was Rhys lying atop her, Rhys who was about to make love to her, the man who had so thoroughly pleasured her beforehand that she had briefly lost all ability to think, move, or speak. It was Rhys, a man she desired, a man who didn't disdain and resent her. A man who wanted her every bit as much as she wanted him. And she relaxed, the tension draining from her body as she waited.

His touch returned to her sex, slicking over her sensitive bud, and he eased forward, gliding into her as if he had been fashioned specifically for her, as if their two bodies had always been meant to join as one. Another thrust, and he filled her, and she gasped at the surprising rightness of it, at the feeling of her stretched around him, his cock buried within her.

But…

Oh, heavens.

That wasn't all. He moved again, deeper still.

She gasped as sensation washed over her, her inner walls clenching on him in welcome, and he lowered his forehead to hers, his ragged breath ghosting over her mouth.

"How is this?" he asked softly, such tenderness and caring in his voice.

"Yes," was all she could bite out. Then, belatedly realizing she hadn't provided the correct response for his question, she added, "Lovely."

"Lovely, hmm?" He kissed her cheek, and she could feel his lips curved in a smile. "I'll have to do better, then."

She wasn't sure he could. Miranda opened her mouth to tell him so, but in that next instant, he shifted, leveraging himself over her again as he withdrew from her almost entirely, only to sink within her again. This time, she savored the sensation, the slippery glide of his cock through her wetness. He pressed deep, even farther or so it seemed, not stopping until she was pinned to the bed, his body perfectly aligned with hers.

The cords of his throat were taut, his movements careful and slow, and it seemed as if his tight grasp on his control was almost too much. She understood, because the pleasure was so intense that she felt as if she might break apart at any moment. As if pieces of her would fly into the very stars above.

This was…

This was good. Wondrous. Better than good. It was everything she had never known she had been missing.

Indeed, words failed to describe what she felt as Rhys

moved in and out of her, eliciting her gasps and moans and cries, wringing bliss from her until she was sure she couldn't bear it. Until the noises hatching from her throat sounded more as if they belonged to an animal than a refined lady. She wrapped her legs around Rhys, matching his rhythm. Her nails raked down his back as she met him thrust for thrust, and then everything within her seized and she was coming again, contracting on him in uncontrollable spasms as a gush of wetness sluiced from her.

He pushed into her again, grunting, gritting his teeth, his jaw clenched. And then his movements quickened, his cock hastily sliding from her, his touch leaving her as he grasped himself in a tight hold. One stroke, and he threw his head back, a strangled cry of sheer erotic elation echoing off the chamber walls as he spilled on her belly and inner thigh.

He collapsed at her side, pulling her against him, and she burrowed her face in his chest, inhaling deeply of his scent, not minding the stickiness of his seed cooling on her heated flesh. Her heart pounded hard as she wrapped her arms around him in return, holding him close.

CHAPTER 10

*R*hys woke to a hard, aching cock and a disappointingly empty bed.

Miranda was gone.

The place where she'd fallen asleep in his arms was cool to the touch, which meant she had left for her own room long before he had arisen. And it was the devil of a thing, that discovery. Not just because he was always the first to leave a lover's bed—clinging women were tedious, and maudlin sentiments more so—but because he realized, as he absently swept his hand over the slight indentation on her pillow, that he hadn't wanted her to go.

He had reached for her and met with emptiness. And it was damned unnerving, the way that emptiness had left him feeling—as he imagined he would if he were missing a part of himself.

He wanted more from her than just one night.

He wanted more from her, quite possibly, than he had ever wanted from another woman.

No.

What the bloody hell was he thinking? Likely, it was his

randy prick guiding him, he reassured himself as he lay back in the bed that still smelled faintly of sexual congress and her sweet scent. He would take himself in hand, and then he would begin his morning, facing this first full day of the house party and whatever it brought with his customary sangfroid.

He had bedded Miranda. He wanted to bed her again. It was a normal, usual red-blooded response. That was it. That was *all*.

Closing his eyes, Rhys reached beneath the sheet and grasped his rigid length. He thought about Miranda holding her delicious breasts together for him and begging him to fuck her. Of thrusting his cock between her full, bountiful breasts while she plumped them up for him. Would he spend on her breasts?

Damn it all, he was harder than hard, a bead of mettle seeping from his tip. With his thumb, he slicked it over his crown, remembering what she had tasted like, how she had writhed and moaned when he had tongued her pussy. And then he had his answer. Miranda would ask him to take her mouth, and he would have no choice but to give her what she wanted. She would part her berry-pink lips, and he would guide his erection over her waiting tongue. She would suck him so good, so hard, moaning around his cock, and…

"Fuck," he muttered, spilling into his sheets like a randy lad.

For a moment, he lay there, his breathing ragged, as he returned to the world and the still-dismaying absence of Miranda. And…he wasn't satisfied.

He wanted her here, but not just so he could persuade her to let him show her the joys of morning bedchamber romps. Not just so he could have his release. But because he wanted to see what she looked like, sleepy-eyed and with rumpled hair. He wanted to watch her while she slept. To kiss her awake. To hold her close to him as the sun rose. He wanted her naked and curled trustingly against him.

What a bloody idiot.

Wincing, Rhys tossed back the bedclothes and stalked to a pitcher and basin, performing some cursory ablutions before ringing for a bath. He needed a thorough soak this morning. Perhaps that would prove the restorative he required. A necessary return to sanity.

But not even submerging himself in hot, pleasant-scented water, which ordinarily cured whatever ailed him, sufficed. He washed and abandoned his still-warm bath in favor of dressing and receiving a quick morning shave from his valet Lavenue, whose presence rendered a trip next door to Miranda impossible. Venturing into her territory during the daylight hours was likely inadvisable anyway, given her stern devotion to keeping the household ignorant of their affair.

With a sigh, he deemed himself suitably respectable and descended to the tawdry whirl awaiting him downstairs. Before he broke his fast, however, there was a matter of supreme importance requiring not just his attention, but that of his fellow founders of the club. To that end, Rhys arranged for a meeting between the four of them in a private salon.

Unfortunately, only three of them were in attendance.

"Where the devil is Richford?" he asked Riverdale and Kingham, irritated by their friend's absence.

"Hopefully sleeping off his bloody terrible mood," King commented lightly, brushing a speck of lint from his coat sleeve.

"I saw him chasing after a masked blonde last night," Riverdale offered with a shrug. "I don't recall if that was before or after naughty charades. Thanks to King's latest potion, my recollection of the evening is delightfully imprecise."

"Lovely," Rhys muttered, annoyed. "We arrange a meeting

of tremendous importance, and Richford is off bedding some wench."

He was more than aware of his own hypocrisy, for he had spent the night with a woman as well. But Miranda was different. She wasn't a mere drunken tryst at a Wicked Dukes Society house party.

"I do so hate to argue finer points," King drawled, "but we haven't arranged a meeting. *You* have. And I have yet to eat breakfast, so this better be damned good."

"I ate an hour ago, and I've already gone for a ride." Riverdale grinned cheekily. "Lazy bastards, the lot of you."

Rhys wasn't in the mood for lighthearted banter. He was in the mood to blacken Lord Roberts's eye.

"We may as well proceed without Richford," he decided. "The matter cannot wait until he has decided he's finished emptying his ballocks."

King made a gagging sound and shuddered. "If you don't mind, I would prefer not to think about Richford's ballocks before half past ten in the morning."

"How about after half past ten?" Riverdale asked.

King pretended to contemplate the question, stroking his jaw. "No, I daresay not then either. Half past ten just seemed a proper sort of time."

"Lord help me," Rhys muttered. "Would the two of you cease nattering like a pair of dowager biddies at the edge of a ballroom? I have something serious I need to discuss with you."

"Why didn't you say so, old chap?" King asked, blinking innocently.

He glared at his friend. "I did say so. Curse your hides, and curse Richford's too."

"What about Brandon and Camden?" Riverdale wanted to know. "Should they not receive the same curse, given their absences as well?"

Rhys growled in frustration. "Yes, to the devil with them all. Now to the matter of import, and the reason I've convened this meeting. Last night, Lord Roberts threatened a woman in the gardens. If I hadn't intervened when I did, there's no telling what would have happened. Given his actions, I believe it's clear he needs to be expelled from both the Society and this house party."

"He threatened someone?" King asked, frowning, his amused expression fleeing.

"Yes." Fury roiled through Rhys anew as he thought of the scene he had come upon, the fear in Miranda's voice last night when she had run into his arms in the moonlight. "She wasn't masked, and Roberts threatened to reveal her presence here to polite society in an effort to hurt her reputation. He also suggested that he would hold his tongue if she bedded him."

White-hot rage accompanied the last revelation. Roberts was bloody well fortunate that Rhys hadn't simply thrashed him to death then and there.

"That is vile," Riverdale agreed, "and decidedly against our rules. Who is the lady in question?"

Damn it, he didn't want to reveal it was Miranda. Not because he didn't trust his friends to keep the matter private and avoid causing a scandal for her. But because he wasn't ready to examine what he felt for her or to admit it to King and Riverdale.

"Does it matter?" he asked. "Roberts was attempting to blackmail a woman and to coerce her into bed with him."

"The woman in question wouldn't happen to be the saucy bit of skirts you brought here to make the cream ice and cornets, would it?" King asked knowingly.

Rhys knew he shouldn't be surprised that King was aware of Miranda being at Wingfield Hall. His friend had an uncanny knack for knowing everything about everyone.

He clenched his jaw. "She has a name, and I'll thank you to refrain from referring to her as a *saucy bit of skirts*."

King grinned. "But I do so enjoy watching how nettled you get over the mere mentioning of her, I must admit. What is she calling herself now? Lady Miranda, Miss Lenox, or Lady Ammondale?"

Bloody hell, either King was omniscient, or he had a spy in the ranks. Neither would surprise Rhys.

"It is Miss Lenox," he ground out. "But the lady is rightfully protective of her reputation. Her presence here is not to become common knowledge. As far as the guests are to know, she has sent a pupil trained by her to delight us with her culinary confections. No one can know the lady herself is staying here at Wingfield Hall. Given the nature of the house party and her divorce being fodder for the gossips, she is concerned that further scandal should fall upon her."

"You ought to have a sword, playing the knight as you are," Riverdale said, shaking his head as if he despaired of Rhys.

He raised a brow, feeling rather murderous at the moment, and positively medieval. "To run Roberts through? I wouldn't turn it down."

King whistled. "I don't believe I've ever seen you so taken with a woman, Whit."

He ground his molars until his jaw ached. "I'm not taken."

But was that true? Rhys didn't want to think about it. Not now. Not after he had made love to Miranda just last night. Not when she had disappeared before morning, flitting away like a seductive, elusive phantom. Not when he had to make certain Roberts would never breathe a word about Miranda again.

Riverdale and King were sharing a look that suggested they didn't believe a thing Rhys said. Before he could tell either of them to go to the devil, the door to the salon opened and Richford stalked over the threshold, resembling nothing so much as a thundercloud brazening his way across an otherwise faultless blue sky.

"Is something wrong?" he bit out.

Clearly, his mood had not improved since the day before. Rhys found himself wondering whatever or whoever it was that had Richford in such high dudgeon. But that discovery would have to wait.

"We're going to beat Lord Roberts to a pulp and then send him out of here," he informed his friend. "He threatened a woman in the gardens last night."

Richford nodded. "I never did like him."

King grinned. "If there is one thing I can approve of before half past ten, it's spilling the blood of arseholes."

The four of them set off in search of the unfortunate Lord Roberts.

THE HOUR WAS late by the time Miranda returned to her bedchamber that evening.

Intentionally so.

She had kept herself from the temptation of Rhys by throwing herself headlong into dinner's intricate dessert preparations. Of course, keeping her hands busy had not prevented her mind from wandering inevitably to thoughts of him. To thoughts of what had happened between them the night before, and thoughts of what must never, ever happen again.

With a heavy sigh, she stepped over the threshold into her darkened chamber. As they had the night before, her feet and back ached. She had spent a great many hours in her preparations for the delicate mushrooms she had created.

The door closed at her back, and she found herself

grateful for a low light that Green must have kept lit for her. But when she noticed a male form sitting in the shadows by the hearth, she let out a squeal of alarm. Until recognition hit her in the next moment.

"Hush." Rhys was on his feet, moving toward her. "It's only me, darling."

"Oh, heavens." She pressed a hand over her pounding heart. "You gave me a fright."

He reached her, and she noted he was dressed formally, as if he had fled dinner to be here with her. "Forgive me. That wasn't my intention."

Goodness, he was handsome. She knew he was, of course, as surely as she knew the sky was blue. And yet, it seemed that each time she saw him, whether in shadows or moonlight, by dawn or full sun, she took note of new facets, rather like a terrain she was learning day by day. The strength of his jaw, the sharpness of his cheekbones, the stubborn tilt of his sensual lips, the golden lashes framing his stormy eyes, the hues of amber glinting in his hair, the breadth of his chest, the strength of his shoulders.

Her reaction to him was infallibly visceral, potent as a warm embrace or a knowing kiss. She wanted him here in her territory, in her private space, the same way she wanted him inside her again. But despite those irreverent yearnings, her rational mind was aware of the consequences should she simply fling herself into his arms and bed yet again.

He could not be here. He should not be here.

And she should not want him.

Miranda forced her countenance into stern admonishment. "You are forgiven for startling me, but not for your presence in my bedchamber. What are you doing here?"

He raised a brow, near enough to touch, to be perilous to her ability to resist him. "Waiting for you."

He said it as if his presence were obvious, as if she ought

to have expected him to be awaiting her on a chair by the hearth in the dim recesses of her bedroom. Something deep within, something forbidden and sinful, sparked into a flame that no amount of reason could douse.

"Why?" she asked, locking her hands together at her waist in a pose that was meant to mimic that of her most fearsome girlhood governess, Miss Biddle.

In truth, she braided her fingers to keep from reaching for him. To keep from cupping his face in her hands and testing the prickle of his gilt stubble on her palms. He was more intoxicating than any wine she had ever consumed. She longed to bask in him. To savor him. To seduce him and make her mark upon him just as surely as he had done to her.

"Because I have yet to see you all day," he said, reaching for her linked hands and folding them in his.

"That seems a woefully insufficient reason." She swallowed hard as he lifted her hands to his lips to skate warm, affectionate kisses over her reddened knuckles.

She winced when his mouth discovered a particularly painful patch of raw skin.

He took note and froze, lifting his head, a ferocious frown replacing the tenderness that had just been lining his face. "Are you hurt?"

"It is nothing," she insisted, for she had injured herself in many kitchens. Cookery was, at its worst, grueling, dirty, dangerous work.

"Your reaction suggests otherwise," he told her grimly, releasing her hands and taking her lightly by the arm instead. "Come."

She knew where he was guiding her, of course. Across the chamber to the door connecting their rooms, like Hades leading Persephone to the underworld.

Miranda dug in her heels, forcing him to stop. "No."

He huffed out an irritated sigh. "Miranda."

She stood firm. "Not in your bedchamber. As I said, it is nothing. A commonplace burn."

The wrong thing to say, she realized as he continued hauling her across the Axminster.

"You've been burned? By God, who is responsible for this? I'll hang him by his ballocks."

Her tired feet rushed after him, her sensible boots pinching her toes and rubbing her heels. All at once, her entire body felt as if it were aflame, and not just from lust, but from weariness and pain. She hadn't the energy to fight him. Perhaps not even the will.

His bedroom was lit with blazing gas lamps, and she blinked at the sudden change as he pulled her into the light. "Tell me, damn it." He held her hands in his oh-so gently, his head bowed over as if in prayer. "Which irresponsible wretch burned you?"

"I did," she admitted. "I spilled boiled sugar over my hand when I was constructing the nougat paste baskets. I ought to have taken greater care, but I was in a hurry. I had a great many baskets to make, and I feared they would be lacking in the proper time to set."

"My God, kitten. This looks as if it hurts dreadfully."

The concern in his voice and touch reached a part of her she hadn't thought existed any longer, and she found herself blinking furiously to keep the unwanted tears pricking her eyes from falling. Not tears of pain, but tears that were far more humiliating. Tears because he cared.

She cleared her throat, willing the unwanted emotion away. "I have experienced far worse."

"Let me wash your hands. I have some ointment my valet keeps on hand for the rare occasions when he knicks my jaw with his razor. A feat which he loves to assure me only occurs when I stubbornly insist upon talking whilst he attempts to shave me."

The wry humor in his voice softened the resistance within her. "Do you?"

"I am a man of endless wisdom," he said. "I have a great many things to impart. Why must I be stopped by a mere shave?"

His bombastic proclamation won a reluctant laugh from her. The man was deadly when he chose to be charming. Look at how easily he had lured her into his lair, and now she was allowing him to lead her to a pitcher and basin on the opposite end of the room despite her insistence that the burn was a minor one.

"You needn't tend to me," she protested lightly, though in truth, she liked his touch. His concern too.

It made her feel...*things*.

Complicated, wondrous, utterly stupid things.

Things she would be better never, ever feeling, especially not for a dazzling rakehell like the Duke of Whitby, who presided over a licentious club and hosted orgies without a hint of contrition.

"On the contrary, I fear I must." He guided her injured hand over the basin and, lifting the pitcher, sluiced cool, clean water over it.

She hissed in a breath as the water washed over the burn. The cook had wished to treat it with butter, but she had refused, knowing from experience that an application of butter only served to make burns worse.

"I'm sorry, darling," he said softly, lathering soap on a small cloth before gently dabbing at her burn. "I don't want to hurt you."

"I know." She forced a smile, still struggling with the new and unwanted emotions churning through her. "But truly, I have experienced far worse, and I shall again."

He rinsed the suds from her skin with care. "Why do you toil like this? You make the finest creations I've ever tasted, but surely not even your divine confections are sufficient reason for subjecting yourself to injury."

She was grateful for the root of his concern, which was for her and her welfare, not for the fact that her culinary aspirations were beneath her station. Ammondale had been disgusted by her "propensity toward being a servant," as he had so disdainfully phrased her dream of running her own cookery school.

"Because I enjoy it," she explained, permitting Rhys to delicately towel her hand dry. "I've always been entranced by the art of cookery, for as long as I can remember. When I was a girl, I would steal into the kitchens and watch our cook, Mrs. Simpson, begging her to share her recipes with me. My nursemaid didn't mind having one less child to look after, so she never breathed a word of where I spent so much time. But as I grew older and had a governess, she told my mother where I was. My mother was horrified that any daughter of hers should have spent so much time in the kitchens, a place that, in her mind, belonged to servants alone."

She stopped before she revealed even more, aware that she was rambling. Rhys's proximity wreaked havoc upon her. But his gaze, focused and intense as he cradled her injured hand in his, was every bit as potent.

"You must think me silly," she said, feeling suddenly foolish for sharing so much.

"Not at all." He shook his head, lowering the towel and releasing her hands. "I think you incredible."

Miranda couldn't quite contain her bitter laugh. "You are the only person of that opinion."

"Surely not." He frowned. "Stay where you are. I'll fetch the ointment."

"Ammondale was disgusted by my interest in cookery," she said, watching as Rhys prowled to a nearby piece of furniture and extracted a tin from a drawer. "He said he wanted a countess, not a servant. He forbade me from visiting the kitchens or speaking with our cook."

"So, he was an autocratic bastard in addition to being a notoriously small-pricked bore," Rhys said as he returned to her.

This time, her laugh wasn't bitter. "You are outrageous, sir."

He grinned. "And you love it."

She smiled back at him, trying to cling to her determination to keep her desire for this man at bay and failing.

"Conceited as well," she commented archly.

"Your hand, madam," he requested with a gallant air.

She dutifully held it out, allowing him to tend to her. Enjoying it, even. He unscrewed the lid on the ointment tin and smeared a dollop on his forefinger before gently layering it over her burn.

"The dessert was extraordinary this evening," he said softly, head still bent as he performed his task. "Everyone was astounded that the baskets could be eaten. The raspberry and chocolate cream ice was delicious, and the ice mushrooms were perfectly formed."

She knew that her latest creation had been impressive, but she didn't want his praise to originate from pity. "You need not say so on my behalf."

"My dear, I can assure you that I speak truth. Grown men were fighting over ice mushrooms. I very much feared Kingham and Richford would come to blows over it."

He had finished applying the ointment to her burn and turned to wash his own hands. Now was the time for her to remind them both of how improper her presence was here and return to her room.

And yet, she could not seem to make herself leave.

"I doubt that they were truly motivated to come to blows," she murmured.

"Would I lie?" he asked, giving her a look that was somehow innocent and yet scorching all at once.

"Yes," she said without hesitation.

He finished drying his hands and pressed one over his heart in dramatic fashion. "Will there be no end to the mortal blows you deal me, my queen?"

She bit her lip to stifle her laughter. "I was not aware there could be multiple mortal blows."

"Nor was I until you arrived in my life with your decadent desserts and your resistance to my charms." He screwed the lid back onto his ointment but left it on the table.

"I fear I am hardly as resistant as I ought to be," she admitted before she could think better of it.

"I'm pleased to hear it." His smile was wickedness personified as he closed the distance between them yet again. "Why did you leave my bed before dawn?"

It was his first acknowledgment of what had happened between them the night before, and it made wanton heat roll through her. Forbidden longing. Desire she didn't want to feel. And shame too. For here was the reminder that she was every bit as sinful as the scandal broth had suggested she was.

"Because I had a great deal of work awaiting me today," she said primly, hoping he could read none of the turmoil passing through her in her face or tone. "And because I had no wish to be caught there by your valet or my lady's maid. And because what happened last night cannot happen again."

"Of course it can."

Oh, how she longed to agree with him. To fling herself into his arms. But it was too dangerous. The risk to him was nothing. He could carry on as he pleased, and polite society would not so much as blink an eye in reproach. But she had already paid the price a woman who dared to seize her independence must inevitably forfeit. And she had no intention of paying it again.

Regardless of how much pleasure there was to be had in this handsome rake's bed.

"No," she told him firmly, pleased with herself for the conviction in her voice. "It cannot."

"Surely I have proven that you need not fear scandal. Lord Roberts has been removed from Wingfield Hall and the Society both. Kingham, Richford, Riverdale, and I have ensured that he won't breathe a word about your presence here if he wants to keep his teeth."

His grim pronouncement should not have brought more warmth to her cold and icy heart, but it did. "You need not have further taken up the matter with him on my behalf."

"Yes, I bloody well needed to," he growled, rubbing at his jaw with an irritated expression on his handsome face. "Any man who thinks to cause harm to you answers to me."

He was being deadly earnest, all the levity and teasing gone from his countenance. No man had ever been so caring, with the exception of Waring, who had been a steadfast source of comfort in her life until he had left for America in the wake of the scandal following her. She felt a pang of guilt anew at being the reason for Waring's absence from England, for which she was entirely at fault. It had been Waring's idea to pose as lovers and force Ammondale into granting her the divorce, but the price he had paid had been every bit as high as the one Miranda had.

"I appreciate your protectiveness during this week," she told Rhys.

"I'm not just speaking of this week."

"After this week, our association will be at an end," she reminded him.

And herself too. Yes, she needed to recall that this was all temporary. Fleeting. Finite. It could never be more than this lone week, which would pass in a flurry and then be forever gone.

"You know that need not be the case," he said, frowning. "Nor can you deny how right it is between us."

"Rhys," she protested, trying to cling to her fortitude.

To summon all her strength.

"You want me." His hands settled on her waist in a possessive hold she knew she could escape with ease if she wanted.

And still, she remained where she was, content to stay for just a few moments longer. To linger in his captivating presence. To breathe in his intoxicating masculine scent. To fool herself into believing there could ever be more for her than one night of passion in his arms.

She licked her lips. "I also want cake for breakfast, luncheon, and dinner, but that yearning is not any more practical."

"My pride objects to any and all comparisons between my cock and cake," he drawled, his head dipping toward hers.

He was going to kiss her. And he was shameless. Sinful. He said words like cock and prick without compunction and stared at her mouth as if he spent all day thinking about kissing her. He cared about her burned hand and listened to her dreams without disparaging them. He protected her. He loved her cream ices.

Oh dear heavens, she was falling under this alluring rake's wicked, wicked spell.

"It's much harder than cake, for one thing," he murmured, so close that his breath whispered over her lips, bearing the faint sweetness of wine.

She wanted to taste it on her tongue.

Belatedly, she realized he was still talking about his cock. The man was incorrigible.

"Your Grace," she protested, trying to summon formality.

"No, you don't, kitten. You cannot *Your Grace* me after I've been inside you and you've come on my tongue."

His voice was low and deep and sinful as his words. Her nipples went hard, and between her thighs, she was embarrassingly aching and wet. All from his nearness and the things he was saying.

Run, Miranda, she urged herself sternly. *Run before you do something you shall regret.*

But that would be the practical, reasonable action to take. Just as never giving in and coming to Wingfield Hall would have been after he made his intentions known. And as she had proven just last night, being reasonable and practical were not nearly as enjoyable as their alternatives.

They were alone in the lamplight and the night. No servants. His hands on her felt like a gift she must not refuse, lest she never again be presented with it. Sometimes, chances were worth taking. Divorcing Ammondale had been. Starting her school had been. And this, this magical, sensual bond that existed between herself and Rhys? It seemed like a chance worth taking too.

She reached for him, feeling as if she had just swum to the surface after being submerged in water, and now she could take a deep breath, filling her lungs with air. Her fingers caught in his white necktie, and she jerked him the rest of the way, pulling his mouth to hers.

CHAPTER 11

*S*he was kissing him.

And ye gods. When Miranda Lenox wanted to kiss, she bloody well *kissed*. Her soft lips were firm and demanding, her sharp little tongue bold and insistent, and the dainty fingers grasping his tie and pulling him to her were a dominant touch he hadn't known would make his prick as rigid as a fire poker.

Until now.

Now he knew. He liked her urgency, her fire, her wild abandon. Not just because a carefree Miranda was such a rarity—though, to be sure, it was. She wore responsibility the way some women wore their jewels. But because he knew what it meant, her unfettered reaction to him. It meant he had chipped away at her walls. It meant her defenses were lying in shattered ruins at her yet-booted feet.

Which reminded him—he needed to get her out of her plain gray gown and hideous ankle boots more suited to a somber housekeeper than a woman of such passion. She tasted like chocolate and sugar with a hint of cream and something else that was as mysterious as it was indefinably hers.

Bloody delicious. That was what she tasted like. Like tonight and tomorrow and a hundred nights afterward. Like his. Like something scarce and indefinable. Something he never wanted to forget or be without. And that in itself should trouble him, but somehow, it didn't.

Her tongue tangled with his, stroking, sliding sinuously, and he groaned, gliding a hand from her waist up the small of her back. The boning of her corset grazed his palm, reminding him anew of all the layers he must strip away to have her naked and utterly at his mercy.

He was taking nothing for granted, of course. His Miranda was skittish as a newborn foal. She needed coaxing and tenderness and persuasion—rightly so, after all she must have endured at her oafish husband's hands. Rhys couldn't simply begin to tear away at hooks and laces and tapes, regardless of how much he longed to do so. No, he would have to woo her and win her. To savor her and pleasure her. To show her just how much she meant to him, which seemed in this moment, her lips sweet and demanding upon his, more than he could have fathomed.

But he was ever cognizant of her reticence. The fact that she had told him she could not stay with him tonight.

Reluctantly, he broke the kiss, moving his other hand from her waist to cup her cheek, holding her still so he could meet her eyes and search her gaze for the mysteries he longed to unlock.

"Stay with me tonight," he said. "Please."

Her kiss-swollen lips parted. And he feared she was preparing to deny him. To deny them both. So he pressed his thumb gently over her mouth.

"Don't say you cannot. Not until you hear what I have to say."

Her dark lashes fanned over her cheeks for a moment, long and sooty. And then they rose on emerald eyes that never failed to take his breath, regardless of how many times he fell into them. She nodded.

"There is a reason I placed us in this wing of the manor house. Have you not noticed that there are no other guests but the two of us?"

He was revealing his rakish plotting to her, and he knew he ought to be ashamed. But part of him hoped his actions might actually work in his favor.

"Yes, but—"

"No," he interrupted, pressing her full lower lip firmly to the top, keeping her from continuing. "I haven't finished yet, darling. I placed us here so that we would be assured of privacy. I also made certain that the only servants about are loyal and trustworthy."

"But Green."

"Green is being paid handsomely for a young lady of no experience. And beyond that, her family is being well provided for. All I ask in exchange is loyalty and discretion."

"Bribery?" She sounded indignant despite the way his thumb muffled the word.

"Hardly. Merely making certain that I am prepared in all ways." He lowered his forehead to hers. "Which I clearly am not. Prepared, that is. I am persuaded that nothing in the world could have prepared me for you."

He meant that. Yes, he was bombastic and ridiculous, and he used his charm and his tongue and his good looks to woo the fairer sex into giving him what he wanted. He had been doing so since he'd been a wet-behind-the-ears lad of fifteen when he had first realized he could use his face and his family name to his advantage. But that wasn't what he was doing here with Miranda. With her, it was as if he were bereft of all artifice, stripped bare and vulnerable. He'd never experienced anything quite like it.

Her nostrils flared as she inhaled deeply, clearly waging war with herself. "You are a notorious rake. Surely you've had ample practice at seducing women into doing whatever it is you wish of them."

"Not with you." It was all he could bring himself to say. Maudlin confessions were not in him. He took the ugliness and worst of life and made a jest of it. He buried his feelings so deep that they could never be resurrected. The lad who had been ruthlessly beaten by the former duke to remove all hints of weakness had learned his lessons well.

Except for the woman in his arms.

Her eyebrows rose. "And that matters?"

"*You* matter." His voice was so raw with emotion that it was hoarse. "I've made certain to protect you and your reputation. No one shall ever be the wiser."

"I will."

He hadn't expected that response from her. Nor the stricken expression on her lovely face.

He longed to kiss her, but he denied himself. The moment was too serious for that.

"Are you saying you regret what happened between us last night, Miranda?" he asked, needing to know.

Because if she did, he would be done. Despite how much it would bloody well kill him to walk away from her, he would. She had been through enough.

"No," she whispered, closing her eyes again as she struggled with herself. "I don't regret it at all, and that is the problem."

Her answer was all he needed. Fierce, potent need shot through him as one.

Rhys leaned into her, pressing his lips to her ear. "If I

lifted your gown and touched you right now, would you be wet for me?"

A breathless sound escaped her, and she clung to him, as if without his support she would fall to the Axminster at his feet. "Rhys, please."

"Please what, kitten?" He licked the whorl of her ear, desperate for a taste of her, then nuzzled the floral-scented hair at her temple. "I'm afraid you're going to have to tell me yourself. Please kiss me? Please lift my skirts and see if my cunny is slick and wet? Please take me to bed? Please give me your—"

She moaned, cutting off the rest of his words, and startled him by cupping his face in her hands and bringing his mouth to hers for a kiss that was nothing short of ferocious. He kissed her back, giving her his tongue as he moved them toward the bed awaiting them. The bed she should never have slipped out of in the dark night, leaving him alone.

The bed where she belonged.

Because at his side, with him, beneath him, atop him, that was where Miranda Lenox was meant to be.

He broke the kiss. "Stay with me."

She closed her eyes, her expression tortured.

"Miranda," he pressed, brushing his lips over hers with tender strokes. "Say you'll let me make love to you tonight."

And a thousand more, he thought, but these were words he knew he must keep to himself. Hell, they were words that frightened even him with their intensity and the way he felt them to his marrow.

"Yes," she whispered at last.

Elation soared through him, desire not far behind. His cock was so hard, he was already leaking, and they had done nothing but kiss. They were both dressed, he in his evening wear from the dinner he had fled after dessert and she in the dove-gray gown she wore like armor.

And it was armor, he realized now. It was her defense against the rumors, the scandal, the rest of the world that would judge her so blasted unfairly. Only he could remove it with her permission.

"Thank you," he breathed and took her mouth, the kiss deep, ravenous, showing her what he felt without needing words.

As their lips clung, he guided them the rest of the way to the bed, until her skirts connected with the mattress, staying further motion. With great reluctance, he tore his lips away again.

"Sit on the bed, darling."

"In my gown? I'm sure it smells of the day's work in the kitchens."

Her protest made his heart lurch. He hated that she toiled away. Despised that she had hurt herself today and, worse, that she had done so many times before. But he had witnessed the pride she had for her culinary confections— and rightly so. Hearing her confessions about how her own mother had regarded her passion for cookery, coupled with Ammondale's treatment, made him more aware than ever that he must not try to dissuade her from her course.

Her work was important to her, and therefore it was to him as well.

He kissed her again swiftly before withdrawing. "It smells like chocolate and a spring meadow and the most beautiful woman I've ever seen."

She struggled to contain her answering smile and failed. "You always know what to say, don't you?"

"Not always, or you would have agreed to the rest of my proposal and not to only this portion," he pointed out. "Now sit, please."

She eyed him warily, as if she was wondering what he could be plotting, but did as he asked, settling her modest bustle on the edge of the bed so that she was perched, long legs just barely grazing the floor.

God, he loved those long, well-curved limbs. He couldn't wait to have them wrapped around him again. But first, he wanted those godawful boots of hers gone.

He sank to his knees on the carpet, holding her gaze. "Your servant, madam. May I have your boot?"

She looked at him, eyes wide, almost as if he had spoken a language she didn't comprehend, until at last she spoke. "My boot?"

"Left or right," he added. "Whatever my queen prefers."

"I'm not your queen."

She was frowning, and he didn't like that. "Yes, you are," Rhys told her solemnly. "And I intend to prove your devoted page."

"Rhys."

"Let me," he said urgently. "Let me tend to you. Let me spoil you. Let me please you."

Miranda sighed, and he knew he had won. "How can I say no?"

She gave him her left foot first.

He took the worn boot in one hand, cupping the leather at her heel as his fingers found the knot she must have tightened that morning and loosened it. She sighed in what he presumed was relief as he slipped the boot off.

Her stockings were fine. Cream silk with an exotic spray of embroidered flowers over the ankle in shades of blue, pink, and yellow. In his haste to bed her the day before, he had taken note of a similar embellishment on her hosiery, but he hadn't taken the time to contemplate the dichotomy of her colorless, unassuming work gowns and her expensive French stockings and bold corset.

Rhys massaged her foot, knowing it must ache after she had spent so much time perfecting the incredible desserts that had been displayed for dinner. "You surprise me," he murmured, using the pads of his thumbs on her arch as he attempted to ease the strain of the tight muscles he found there.

"My stockings are for me," she said softly.

He wondered if there were any other indulgences she allowed herself beyond her undergarments and had to tamp down the impulse to offer to shower her with everything she could possibly want. There would be time aplenty for that later, after he persuaded her to become his mistress.

"Who are your gowns for?" he asked, working her foot gently.

She made a purring sound of pleasure as he massaged. "They are for everyone else."

"Not for me." He winked up at her. "I happen to prefer you out of your gowns. And everything else too."

A flush crept over her cheeks. "Rhys."

"Do you know why I tell you such wicked things, kitten?"

"Cease calling me kitten." There was scarcely any protest in her voice now.

Her lashes were lowered, eyes closing. He hoped it was a sign of relaxation rather than exhaustion. The notion of her injuring herself earlier was nettlesome enough. He didn't want her working herself to death on his behalf.

"Why? I think it suits you. You're adorable, but you also have claws."

"Adorable?" Her lashes fluttered, brilliant emerald once more searing him to his soul. "No one has ever referred to me thusly before."

"Then no one has seen you as I have." And Rhys couldn't deny that he liked that. Liked it very much indeed. "Seeing you with your defenses down is a potent aphrodisiac. And you never did answer my question."

Her brow furrowed. "What question?"

He smiled, thinking he was accomplishing his task splendidly. "Why do I tell you wicked things?"

"Oh." She bit her lip, and the urge to kiss her was so strong he almost sprang to his feet and pressed his mouth to hers. "Because you are a sinful rake."

"Wrong, kitten. It's because I love it when you say my name."

Absolute truth. And Rhys was, quite unapologetically, a man who had no qualms about lying when it suited him. Not in this instance, however. Everything he said to Miranda was true.

He'd ponder that realization later. For now, he had another boot to remove.

Gently, he placed the foot he'd been massaging on the Axminster, before holding out his hands. "Next."

She settled her right boot in his hands. "You needn't play lady's maid, you know."

"Lady's maid? I'm offended." He untied the knot and loosened the laces. "I'm a page, darling."

Her lips twitched as if she were fighting off a smile. "Forgive me."

"Always." The boot slid away, revealing the same colorful spray of embroidery on her stockings. "How long have you been on your feet today?"

"Most of the day."

"By God, woman. No wonder your feet are so bloody sore." He pressed his thumbs into her arch, the same tenseness that he'd found in her other foot greeting him. "What about when you ate dinner? Did you not sit then?"

"I didn't eat dinner. I was too busy arranging the mushroom baskets to my liking."

He paused, looking up at her. "You've had nothing to eat since luncheon?"

"I'm not hungry."

"I hired you to make cream ice, not to starve yourself." He placed her stockinged foot on the carpets and rose, determined to rectify this grievous wrong at once.

"Where are you going?" she demanded to know.

Rhys stalked to the bellpull. "To order something for you to eat."

"No, you cannot." She flew from the bed, rushing across the room, and caught him just before he reached the cord. "Please, Rhys. It would be ruinous. You cannot request a tray of food for me to be delivered to your bedchamber."

Hell. She wasn't wrong about that. But there was another way he could procure her a meal. One that didn't involve servants.

He nodded. "I'll fetch a tray for you myself, then."

Her eyes went wide. "That would be an even greater disaster. Everyone belowstairs will know why you are procuring food for me."

"It's none of their concern who the food is for," he growled. "They're paid handsomely to have no opinion on such matters. But if they ask, I'll tell them it's for me."

"I'm truly not hungry," she protested. "There's no need for you to go to the kitchens and fetch me dinner. I can wait until the morning without perishing, I assure you. I often get so caught up in my work that I skip the evening meal."

But Rhys's mind was already made.

"There will be no skipping of dinners whilst you are under my care," he informed her. "I'll go and fetch you a tray, and you are to wait here until I return. Understood?"

Her expression turned mulish, and he could tell she didn't like the way he had taken command of the situation. But quite likely, she was also hungry, despite her protestations otherwise.

"I'm not asking for your permission in this, Miranda," he added sternly. "You need to eat."

As if on cue, her stomach issued an angry growl. She flattened a hand over her midriff, looking mortified by her body's indecorous reaction to the promise of sustenance. "Very well. If you insist."

"I do." He drew her to him and kissed her swiftly. "Now, please sit and relax. I'll be back in a few minutes."

As he slipped from his bedroom, leaving Miranda behind, part of him wondered if she would do as he asked or if she would steal back to her own chamber.

"Stubborn woman," he said under his breath as he stalked down the empty hall.

It was only when he reached the kitchens that he realized he'd been grinning like a fool the whole way there.

"WOULD YOU LIKE ANYTHING MORE?" Rhys asked from where he was reclined in a pile of pillows by the hearth. "There is plenty remaining on the tray."

Between them, the remnants of his kitchen spoils were a temptation that, like the man himself, she shouldn't indulge in. Miranda's stomach was full—he had somehow ransacked the kitchens and emerged with a veritable feast for her, which he had brought on a large tray just as he had promised. No servants. No one the wiser, even if she did wonder if the domestics hadn't found the sight of a duke both obtaining and delivering his own food a bit eccentric.

She shook her head. "Not another bite."

"Wine?" He held up one of the bottles he had also managed to acquire in his absence earlier.

The Duke of Whitby was a very industrious man. In all matters, she was beginning to suspect.

She glanced at her glass, finding it almost empty, and

knew she ought to refuse his offer but extended it toward him instead. "Perhaps just a bit."

There was the embarrassing reminder, of course, of what had happened the last time she had imbibed too much wine at dinner. And her resulting sobriquet, which he seemed to enjoy using more with her every protest.

He finished pouring her wine and met her gaze, the mask of effortless rakish charm he so often wore gone for a moment. In its place was a look of frank affection, as if he enjoyed spoiling her.

But that was silliness, was it not? Tending to her was all a part of his seduction. And it was working too. She couldn't recall the last time she had felt so very cared for. Not since before Waring had left England for America's shores. But with the marquess, the feelings burgeoning within her had always been friendship and a deep appreciation for his aid. With Rhys, it was something else. Something bigger and almost frightening.

Holding his gaze, she took a slow drink from her wine. At his back, the fire crackled, the flickering light playing in the golds and hints of red in his hair. His feet were bare, and he had removed his coat and necktie, leaving him in shirtsleeves and trousers and waistcoat. The buttons at his throat called to her now, taunting. Above his collar, the protrusion of his Adam's apple bobbed as he took a swallow from his own glass.

"Dinner was lovely," she told him, suddenly flustered by his regard and the heat from the fire, which mingled with the warmth inside her. "It was kind of you to fetch me so many offerings and deliver them to me."

He inclined his head. "Your loyal page, my queen."

"Thank you for everything that you have done for me this evening," she said quietly. "It was quite unnecessary."

"On the contrary. It was absolutely necessary. I cannot have my queen go to bed hungry."

"I do believe you revel in being as outlandish as possible," she quipped lightly, before hiding her smile in her wineglass.

Oh, he was amusing. Too amusing. Too handsome. Too kind, too considerate, too charming by half. He was too much of everything, and she wanted it all.

The hour was late, and she knew she needed to go to bed. Alone. In her own chamber. The impromptu dinner's interruption had shattered the earlier erotic spell between them. She should have gone by now.

She had wandered about his room during his foray to the kitchens, deliberating what to do with herself. Thinking she should leave until her stomach rumbled. Paging through a book of poetry at his bedside and wondering if he read it until he fell asleep. Or perhaps even first in the morning.

And then he had returned, grinning and handsome, bearing a massive tray laden with more food than she could dream of eating in one sitting, a bottle of wine tucked precariously under each arm. He had made a nest of pillows for them on the floor by the fireplace and had decanted wine and made up a plate to her specifications. She had eaten, and he had regaled her with tales of the rumors swirling amongst the revelers below, bringing her to so much laughter, in a few instances she'd been near tears.

"Are you sure I cannot convince you to eat anything else?" he asked softly, tearing her from her thoughts.

She swallowed her wine. "No, thank you. You are too kind to look after me."

"If selfishness is kindness, then I am guilty."

"How is fetching me dinner and rubbing my aching feet selfishness?" she couldn't help asking, even though she knew it was dangerous to linger, to further question him.

She ought to scurry back to her room like a mouse saved

from certain death at the paws of a merciless cat. But she remained, holding her wine, watching him, awaiting his answer, enthralled.

He slowly slid one foot flat upon the floor, leaving his knee bent and drawing her attention for a moment to how handsome his feet were. And what a startling intimacy. She didn't recall ever even seeing Ammondale's feet bare, but she was sure they would have been pale and unattractive, marked by spindly toes and dark hair.

The very notion of her former husband's feet made her grimace, so she took another sip of wine.

"What are you thinking about now?" Rhys asked, his tone curious as he rested his forearm over his knee.

She swallowed hard, nearly choking. Good heavens, what was she to tell him, that she had been ogling his feet, of all things? Comparing his to Ammondale's? No. She couldn't bear such a mortifying confession.

"Nothing," she lied, offering him a bright smile she hoped would fool him.

"Hardly nothing, I think. You're blushing."

She bit her lip, wishing she didn't like him so much. Wishing he hadn't proven himself to be considerate and kind, silly and whimsical, intelligent and protective. Little wonder his eyes were the color of a sky after a storm. The man himself was a storm, fierce and powerful. Capable of changing everything in his wake.

"And now you're biting your lip," he observed. "I do so hate when you torture your pretty mouth so."

Miranda stared at him, drinking in his masculine beauty and smooth charm. There was something so lovely and domestic about this arrangement on the floor, bolstered by several bedrooms' worth of pillows he had pilfered. Although she had lain with him, she found something more potently intimate about this moment, about the lamplight glistening in his eyes and the boyish pose he affected for her benefit, the food he had brought her on the tray between them, her stockinged feet facing the dwindling flames in the hearth. It was, in fact, the most intimate moment she'd shared with any man, and that realization was terrifying.

Because it made her understand she wanted more of it. A perilous desire, that. He was an unrepentant rake, the sort of man who wanted her as his mistress, and she was a divorcée, a scandalous woman who needed to retain her faultless reputation if she was to survive.

"You're still biting your lip," Rhys said into the silence. "And you have yet to tell me what is churning about in that clever mind of yours."

"Your feet," she blurted, because she couldn't very well say any of the rest of it. "I was thinking that you have handsome feet."

He chuckled, the sound soft as velvet, low and deep. "Handsome feet?"

Her ears went hot, and she was painfully aware of how foolish her admission sounded, particularly when repeated back to her. Even if it was true.

"Yes," she managed. "They are very pleasing to look upon, which ought to come as no surprise, given the rest of you."

Oh heavens. That was surely the wine loosening her tongue, wasn't it? She wasn't even sure.

A crooked grin curved his sensual lips. "You like my feet, kitten?"

She blew out the breath she hadn't realized she'd been holding. "Cease calling me kitten."

"I fear I cannot."

"Why?"

His grin deepened. "Because I like it far too much. And, I think, I like you far too much, Miss Miranda Lenox."

The feeling was mutual. But she didn't dare return the words or the sentiment. Doing so was far too perilous.

"I've never heard of anyone liking someone far too much," she said instead.

His levity faded. "Nor have I. Not until you. And that is why we both ought to get some sleep this night."

With a sigh, he rose, towering over her and extending a hand.

Startled by the abruptness of his reversal, she settled her palm in his, allowing him to pull her to her feet with one graceful tug. Of course, tired as she was—and perhaps a trifle disguised from the wine, if she were honest—she swayed on her feet, falling into his chest. He caught her, holding her to him, and even through the layers of her corset and gown and underpinnings, she felt the undeniable ridge of his cock against her.

Which was why it was so very confusing when he kissed her cheek and murmured in her ear, "You should go and get some rest, darling. I don't want your exhaustion on my conscience along with your starvation."

"I was hardly starving," she protested, "and I'm not tired."

But the yawn she promptly stifled proved otherwise to the both of them.

He lifted one imperious, ducal brow. "You see, kitten? You need your rest."

Her lips parted to protest. Surely he didn't intend to…not bed her? That had been his design from the moment she had arrived in her chamber to find him waiting for her.

Had it not?

Rhys smiled. "Tomorrow is another day, and you are worth the wait, darling."

She didn't protest as he walked her to the door adjoining their chambers, plucking the wineglass she hadn't realized she had emptied from her fingers just before sending her back to her own territory.

"But…I thought…" She allowed her words to trail away, realizing she was stammering.

"Besides, we have much more time awaiting us when we return to London and I have you all to myself."

He kissed her. And then, with a gentle push, she was once more in her own bedroom, and the door clicked softly closed.

Miranda was so shocked by it all that it wasn't until she was unbuttoning her bodice and preparing herself for bed that what he had said returned to her.

The arrogant man still believed she would be his mistress.

She snorted indelicately, unhooking her skirts and letting them fall. The Duke of Whitby was doomed to be disappointed.

CHAPTER 12

"Why are you so bloody happy this morning, Whit?" King asked grimly from the other side of a mountain of Bayonne ham and poached eggs.

"One might also beg the question of why you are so hungry this morning," he returned to his friend with a cheerful smile before he took a bite of his own bacon. "It looks as if you're eating for three."

King pinned him with an icy glare. "Pray, don't be defensive just because you're wearing country tweed paired with a waistcoat that would have better served as a maiden aunt's drawers."

"A truly crushing insult, old chap," he praised, unaffected by King's slur against his attire.

He raised his demitasse of coffee in salute.

King wasn't appreciative of his praise, however. His friend's eyebrows snapped together. "Riverdale, check to see if Whitby is feverish."

Riverdale glanced in Rhys's direction and shuddered. "Christ no. I'm not touching him. For all I know, he's contagious."

Rhys chuckled. "Where the devil is Richford this morning? Surely he ought to be on the receiving end of some of your mockery. I rather miss his scowl."

Their friend was, once again, conspicuously absent. Rhys might have been more troubled by Richford's unusual behavior if he weren't so damned pleased with how his courtship of Miranda was proceeding. Because that was how he was thinking of his slow and steady campaign to woo her into becoming his mistress. He hadn't bedded her last night. Instead, he had taken himself in hand and gone to sleep, then risen in the morning with a cockstand of steel only to tug himself to completion again.

Not sufficient, of course, but a man needed to remove the poison, and at the moment, he was—surprisingly enough—more interested in taking care of Miranda than himself. A novel experience, that.

"I haven't seen Richford since yesterday," King said. "He's probably off somewhere growling at his blonde goddess."

"Blonde goddess?" Rhys repeated, curious. "Is this the mystery woman Richford has been chasing about?"

"We reckon it is," Riverdale confirmed. "King made one of his elixirs last night after you disappeared. Richford drank half of it himself, the selfish arse. And then he started carrying on about a goddess he couldn't touch or some such rot. Something about her being a Gorgon who would make his cock fall off."

"Christ." Rhys shuddered. "No talk of Richford's cock at breakfast, if you please. I don't want to have to vomit my eggs. I have a delicate constitution."

"It's possible he was delirious," King added with a shrug. "I added a bit too much of a particular ingredient that tends to have such properties."

Rhys shook his head. "I don't even want to ask."

King grinned. "Then perhaps it's best you don't, old chap."

"Right." He concentrated on the task of finishing a rasher of bacon.

"Where were you, last night, Whit?" Riverdale asked slyly. "You slipped away just after dinner."

Fortunately, none of the other club members was seated near enough at the massive table to overhear the conversation. Rhys had no wish to leave Miranda vulnerable to becoming fodder for gossip again.

"I wasn't aware I needed to ask your permission to conduct my private affairs," he drawled.

"Private affairs?" Riverdale repeated. "Ah."

"It would seem Richford is not the only one among us who has found a goddess," King quipped, cutting into his Bayonne ham. "One can only hope that your particular goddess is not as dangerously capable as his."

"Quite," Rhys said, grateful his friend hadn't mentioned cocks falling off again.

How terribly grim.

And there was nothing at all grim about today. Because Miranda was almost precisely where he wanted her. She had yet to agree to become his mistress, but he was reasonably confident that in one more night, perhaps two, he would have her concession. She couldn't resist him.

The feeling was mutual, of course.

And that was a problem he wouldn't dwell on at the moment. He had a breakfast to consume.

"Have you seen Richford this morning?" Riverdale was asking King now, frowning.

"What am I, his mother?" King shook his head. "He is a man grown. He can look after himself."

"You don't think your potion was too strong, do you?" Riverdale pressed.

"It wasn't fashioned of arsenic, you know."

"What *was* it made of?" Riverdale countered.

"If I told you, it would no longer be a secret," King said patiently, in the tone he might have used for a very small child.

Riverdale responded by taking up a forkful of poached egg and launching it at King from across the table. The soft yolk landed with a thud upon King's coat, and their friend's reaction was the same, Rhys imagined, as it might have been had Riverdale challenged him to pistols at dawn.

"Did you just throw egg at me?" he demanded, incredulous.

"Yes," Riverdale said, grinning. "I do believe I did."

King used his napkin to wipe the egg piece away with a flick of his wrist. "That's an act of treason, you know. Wet egg yolk is despicably difficult to remove from fine silk."

"Is it?" Riverdale asked innocently. "I was rather thinking it made an excellent brooch."

King glowered. "I don't wear brooches, you arse."

"The two of you are little better than a pair of squabbling children," Rhys commented lightly, still utterly unaffected by the vignette unfolding before him.

King responded by hurling a hunk of Bayonne ham at Riverdale. The piece hit him in the temple with a resounding thwack. Their friend's astonishment was comical. Shock followed by an icy calm.

"You know what this means, do you not?" Riverdale asked.

"I'm sure I don't," King said mildly, returning his attention to his plate.

"War," Riverdale declared.

And then the egg and ham began to sail through the air.

THE ICES for this evening's *Glace à la Dudley* were in their molds and would spend the next two and a half hours in their ice caves. Miranda had devoted the morning and most of the afternoon to making both a cream ice and water ice, the latter of which had been quite rigorous. She had pounded bananas, juiced oranges and a lemon, chopped pistachios and preserved ginger, and added the perfect combination of carmine and apricot yellow to form the water ice. For the cream ice, she had blended rose water, cream, vanilla, and kirsch syrup, before coloring the roses in her molds with more carmine and sap green.

Whilst the ices and molds were chilling, Miranda slipped from the kitchens, pleased with her creations and yet oddly on edge. With a heavy sigh, she meandered through the labyrinth of servants' halls to the stairs, mounting them swiftly on sore and tired feet, trying not to think about the Duke of Whitby.

And failing utterly.

Not wanting to risk herself by venturing to the gardens for air again, she made her way instead to her room, knowing Rhys would be playing host to his guests. She intended to throw herself into the task of planning tomorrow's dessert, to be paired with salmon filets, quail *à la Chaponnay*, an assortment of potatoes, and asparagus in Hollandaise as the *entrées* and *relevés*.

Perhaps her Monte Carlo violet ice would make a nice accompaniment, she thought. Or nougatine with almond cream. There was the princess basket as well, which always looked lovely filled with an assortment of ices formed to resemble fruit. Then again, she had offered nougat baskets yesterday with her chocolate mushroom-shaped ices.

Miranda reached the ordinarily deserted hall where her chamber was located and was surprised to see another woman bustling toward her. A lovely woman, with golden hair and a pink silk gown that proved she was no servant. Who was she, and what was she doing in this largely deserted wing of the manor house?

Frowning, she drew up short. Was it someone looking for Rhys, perhaps a former lover or admirer? Regardless of who the woman was, she looked as startled to see Miranda as Miranda was to find her there.

The woman came to a halt, her skirts swaying as she pressed a hand over her heart. "Good heavens, you gave me quite a fright."

"Forgive me," Miranda apologized, taking note that the unexpected woman appeared a bit younger in age, with brilliant blue eyes and something about her countenance that was vaguely familiar.

"Oh, I didn't mean to suggest the fault was yours," the woman said, smiling warmly. "I simply meant that I wasn't expecting anyone to be in this wing of the manor house."

"Nor was I," Miranda offered, thinking belatedly that she ought to have donned a mask, for although the other woman appeared friendly, it was possible she might be a gossip. "I expect you are one of the houseguests?"

"I…" The blonde faltered, looking suddenly uncertain. "Not precisely. And you?"

A strange response, Miranda thought, uncertain of how she ought to answer the same question herself. "Not precisely either."

The blonde's smile faltered. "How interesting."

"Indeed."

They stared at each other for a tense moment.

"I do hope you won't mention seeing me here," the woman said, breaking the silence. "It wouldn't do for anyone to know I am present at such a gathering, you see."

Miranda offered her a wry smile. "Once again, we find ourselves in similar circumstances. I would appreciate your secrecy as well."

"That is easily promised. I haven't any notion of who you are."

"Nor I you."

"Well, then." The woman beamed at her. "I shall forget our paths ever crossed, and you may do the same for me."

Miranda inclined her head. "Of course."

The blonde made to move past her in the hall but hesitated suddenly, biting her lip. "Are you...staying in this wing of the manor house?"

This was dangerous territory. Miranda wasn't certain how she ought to answer. The woman had yet to explain who she was or why she was wandering in this particular hall herself.

"You need not answer," the woman hastened to say. "Curiosity is one of my downfalls, or so I've recently been told by a very overbearing and frustrating arrogant oaf."

There was such feeling in those words that Miranda found her own curiosity heightened in turn. For the second time, she wondered just who was this beautiful young lady, who claimed to be *not precisely* a houseguest?

"You sound quite provoked by the gentleman in question," Miranda observed politely instead of asking the questions she yearned to blurt.

It was no business of hers.

Even if the woman had come in search of Rhys, what hold did Miranda have upon him? She had no intention of becoming his mistress, and last night, he had returned her to her own room as if he were a kindly guardian tending to a wayward ward. He had rubbed her feet, fed her dinner, and closed the door in her face.

The reminder was rather lowering—and just what she needed.

"Dukes are the most conceited, smug, supercilious beings," the blonde was saying with an air of authority that Miranda thought newly perplexing. "Particularly when they think they know better than you do, even if the opposite is true."

"I cannot say I would argue with the smugness," Miranda commiserated, thinking of Rhys and his insistence that he would have what he wanted from her.

As if her agreeing to be his mistress were a foregone conclusion.

"You must know m—" the other woman began, and then paused, seemingly correcting herself as she continued "—the Duke of Whitby."

Even more odd.

What had she been about to say?

And how could Miranda answer without implicating herself?

She was weighing her response when the blonde's blue eyes suddenly went wide. "Oh heavens, what a silly goose I am! I've forgotten something that's very important. If you will excuse me?"

The mysterious lady didn't even await Miranda's response. And, adding to her perplexing behavior, she whirled on her heel and rushed past, disappearing down the servants' stairs. In the next breath, Rhys rounded a bend in the hall, grinning broadly when he saw her.

"If it isn't just the lady I was looking for," he announced, sounding pleased with himself.

Miranda had failed to hear his arrival, but now she couldn't help but wonder if the woman in the hall had, and if that had been the reason for her hasty retreat. If so, that certainly made the mysterious blonde's behavior even more curious. But what did it prove?

"You were looking for me?" she asked, trying to tamp down the unwanted surge of desire that overtook her as he neared, bringing with him his potent masculine allure and his decadent scent.

How she longed to throw herself into his arms and kiss him, regardless of all the reasons she must not. And even if the lovely woman in the pink silk had been attempting to seek him out.

"You are an elusive woman to find," he told her, grinning in a way that called attention to the charming divot in his chin. "I went looking for you in the kitchens and was told that you had left your ices to freeze in their caves."

"You shouldn't have gone looking for me in the kitchens."

"Why not? I had a pressing need to confer with you regarding tonight's dessert."

She instantly felt guilty for chastising him. "You do? Is something amiss?"

He winked. "Of course not. That is merely what I told the cook when I went looking for you. I wasn't about to tell them that I intended to spirit you away and shag you senseless, now was I?"

She gasped. "Your Grace."

"Do you know that when you reprimand me in that outraged governess voice of yours, it makes my cock despicably hard?" he drawled.

Her face was flaming. The gentlemanly swain of the night before had disappeared, it would seem. And in his place was the grinning, reprehensible rakehell who delighted in saying all manner of wicked things.

"You are a rogue, sir," she told him primly. "Was there a true reason you sought me out, or was it merely to utter such inanity at half past two in the afternoon?"

"You like my inanity," he teased lightheartedly. "Confess, kitten. And yes, there is another reason I sought you out. However, I would have it be known that there is no better reason than spiriting you away to shag you senseless."

He was outrageous, and the vexing man had called her *kitten* yet again. She tamped down her smile, refusing to allow him to see it.

"What is the reason then, Your Grace?" she asked, keeping her voice cool and polite, as if he hadn't repeated his sinful words and started a fire burning deep within her.

"Luncheon," he said, surprising her yet again. "I decided to make certain you are fed today."

She chuckled. "You make me sound as if I am a dog or a small child."

"Hardly. However, I have noticed that you possess a distinct ability to place everything and everyone before yourself, particularly in regard to your work. It's my solemn duty to subvert you at all costs."

Miranda tried with all her might to remain impervious to him. And failed. He was looking at her expectantly, little different than her brother had as a lad when someone had agreed to go fishing with him—pure, unfettered delight.

"I don't see any luncheon here," she pointed out, taking a glance at the empty hall surrounding them, its damask-lined walls anointed by an array of gilt-framed portraits.

"We'll have it in one of the private salons downstairs," he announced, still sounding quite pleased with himself.

"Downstairs?" Her alarm was instantly raised. "You know that I cannot go downstairs with you, not after what happened with Lord Roberts in the gardens."

Although Roberts himself was gone, there was no guarantee they wouldn't come across someone else who recognized her as he had and sought to cause problems.

"You can wear one of the masks I gave you," he countered.

"I fear the masks aren't sufficient." She shook her head. "There's a chance I'll be recognized. The risk is far too great."

"Ah, but the reward will more than outweigh it, I promise. Besides, I've made certain that the guests are otherwise occupied in the library and the billiards room. There will be no one about to see you."

"There will be servants," she pointed. "They are familiar with me by now from my time in the kitchens, and my gowns are all gray. None of your club members would dream of going about dressed in my sensible day dresses."

"You could wear one of the gowns I gave you," he suggested.

Predictably so.

"We have discussed this before, Whitby. I cannot wear them."

"Cannot or will not?"

"Both."

He frowned. "You must eat, kitten."

"And you must cease calling me kitten."

"Perhaps I shall, but only if you agree to join me for a late luncheon."

She glared at him, irritated by his stubborn insistence and tempted beyond all ration and reason. "This is but a lark to you, but to me, it is everything. It is my reputation, my school, my future. Without what remains of my good name, I have nothing."

His gaze searched hers, presumably reading the determination there, because he sighed heavily. "It would appear we are at an impasse."

She smiled, another surge of tenderness for him moving within her breast. "Thank you for your concern. You needn't worry over me, however. I can find some tea and toast to tide me over until later."

"Of course I must worry over you. No one else does, and you most assuredly do not worry over yourself."

She found it astonishing that this golden devil of a rake would be so bothered by whether she took luncheon.

"I am a woman of independent means," she said. "I look after myself."

"Woman, it is as plain as the nose upon my face that you do not look after yourself." He offered her his arm. "Now, come with me, if you please. I have a new plan, one that doesn't involve you venturing anywhere you might be spied."

She wasn't sure she liked the sound of that either.

Miranda narrowed her eyes at him. "What is your new plan?"

He sighed. "Oh, kitten. Cease looking at me as if I've just announced my intention to become a highwayman of old and go about robbing carriages and stealing family jewels."

She bit her lip to keep a chuckle from escaping. He was so very expressive. And impossible. And endearing.

And, and, and. Her foolish heart could go on. It was steadily becoming far too fond of the Duke of Whitby. As was the rest of her.

"My name is not kitten," she reminded him pointedly.

"If you had seen yourself curled against me in slumber, you would know how utterly appropriate the sobriquet is," he insisted, apparently unmoved by her irritation.

He reached for her hand then, the connection of his skin on hers sending a jolt of awareness through her like a live electric spark. "Please," he added, with meaningful emphasis. "Trust me, Miranda. Come with me."

Tell him no, urged her inner voice of reason.

And she knew she ought to do so. Knew she would be better served returning to her bedroom as planned and throwing herself headlong into the planning of the next day's cream ices. She wanted to impress the guests. The distraction would be welcome and, most of all, safe.

"Please," he added softly. "You won't regret it, I vow."

Miranda nodded, relenting despite all her misgivings. "Very well, then."

She allowed him to lead her down the hall, the persistent suspicion she would regret her capitulation despite his solemn promise dogging her with every step.

CHAPTER 13

*R*hys drank in the sight of Miranda at the other end of the picnic blanket he had spread for them. They were in a small clearing that was rendered private by a copse of trees at their back, just far enough from the manor house that they needn't fear being disturbed.

He didn't recall ever feeling so bloody happy and content.

A rarity for him—content to simply be in her presence. To eat with her, talk with her, laugh with her. He hadn't even done anything more forward than taking her hand in his earlier, and yet…that didn't matter.

Because she had agreed to come with him, and he had learned more about her and her passion for cooking, her students, and her school. And there was something deliciously intoxicating about merely being in her presence. Having her here with him was enough.

When Miranda relaxed and all the starch leached from her capable form, the tension fleeing, her beauty was even more pronounced. He thought he could happily stare at her for hours, days, years, and never grow tired of watching, of discovering new details he had heretofore missed. The woman was a masterpiece. And he'd never in his life held the slightest inclination toward taking up paint and brush, but some maudlin part of him longed to capture her thus on canvas. To preserve her forever as she was, lips reddened from the wine he'd persuaded her to drink, sunshine glinting in her raven hair.

She wasn't even wearing a hat. There hadn't been time to stop for one. They had slipped out through one of several hidden passages Wingfield Hall possessed, and onto a side path that had led them to this spot. It was a place he had previously thought ideal for a seduction. But today, he had put it to better use as a location for a picnic.

"This truly is a lovely, secluded little spot," she said, looking around at the tranquility of the rolling grasses around them.

"You see? I told you. No one knows how to steal about in secret better than I do, darling." He winked, but he very purposefully neglected to mention the reason for that.

He had become adept at fleeing a bored wife's bedroom just in time to avoid an unpleasant confrontation with an irate, cuckolded husband. And naturally, the house parties being held at Wingfield Hall had lent themselves to the further investigation of the sprawling manor house. He had discovered the secret passages in short order and used them whenever it suited him.

"In this instance, you were not wrong, Your Grace," she allowed, fidgeting with the drapery of her dove-gray skirts.

Her insistence upon reverting to formality between them was not lost on him. It was her attempt to rebuild the walls she was so set on erecting. The walls that allowed her to tell herself she would never be his mistress. Walls that were an illusion, as it happened. He would be more than happy to prove them so.

"Kitten, if you don't cease calling me *Your Grace*, I'm going to have to resort to nefarious means of persuading you otherwise," he warned lightly, loving the fire that sparked in her eyes whenever he used the pet name for her he had settled on in partial jest.

She had been like a trusting kitten that first night, and he hadn't forgotten. Nor had he forgotten the way her curves felt pressed against him, how warm, how soft, how right. He intended to feel them again.

Soon.

A sultry smile curved her lips. "Perhaps I'll stop calling you *Your Grace* when you stop calling me *kitten*."

God, he wanted to kiss her. He was beginning to think himself rather a bit obsessed with Miranda. Ever since their meeting at her school, he'd been perpetually randy, haunted by thoughts of her when she wasn't in his presence, and consumed by the need to touch and taste her when she was. Last night, he had even dreamed of her, for Christ's sake. It was a troubling progression indeed for a man who ordinarily tired of his lovers the moment the passion between them inevitably cooled.

And yet, conversely, the more time he spent with Miranda, the more he wanted her.

At this very moment, he thought it reasonably possible that he would crawl through fields of burning coals and broken glass just to be inside her again.

He pushed these heavy notions aside in favor of grinning back at her, as if he hadn't a care in the world. "Now that I think upon it, I rather enjoy hearing you call me *Your Grace*. It makes me think of other circumstances in which you might say it. For instance, *oh Your Grace, please f—*"

"Rhys," she interrupted, her tone scandalized.

"What?" He gave her his most innocent look. "I was about to say *oh, Your Grace, please fetch me my smelling salts. Because you are so unfairly handsome that I fear I am about to swoon*."

She laughed at that—her levity an uncommon prize indeed, and one he would happily claim as his own. Miranda's laughter was throaty and mellifluous, and like everything she said or did, it made him want to fuck her with a desperation that was truly bordering on pathetic. His cock was being maddeningly insistent at the moment.

"I suppose you often have ladies swooning over you," she said when her laughter had subsided. "However, I hate to disappoint you. I don't own any smelling salts."

"However shall I revive you when you faint, then?" He gave her a wicked grin. "I'm certain I can think of at least one means of doing so."

She compressed her lips in that way she had when she was trying valiantly to keep from letting her amusement show. "You are outrageous."

"And as we have already established, you enjoy it."

He was teasing her, his tone light, but there was something in her emerald eyes—a deep, searing recognition—that stole his breath. Although there were plates and cutlery separating them, he was half tempted to thrust them all aside and go to her.

"Thank you for *déjeuner*," she said, growing serious. "It was very kind of you to go to so much effort, just for me."

"Ah, but as I've already said, I'm a selfish man. It wasn't just for you. It was for me, also."

"I am sure you were hungry as well."

Yes, he was. He was positively bloody ravenous. But not for food.

Rhys held her gaze, keeping that to himself. "I could have taken my repast earlier. But then I wouldn't have had you for company. I wouldn't have had the privilege of your laughter and smiles. I wouldn't have had this glorious image of you in the sunshine, the light glinting off your gorgeous hair."

At his words, she patted her head, looking self-conscious.

"I ought to have worn a hat. It's most unseemly to be out of doors without one."

Rhys busied himself with packing some of the empty crockery back into the picnic hamper. "I like you this way. To the devil with hats. Besides, I haven't one either. We have flouted all the rules together. Doesn't it feel lovely?"

"Too lovely, I think, and that is what makes it so very dangerous."

He paused in the act of clearing up a stack of plates, glancing back up at her. "Dangerous to whom?"

"To me, of course." Once more, she was solemn. "To my ability to resist you."

His already frayed restraint snapped, like a rope that had been sawed through, leaving only a single strand to hold it in place. Gone.

He swept everything remaining between them on the blanket out of his way with one fluid motion. "Then don't."

MIRANDA WASN'T certain which of them moved first. All she did know was that one moment, Rhys was unbearably handsome across the blanket, daring her to be bold, and the next, she was clutching a fistful of his neckcloth, holding him to her as he kissed her passionately. Their lips clung voraciously, tongues tangling, teeth nipping, desperation and desire prodding them both beyond their breaking points. Her other hand was somehow in his hair, fingers grasping silky, golden strands.

He growled, the low rumble setting off an answering reaction in her nipples and between her legs. The ceaseless ache that punctuated his presence grew stronger, fiercer. Oh God, she wanted this man. Wanted to take his cock deep inside her. Wanted to claim him, to take her pleasure from him, to make him hers.

Miranda was a creature of need only, reborn in the sunlight with the verdant grass springy and soft beneath the picnic blanket. With the scent of earth and amber, of musk, of forest and man and helpless desire. A wildness overtook her, caution becoming dim and murky, like a language she had learned years ago and no longer used.

She wanted more from him than mere kisses.

Miranda took his lower lip in her teeth, biting him enough to make it sting, driven by some instinctive urge to make him come undone. He growled again, his fingers sinking into her tightly coiled chignon. Hairpins were plucked free by the handful, raining on the blanket. She didn't care.

From his mouth, she moved across his jaw, exploring, needing. Beneath her lips, the stern angle of bone was covered with short, golden whiskers that lightly prickled as she peppered kisses everywhere her mouth traveled. The knot of his neckcloth loosened and opened, and she tore at it frantically before laying her lips over the hot male flesh she found there, the pulse of his frantically thudding heart, the protrusion of his Adam's apple.

This was still somehow insufficient. She tore at his shirt, feeling the satisfying pop of buttons. He shrugged out of his coat, and then his waistcoat was gone too as her hair fully unraveled down her back in heavy skeins. He preoccupied himself with the line of fastenings on her bodice as she pulled at his shirt, until the twain ends hung apart, revealing the muscled expanse of his chest. Inhaling deeply of his scent, she kissed along his clavicle, kissed his flat nipple, flicked her tongue over it.

"Miranda," he ground out, her name part warning, part plea.

She felt infinitely powerful and deliriously powerless all at once. She had this beautiful rakehell at her mercy, and yet he also had her helplessly in his thrall, captive to her own desire. Her bodice sagged. He rent the top of her chemise in two and gave her corset a swift, sudden tug that made her bare breasts spill over the top. Cool, gilded air greeted her hot, aching skin. And then his hands were on her. Big hands, knowing hands, cupping and stroking, his long fingers plucking at her nipples until she cried out against him and lifted her face to receive his kiss.

This time, it was a long and plundering meeting of mouths. His thumbs rolled over the peaks of her breasts, and then he pinched, sending arcs of pure, wonderful sensation shooting through her. She kissed him, giving him her tongue, suckling his. He tasted like meringue and cerise pudding from their luncheon and sweet, heady desire.

Oh heavens, this was wondrous and foolish. Her breasts were bared to the light of day, and they had pawed each other's clothing apart. They were feeding each other kisses so carnal she thought she might spend just from his hands on her breasts and his tongue in her mouth. Anyone could come upon them. Someone could find them at any moment. But somehow, wicked sinner that she was, the knowledge of this danger only served to heighten her own need. Only made her want him more. As if sensing her eagerness, he squeezed her nipples harder.

"I need you inside me," she murmured into his kiss.

Another low rumble emerged from him, and she felt the frantic fumbling of his hand on his trousers, releasing buttons and opening the fall. He caught her lip in his teeth and tugged.

"Ride me, kitten."

She ought to have been irritated by his insistence upon calling her by the silly sobriquet. And yet, it only made her want him more. Still kissing him, she reached between them, wrapping her fingers around the rigid thickness of his erect cock. With a moan, she stroked him up and down, loving the way he felt, so smooth and yet so firm, hot and insistent. Slicking the pad of her thumb over the head, she found his mettle leaking and swirled it over him, making him groan.

He was as ready for her as she was for him.

But she had never made love out of doors. She didn't begin to understand the mechanics of how she was meant to ride him, as he had urged.

"How?" she asked hesitantly, wanting to please him more than she wanted, even, to please herself.

What a strange, unfamiliar feeling this was. Not just to revel in her own desire. But to revel in another's too. To experience such carnal yearning, the likes of which she hadn't imagined were even possible.

"I'll show you."

Gently, he disengaged himself from her, sliding his cock free of her grip. Then he shifted his positioning, moving away from her and seating himself on the blanket, his long legs stretched before him. For a moment, she was transfixed by the sight of him, his golden hair in disarray, his shirt hanging apart to display a delicious wedge of chest, his trousers undone to reveal his cock, stiff and ruddy, a pearlescent bead on the tip. His gaze hot on her, he grasped himself at the base, stroking.

An answering ache throbbed deep. She wanted him to slide inside her. To fill her. How sinful it was, the sight of him basking in the afternoon's glow, surrounded by green grass and blue sky, so thoroughly male and beautiful, half dressed and watching her with a heavy-lidded stare as he fondled his cock.

It was too much. She thought she might explode from the pent-up yearning.

Rhys held out his other hand to her. "Hold up your skirts and come here."

Following his instructions, she grasped handfuls of her gown, grateful that it was not nearly as voluminous and cumbersome as fashion would decree, but instead made for ease of movement.

"On your knees," he added.

She did as he bade, moving to him across the blanket. He guided her so that each knee was on either side of his hips, and she was poised over him.

"Perfection," he praised, lowering his head to take one hard nipple into his mouth and suck greedily.

A gasp tore from her, and she arched her back. He moved to her other breast, taking the pebbled bud in his mouth anew and groaning as he suckled, his tongue lapping over her aching flesh.

When he released her, she was panting, trembling on her knees as he palmed his cock between them.

"Closer," he instructed, helping her to sidle over him, until her lifted skirts obscured his length from view, and the blunt head of his cock strummed lightly over her inflamed flesh.

He felt so good.

She whimpered, trying not to fall on him.

How in heaven's name was this meant to work?

"Easy, darling," he crooned, gliding his cock up and down her seam now, through her swollen folds, slicking himself in the wetness that seeped from her. "Are you ready for me?"

"Oh yes," she managed, her thighs clenched in anticipation.

"Then sit on my cock."

Wrong words, sinful words, wicked words. Words that made her moan and do his bidding, sinking down on him. He helped her, guiding himself to her entrance as she lowered herself, and then his cock was there. In her, invading her. Demanding as she impaled herself on him, every glorious inch sending uncontrollable pleasure through her.

Finally, she was seated atop him, and he filled her completely, the angle of his penetration so exquisite she almost wept as he lavished attention upon her breasts anew, his clever mouth making her tighten on his cock.

"Ride me now," he urged, his hands settling on her waist, showing her what he meant.

She rose, his length gliding through her, and then sank back down, filling herself with him. It was too much. It was exquisite.

"Oh God," she keened, half certain she was about to die. "Rhys."

Her hands found purchase on his broad shoulders, and he sucked her nipples as she began moving faster, with greater intent.

"Find what feels good to you," he urged against the curve of her breast, before flicking his tongue cleverly over the peak. "Make yourself come on my cock."

A strangled noise escaped her that was not even a word. She rode him faster, harder, bouncing on him until her breasts jiggled, angling her body in a way that made him stroke that place inside her that seemed specifically made for pleasure.

"Yes," he urged, his expression taut with his own withheld desire, allowing her to use him. "Take your pleasure from me."

Harder, faster. She watched him as she fucked him, thinking it the most intense experience of her life. That nothing before could have prepared her for this fierce abandon. For the glory of making love to him purely because she wanted to. Because she could.

"Fuck, Miranda," he ground out, moving beneath her, his

hips following the rhythm she had set. "Your cunny is so wet."

These vulgar words were offered as praise. She loved it. And, it was possible, she loved *him*. The thought jolted through her in the same moment Rhys slid a hand under her skirts, his thumb unerringly finding her clitoris and stroking.

She spent with a cry that sent a bird noisily winging away from a nearby tree branch, pure bliss rocketing through her like fireworks blossoming across a night sky. She clenched on him, bringing him deep inside her as wave after wave of release hit, rocking on him, selfishly taking everything she could, all the pleasure, in case she would never again know such ecstasy. She was still riding him when he stiffened beneath her.

"I'm going to come," he rasped suddenly.

Through the rushing in her ears from the force of her release, the warning in his voice spurred her onto her knees. His cock slid from her, and then he gripped himself, the hot spurt of his seed painting her inner thigh.

He had been close to spending within her. Agonizingly close. And it astonished her to realize she had wanted him to. That some part of her had thrown caution to the wind in favor of pleasure.

It was in that moment, her heart pounding, skin flushed, hair unbound, half naked and covered in the Duke of Whitby's spend, that she realized there was one person even more perilous to her future than he was.

And that was Miranda herself.

CHAPTER 14

*T*he dinner gong would be sounding in approximately an hour and a half's time. Likely, Rhys ought to be presiding over the house party guests. There had been rumbles that morning of naughty *tableaux vivants* being staged. Christ knew what could have happened since breakfast. And yet, he found himself entirely disinterested in revels that would have, a mere month ago, amused him.

Instead, he was taking the air. Pacing the garden maze. Trying to gather what remained of his wits, it was true. Because earlier that afternoon on a picnic blanket, they had been ruthlessly scattered to the wind by one beautiful, stubborn, sensual woman.

Miranda had ruined him.

Ruined him for Wicked Dukes Society house parties. Ruined him for lovers. Hell, he didn't even want to play billiards, dice, or cards. He didn't want a brandy and soda water or a glass of wine. He didn't even want to trade ribald jests with his closest chums.

Because all he wanted was her.

Miranda.

More Miranda. More than he'd been able to have thus far. More than stolen moments in the shadows and clandestine, half-clothed romps in the outdoors. He wanted her to agree to be his mistress, and not just for the next month but for the next bloody year. Perhaps even longer. He was insatiable for her.

He'd never been afflicted thusly, and he had to admit as he rounded a bend in the boxwood hedges that the intensity of his attraction to Miranda frightened him. He was attuned to her, desperate for her, an utter fool for her. Since they had parted ways earlier so she could return to her molds and inspect the progress of her ices for the evening's dessert, he had been adrift. Half wild with the need to follow her to the kitchens and watch as she worked, rather like an eager pup who could not stop trailing in his mistress's wake.

"Stupid," he muttered to himself. "You're so bloody stupid, Rhys."

And yet, no amount of inwardly issued chastisements served to abate the all-consuming need for her. He was plotting all the ways he could persuade her to agree to his madcap scheme. The promise of further funds was always an option, though not the most enjoyable one. He would far prefer to woo and seduce her into agreement.

Yes, the latter would be infinitely more delightful. Perhaps he could arrange for a warm, soothing bath for her this evening. He could help her to bathe, wash her hair, and afterward, he would dry her off with his tongue.

Indeed, that would—

His plans for seduction were abruptly interrupted by the distant sound of voices, one male and the other female, rising heatedly from somewhere within the garden maze. Not another damned contretemps in the gardens. His first thought was of Miranda. Surely, she would not have ventured here after what had happened with Roberts. Would she?

Frowning, he started moving, hastening his steps as he made his way through the twisting and turning maze, in search of the voices. But try as he might to tread lightly, the crunching gravel beneath his soles must have alerted the couple that they were not alone. The voices suddenly stopped.

Rhys continued on, determined to discover who it was and reassure himself that nothing else untoward was unfolding here at Wingfield Hall beneath his watch. If yet another woman were being accosted…

He turned a corner and nearly collided with a man who had been barreling toward him. A man he recognized.

"Richford?"

His friend drew up short, looking equally surprised to see him. "Bloody hell, Whit. You gave me a fright."

Rhys's suspicions were instantly raised. What the devil was Richford up to? This was getting deuced strange.

"What are you doing skulking about in the gardens?" he asked.

Richford drew himself up, his expression turning haughty. "I do not skulk."

Rhys raised a brow. "As you wish."

"I don't."

He shrugged. "I thought I heard you arguing with some-one. A female someone."

Richford stiffened. "You must be hearing things. I say, you weren't indulging in another of King's potions, were you?"

"Riverdale said something about you and a blonde. Are you dallying with one of the club members?" Jesus, he hoped it wasn't a servant because domestics were decidedly forbidden.

But nothing else made sense about the way his friend was

being so oddly elusive and defensive since their arrival here at Wingfield Hall.

"I don't dally either." Richford scowled. "Is Riverdale your spy now?"

"Do I have need of one?"

"Of course not," Richford said hastily.

Too hastily.

"Something is afoot," Rhys insisted. "Tell me what it is."

"Nothing is afoot."

"You never did have a face for cards. I can tell when you're guilty, old chap."

It was true. Of all vices, Richford was notoriously bad at anything that involved not revealing his thoughts to his opponents. Which also made his evasiveness all the more suspect and concerning.

"Nothing is afoot. I am merely here in my capacity as one of the leaders of the club, given that two of our members were not able to attend because of women and weddings and other such bloody rot."

"Christ, don't tell me you've fallen in love with someone," he guessed.

It was the only explanation that made sense. The brooding, the disappearances, the mysterious blonde woman.

"In love?" Richford choked, sputtering, a telltale red creeping along his cheekbones and up his throat. "Of course not. Don't be daft."

"You don't dally, you've been chasing about a blonde, and you're acting damned odd. But I'm to believe that nothing is amiss?"

"Yes, that is what you are to believe, Whit. Because that is what I bloody well told you."

"I know that is what you told me, but I also happen to know it's a lie. What I don't know is why you're so intent upon deceiving me."

And he didn't particularly like it either. The six friends had a pact, an understanding. They were the brothers each had never had. And they didn't deceive one another.

Richford scowled. "You're not my goddamned mother, Whit. Leave well enough alone."

"That rather stings," he admitted. "Fair enough. If you don't want to tell me—"

"I don't," Richford interrupted.

"—then I shall simply have to bide my time and discover what is going on myself," he finished with a triumphant air.

Because they both knew he would. Rhys was nothing if not determined. He didn't like secrets, and he didn't like lies. His hideous childhood had been rife with both. And there was something Richford was keeping from him.

"Don't pry where you aren't wanted," Richford said. "You may not like what you find."

That was rather cryptic.

Rhys frowned at his friend. "What is that supposed to mean?"

"It means that I don't want you interfering in my affairs," his friend growled. "If there was something I wished to tell you, I would have done so by now."

With that curt rejoinder, Richford stepped around him and stalked away.

Rhys stared after his departing back until he turned a corner, wondering just what his friend was hiding.

As she had the previous two nights, Miranda returned to her bedroom tired but pleased with how her creations had emerged from their ice caves. Her feet ached, her back was equally sore, but she was eager to hear how the guests had enjoyed the *Glace à la Dudley* she had prepared. She'd been especially happy with the presentation of the roses on the tops of her molds.

And like the night before, when she entered her room, Miranda was startled to find someone awaiting her. This time, it was an expectant Green, with a clawfoot tub prepared with steaming water at the center of the room.

"Mrs. Loveless," Green greeted.

For a moment, Miranda wondered whom the lady's maid was speaking to. Weary as she was from her exertions in the kitchens, she even briefly glanced over her shoulder. Until she recalled that Green didn't know her true name, and she turned back to the servant with a guilty start.

"You've prepared a bath," she said, her aching muscles all but clamoring for her to dip into that hot water and soak.

"As you requested, ma'am," Green said, arranging an assortment of soaps and shampoos on a low table which had been laid by the tub, along with some towels and stoppered glass bottles.

She blinked. "Oh, but I didn't request a bath."

Now that it was here, she most certainly wouldn't refuse it, however. She had been performing her ablutions with the pitcher and bowl and a small hip bath since her arrival. The oversized tub looked nothing short of heavenly.

"His Grace told me that you did." Green frowned. "I'm sorry, ma'am. Do you wish it to be removed? I'll send for the footmen who brought it here and filled it."

"No," she hastened to say, heat warming her cheeks at the revelation that Rhys had made such a personal request on her behalf. It was unseemly. As unseemly as sharing adjoining chambers. "That won't be necessary, Green."

Calling for the bath had been presumptuous of him. She ought to give him a proper tongue-lashing over his temerity when she saw him next. But for now, she was tired and her feet were sore and she would like nothing better than to settle into the warmth awaiting her in the tub.

"Would you care for my assistance, Mrs. Loveless?" Green asked next. "I could wash your hair for you. If you'd like, of course."

"That won't be necessary." She summoned a smile for the lady's maid's benefit. "I will ring for you when I've finished."

It had been nearly a year since she had settled into her own modest rooms following the divorce from Ammondale, when she had begun her life anew. She had been without a lady's maid for all that time, and Miranda had rather grown accustomed to looking after herself. Besides, a foolish part of her hoped there was a hidden meaning in Rhys's request for the bath, one that went beyond her mere comfort.

Green nodded. "Of course, ma'am."

She dipped into a hasty curtsy and left the room.

Once alone, Miranda wasted no time in removing her bodice and skirts, laying them out with care over the back of a chair. Next came her petticoats, easily untied and draped along with her gown. With that gone, she spun about, intending to remove her boots, when she caught sight of her reflection in the mirror.

Good heavens, she had forgotten about her partially torn chemise. How fortunate that she had sent Green away. Surely the lady's maid would have wondered how Miranda's under-garment had been so badly ripped when the rest of her garments had remained intact.

Heat crept up her throat as her thoughts returned to what had happened that afternoon during the picnic lunch she had shared with Rhys. The both of them had been overcome. She had done damage to his clothing as well, she recalled with a hint of rising embarrassment at her actions.

It would seem she was every bit as wicked as the gossips had claimed. Because surely no decent woman would lie with a man who was not her husband, in the midst of the day, on the grass where anyone could have come upon them. And yet, another part of her, long suppressed and tamped down, thrilled at the memory. That part of her wanted more.

More adventure, more seduction, more forbidden pleasure.

She untied her boots and unlaced them, slipping her feet free of their stiff leather confines. She was clad in her drawers, damaged chemise, and corset. But instead of taking off the remainder of her garments and slipping into the bath, she was suddenly tempted to go to him instead. To forget caution and ration and reason and seize what she wanted. What they both wanted.

Her body was instantly flooded with sensual awareness. But then she reminded herself sternly that here was her chance. She should cling to her defenses and refuse to surrender to her foolish desires. Twice had been enough. She needed to deny him. To deny herself.

But there was a poignant, persistent voice within her that emerged just then, one that wondered why.

Why must she deny herself? Had she not been putting everyone else first all her life? Beginning with her parents and her duty to them, marrying as they had wanted. Then to her husband, Ammondale, in a marriage that had only served to make her miserable. And when she had finally escaped and found her freedom, she had become constrained by the need to restore the reputation that had been so thoroughly spoiled by her divorce. The need to provide for herself so she would not go destitute or be forced to rely upon the charity of friends or distant family who might be willing to look the other way.

Why not take this for herself? Why not take Rhys?

She could have him. All of him to herself. Could have his kisses and his wicked mouth, his outrageous teasing and his clever hands and even more cunning tongue. Could have the pleasure he brought her, have his companionship. She could have everything she had never dared could be hers but now hung within her tenuous grasp.

Do it, urged that inner voice.

If no one ever discovered the truth, what would be the harm? One month of passion, and then a life afterward of penance. It suddenly occurred to her that there was a way she could spend a month with him and still retain her pride. Possibility rose inside her, joining hope for the first time in as long as she could recall.

And, that quickly, her decision was made.

She was going to seize this opportunity. She was going to be the Duke of Whitby's lover for the next month. And strangely, the realization didn't leave her feeling worried or fearful within. Instead, it made her feel lighter than she had felt in years. Not since well before she had walked through the church and committed herself to a lifetime of marriage with a man who had disdained her.

With purposeful strides, she crossed the room, stopping at the door that adjoined her chamber to Rhys's and knocking. Hesitantly at first, and then with greater force as she took hold of this newfound freedom.

By the fourth knock, he was there, tearing the door open to tower over her as so few men did. He was clad in a dressing gown of black silk, the contrast between the dark fabric and his golden hair making him look like some sort of wicked immortal. His hair was damp at the ends, she noted, as if he, too, had been bathing. His stormy-sky eyes met hers before flicking downward, to where her ripped chemise put her breasts on display above her corset.

Belatedly, she saw herself as he must, realizing that her nipples were almost showing. Her corset was loosened, her feet clad in embellished stockings peeping from beneath her drawers, the hem of her chemise stopping at her knees.

"Did you take your bath?" His voice was velvet and seduction.

She almost smiled at his low question. Her hair was yet to be unbound, and she was wearing her undergarments. Did he truly think she had emerged thus from the water?

"Not yet," she told him, a sudden fit of nerves making her hand tremble on the latch.

Could she do this?

"My God." He raked a hand through his hair, leaving it charmingly ruffled in his wake, the lack of perfection so at odds with the handsome symmetry of his face. "What a beast I am. I've torn your chemise. I'll buy you a new one. Two. Three. Half a dozen. Hell, I'll buy you a whole bloody chemise store."

A chuckle escaped her. "I fear there is no such thing as a chemise store."

"Wherever a lady makes such purchases," he elaborated. "I'll buy you an entire new wardrobe to replace them, at the establishment of your choosing."

It wasn't new chemises she wanted from him, although she did appreciate the proposal. Nor was it the small fortune he had offered her to be his mistress for a month.

"That is kind of you, but I'm not concerned about the garment just now." She stepped back. "Would you care to join me?"

"I thought you'd never ask, kitten." He crossed the threshold.

His light, teasing tone vanquished some of her nervousness. It wasn't every day she propositioned a gentleman. Indeed, she had never done so, not in truth. The pretense of an affair with Waring had been his idea, the means of finally forcing Ammondale's hand. But they had never even shared a kiss. Their friendship was strictly platonic, and although she harbored a deep sense of gratitude for his intervention on her behalf, she had never been even slightly tempted to invite him into her bed.

"It was most considerate of you to arrange for a bath to be brought up for me," she said, moving back across the room toward the steaming tub. "But unfortunately, I need someone to wash my hair, and Green wasn't able to assist me this evening."

That was because Miranda had sent her away. But tonight, she was challenging Rhys at his own game, which meant she wasn't opposed to a bit of subterfuge. And he didn't need to know the full truth. No, Miranda fully intended to taunt him and tease him as he did to her this night.

She stopped before the mirror and began to pluck the pins from her hair, leaving them on a small silver tray. Miranda felt him approach, a frisson of awareness traveling up her spine to make her skin prickle.

And then he stood behind her, tall and golden-haired, dropping a kiss on the nape of her neck. "I would be more than happy to play lady's maid for you. It's the least I can do as atonement for being a ravenous monster earlier and tearing your chemise."

As he spoke, his hand settled on her chest, in the space between the rent ends of her undergarment, directly over her bare flesh, his fingers splaying above her madly thudding heart. She swallowed hard at a rush of longing, allowing herself to lean into his solid frame. The undeniable prod of his cock against her made an answering ache pulse to life deep within her. If she had any lingering doubts, they were banished by the rightness she felt, his warmth and strength radiating into her.

"Thank you," she said. "Your assistance is most appreciated."

"Mmm," he hummed, his face buried in the side of her throat now as he inhaled deeply. "I love your scent."

She smiled, thinking that although she had added some scent to her throat that morning, it had likely dissipated. If she smelled of anything, it was likely the kitchens. But she wouldn't argue, because she liked the way his mouth felt on her skin, open and seeking, as if each part of her was a wonder that required exploration.

Feeling bold, she reached for him, sifting her fingers through his hair. There was something intimate and deeply… cozy about him in her chamber, both of them in varying states of undress, his face buried in her throat. What a luxury it was, to have him here without allowing in any of the guilt that threatened, the worry, the fears.

"I have been thinking about your proposition," she ventured, needing to get the words out before they proceeded.

He stilled, his head lifting though he remained as he was, one hand on her waist and the other flattened over her heart. His gaze met hers in the looking glass, his fingers dipping ever so slightly to slide inside her corset and curve around the slope of one bare breast. He brushed the edge of her nipple lightly once, twice.

"Oh?"

"Yes." She wetted her lips, unable to keep from arching into his touch. "I have."

His hand slid deeper, his thumb strumming over the sensitive peak. "And I hope that you have reached the only conclusion there is for you to reach."

"I don't want to be your mistress," she blurted.

CHAPTER 15

*R*hys stilled. "You don't?"

"No." She shook her head slowly, then rested it against his chest, relaxing into him even further. "I want to be your lover."

"Silly." He kissed the shell of her ear, still holding her gaze. "You can be both."

"Not whilst maintaining my self-respect," she protested firmly. "I don't want ten thousand pounds. I don't want to be your kept woman. All I want is to be your lover. For the next month and no more."

There. She had said it. Now that the words had left her, the last of her trepidation slid away as well, replaced by desire as he swirled his touch over her breast, somehow finding the space within her loosened corset to further torment her.

"You will be mine for the next month?" He nuzzled her throat, withdrawing his hand from her corset and leaving her bereft.

But she didn't hesitate in her response. "Yes."

Both of his hands were clamped on her waist now in a

possessive hold as his eyes seared hers in the mirror. "I don't share, kitten."

"Nor do I."

"Good." He spun her about with such speed that she flattened her palms on his chest, clinging to him. "Say it again."

"I'll be your lover for the next month."

He shook his head slowly, his stormy stare fixated upon her lips. "Tell me that you'll be mine."

"I'll be yours."

Saying the words came naturally. Because they felt right. And the act of giving herself to this man, of embracing the pleasures she had so long been denied in her unhappy marriage, felt better than right.

"I've been waiting an eternity to hear you say that," he told her.

She couldn't resist gliding her hands up his chest, over silk warmed from his body, to cup his handsome face. The prickle of his golden whiskers enthralled her, as did the freedom to touch him thus. To long for him without self-loathing. To simply accept that she could have this man for herself, even if it was finite.

"You haven't known me for an eternity," she pointed out softly, thinking every facet of his countenance a marvel.

His cheekbones were blades, his mouth sensual and full, his jaw determined and masculine. Even his brows, a shade darker than his golden hair, were elegant and defined, somehow making his brilliant eyes stand out in stark relief against his sun-dappled skin. Everything about him was different. Unique. Familiar and yet new, almost as if she had not allowed herself the freedom to truly take all of him in until now, this moment.

"It feels as if I have," he said, his voice for once lacking its customary flippant teasing. "It feels as if I've always known you. As if there is no one I want to know more."

His words struck a place inside her that she'd previously believed buried and hidden away. He stole her breath with those confessions, and not just because she felt the same way, but because she had already surrendered. There was no reason to ply her with rakish charm. She was his.

"I feel it too," she murmured, a rush of tenderness careening through her, raw and dangerous and just a little bit wild.

All for this man, who was vexing and beautiful, complicated and enigmatic, who was passionate and bold.

His mouth was on hers, ravenous and hot. It was a kiss that didn't so much claim as it plundered, leaving her stripped of all defenses and artifice. She opened her mouth for his questing tongue and didn't care. Everything that wasn't Rhys ceased to exist.

She sucked on his tongue and reveled in the growl that emanated from his chest, in the way his fingers found the knot on her corset and frantically worked it apart, loosening her laces until satin and boning gave way. Hooks and eyes came open, and then her corset was falling. Hairpins were next, a waterfall of them raining to the floor as he pulled them free of her chignon. Hair tumbled down her back in a heavy coil that fell apart like her resistance.

She caught a handful of his hair and held him to her, feeding him voracious kisses in return. There seemed to be an undercurrent of fire between them, more intense than those that had come before, not just of desire, but of understanding. Acknowledgment. There was something deeply powerful about embracing this part of herself, a part she had restrained for so long and which had been longing for release.

A tearing sound filled the air, and then the kiss of cool night air whispered over her bare breasts. She broke the kiss to see that Rhys had rent her chemise the rest of the way.

"It was already beyond mending," he murmured and then cupped her breasts in his big hands, his thumbs unerringly finding her hard nipples and stroking until she was on her toes, making kittenish sounds that didn't belong to her. If she didn't soon step into the bath, she would never make it. And she very much wanted to be free of kitchen drudgery tonight. She wanted to be clean and soft and-sweet smelling for him. So she found the buttons on her drawers and plucked them free, sending them to the floor.

"So beautiful," he rasped.

She had never felt particularly beautiful—and less so since she had begun her new path in life. But he made her remember that old part of herself she had long since buried beneath mountains of duty and obligations. The young woman who had been blithely hopeful, who had dressed with care before balls and danced with suitors and who had naively believed she would marry a man who loved her, have a bevy of children, and live happily until her last day. He made her want to be herself, but wiser.

He made her feel beautiful and unencumbered, free and bold and wanton. She reveled in it. In him.

"You should get into your bath before it grows cold," he said. "Let me help you with your stockings."

She nodded, not wanting to lose his touch, and yet knowing he was right. The water would soon cool, and she needed to wash the toiling of the day away. He rolled down her garters and stockings with great care, then helped her into the tub. With a sigh of pure bliss, she sank down into the water, all the way up to her chin.

"This is heavenly," she said, enjoying herself immensely, for the tub in her modest accommodations was a mere hip bath.

She had forgotten the luxury of a large, deep tub, the water covering her entirely. Here was her reminder of what she had been missing, and she would enjoy it whilst she could.

"I see your lady's maid was at least efficient in setting out the soap and shampoo," he commented, selecting a small, round bar of soap and a cloth before pushing a mahogany stool nearer to the tub with his bare foot.

She knew a moment of guilt at her deliberate fib. "I may have dismissed her in the hope that someone else might wash my hair for me instead."

"Oh? Have I a competitor for this role?" He settled the soap and cloth in his lap and then began rolling up the sleeves of his dressing gown, one by one. "Perhaps I need to challenge someone to pistols at dawn."

She lifted a hand from the bath, water dripping from her fingertips, and flicked a hint of spray in his direction playfully. "No duels over me, if you please. There is only one man I want to wash my hair."

The second sleeve was rolled to his elbow, putting his comely forearms on display. It was a part of a man that was so oft hidden from view, and Miranda had never been particularly bothered by it either way. But one look at Rhys's forearms made her understand why men were meant to wear sleeves for the sake of propriety. His forearms were, like the rest of him, disturbingly attractive.

"The man in question had better be me," Rhys said with mock warning before taking up the soap and cloth and dunking both into the water. "Now, where shall I begin, my queen?"

She giggled at his silliness. "I didn't know that pages are tasked with bathing their queens."

"This one is. I take my duties very seriously." He shifted, scooting his stool to the foot of the tub. "I believe I'll work from bottom to the top." Rhys held out one hand, palm up. "Your foot, oh queen."

She bit her lip to keep another giggle from falling from her lips at his ridiculous insistence upon pretending she was a queen and he her loyal vassal and lifted her right foot. He took it and began soaping up the sole, the abrasion of the cloth on her sensitive skin making her jump.

"Ah," he drawled, as if he had just made an immense discovery, casting a glance in her direction. "My queen is ticklish."

"Only with light touches," she said as he made another pass of the soapy cloth along her arch, and she flinched again, her reaction instinctive.

"This is information that could prove most useful to me. A word of warning, kitten, you must never allow me to have the upper hand. I'll be shameless at exploiting it."

He finished washing her foot, then worked his way up her ankle and along her calf, taking his time, his fingers gently exploring along with the soap and cloth. She had no doubt his warning was complete truth. The Duke of Whitby was a man who unrepentantly seized whatever he wanted, using any means necessary. He had certainly done so with her. And yet, as she soaked in the bliss of the hot bath and he tended to her, Miranda couldn't summon even a modicum of outrage.

"I also kick when tickled to excess," she cautioned him as he finished with one leg, having washed her thigh whilst avoiding moving too high. "My younger sisters dearly loved to tickle my feet whilst I was sleeping. You can imagine what happened when they stood too near one morning."

He chuckled as he soaped her left foot. "Never say you kicked the poor girls."

"I caught Daisy in the nose," Miranda confirmed. "And I managed to get dear Elizabeth in the middle before I woke fully. Daisy was wretched, blood dripping everywhere. I hadn't known a nose could bleed so much until that morning."

"I shall endeavor to keep my nose far from your dainty feet, in that case."

"And to keep from tickling me," she added pointedly.

"I'm afraid I can make no such promises on that account." At his words, he trailed his forefinger lightly over her sole, making her jerk.

He was saved from a kick by his other hand, which was wrapped firmly about her ankle, holding her still.

"Two can play at this game, you know." She flicked another spray of water in his direction, leaving damp spots on the black silk of his dressing gown. "I shall discover where you are ticklish and get even."

"I'm afraid you'll be doomed to failure." He worked the cloth over her shin, up to her knee, soaping as he went. "I am not ticklish in the slightest."

"Nowhere?"

"Not anywhere," he confirmed, sounding smug.

"Vexing man," she muttered, her evil plans suitably dashed.

"I pride myself upon it." Partially rising, he shuffled his stool toward the middle of the tub with one foot, the soap and cloth still in hand. "Are there any other sensitive areas of which I should be made aware, darling?"

His question was wicked. He was, in fact, quite near to an extraordinarily sensitive place. A place that was desperate for his touch. A place where she was not at all ticklish.

She slid her bottom along the tub, propping herself up into a sitting position, taking care to cover her breasts with one arm as they bobbed at the water's surface. The other, she extended toward him. "I can bathe myself, you know. I daresay I don't need your help."

"But I want to help. I like taking care of you. Let me, Miranda."

There was something so very earnest in his gaze, in his

voice. He wasn't demanding, and he wasn't quite asking either. But she believed him when he said he liked taking care of her, that he wanted to do so. And she liked it too. Liked it far too much.

"Very well," she relented, lowering her hand so that it was below the surface of the water again, surrounded by warmth.

"You are far too capable, I think. It will be good for you to let me tend to you."

Her mind whirled as she tried to think of ways he might accomplish something so astounding when they were back in London and she was once more helming her school. But no, she mustn't ruin what time she had in this idyll with him. She would fret later.

"Sometimes, I worry that I'm not capable enough," she admitted quietly as he continued his ministrations, plucking her hand from the water and soaping it carefully before moving to her wrist and then higher still. "What if my school is doomed to failure, even with the funds you've given me? If I cannot attract a sufficient number of pupils, I will never be able to continue when my coffers run dry. I don't know what I would do should that come to pass. For so long, I have carried on, with the school as my sole objective."

She didn't reveal the rest of what worried her—that she would be forced to beg for a roof over her head or for her supper, accepting the alms of her friends forever. When she had left Ammondale, she had been so certain of her future. So determined to succeed. And yet, it had proven a struggle, and many days, she had felt as if she were attempting to dig herself out of a hole that was far too deep, thanks to the scandal of her divorce.

"Your school is not doomed," he told her softly, the cloth traveling along her shoulder now, following her collarbone. "Your creations are nothing short of glorious. Not only do they look beautiful, but they taste divine." The cloth dipped, and he soaped her breast. "Beyond all that, your determination to succeed and your steadfast devotion to your school will make failure an impossibility."

She wished she could be so sure. The cloth moved over her aching nipple, and she stole a glance at him through her lashes. His countenance was stern and yet tender, the mask he so oft wore—that of cavalier rake—stripped from him. He washed her stomach, her other breast, and then her arm in silence as she contemplated his words.

"Thank you," she said.

Not because his words were kind and much-needed—which they were. But because he believed them. Because he believed, quite specifically, in her.

"You needn't thank me, kitten." He gave her a wry half smile as he swirled the cloth over her skin beneath the water's surface. "I'm simply stating truth. I admire you. I've known many women, but not one who is so willing to be bold and to seize what she wants."

The cloth ghosted over her most intimate flesh right then, making her think of what else she wanted. But just as quickly, he moved away, finishing his task before taking up her shampoo. "Time for your hair."

Obligingly, she leaned her head back and dunked it low, enjoying the play of the hot water on her scalp. How wondrous it felt, being washed by him. She felt like a creature of pure hedonism. A wanton.

And for the first time, that feeling came without shame.

She could seize what she wanted. She could indulge in this secret affair.

When Miranda lifted her head from the water, Rhys was already situated behind her, his hands ready with the sweet-scented shampoo. Roses and orange blossoms hung heavy on the air. Her senses were intensely heightened, so much so that when his fingers began to massage her scalp, she purred like a cat, her eyes fluttering closed.

She felt the soft graze of his lips on her forehead, as quick and light as a butterfly, so rushed she would have thought she'd imagined it if he hadn't lingered long enough to press another kiss to the bridge of her nose. Miranda opened her eyes and reached for him, not caring that her hand was wet, cupping the back of his head and holding him to her as she kissed him, openmouthed and hungry, upside down.

The sensation was novel, her upper lip fitting over the fullness of his lower. She fed him her tongue, and he suckled, his fingers pausing their massage on her scalp as he surrendered himself to the kiss. She was ravenous for him anew, twisting in the bath, her breasts rising above the surface, water splashing from the tub, soaking his dressing gown. And she didn't care. He groaned, his tongue gliding against hers.

When it was finally over, she was dizzied with want, and his breathing was ragged.

"I do believe I'm clean enough," she murmured, dunking her head backward again, allowing the shampoo to rinse from her hair.

He watched her, his face hovering above, unreadable. She wondered what he was thinking. His hands were yet lathered with shampoo. No one had ever treated her with such care. Her marriage with Ammondale had been loveless and cold. He had resented and disapproved of her, and she had grown to loathe him for his callous treatment. Being with Rhys was like exploring a new city. She wanted to savor every moment. To explore every corner, experience everything.

"If I could paint, I would capture you here in this moment," he said, his voice low, silk and sin and velvet. "I'd call it *Aphrodite at Her Bath*."

What a fanciful notion. She stared at him as she floated in

the water, her hair spread like a halo on its surface, and realized she was falling in love with him.

"You would cause quite a scandal with such a painting," she pointed out breathlessly, shifting to a sitting position once more and turning in the tub so that she faced him.

He dipped his hands in the water, rinsing them. "No one else would ever know it existed. I'd be far too jealous to allow anyone else to see it. The painting would be for my eyes only."

She stood, water running down her body in rivulets as his eyes feasted on her. "I've finished my bath, page. Perhaps you could help me to dry off."

He stood with a helpless sound of need. "What you do to me, woman."

And then he snatched her from the tub, taking her up in his arms and carrying her to the bed. She was still soaked, and she shivered at the chill air on her wet skin as he laid her in the center of the mattress.

He clawed at his dressing gown like a man possessed, flinging it to the floor. She had a moment to drink in the sight of him—all stern, masculine angles and sinewy muscle, his cock ruddy and ready—before he was upon her. He settled between her thighs, nudging them wide, and then lowered his head, lapping at her clitoris with slow, steady strokes that had her writhing beneath him. Then he sucked, the sound wet and sinful, as he sank two fingers deep inside her.

The steady seduction of the evening—words and washing and so much more—already had her at desperation's edge. When he twisted his fingers and nipped her simultaneously, she came apart, clenching on him as she reached her release fast and hard.

"My name," he growled, his fingers still buried deep within her. "Say my name when you come."

She was breathless, feeling like a new woman entirely as she said, "Make me come again, and I will."

"Challenge accepted." He flicked his tongue over her in a few more wicked circles, thrusting in and out, rubbing her inner walls in a way that made her toes curl into the bedclothes.

And then he withdrew, moving up her body as he rained kisses on her stomach, her breasts, her throat. He slicked his cock over her folds, the sound somehow more obscene than when he had suckled her pearl, and it made her even wetter. She hooked a leg around his hip, opening herself to him.

He took her mouth in a kiss that tasted of her own desire and a faint hint of roses, and she clung to him as he canted his hips, driving inside her with one swift movement. She was filled, so deliciously full of him, and the urge to keep him here, to wrap herself around him and never let go, was strong. But so was the need to seek more pleasure.

Her hips moved against his, one foot flat on the mattress so she could follow him as he found a rhythm. His pace increased, his cock gliding in and out of her slick passage. It was good, so good. She kissed him furiously, their hips slamming together, almost ready to spend.

But just as she was about to fall apart, he abruptly withdrew, his lips leaving hers as his rigid length slipped free.

"Rhys," she protested.

"I know," he murmured.

She wondered if he did, if he could possibly comprehend the violence of the need careening through her just now. But then it ceased to matter because his hands were on her, flipping her to her stomach, guiding her so that her knees were curled, her bottom in the air. He caressed her cheeks, lightly squeezing and massaging, and then he nudged her legs farther apart, one hand still on her rump as the other slipped

233

to her opening, his fingers gliding into her, bringing her a measure of relief.

"You're so pretty and perfect, your pussy pink and wet and ready for me." His voice was a deep, decadent rasp. His fingers pumped in and out of her slickness, the pleasure almost too much to bear. "Tell me what you want, what you need."

"You," she managed, cheek pressed to the bedclothes, heart pounding, body entirely his to plunder. "I need you, Rhys."

She was completely on display to him, utterly at his mercy, and nothing had ever felt more right. His fingers left her, quickly replaced by the blunt head of his cock pressing, stretching. He filled her with one flex of his hips, the sensation new and yet familiar all at once, so deep inside her that it was almost on the verge of pain. Agonizing in the very best way.

"I wish you could see how beautiful you look, taking my cock," he ground out, his voice strained.

She moaned. There was no answer, no thought. There were no words left in her. There was only feeling, the building up of her need, growing more insistent with each thrust and withdrawal. He held her hips and shoved himself into her again and again, his ballocks slapping against her with each thrust. They were mindless and one.

She came again, just as he had wanted, crying out his name into the twisted bedclothes. He followed in the next few breaths, slipping from her body and covering her lower back in the hot spurt of his seed.

Miranda remained as she was, too sated to move despite her position, scarcely aware of Rhys leaving the bed and returning with a damp cloth that he used to clean her. Then he padded away, lowering the gas lamps before joining her in the bed again, pulling her so that their bodies were perfectly aligned.

"The tub," she protested, nuzzling his chest and reveling in his protective warmth. "I should ring for the footmen to take it away."

His lips grazed the top of her head. "They can take it away in the morning."

How she wished the morning would never come. But it inevitably would.

"You can't sleep in my bed," she warned, already half asleep. "Green can't find you here."

"I know, kitten." He stroked her back and pulled the covers over her, and she didn't even protest his use of the sobriquet this time.

Because she was deliciously satisfied and in Rhys's arms, the reassuring thrum of his heart against her ear. Her life had never, ever been as glorious as it was now, in this moment of quiet with him, the moonlight seeping in the far windows, all the world asleep.

CHAPTER 16

*H*ad he ever been happier?

If he had, Rhys couldn't recall.

He was presently ensconced in the inviting warmth of his bath, Miranda on his lap, his half-hard cock pressing against her luscious arse. His arms were wrapped around her waist, her head tucked against his chest, his chin resting atop her crown. He never wanted to move from this bath, from this moment. Never wanted her to leave his arms.

Obsessed.

Yes, he was that. Unapologetically so. Obsessed with her, desperate for her, hopeless for her. Miranda had entranced him. He had fallen beneath her spell, and he didn't even give a damn about it. The days of the house party had passed in a haze of desire and contentedness that no amount of good-natured mocking on the part of his friends had dispelled.

"It's a pity we must return to London tomorrow," she said into the quiet of the bedchamber. "I've rather grown fond of it here at Wingfield Hall."

He inhaled deeply, drinking in the scent of her damp hair

and skin. "You've grown fond of this pile of stone, have you? Fonder than you are of me?"

Her dainty fingers were idly drawing patterns on his forearms. "You know what I meant."

Of course he did, but he still wanted to hear her confess it aloud.

"I'm afraid I don't, kitten. Tell me."

She huffed a little sigh he found endearing. "I am fond of you as well."

"Oh, how my queen wounds me," he teased, shifting so that he could kiss the shell of her ear. "I should have thought you more than merely fond of me by now."

"I am fonder of you than I ought to be," she said archly, turning her head to give him a meaningful look. "By far."

He kissed her, unable to help himself. Her lips clung, warm and silken and delicious. "I do believe I know the feeling," he managed when he broke away at last.

"I shall miss this place," she told him, turning her head and resting it against his chest again.

He would miss it as well. Not Wingfield Hall, but what had happened between them here. Part of him feared returning to London would only further complicate their relationship. He wanted to install her in his house in St John's Wood, buy her dresses from Paris, cover her in diamonds and emeralds the color of her eyes. He wanted every second of each minute of her day and all her nights too. But she had denied his every request to gift her with anything, whether funds or necklaces or Worth gowns, and neither would she agree to moving in to St John's Wood. She would meet him there in an unmarked carriage, the better to keep their secret and preserve her reputation.

Rhys already hated it. But he would do anything he had to in exchange for more time with her.

"We need not leave," he cajoled, thinking of how glorious

it would be to frolic freely with her here for the next fortnight at least. Hell, perhaps even the whole bloody month. "Not yet."

They could linger after the others had gone. The notion held untold appeal. The estate belonged to Brandon, after all, and the next house party was three months away.

"I haven't even shown you the grotto yet," he added, thinking of the cavernous room with its delightfully warm pool that the Wicked Dukes Society had made modern improvements to not long ago.

But Miranda shook her head. "I don't dare. As it is, I've been gone from the school for too long. And if I were to linger, I would have no excuse for being here. We have managed to keep our liaison a secret from the servants, but what would they think if I were to remain here with you alone?"

"Perhaps they would think that I've kept you on to make your glorious desserts for me alone," he tried hopefully.

"They're already suspicious of me," she said. "I can feel it when I'm in the kitchens."

He stiffened, his protective instincts surging to the fore. "Did any of them dare to make even the slightest suggestion that you and I are lovers?"

"No," she hastened to reassure him. "But I wouldn't blame them if they had."

"I would. No one causes problems for you without having to answer to me." His words were vehement as they left him.

His protectiveness where she was concerned had not ended with the odious Lord Roberts. As the week progressed and they had become even closer, the way Rhys felt for her had only grown deeper and stronger. He would use whatever means he had at his disposal to defend her and to keep scandal from her name.

"That is sweet of you, Rhys, but you cannot browbeat everyone into silence on my behalf."

"The beating I have in mind has nothing to do with brows."

"Rhys." Water sloshed as she turned back toward him, her tone chastising.

"You are mine," he said unapologetically. "Woe be to anyone who attempts to hurt you."

Something in her face softened. "For the next month."

Ha! He would not tire of her in the next month. If the last week had taught him anything, it was that every second spent with her only made him long for a thousand moments more. But he held his tongue about that for the moment, deciding to fight one battle at a time.

"We could spend the month here," he tried again.

"To the demise of my reputation and my school both," she countered, using that prim tone of hers that made him want to kiss her and then bed her until she was breathless.

He loved it when she disapproved of him. He was a perverse bastard, he knew. But then, he loved it when she was pleased and sated, when she was laughing at something ridiculous he'd said just to make her eyes twinkle. When she was moaning his name…

That last thought had his cock twitching to attention.

The look she gave him said she had felt it.

"Am I to be blamed?" he asked rhetorically, defending both himself and his wayward cock. "I can't help myself where you are concerned. I'm selfish."

"As much as I would love to do so, we cannot stay here together."

He sighed, knowing she was right. "Very well. But I do hope that if I'm forced to return to London, you will at least pacify me with your delicious confections."

She turned fully in the tub, retreating to the opposite end. "What did you think of this evening's *Ananas Glacé à la Redalia?*"

He grinned, thinking of the pineapple-flavored cream ice she had lovingly molded into the shape of real pineapples, complete with pistachio cream ice for the leaves. "The pineapple was divine, but all I kept thinking about was how lovely it would be to swirl it over your pretty nipples and then lick it off."

"Wicked man." She splashed him lightly, but her words had no bite.

"Always." His gaze dipped to the water, where said pretty nipples were pert and pink and begging to be sucked. "If I behaved, I don't think you would like me very much, darling. I'd be dreadfully dull. Only think of how tiresome it would be if I wanted to recite sonnets all day or read theological texts or debate tedious subjects no one else cared about."

She bit her lower lip, clearly trying to stave off a smile of her own. "You are incorrigible."

He winked. "I pride myself on it."

Miranda's countenance turned serious then. "You truly liked the Redalia Pineapple Ice?"

"God yes. I like everything you make. And I like *you*, full stop." It was the closest he could bring himself to making an admission to her.

Hell, it was the closest he could bring himself to making an admission to himself. He wasn't just obsessed with Miranda. He liked her. Too much.

"I like you too." Her soft voice wrapped around his heart, squeezing it like a mighty fist.

But he didn't want to wallow in complications like emotions. He wanted to plan the next month at least. To make certain that nothing changed between them after they returned to London.

Beneath the water, he found her foot and began gently massaging. She was ticklish, yes. But she adored having her feet rubbed. And he found he enjoyed making her feel good in whatever way he could.

"When do you typically end your classes in your school?" he asked.

"Late afternoon," she answered, making a soft sigh of contentment that sounded rather like a cat trilling her delight. "No later than five o'clock, usually."

Hmm. That was rather a bit later than he would have preferred, but he could still dine with her each evening. And he didn't wish to interfere with her school, even though the selfish monster within him certainly would have liked to have her all to himself.

"I'll send a carriage round every day at one quarter past five," he said.

Her response was instant. "No."

This was not what he had expected to hear.

He raised a brow. "No?"

She shook her head, and he was briefly mesmerized by the silken raven curls clinging damply to her breasts. "That is far too early."

"How? You'll have one quarter hour to do whatever you must after the last of your students disperses for the day."

"Because there is a great deal more to my day than merely teaching my students. I need to balance the ledgers, make certain I have the next day's lessons organized and that all the ingredients are purchased. I must see that the day's fresh ingredients that have not been used won't be wasted…"

"It sounds like rather a lot of work," he mused and not without an edge of distaste.

Bad enough that she had been toiling in the kitchens this last week at Wingfield Hall. Even if she enjoyed her cream ice creations and her molds and perfecting her recipes, her work was not without suffering.

He had taken note of the many hours she poured into her task, the way she returned each night weary and with an aching back and feet, and sometimes sporting burns on her hands. Rhys was many things, but he had been raised his father's son, the duke. The very notion of earning his living was anathema, and he was fortunate enough that his family wealth had left him with an almost hideous amount of funds at his disposal. The money he earned from the Wicked Dukes Society was a mere pittance in comparison, one he reserved for his sister's ever-growing dowry.

"It is a lot of work," Miranda agreed, pulling her foot from his grasp and frowning at him. "But it is important to me."

Well, Christ. That explained the hurt expression on her lovely face.

"I didn't mean to suggest it isn't important," he hastened to explain. "I just don't like the notion of you working so hard. Could you not hire others to assist you?"

"I couldn't before," she said quietly. "The funds earned from my pupils didn't support more than a handful of employees, and I needed to continue investing part of my earning back into advertising and supplies."

But she could now that he had paid her such a princely sum for this week. Guilt cut through him.

"Let me pay you more for this week," he said.

"You've already paid far more than the week's desserts were worth."

"Not to me," he insisted stubbornly. "If you'll not accept more for this week, then please take what I offered for the month."

"I cannot," she denied, her tone every bit as mulish. "I'll not be a kept woman. You know what my terms are."

Yes, he bloody well did. But that didn't mean he had to like them.

"When would you have my carriage arrive, then? Midnight?"

"Your carriage can't be waiting for me at the school either. What would my students say? Or my employees, for that matter? Someone will most assuredly take note."

"The carriage will be unmarked."

"It will be exceedingly fine," she countered. "Others will see the difference."

"Well then, how do you expect me to see you every night?" he asked, frustrated and feeling not just a little bit like a child who was being deprived of his favorite toy.

"I didn't imagine we would see each other every night."

He was astounded. "Of course we will see each other every night, just as we have here at Wingfield Hall."

"But we won't be at Wingfield Hall."

"Ye gods, woman." Having had quite enough of this argument—for he would have his way, he was determined—he caught her waist and hauled her back onto his lap.

She landed there sideways and with a lack of grace he found utterly irresistible as water sloshed over the sides of the tub.

"Rhys," she protested.

"I need you," he said simply.

Because it was true. He *did* need her. Did she not see? He needed her every waking hour. He needed her in his bed, in his arms. But he would persuade her of that later. For now, he would show her how badly he needed her here, in this moment.

Her emerald eyes went wide. "In the tub?"

"Oh, my innocent little kitten." He grinned, pleased at the idea of further debauching her. He had been quite remiss and neglected to show her the joy of making love in the bath.

"Is such a thing possible?" she fretted.

"Quite."

"But the water. Surely—"

He kissed her, silencing further protest, and then he reached for her hand, settling it over his straining cock. And then he proceeded to show her, in exacting detail, just how possible making love in the tub was.

THE CARRIAGE AMBLED along the same country roads she had traveled one week ago, but as Miranda stared out the window at the passing Hertfordshire scenery, she felt as if a lifetime had passed instead. So much had changed. If someone had warned her before she had left London that the sennight facing her would change her in a way that nothing else in her nine-and-twenty years had, she would have laughed. She would have sworn it was impossible for her life to be so thoroughly upended in a mere seven days.

She would have been wrong.

So very wrong.

And if someone had warned her she would lose her heart to the devastatingly handsome, magnetic rake who had cozened her into making ices for a depraved house party, she would have scoffed. But here she was, on her way back to London and a life that no longer seemed as certain as it had before she'd left. Returning was bittersweet. Because it was the beginning of the end.

Yes, she had fallen in love with the Duke of Whitby. Miranda could admit it to herself, if to no one else. Definitely not to him.

Her embarrassing, naïve mistake needed to be held closely to her bruised and battered heart. Nothing could come of it. She was content with her school. He was content to seek pleasure. His words in the tub the night before had made that clearer to her than anything else.

Rhys was a sybarite.

Their arrangement was temporary. He would move on to someone else, and she would throw herself into her school, her recipes, and her ice caves. She had the funding she needed to grow her businesses, and she would be content with that. Falling in love with him had been not just foolish, but futile.

She knew that, of course. She was a practical woman. This affair was meant to be her taste of passion, enough to last her a lifetime. She hadn't expected feelings for him to develop or grow so quickly. But like a determined, invasive weed in a garden, they had. Five interminable years of marriage with Ammondale, and she hadn't felt a thing other than sadness, pain, and regret. One week with Rhys, and she was helplessly in his thrall.

That was her mistake, lowering her guard. And he had stormed her like an enemy taking a castle. But she could carry on. She simply had to keep her emotions to herself.

She turned away from the window, determined to distract herself from such complex, unwanted thoughts. Rhys was seated opposite her, his long legs elegantly sprawled before him, crossed at the ankles. His hat was on the leather squabs along with his gloves, his golden hair catching the sun filtering through the blinds and glinting. His vivid gaze was upon her, and she wondered how long he'd been studying her without her realizing.

"You are quiet," she said. "Is something amiss?"

He was, she had learned, a loquacious man, always talking, teasing, probing. Miranda was the opposite, quite accustomed to living in the space within her own head. Ammondale had never been interested in her thoughts, and she had learned over the course of their unhappy union to simply keep them to herself. But like his sensuality, Rhys embraced discourse.

He passed a hand over his sharp jaw, sighing. "It is nothing. At least, I think it's nothing. But I cannot shake the notion that there was something decidedly off about Richford this last week. He has been surlier than usual, disappearing at odd times, and I learned just this morning that he left without word yesterday. It isn't like him."

The Duke of Richford was one of the six founding members of the Wicked Dukes Society, having come up together at Eton. Rhys had shared a great deal about their long-standing friendship with her, and how years ago in drunken revelry, they had settled upon the idea of their club. Miranda hadn't been a part of the fast set in which Rhys and his chums had run, but she had crossed paths with Richford in her old life on a handful of occasions. She recalled a handsome and forbidding man, with a neat beard and dark-gold hair.

"Perhaps there is something in his life that is troubling him," she ventured. "Something with a family member? An illness?"

He shook his head. "It wouldn't be like Richford to keep such a thing secret."

That was curious, indeed. Miranda was grateful for the diversion. Anything to keep from thinking about how she had been imprudent enough to fall in love with Rhys.

She pondered what he had said for a moment. "What do you mean when you say he has been disappearing?"

Rhys scrubbed his hand over his jaw some more. "No one knew where he was. He wasn't at any of the revelries, from what King and Riverdale said."

Nor had Rhys, but that had been because they had been together.

"He may have been otherwise occupied," she said gently.

"But with whom? None of the guests." He frowned.

Understanding dawned. "Are you concerned he was dallying with one of the domestics?"

"I…it wouldn't be like him to do so. We have strict rules that we adhere to, and refraining from bedding servants is decidedly one of them." He shook his head, looking lost in his own musings. "But Riverdale said he saw him with a lady at some point, so it certainly seems as if perhaps a woman was to blame. Still, I cannot fathom who. All the guests left this morning as planned, everyone accounted for."

"That is odd," she agreed. "I suppose that when we reach London, you might seek him out and make certain all is well."

The reminder that they were presently *en route* to London was an unwelcome reminder. How easy it had been to pretend as if their idyll at Wingfield Hall would simply never end. And yet, it had. Just as their month as lovers inevitably would too.

"Bloody hell," Rhys muttered. "London is the last place I want to be at the moment."

She felt the same. But they couldn't hide away in Hertfordshire forever, and she knew it.

"It will be good, in some ways, to return to our routines," she said, summoning a smile for his benefit.

"Will it?" He was suddenly sullen. "It hardly feels that way. I want nothing more than to turn this carriage around and spend the next month ravishing you everywhere I can and in as many ways as possible."

His words brought her desire to life, chasing the melancholy.

"You can still spend the next month ravishing me," she pointed out. "Only, we shall be in London."

"Where you will be working yourself ragged until God knows what hour every day," he grumbled.

"There will be time for us," she promised. "I'll make it so."

She only hoped she could manage the subterfuge that would be required to keep anyone else from discovering their secret. Because she truly could not afford to allow any further damage to come to her reputation. Her future and her school's success depended on it.

"Of course you will." He sighed heavily. "Listen to me, prattling on like an arse. I'm sorry, love. I'm in a rare mood. Don't take anything I say to heart."

"You're worried about your friend. I understand. I haven't many good friends any longer after the scandal of the divorce, but I treasure those who have remained steadfastly loyal."

The number of ladies she'd believed were her friends, who had faded in the wake of the wretched gossip surrounding her, had been shocking. There had been so many, when she had been Countess of Ammondale, who had avowed their friendships were lifelong. Only to disappear in her time of need.

"Bloody hell." He frowned. "Anyone who didn't remain loyal to you wasn't worthy of your friendship."

"I expected some of it, of course," she said, confiding in him about what had been a staggering loss at first, but had grown easier with time. "I knew that there were some ladies who would not wish to be associated with a divorced woman. It was a risk I gladly took so that I could be free. But there were others whose defections hurt more. It was quite sobering to realize suddenly that someone who professed she considered me a sister had only sought my friendship for her own selfish gains and not because she was truly my friend."

Lady Clarissa Leland had befriended Miranda for her familial connections, and she had promptly set her cap at Miranda's brother. In the end, it wasn't George whom Clarissa had married, but George's friend, the Earl of

Hayward. Miranda still recalled her shock upon paying a call to Clarissa and being told by a frosty butler that her ladyship was not at home. The shock had turned to sadness upon her receipt of a letter from Clarissa which had laid bare her true feelings. The bonds of sisterhood had not just been thoroughly broken—they had never existed from the start.

"I'm sorry," Rhys said, cutting through bitter memories. "I cannot begin to imagine how difficult the divorce and ensuing gossip has been for you."

Like her marriage to Ammondale, her divorce was not a subject Miranda preferred to dwell upon. Nor was the sad way that seeking her own happiness had led most of the people in her circle to sever ties with her.

"It was difficult," she agreed, thinking of the countless days she had spent agonizing over those who had betrayed her, who had claimed to love her and then proven the opposite. "But I will forever believe that it made me stronger. And I need to be strong, if I am going to succeed with my school and other endeavors."

"Your quiet strength is one of many traits of yours that I admire."

What an enigma this man was. Sometimes, he surprised her by offering words of such deep reflection, words that held profound meaning and were precisely what she needed to hear in the moment he uttered them. And other times, he made her laugh with outrageous statements, sweeping hyperbole, and silly quips. This was part of why she loved him so. She made an alarming sound, quite unintentionally, in her throat as she choked back a sob and a laugh all at once, tears pricking her eyes.

"Oh dear. You're not weeping, are you?" he asked, leaning across the carriage to peer at her with comical effect.

She sniffed, blinking furiously. "No, of course not."

He reached for her, taking her chin in a gentle hold. "I didn't intend to make you sad."

"You didn't," she hastened to reassure him. "You don't. You make me happy." Frighteningly so.

And she knew she must not grow too accustomed to it, for one day too soon, this little understanding of theirs would come to an end as well.

"Good, because when you get tears in your eyes, it makes me want to set fire to the very world and watch it burn to ash."

She smiled. "That is very bloodthirsty of you."

"I'm a bloodthirsty chap, I find, when it comes to you." He swiped his thumb along her lower lip, his stormy gaze dipping there as well. "I am sorry about all the suffering you've endured, but I am selfishly glad that you divorced that bloody arse Ammondale. Because now I can have you to myself."

"Marriage was not what I had imagined it would be."

"Oh?" His thumb traced the upper bow of her lip now, the touch light and delicate. "What did you imagine it to be?"

"Happy," she blurted. "I thought that my husband would fall in love with me and that I would do the same with him in time. That we would laugh together and talk together, that we would attend balls and the theater, and that one day our children would fill the nursery and our hearts."

She stopped herself before she revealed more or said something she would regret.

He cupped her cheek, his warmth and tenderness comforting her, his touch making desire burn to life too. "What was it instead?"

Miranda found that she wanted to unburden herself to him.

"He was cold and resentful toward me. I later discovered that he had wanted to marry his mistress, and his father, the duke, had forbade the match. He never forgave me. Nothing I ever did was good enough. Nothing I said pleased him. He spent most of his time out of the house, which was a blessing at first, until I realized that his mistress was with child and that all the time he had spent away had been with her instead."

The betrayal she had felt at the knowledge had not entirely faded. How she had wanted a family of her own. And then to discover that her husband had begun one with the woman he truly loved instead… The duplicity had nearly broken her. In the end, it had been what had driven her out of the marriage. There was only so much unhappiness she had been willing to bear.

"My God, Miranda. I'm so sorry."

"I'm not. I'm contented now. My school gives me a sense of purpose I was missing before." She stopped herself before she said more.

And being with you makes me happier than I ever imagined it was possible to be.

It had been there, almost falling from her wayward tongue. She bit her lip to keep the truth from spilling forth.

"I understand the need to have something purely for yourself," he told her softly, stroking her cheek. "To find your own contentedness apart from what is expected of you. That was what the Wicked Dukes Society was for me when it began. And now, over the years, it's taken the place in my life that I imagine a wife would have. My obligations and responsibilities are to the club, my mother, and my sister alone."

"Did you never wish to marry or have a family?" she blurted.

It was reckless, that question. Miranda had no right to ask it, and she very much feared the answer.

"I prefer my life this way." He gave her a rueful grin,

tucking a tendril of hair behind her ear. "Like you, I've no wish to be tied down in a marriage that will inevitably be a misery. My parents' marriage was bloody wretched. By the end, they hated each other. I have no desire to repeat their misfortune. I decided long ago never to visit that kind of agony upon myself or another."

Miranda tamped down the inane disappointment within her at his response. What had she expected? There was no future for them. Nor had there ever been one. She was a divorcée tainted by scandal, a woman who earned her bread. He was a voluptuary who lived his life one pleasure at a time.

One month.

That was all they had. All they could ever have. And she needed to be satisfied with it.

"You're wise to feel that way," she forced out, along with what she hoped served as a carefree smile. "My own experience with matrimony persuades me that it isn't worth attempting ever again."

The reminder was for herself. Her marriage with Ammondale had been terrible. She had vowed never to marry again, and nothing had changed just because she had taken a lover.

"Why are you on the opposite side of this damned carriage?" Rhys asked, his voice low and soft, velvet on silk.

"Because there is more room if I sit here," she pointed out primly, turning her head to press a kiss to his palm.

He winked. "There is room aplenty for you on my lap."

She laughed, grateful for the return to lightheartedness. "I'm not sitting in your lap the whole way back to London, you rogue."

A mischievous grin curved his lips. "Who said you would merely be sitting?"

There was no misunderstanding the sensual intent in his voice and eyes.

Her levity faded, overtaken by desire. "In a carriage?"

He gave her that wicked sinner's rakish grin that never failed to cue an answering rush of need within her. "Oh yes, kitten. Most definitely in a carriage."

He held his hand out to her, and she settled her palm in it without hesitation.

CHAPTER 17

*R*hys pinched the bridge of his nose, trying to ward away an impending headache, and glared at his mother, who had just fluttered into the breakfast room, resembling nothing so much as an agitated owl. Evidence of her distress could be seen plainly not just in her distraught expression but in her silver hair, which was loose and unbound from its customary coil. She was also wearing a dressing gown.

Mater never left her rooms without her hair coiffed, and she most certainly never wandered about in *dishabille*. Perhaps, he thought unkindly and with a hint of disinterest, the old bird had finally gone senile.

"What is the matter, madam?" he asked calmly, watching as she wrung her withered hands and blinked behind her gold-rimmed spectacles.

She exclaimed something unintelligible that he swore sounded like *Mignonne casts dreary*. Her dudgeon was so very high, which was also most unlike her. If she had been the sort of mother that had instilled a deep and abiding sense of love in her children, he might have been more concerned. As it was, he was rather displeased to have an interruption of breakfast when he had yet to enjoy his bacon.

Rhys stood belatedly, recalling that he was sitting in the presence of a lady, even if said lady was perhaps mad and someone he resented for his unhappy childhood. "Who the devil is Mignonne, Mater?"

"Your sister!" his mother wailed.

"You mean Rhiannon?" He frowned, realizing that his sister wasn't present at the breakfast table yet this morning.

He hadn't thought much about it; Rhiannon kept whatever hours she chose, flitting about like a butterfly from one social engagement to the next. He had arrived in London late in the evening, and after a carriage ride with Miranda that had been spent in delightful distraction, he'd been so tired he had simply gone to bed. No one but the servants had been about.

"Yes," his mother said unhelpfully, still twisting her hands together and looking as if someone had announced that her prized collection of jewels had been thieved.

Which would have made more sense in this moment than anything to do with his sister. Because Mater didn't care about anything other than herself and her collections. Oh, she wasn't malevolent. She was always perfectly pleasant to converse with. However, she simply didn't care about her children. She never had.

Rhys had long suspected that to her, he and Rhiannon were obligations forced upon her by his father. The heir, although not the spare. Several years of miscarriages and one stillborn son had finally persuaded the former duke to put an end to his quest to secure the Whitby line.

"What about my sister?" he asked, when it seemed Mater was not inclined to elaborate.

"*She's missing,*" Mater announced, her words rambling together without pause, punctuated by a wail.

This was more emotion than he'd seen from his mother in…well, ever.

Rhys blinked. "Did you say she is missing?"

"Yes," Mater cried, wringing her hands some more.

And that was when worry hit him, like a fist to the gut. True concern from Mater, and his sister was missing. Just what the devil was going on here?

"What do you mean, Rhiannon is missing?" Rhys hissed at his mother, sure he had misheard.

"P-precisely that," Mater snuffled. "She's g-gone."

He stalked toward his mother, stopping before her. "Details are important at a time like this, madam. When did she go missing? Where did she say she was going last?"

"I…I c-cannot be c-certain."

"What can you not be certain of?" he demanded, frustration surging along with worry.

He could scarcely make sense of what she was saying.

"I d-don't know w-when she went missing."

Rhys sent a silent prayer heavenward for patience. Mater was sobbing now, verging on inconsolable, which only rendered getting lucid answers from her even more difficult.

"I saw her the day I left a week ago," he said slowly. "Did you see her after that?"

Mater's face crumpled. "You were gone f-for a w-week? Where w-were you? Did you take h-her with you?"

Dear God. If he weren't so worried about his sister, he would most definitely be insulted that his mother had failed to note a weeklong absence on his part.

"I went to the country," he snapped. "To a house party. And no, Rhiannon was not with me. Nor would she have been invited. Do you mean to tell me that you have not seen her this last week at all?"

"I…I couldn't say." Mater's face crumpled even more, and fresh streams of tears rolled down her cheeks.

"Bloody hell," he muttered, raking a hand through his hair. "I left her in your charge, madam. You are her mother."

Not that the title meant a damned thing to Mater. She had never looked more selfish and small to him than she did now, her nose red from weeping tears that were undoubtedly more for herself than for Rhiannon. Likely, she feared how such a scandal as a disappearing daughter would reflect upon her.

"She is th-three and t-twenty," Mater protested. "How am I meant to w-watch her?"

"You are meant to make certain that she is safe," he growled. "To ensure that no harm befalls her. You are meant to be chaperoning her, to be at her side. That is the duty a mother owes to her daughter, at the very least, madam."

"B-but you know how Rhiannon is. She is r-rebellious. She d-doesn't want my interference."

That much was likely true, though Rhys doubted very much that Mater had even tried to offer any influence over Rhiannon. Christ knew she hadn't with him. She was like a dazzling little butterfly, mysteriously flitting about, his flesh and blood and yet almost entirely unknown to him.

"Do the servants have any notion of where she has gone? Have you checked her bedchamber? Did she leave a note?"

He paused, realized that he was biting off every question that occurred to him and that from Mater's dazed expression, she could not possibly keep up.

"Are you attending me, madam?" he demanded. "Have you nothing to say?"

"Mrs. Hatch said that she l-left a week ago," Mater said at last. "I've no n-notion where she's g-gone."

Rhys stared at his mother, aghast. "You mean to suggest that my sister left this house a week ago, and you didn't notice her absence until today?"

Mater went pale, guilt and a fresh sob crumpling her countenance.

"Bloody hell," he muttered to himself, striding past his mother, breakfast forgotten.

He needed answers, and it was more than apparent that Mater didn't have any. Rhiannon had been missing for an entire damned week.

Dear God. He shuddered to think the trouble his hellion sister could have landed herself in during that time. He needed to find Rhiannon.

Posthaste.

THE TROUBLE with pretending she had spent the last week visiting her Great-Aunt Bitsy, Lady Rhiannon Northwick thought to herself rather grimly, was that her brother wasn't stupid. He would have questions. Questions to which she didn't have suitable answers.

Such unpleasantness could have been easily avoided if not for the interference of one stubborn, maddening man. A man she would not think about now. Nor ever again, if she could help it.

Impossible, said a voice deep within herself.

A voice she promptly ignored. What she couldn't ignore, unfortunately, was the burning memory of his kisses. His hands on her. His searing eyes that had seemed to see a part of her she hadn't known existed…

No, she chastised herself inwardly. She must be strong. She must not allow her girlish infatuation with a certain handsome, conscienceless rake to weaken her resolve. He had made his feelings about her more than abundantly clear, dashing her heart to pieces in the process.

And that was why she was presently arriving a day too

late back at the home she had left a short week ago. She had set off with such hope in her heart, so hopelessly naïve. How horridly wrong her plans had gone.

He had left without warning, without a word. Had disappeared. And then she had found him, much to her everlasting regret. Rhiannon squeezed her eyes tightly shut against a painful rush of heartache and betrayal.

His words still echoed in her mind.

You will thank me later, minx.

Minx, he had called her, daring to use the pet name for her that she had once found so endearing. Now, it felt like a dagger plunging into her flesh, glancing off sinew and bone, making her bleed.

Her hired carriage came to a halt before her brother's town house. Rhiannon didn't know what awaited her within, nor how she would brazen her way through her explanation. If she even could.

But there was one matter of which Rhiannon was deadly certain.

She would never, as long as she lived, forgive the Duke of Richford for what he had done to her.

As Rhys had promised in his missive, the unmarked carriage he had sent for Miranda was waiting around the corner of the Lenox School of Cookery that evening. It was discreetly tucked away on a side street where no one would take note. And yet, as she prepared to enter its confines, she knew a moment of trepidation as she passed a guilty look over her shoulder.

No one watched.

She stepped up and into the conveyance, startled to find that it wasn't empty.

Rhys was within, dressed in elegant evening finery, looking serious and unfairly beautiful. Her heart soared at the sight of him. Throughout the course of her busy day, she had done her best to distract herself from thoughts of him. But diverting herself had been an impossibility. She'd spent the time since she had seen him last in a haze of longing and desire. And she couldn't deny that she had missed him. Desperately so. Hertfordshire—and Rhys—had quite spoiled her.

"God, I missed you," he muttered, taking her into his arms and hauling her across his lap as the carriage door closed.

Her petticoats were bunched beneath her bottom, her skirts awkwardly twisted, and anyone could have seen him pulling her into his lap had they but glanced in their direction before the door had shut. But somehow, all that ceased to matter the moment she threaded her arms around his neck and looked up into his summer's-storm eyes.

"I've missed you too," she confessed softly.

His mouth was on hers in the next breath, ravenous and hot. She kissed him back with all the need and longing that had been building within her since they had parted ways the day before. How had it been only one day that had passed since she had seen him last? It felt more like a lifetime.

She was breathless by the time the kiss was over, her nipples hard, the insistent ache between her legs so demanding that she pressed her thighs together in an effort to quell it. Miranda sifted her fingers through his silken hair, studying his handsome countenance, so serious and stern, the customary teasing, devil-may-care rake nowhere to be found this evening.

"Is something wrong?" she asked.

"Yes. I'm not inside you right now."

He kissed her again before she could chastise him for saying something so vulgar. His lips moved over hers, lingeringly, deliciously. But Miranda knew him well enough to sense when something was weighing heavily on his mind.

She tore her mouth from his. "Something is amiss. Tell me."

He sighed, the sound weary. "It's my sister."

Miranda recalled the fondness in his voice when he had spoken about her. They were close. His solemn expression worried her.

"Is she well?"

"Yes. No. Hell." He rubbed his jaw. "I don't know."

Miranda smoothed a lock of hair from his forehead, a surge of tenderness and protective concern rising. "Has she taken ill?"

"No, thank God. She is well enough. But whilst I was away, she disappeared for a week. She returned this afternoon, claiming to have been visiting our Great-Aunt Bitsy in the country."

Miranda frowned. "*Claiming* to have visited your great-aunt? You don't believe your sister?"

He sighed again, looking torn. "It isn't like Rhiannon to deceive me, but her story makes little sense. Our mother had no notion my sister was going or where she had gone. Great-Aunt Bitsy would have invited Mater as well as Rhiannon, and our mother received no invitation that she can recall. Great-Aunt Bitsy may be eccentric, but she would not have approved of Rhiannon traveling to her unchaperoned."

"Your sister traveled alone?"

A muscle worked in his jaw. "And without informing any of the servants or our mother where she had gone or when she might return. She took a hired hackney, for Christ's sake. Anything could have happened to her."

"That does seem rather reckless," she allowed. "But perhaps there was a reason for her actions."

"I don't doubt there was, nor do I doubt the timing. She

left when she knew I would be gone, and she was more than aware our mother would fail to take note of her absence until it was too late."

Suddenly, Miranda understood the underlying reason for his concern. A young lady who would deliberately go on an unplanned jaunt alone, and when her protective older brother was conspicuously absent, was suspicious indeed. There was one likely reason for her unexpected disappearance.

"You suspect your sister of meeting with a beau," she guessed.

His expression turned haunted. "Yes. If any scurrilous rogue has dared to ruin my sister, he will wish he was never born. I'll see to it myself."

"Have you any proof that she was with someone else? What of your great-aunt? Has she confirmed your sister's story of the visit?"

He shook his head. "Great-Aunt Bitsy is not a prompt correspondent, I fear. I've sent off a letter in her direction, but I don't expect to have a response any time soon, if at all. She is forever fretting over her menagerie of animals and often ignores her correspondence for weeks at a time. Short of paying her a visit myself, I'm not likely to have an answer. Rhiannon, of course, would know this as well."

"You are a good brother, Rhys." She caressed his cheek, love for him welling up within her, threatening to overflow.

How would she be able to carry on in one month's time? To live her life without him in it? The thought left her desolate. She couldn't bear to consider it.

"If I were a good brother, this wouldn't have happened," he countered grimly. "I ought to have made certain she had a companion to watch over her. I should have known Mater wouldn't be any match for Rhiannon when she sets her mind to something."

"You couldn't have known that your sister would leave when you were gone. How many occasions have you left without anything untoward happening at all?"

"Many," he admitted.

And for a moment, she knew a pang of jealousy for each of those occasions, many of which had likely been Wicked Dukes Society house parties. For the lovers he had known before her. For the lovers he would take after her.

Miranda blinked against the sting of tears she refused to allow to fall. "You see? You could not have known."

Just as she couldn't have known how quickly she would lose her heart to this man. How was it that only a little over a week had passed since they had gone to Hertfordshire together? She could only hope the next month would progress torpidly. That she could savor these moments with him, when he was hers.

"You are too good for me," he said, kissing her softly. "I don't deserve you. But as it happens, I'm a selfish and greedy chap. I'm not about to challenge the fate that brought me into your path."

She smiled against his mouth. "It was my cream ice that brought you. Hardly fate."

"Your cream ice is bloody delicious," he agreed, his voice low and silken as he pressed kisses to the corner of her lips, then her jaw, alternating words with decadent brushes of his mouth. "But not nearly as delicious as you are. Have I told you how much I missed you, kitten? I could devour you here and now."

And she wanted him to, wanton that she was. Miranda chased his lips with hers, kissing him, their tongues tangling. A moan stole from her. His hand was moving, gliding under her voluminous skirts, trailing past her knee.

She had ridden him on their carriage ride back to London the day before. The memory of how wonderful it had been, rocking in time to the swaying conveyance, brought the need between her legs to an aching throb. The sinful, forbidden nature of their frantic coupling had imbued the act with an eroticism that had made her climax even more potent than usual. He was turning her into a voluptuary as well, and she didn't even mind.

She had been missing more than she could have comprehended in her frigid, unhappy marriage. And she knew that regardless of how devastated she would be to part ways with Rhys at the conclusion of this month, she would be forever grateful to him for showing her the pleasure that could exist between a man and woman.

Miranda sucked on his tongue as his fingers skated up her inner thigh, and although she was somewhat hampered by the cumbersome fabric of her petticoat and gown, she was able to part her legs just enough for him to breach the slit in her drawers. The first stroke over her aching sex made her gasp.

"You're already drenched, darling," he murmured, kissing down her throat, sucking on her pulse, making her burn. "Have you been this soaked for me all day?"

Miranda was beyond shame. "Yes."

Concentrating on her ledgers had been nearly impossible. She had been restless on her chair, wishing for a release she knew she couldn't have until the evening.

He cupped her mound then, his touch possessive but tender. "Who does this wet, wicked pussy belong to?"

His sinful words wrung another moan from her. "You."

"You're damned right it does," he growled with satisfaction, his fingers parting her folds to find the seat of her desire hidden within.

He strummed over her swollen clitoris, sending sparks of pure bliss radiating from her core. He had distracted her with his concern over his sister, but now, all the need that had been eating her alive through the hours they had been apart returned tenfold. His thumb swirled in knowing circles, the pressure he applied increasing, as he sank two fingers deep inside her.

She grasped his hair as he tongued the hollow behind her ear. Oh dear heavens, it felt so good. So wrong. The second day she had surrendered to her desires and allowed him to pleasure her in a carriage. But she didn't care. No one could see what was happening within the haven of the brougham. Everything else ceased to exist but for the two of them.

"Rhys," she whispered, his name torn from her as she rocked against his touch, seeking more. "Please."

"Please what, kitten?"

She ought to have objected to the silly pet name. But she was beyond rational thought. There was only sensation, her body spurring her on, the need for completion supplanting all else.

"You know what," she murmured, grasping a handful of his hair and pulling his lips back to hers for a drugging kiss.

He licked her lower lip, then gently nibbled there, his fingers gliding in slow torment in and out of her, whilst his thumb continued to gently tease. She was close, so close.

Miranda made a noise of frustrated yearning.

He withdrew his hand, resting his wet fingers on her inner thigh, stroking her there as his thumb, too, left her sex. "I'm afraid you'll have to say the words, darling. I need to hear them."

He brushed his lips over hers lightly once, twice. Thrice.

Her breaths were coming in ragged gasps. She so desperately needed to come. But he wanted to have the filthy words from her. He was pushing her once again, beyond the bounds of her comfort. And she both loved and hated him for it.

"Rhys," she tried again, shifting on his lap. "Touch me. Please."

"I *am* touching you," he drawled, caressing her thigh again. "Is this not where you want it?"

She compressed her lips. "No."

He raked his teeth along her jaw, then caught her earlobe between his teeth and bit, making a liquid rush of desire go straight to her center. "Where, kitten? Tell me."

Miranda licked her lips as his hot breath coasted over her throat. She couldn't say the word. Could she? It was scandalous. A word she had never uttered before, nor even heard until him.

She couldn't.

But this need was unbearable. If she didn't have relief, she would surely perish from it.

Miranda opened her mouth, prepared to concede defeat.

The carriage rocked to a halt.

"Oh dear. It would seem we have arrived at our destination." His grin was knowing, the rogue, making the corners of his eyes crinkle, amusement shimmering in those stormy blue depths.

He withdrew his hand from beneath her skirts and, as she watched, sucked his glistening fingers clean. "I reckon that will have to suffice until dessert."

The scoundrel! She was positively aflame.

Gently, he gathered her up in his arms and deposited her on the opposite bench just before he rapped on the carriage roof to signal they were ready to disembark.

"Don't forget your veil, kitten," he reminded her solicitously.

Oh! Miranda looked around, at a loss. She had quite neglected to bring a piece of millinery that had one.

"I…I seem to have forgotten one," she stammered, her brain struggling to keep up with the haste of the events as they unfolded.

One moment, she had been about to come, his fingers

deep inside her, and the next, they had arrived at their destination, and she didn't think she would ever be the same.

"Fortunately, your page has come prepared, my queen," Rhys said, grinning as he reached beneath his seat and extracted a hat box. He lifted the lid and offered her a jaunty hat that had been trimmed with a dark veil that looked more appropriate for mourning than an evening assignation.

She stared at the hat, wondering where he had procured it, and for whom. Had he given it to past lovers? Would he use it again? These were unwelcome and foolish thoughts that she banished, lest she linger on them too long and they were allowed to take root and grow.

This was naught but an affair. A fleeting relationship devoted to the pursuit of pleasure. He owed her no loyalty. They were lovers. Nothing more, even if what she felt for him suggested otherwise.

"Thank you," she forced out, her voice thick with restrained emotion and desire both.

She took the hat and replaced her own with it, settling the veil over her face to shield her features from curious stares and save her from scurrilous gossip.

If only her heart were as easily protected. But it was far too late for that. The carriage door swung open. She blinked as the cool evening air flooded within.

Resigned to her fate, Miranda descended from the brougham.

CHAPTER 18

*R*hys watched the lamplight in the dining room at his St John's Wood house playing lovingly over Miranda's glossy ebony hair, marveling that this beautiful, complicated woman was here with him. That she was his.

For now, he reminded himself.

Or for as long as he could persuade her.

Forever.

The word flew into his mind, wild and fleeting. Impossible too. She had made her opinion on marriage clear; her obligation was to her school. And likewise, he had no wish to marry. He was perfectly contented to be the last Duke of Whitby, having neither brothers nor uncles nor cousins, distant or otherwise, to inherit.

At least, he thought he had been contented. Some maggot seemed to have wormed its way into his brain, leaving him occasionally susceptible to the odd rush of yearning to see a little girl with his blue eyes and Miranda's raven curls. Or a young lad with emerald eyes and wavy blond hair.

"What are you thinking?" she asked him, her voice like a caress.

He couldn't very well admit that he had been harboring maudlin sentiments about the children they would never have together. So he took a slow sip of his wine in the hopes that the *Chateau Margaux* would chase such unwanted notions from his mind.

"I was thinking about how lovely you look tonight," he improvised.

Which wasn't a lie. He had been admiring her. Even dressed as she was in one of her demure gray silks, she was the most gorgeous woman he had ever beheld. It had taken all the control he possessed to keep from ravishing her in the carriage on their way here. He'd been just about to make her come when the carriage had rolled to a stop, and he had decided to make them both wait. To heighten the sensuality, the need.

"You are far too generous." She gave him a wry smile from across the table. "I'm sure I look like someone who has been balancing ledgers and instructing students on the merits of clear and pureed soups all day."

"Not at all." He held her stare. "You look like the most beautiful woman I've ever met."

A becoming flush stole over her cheekbones. "Do cease flattering me. You've already won me, you rogue."

But he hadn't won her. Not truly, had he? And the knowledge left an ache in his gut. One he had never felt before.

"I'll own that I'm a rogue," he allowed, tamping down those unwanted feelings. "However, I would never offer empty flattery. You are every bit as incomparable as your desserts."

"Speaking of my desserts, I was thinking of bringing some of my molds and an ice cave here," she said. "I thought that perhaps you might enjoy an occasional cream ice over the course of the month, and it would be easier for me to prepare it here in the kitchens than to freeze the mold at the school and bring it with me."

The month—an unwanted reminder that their time together was finite. Unless he could persuade her to give him more. Before her, he had never wanted more from anyone. But Miranda was different.

He knew it to his marrow.

"I would love nothing better than to indulge in your ices, but I don't like the idea of you continuing to work after you've spent the day at your school," he pointed out, keenly aware of how hard she toiled. "I want you to relax when you are with me here. I want it to be your respite."

"That's very considerate of you." Her smile warmed. "Perhaps on days when the school is not in session, then?"

"As you wish. When we are together, however, I don't want you to feel as if you must tend to me."

"Perhaps I like tending to you," she said softly.

That warmed him more than the wine. Dear God, she was a gem. Ammondale ought to have his head examined for treating her so callously. But then, if the earl had been a proper husband to Miranda, Rhys never would have had the opportunity to get to know her. And he couldn't fathom his life without her in it.

A sobering thought, that.

"I have a great deal that requires tending," he teased her to distract himself and lighten the conversation. "One part of me in particular, kitten."

That won him a laugh from her. "Will you forever insist upon referring to me thus?"

He winked. "Yes. I will. For one thing, I like to ruffle your feathers. For another, when you chastise me, it makes my cock hard."

But then, in her presence, *everything* made his cock hard.

She bit her lip, clearly trying to keep from laughing again. "You are an unrepentant scoundrel."

"Would you have me any other way?"

"No." She shook her head, her expression turning serious. "I don't think I would. But fortunately, though you may be a rogue, you are a generous one. I've already received some inquiries about my employment agency. I presume you are the source."

He had indeed been planting the seed in as many places as possible during the house party.

"I'm pleased to hear that some of the guests have contacted you so soon," he said. "I cannot say I'm surprised, what with the way everyone was perpetually raving over your ices each night. I quite expect the demand for your charges will exceed the number of pupils you have, forthwith."

"Thank you, Rhys."

"You needn't thank me. Your hard work and dedication are responsible for your success."

"But without the funds you paid me for the house party and your recommendations, my school would still be struggling." There was a tenderness in her verdant gaze that touched something inside him.

He cleared his throat. "Yes, well. I can assure you that my motives were not entirely noble."

Hell, when they had begun, his motives had been anything *but* noble. He had wanted her in his bed, full stop. But now? Ye gods. Now, he couldn't quite tell what his motives were where she was concerned, and that terrified him more than anything else. Because he was very much beginning to fear that he, a man who had always considered his romantic entanglements purely carnal in nature, was beginning to fall for Miranda after a mere week of bedding her.

"You want me to believe the worst of you, but there is far more to you than the jaded rake," Miranda insisted quietly.

No one had ever looked at him as she was. It was a potent, heady sensation.

"Come to bed with me," he said, needing the diversion of the physical rather than the intellectual, which felt suddenly far too dangerous with her.

Their meal was finished, and in the absence of the discreet servants who had whisked themselves belowstairs, he was free to do as he liked with her, just as she was at liberty to do what she wished with him.

"You're trying to distract me," she observed.

Quite correctly.

"Is it working?" he asked cheekily.

A reluctant smile played at the corners of her full lips. "Your charm is deadly, Your Grace, as I'm sure you are already aware."

She rose to her feet then, and he followed suit, feeling rather like a callow youth in such a haste to touch her that he was about to spend in his trousers. That was the effect she had on him. Regardless of how many times they made love, he only seemed to want her more.

"So I've been told, but I'm gratified that you find it so." He skirted the table and offered her his arm formally, as if they were about to enter a ball together instead of on their way to shag like mad.

She settled her hand in the crook of his elbow. "How could I not?"

"So you find me irresistible?" he teased as he guided her from the room and down a short hall to the staircase.

"I'm sure you already know the answer to that question." Her tone was arch, but then she sent him a seeking look and asked him a question that nearly had him tripping on the first step. "Is this the house you reserve for all your paramours?"

Thankfully, he grasped the banister before he planted himself face first into the stairs. "It is a house I have used when discretion is needed, yes."

Mater and Rhiannon lived in his town house, and neither of them had ever crossed paths with the lovers he took. A strange sensation lodged in his chest. Bringing Miranda here suddenly felt inherently wrong.

"Of course," she said quietly.

Damn it.

Rhys stopped her there on the stairs, turning toward her. "You're not my paramour."

He didn't know precisely what she was to him. There was no word in his lexicon to accurately describe her. All he did know was that she was necessary. Like air in his lungs, sun in the sky, like rain on a drought-ridden field. He simply had to have this woman.

Miranda smiled softly. "I know." She tugged at his arm. "Now, come to bed with me before I perish from wanting you."

His cockstand was instant, all noble attempts at sorting out his tangled emotions effectively abandoned.

"As my queen commands," he told her, guiding her up the rest of the stairs to the room he kept as his own.

They scarcely made it over the threshold before she took him by surprise, kissing him soundly. His hands settled on the curves of her waist, and he answered her by giving her his tongue. She tasted sweet, like wine and the vanilla mousse that had completed their dinner, and he couldn't get enough. He wanted to gorge himself on her, to devour her.

But she had other ideas.

Her hands flattened on his chest, lightly pushing as she broke the kiss.

"Wait." She was breathless, her eyes glistening, her lips berry-red. "You said as your queen commands, did you not?"

His cock pulsed. "I did."

"Then disrobe for me," she ordered him.

Sweet God. This woman was going to be the death of him.

Rhys shrugged out of his coat, allowing it to fall to the Axminster. He toed off his shoes, then worked frantically at buttons, not stopping until he was bare-chested and clad in nothing other than his trousers.

"More?" he asked, holding her rapt gaze, his fingers on the fastening at his waistband.

"Not yet. I need some assistance."

Ceding control to her was a more potent aphrodisiac than he could have imagined.

"Tell me what you want me to do."

"Help me with my gown," she said softly.

The demure line of buttons on her bodice was no match for his nimble fingers or his desire to get her naked. It was gone in less than twenty seconds, followed swiftly by her skirt and petticoat, until she stood before him in her embroidered stockings, drawers, chemise, and a bold corset that was light-blue silk trimmed with white lace and embroidery.

She was so stunning he had to take a moment to simply admire her, the flare of her hips, the nip of her waist, the bountiful, lush breasts pooling over the top of her corset.

"What else would you have me do?" he rasped, already half crazed with lust.

Miranda turned, presenting him with her back. "My corset next."

The back of her was every bit as tempting as the front, her bottom round and full, her pale shoulders partially on display, along with the elegant nape of her neck.

"With pleasure." He untied the knot on her laces, unable

to keep from pressing kisses everywhere he could find bare skin.

Her scent enveloped him—rose and orange blossom and Miranda. The laces loosened, and she turned toward him again. He gripped her busk, removing hooks from eyes, until the last was unfastened and her corset landed on the floor with an ever-growing mound of their garments. Her pink nipples tented the thin fabric of her chemise, and he couldn't resist cupping her breasts, rolling the stiff peaks with his thumbs.

"Is this your revenge on me for making you wait in the carriage?" he asked softly.

She arched into his touch with a low purr of sensual appreciation. "If it is?"

"Then I foresee a great deal of playing with your pretty pussy on carriage rides until you're almost ready to come," he murmured wickedly. "Now, tell me what you want me to do next."

Miranda met his gaze boldly. "I want you to fuck me."

Pure, molten need washed over him, so potent and all-consuming that for a moment, he could scarcely think. But all too quickly, his body took the reins from his mind.

"I'd love nothing better," he growled as his hands flew over her remaining undergarments.

The chemise sailed over his shoulder. The drawers glided down her hips. He tore at his trousers with considerably less elegance, shucking them and his stockings until he finally took Miranda in his arms and carried her to the bed. Once there, he laid her on the bedclothes, admiring how sinfully beautiful she looked in nothing more than her garters and embroidered stockings. She was all pink and cream, curves and sleek, feminine allure. He had to have a taste.

His cock rigid and aching, he parted her thighs and buried his face between her legs, concentrating all of his attentions upon her pleasure. His tongue flew over swollen, hot flesh, the taste of her—musky and sweet—better than her most decadent cream ice. Cupping her rump in his hands, he held her to him like a feast and devoured her, licking and sucking, fucking her with his tongue until she was crying out and coming on his face, and he was coated in her dew everywhere.

And then he couldn't wait. She was still throbbing with the contractions from her climax when he rose over her, guiding his length into her. Slick heat greeted him, her muscles lovingly clinging to his cock as if welcoming him home. She was so perfect, wrapped snugly around him, her body soft and perfumed and lush beneath his. He was undone, losing himself as he thrust in and out of her, his ballocks already drawn taut.

She raked her nails down his back, wrapping her legs around her hips as she matched his rhythm, pumping into him, taking him deep. The time for games was over. They were mindlessly one, both of them seeking, straining for their release. It was messy and it was perfect, his hips slamming into hers again and again, until she had slid up the bed and into the headboard. Cradling her head with one of his hands, he continued pounding into her, his knuckles rapping off the carved mahogany as she clutched him tighter, her inner walls milking his cock.

He suckled a pointed nipple, wringing a moan from her, and reached between their joined bodies to find her clitoris and stroke. She convulsed on him with so much force that she nearly drove him from her, but he shoved his cock deep, riding out the ripples of her release as she came, drenching him anew. The urge to spend inside her rose up, so strong. To fill her up with his seed, fill her so full of him, to watch it seep from her pussy afterward, to know that she was covered in him...

He tore his mouth from her breast, muttering a savage oath. Reluctantly, Rhys withdrew, fisting his cock as he came all over her belly and inner thighs. The sight was erotic— Miranda lying there with lashings of his seed decorating her pale form. He rubbed it into her skin, claiming her in the only way he could.

And then he collapsed atop her, heart pounding, not caring about the sticky mess coating them both. They could take a bath together later. He would wash her clean and then relish every moment of making her filthy again.

His wilted prick twitched anew at the thought.

Miranda held him tightly to her, a soft chuckle stealing from her. "Again?"

He kissed her slowly, lingeringly, feeding her the taste of herself on his lips. "For you, it would seem I'm insatiable."

"Mmm," she hummed, her brilliant gaze dipping to his mouth. "I feel the same way."

Rhys took her lips again, sending up a fervent, futile prayer that the next month would last forever.

CHAPTER 19

*M*iranda woke with a jolt, realizing she had fallen into a deep, sated slumber after making love with Rhys. The lamps were out, and the fire had burned to glowing coals in the grate, leaving the bedchamber darkened, nothing but the moonlight stealing in through the curtains for illumination.

What was the hour?

She sat up in bed, feeling about in the darkness for the pocket watch he kept on a bedside table to facilitate her returns home. Miranda snatched it up, peering through the murky light to see the time. In all the weeks of their clandestine meetings, she had never lingered so long at his house in St John's Wood.

And the weeks had passed by in a flurry of heated kisses, sumptuous dinners, and decadent lovemaking.

Three days.

Impossible to believe that was all they had remaining.

Her heart stuttered at the reminder that their time together was rapidly dwindling, just like the night and its protective darkness likely were. The pocket watch slid from her grasp, falling to the Axminster with a muffled thump.

"Miranda?" Rhys's deep voice cut through the silence from next to her in bed, slumberous and raspy. "What is it, darling?"

"I must have fallen asleep," she explained. "I was trying to find the time, but I dropped your watch."

His arm slid around her bare waist beneath the bedclothes, warm and possessive. "Don't go."

She was tempted to linger. He could never know how much she treasured these moments alone, when they were close in the aftermath of their shared passion, all seemingly right with the world. When their affair was over, she would return to these memories, she knew, again and again.

Hollow comfort.

"I must," she told him softly, hating that she could not stay here with him, that she could not wake in his arms to the morning light.

That they could never acknowledge what they were to each other. But there was no future together. It was an inevitable truth she faced each morning that took her one day closer to what would be their last.

He pulled her gently against his chest, nuzzling her throat. "You are the stars in my night sky, glittering and mysterious. I want you all day long, and yet you leave me before the rising of the sun."

His words were unexpectedly poetic, tinged by his flair for the melodramatic. So very Rhys.

Oh, how she loved this man. How she would miss him when they soon had to part.

Miranda sniffed, blinking furiously against impending tears.

Three more days, she told herself. *It isn't over yet.*

"Such is the way of it for us," she reminded him softly,

caressing his forearm, which was still slung around her waist. "I need to return home whilst it's yet dark."

"Or you could stay here." He cupped her breast, gently massaging. "Remaining would be far more pleasurable than leaving, I assure you."

She smiled sadly, desire sparking back into flame despite the heavy emotion weighing on her heart. "You needn't convince me of that. There is nothing I would like better than to stay in this bed with you all night and all day."

"Mmm." He pinched her nipple lightly, sending a twinge of desperate yearning to pool between her thighs. "Then why don't you?"

"You know why." She took his wrist in a firm grasp and plucked his hand from her breast. "Besides, I shall see you later tonight, won't I?"

"Of course, but you don't even have to go to your school today. Why not linger just a bit longer?"

"Because I cannot risk being seen returning to my home at dawn," she countered. "Particularly not in a brougham that isn't mine."

"Blast."

She slipped from the bed and retrieved his pocket watch from the floor, holding it up to the moonlight to discover that the hour was even later than she had supposed. "My goodness, it's nearly dawn."

Panic set over her, chasing any lingering desire.

"Bloody hell," Rhys grumbled, rising as well. "Don't worry, darling. I'll see to it that you're safely returned to your home before the sun rises."

By lamplight, they both hastened to dress, Rhys playing lady's maid for her and helping her to fasten her corset and button her gown back into place before restoring her hair to its customary chignon. He threw on his trousers and other garments with a swift agility that suggested this was not the first time he had dressed in a hurry. She tried not to think about that as they dashed to his waiting brougham together.

And as the carriage bounded over the roads that would return her to her modest home, she tried not to think about the women who would, inevitably, take secret early-morning carriage rides with Rhys. The women who would have the privilege of smoothing down his wayward golden waves, of lacing their fingers through his, and of leaning into the comforting strength of his solid frame.

By the time they reached the small house she shared with her maid of all work, the disapproving White, the sun was indeed rising in a leaden London sky. Dawn was painting gray light over the city that was bustling back to life. Securing her hat and veil, she began to descend from the carriage.

"Miranda, wait."

Rhys's soft call had her turning back to him.

"You forgot something."

Her brow furrowed. "Oh?"

What could it be? She had everything she had brought with her the night before, down to her reticule and gloves.

"This." He moved toward her swiftly, flipping back her veil and taking her lips in a kiss that left her breathless. "I'm going to call on you later today."

"Rhys," she protested. "You can't."

It was far too risky. Too obvious.

"Of course I can. Please, darling. For once, I want to call upon you like an ordinary suitor. We can have tea and be boring, and I won't even talk about your nipples."

She laughed, charmed in spite of herself. And tempted too.

"I don't think it would be wise," she hedged, worrying her lower lip.

Rhys kissed her again. "To the devil with wisdom. I want

a normal afternoon with you. There is no school today to otherwise distract or keep you from me. Say yes."

Miranda hesitated.

"Please." The boyish smile of hope he gave her melted her heart.

"Very well," she relented before she could think better of her capitulation. "Yes."

"Thank you." He kissed her once more. "Until later, kitten."

As she turned to go a second time, still dazed, her heart beating far too fast, she thought she saw movement from the corner of her eye. But when she turned in that direction, there was no one there.

Perhaps it had been her veil, tricking her into thinking she had seen someone.

Yes, surely that must have been it.

THE EARL OF AMMONDALE's pale gaze was as glacial as his demeanor.

"You're certain of this?" he demanded, his voice resonating with quiet fury.

Viscount Roberts, whose broken nose had finally healed, smiled at his friend. They were discreetly seated at a private table in their club, enjoying cigars. "I'm certain. I have suspected the Duke of Whitby and the former countess were involved. However, I've never been able to witness them together until this morning, just before dawn, when I was traversing her street on my way back home."

The sight of one Miss Miranda Lenox, former Countess of Ammondale, descending from an unmarked carriage at dawn and being soundly kissed by the Duke of Whitby had been just what Roberts had been waiting for. Ever since his ignominious return to London, with a badly beaten face he'd needed to hide, thanks to the sin of meeting Miss Lenox in the gardens at Wingfield Hall, Roberts had been waiting. Biding his time. Watching. And his patience had finally paid off that morning after several weeks of being thwarted by similar carriages and London traffic.

"I had hoped she would have seen the error of her grievous sins when the Marquess of Waring left for America and she remained here in London," Ammondale said, his mien grim. "I couldn't have imagined that she would make herself a whore for another man so soon, particularly given that she began that disgusting little school of cookery. I had hoped she might have a modicum of care for what remained of her reputation, in deference to the damage she has done to my good name."

"Regrettably, she does not," Roberts said. "Or else she would not be cavorting with such a despicable rake."

Ammondale eyed him. "What were you doing out at such an hour?"

"I was returning home from a call to Roberta," he said, referring to his mistress.

Although, in truth, he had been waiting for the carriage he had seen Miss Lenox get into at her school to return with her in it. As it happened, the process had taken hours. She and Whitby had clearly been enjoying each other's company.

Roberts had been anticipating his revenge ever since he had been unceremoniously removed from the Wicked Dukes Society. Ever since he had been attacked by Whitby, Kingham, Richford, and Riverdale. Yes, he would gain his revenge. One person at a time.

Miss Lenox was first, and she was about to learn that she had made a grievous error by whoring herself for the Duke of Whitby.

"Thank you for entrusting me with this information,"

Ammondale said then. "She cannot be allowed to continue making a disgrace of herself."

"What do you intend to do?" Roberts asked, hope rising.

Ammondale gave him a chilling smile. "I'm going to ruin the bitch."

MIRANDA'S MAID of all work greeted her with unsmiling solemnity that afternoon when she returned from a call to her friend Rosamund, the Duchess of Camden. Rosamund was one of the few society ladies who had remained a true and loyal friend to her in the wake of her scandalous divorce from Ammondale, along with Lottie, the Duchess of Brandon.

"You have a guest awaiting you in your sitting room, madam," White announced.

With her modest means following the divorce, the lone domestic had been all Miranda could afford for her home. Now that she had the funds from Rhys, however, the temptation to replace the perpetually Friday-faced woman with a servant who was more congenial was strong.

"Thank you," she told White, stomach flipping with a mixture of worry and anticipation.

Rhys was here. And he was earlier than she had anticipated. Oh, what had she been thinking in the midst of the night when she had agreed to such a nonsensical request from him? Paying a call upon her as if he were a suitor.

It was dangerous.

Foolish.

Stealing about under the cover of darkness was one thing, but at least they could be covert and surreptitious. Calls by the light of day could be cause for wagging tongues, particularly given Rhys's reputation and Miranda's own past scandal.

Miranda removed her hat, wrap, and gloves whilst the maid of all work lingered, unsmiling.

"The guest in question is a *gentleman* caller," White added, her disapproval evident.

"Indeed," Miranda said, feigning a lack of concern she didn't feel as she hung up her wrap.

"I warned him it was most unseemly, his presence here in an unmarried lady's residence," White added sharply.

Miranda almost reminded the other woman that she had been married once, but mentioning her divorce seemed counterproductive to White's bilious constitution.

She smiled instead. "Thank you for your forethought, White. I do believe he is here to discuss some business related to my school. Nothing untoward, I assure you."

Ha! If she only knew. Thank heavens White was a heavy sleeper. Miranda had become adept at sneaking in and out of the house to the sound of the maid of all work's rhythmic snores.

"As you say, madam." The maid of all work gave a stern sniff of disdain.

Miranda truly did not think she could carry on with such a supercilious woman in her household, but that was a matter for later. For now, Rhys was awaiting her. "I will see to him, then."

"Shall I bring a tray of tea?" the maid of all work wanted to know.

"I'll ring for it," she decided, knowing Rhys well enough by now to understand that despite what he had promised about behaving, anything could happen.

She had no wish for White to walk in upon a tableau that would set her tongue wagging. He was a rogue to the core after all. And Miranda was woefully incapable of resisting him, particularly when he plied his rakish charm.

Leaving White at the door, Miranda made her way to the sitting room at the hall's end. As she crossed the threshold, she halted, shock washing over her. For the familiar figure awaiting her within—tall, dark-haired, and blue-eyed—was decidedly not Rhys. Rather, he was a dear friend who had sacrificed much on her behalf so that she could escape her hateful union with Ammondale.

"Waring," she greeted, astonished.

"Miranda." The Marquess of Waring offered her an elegant bow that seemed better suited to a formal gathering than to her modest private sitting room.

In the clutter of her books and pictures, her writing desk and scribblings and models for ice caves and working proto-types, he was decidedly out of place. And far more serious than her dear friend ordinarily was.

"What are you doing here?" she asked, still astonished at his presence.

Following her scandalous divorce, he had decamped across the Atlantic. He had business dealings that took him there, and he had graciously wished to distance himself to quiet the salacious gossip concerning the two of them, none of which was true, had the gossips but known it.

Waring gave her a small smile, clasping his hands behind his back. "You are not pleased to see me, then?"

"Of course I am," she reassured him, moving deeper into the room.

For she *was* happy to see him. His letters had been few and concise. She had missed his steadfast presence in her life, which had begun during the misery of her new marriage and had lasted the duration.

She reached him and opened her arms. Waring embraced her as he always did, with tenderness and yet reverent care, as if she were fine Sèvres porcelain he feared might break lest he grow too exuberant. Miranda rejoiced in the familiar, comforting warmth of his strong arms, noting he held her just a moment longer than strictly necessary before releasing her and stepping away.

His light-blue gaze roamed her face, as if searching for signs of change. She wondered if he found any and treated him to the same. His hair was longer than fashionable, and he had grown a beard in his absence. Perhaps his new hirsute appearance was down to his time in America.

"You look well," he said at last, breaking the almost awkward silence.

"As do you," she returned politely. "You have a beard now."

He scrubbed a hand over his jaw, and she noted for the first time that the dark hair was stippled with hints of silver. "You don't like it?"

"I suppose I'm not accustomed to it."

"I thought it rather dashing."

"I think it very American."

They shared a laugh, and suddenly, it was as if he had never been gone, the initial uncertainty of their reunion shattered like an unwanted pot tossed into the dustbin.

"I've missed you, Ran."

His words were tinged with emotion she didn't recognize, even if his old, familiar endearment for her was.

"I have missed you as well." She gestured to the settee behind him. "Shall we sit? I'll ring for tea. How long are you staying in England?"

"Tea would be just the thing."

Miranda moved to the bellpull and gave it a tug before she turned back to the seating arrangement.

"And as for how long I'm staying, forever, I should think," Waring added.

He said the last as Miranda settled in an overstuffed chair opposite the settee. The act was undertaken with a distinct lack of grace, thanks, in part, to her renewed surprise.

"You mean you won't be returning to America?" she asked.

Just prior to his departure, Waring had been considering the move a permanent one, pleased to leave his estates in the care of his capable younger brother.

He shook his head now. "I discovered there was something of great import I left behind."

The look he gave her was meaningful, and just as quickly as the mood between them had lightened, becoming familiar, it shifted yet again. There was a new intensity in his eyes, in his voice. Almost as if… But no, surely not. Waring considered her a sister. He had always said so, and she felt for him as if he were another brother, only one to whom she was even closer than George.

"I expect you must have missed your brother and your estates," she guessed.

"I missed more than that," Waring told her quietly.

She blinked, thinking she was misreading the expression on his face, one of such honed concentration. It was a look he hadn't given her since he had volunteered himself as sacrificial lamb in the matter of her divorce from Ammondale. One that had been so fleeting at the time that she had decided she must have imagined it.

"What else did you miss?" she asked, fearing she knew the answer.

"Do you need to question it, Ran?"

She was spared from having to answer by the discreet tap on the door signifying White had arrived with the tea. Apparently, White must have had it at the ready, and Miranda had never been so thankful for her disapproving maid of all work as she was in that moment. The bustling presence of the steel-haired domestic broke the subtle tension of the room. When she had excused herself and Miranda and Waring were once more alone, Miranda prepared tea for them.

The distraction was a welcome one, for there were emotions in her old friend's eyes she had never thought to see. Emotions that made her belly tighten with dread, because she could not return them. Not after Rhys.

In silence, she presented Waring with his dish of tea.

"Just as I like it," he said. "You always remember."

"It is a small thing," she protested. "I remember the way everyone takes their tea."

"Is it small?" he returned, his expression unsmiling. "I do not find it so."

"Perhaps you should," she cautioned, fraught with the expectations she suddenly sensed in him.

Expectations which made no sense. He had never treated her as anything more than a sister. Had never expressed a masculine interest in her. And yet, here he was in her sitting room, staring at her with a far too warm regard, saying things that her old dear chum would never have said.

"Tell me how you have been in my absence," he urged, seemingly content to change the subject for now as he sipped at his tea. "I understand the scandal has withered on the vine."

"And yet the vine persists." She couldn't keep the bitterness from her tone as she thought of the wagging tongues that continued to whisper about her, the threats from people like Lord Roberts that were never far.

"It will, in a way, until you marry again," Waring said, his voice solemn.

"I have no intention of marrying again, so I suppose I shall always be forced to endure it." She managed a smile she didn't feel.

It wasn't that she wanted to wed, she reminded herself sternly, tamping down the traitorous twinges in her heart that had become more insistent over the course of the last month she had spent as Rhys's lover. But there were times when she wished she didn't have to face the fear of losing everything she had struggled to build because of her past and the way it would forever taint her future.

"Perhaps you might be persuaded to change your mind on the matter," Waring proposed mildly. "Enough time has passed since the divorce. You are a young and vibrant woman. Everyone will expect you to marry again."

She settled her tea in the saucer with a rattle. "They can expect whatever they like. It doesn't mean that I shall do so."

"I didn't mean to suggest that you should wed to appease polite society's expectations," Waring said softly, "but for your own sake. Do you not wish for a husband and a family?"

Her heart gave a pang at his question. For she knew what her answer must be.

"I have always wanted children," she allowed, "but not at the expense of my freedom. I found the price too much to pay."

"With Ammondale, yes. But have you ever considered marrying someone else?"

For a wild, foolish moment, she thought of Rhys. But then she banished all such ridiculous notions. He had told her in no uncertain terms that he never wanted to wed. He wanted her as his mistress, not as his wife. She had accepted it, just as she had accepted that she had fallen hopelessly in love with him.

"I have not," she told her friend calmly, hoping he would grasp her meaning.

"You and I have always had an understanding, I believed," he said with painstaking care, proving her wrong. "Have we not?"

She opened her mouth to answer him, uncertain of how to proceed, when another interruption distracted her. This time, however, it wasn't White knocking efficiently at the sitting room door to announce her arrival, however. Rather, it was the door opening to reveal Rhys, who strode into the room with his hat still dangling from his fingers and his gloves clasped firmly in one hand.

A knot of dread tightened in her stomach.

His stormy gaze flicked from Waring to Miranda, lingering on her, and she felt the effect of his stare like a jolt of electricity. It was as if he sucked all the air from the room, and her heart instantly beat faster.

"Good afternoon, my dear," he drawled. "Your maidservant informed me you already had a gentleman caller, but I didn't think you would mind the intrusion since we are meant to be taking tea together."

What must he think, finding her here alone with Waring? She wished she knew, but his countenance was carefully neutral.

He bowed formally to her and then turned to Waring. "The Duke of Whitby, sir."

"Your Grace." Waring inclined his head. "I am Waring."

Rhys's golden brow rose. "Ah. I don't believe we've traveled in the same circles."

"No," Waring clipped, his expression closed and stern.

"Would you care to sit?" Miranda invited. "We were taking tea when you arrived."

What was the protocol for having tea with one's present lover and the man everyone thought to be one's former lover? A man who had just intimated that he wished to marry her? Heat crept up Miranda's throat.

Rhys flashed her another look she couldn't quite read. "Tea would be lovely, but I confess, I didn't expect a small gathering."

"Waring has only just returned from abroad," she explained, guilt weighing heavily upon her. "His call was a pleasant surprise."

She didn't blame Rhys for his reaction. Had she walked in upon him indulging in tea with another woman, she didn't know what she would have done. But what other choice did she have? She couldn't turn away Waring. Not after all he had done to help her. Her loyalties were hopelessly confused and torn.

"A pleasant surprise indeed," Rhys said dryly, seating himself in the second chair.

Miranda dutifully fixed him a cup, only belatedly realizing Waring's shrewd gaze pinned to her as she added sugar and milk to Rhys's liking.

"You are familiar with how the duke prefers his tea," Waring commented lightly enough, but she heard the underlying question.

"She is familiar with how I prefer a great many things," Rhys was quick to add, flashing a smug smile in Waring's direction.

The implication was clear. She would give him a stern piece of her mind later when they were alone. For now, she could do nothing but attempt to salvage the civility of the conversation.

"Such as cream ice," Miranda added pointedly through gritted teeth as she passed him his tea. "His Grace has taken an interest in my school, and he has been helping me by encouraging the members of his set to use my employment agency."

"How generous of him," Waring said, his lip appearing to curl ever so slightly beneath his new whiskers in a sneer of contempt.

The two gentlemen did not like each other, and that much was plain. What Miranda could not tell for certain was whether Waring was trying to protect her or if he considered Rhys competition. If the latter were the case, that meant the man she had considered a dear friend for years had somehow developed tender feelings for her, and she didn't know what to do with that knowledge.

Or what to do about it.

"I'm a generous chap," Rhys said with a grin before taking a careful sip of his tea. "My dear Miranda, this is heavenly."

"Is it?" she asked, knowing he was partial to coffee rather than tea.

"Mmm," he hummed. "Much like everything you make. I say, have you sampled Miranda's cream ice and cornets, Warting?"

Thankfully, Miranda had yet to lift her own cup to her lips, or she would have sprayed it everywhere at Rhys's less-than-subtle dig. The outrageous devil.

"*Waring*, Your Grace," she corrected him gently. "I believe you misheard."

"Quite." He sent Waring a patently insincere smile. "Do forgive me, my lord."

"Perhaps your hearing is going," Waring returned. "I understand it happens to those of us who have reached a certain age."

"And I am certain you would know, given the profusion of hoary hair in your beard," Rhys quipped.

"Miranda was just telling me how lovely my beard is," Waring proclaimed. "Weren't you, Ran?"

"Ran?" This time, it was Rhys's lip that curled.

Miranda was beginning to feel as if she were a bone that had been laid between two dogs, watching as they bared their teeth and snarled and growled and otherwise attempted to stake their claim and scare the other away. It was a most unsettling sensation, and not one she particularly liked.

"His lordship and I are old and fond acquaintances,"

Miranda interrupted, giving the both of them a look of stern admonishment. "Waring is a dear friend to me, just as His Grace is also a cherished friend."

"And I am honored to be your *friend*, my dear," Rhys told her gallantly, putting an indecent emphasis on friend, as if she had said lover instead.

"Just what are your intentions where Miranda is concerned, Whitby?" Waring asked, taking Miranda by surprise yet again.

He had always been staunchly protective of her, particularly when it came to Ammondale, but she had believed it was a brotherly protection. That of a friend. Not a lover. However, given the way he had been acting ever since his surprise appearance in her sitting room, she could no longer be sure.

Rhys gave Waring a withering look. "I'm sure it's not any of your concern what my intentions are, as you suggest, if indeed I have any. Although, I daresay, the same could be said of you. Did you not cause Miranda suffering enough? An honorable man would have remained in America and allowed the gossips to wear themselves out."

Oh dear. Rhys *did* know precisely who Waring was to her. She ought not to be surprised, she supposed. He had known that the gossips had called her the Fallen Countess. It stood to reason that he would know the rest of the sordid tale too. The urge to explain was strong, but not now when she and Rhys were not alone.

"An honorable man wouldn't have a reputation like yours," Waring returned, his voice rising.

"An honorable man would not go sniffing about the skirts of a married woman," Rhys countered.

"Ha!" Waring sneered. "Do not tell me you have never cuckolded a man. I'll not believe it for an instant."

Miranda had endured quite enough of their masculine

posturing. At the moment, she was every bit as cross with Waring as she was with Rhys.

"That is enough," she interrupted sharply. "The two of you cease this nonsense at once. I do not wish to hear another word of it."

Their gazes swung to her, both blue and yet each so different. One turned her insides to molten fire, and the other made her feel safe and comforted. One was dangerous, and the other was innocuous. One had helped her in her time of need, and the other had invaded her world and turned it upside down in the very best way.

Still, their behavior was equally childish and abominable.

The heat that had been crawling up her throat reached her cheeks. "I'll not be fought over as if I am a bone and the two of you are territorial mongrels, snarling and snapping your jaws. If neither of you can keep a civil tongue, then you may go."

"I believe she's talking to you, Wartly," Rhys taunted.

Waring glared back at him, his fists clenched. "Clearly, you were the recipient of her harangue."

"*The both of you,*" she interrupted, frustrated with their antics. "I was speaking to the both of you."

"Miranda," Rhys began.

"Ran," Waring said simultaneously, a note of hurt in his protest.

She replaced her dish of tea on the tray and shot to her feet. "I think it best if the two of you go."

Miranda hated the hurt on her old friend's face. He had just crossed an ocean—and seemingly to return to her. But the expectations he had arrived with did not match her own. She cared for Waring, but she loved him as a brother.

And as for Rhys, he had her heart, but loving him did not matter when there could be no future for them together. He had made his opinion of marriage more than clear. His offer to her had been finite and founded purely in the physical.

She had to think of her school. Of her own future. Before her was a stark representation of the choices she must make. And she knew, to her marrow, what she must do. Even if it broke her heart.

"Please," she added, emotion making her voice thick. "For my sake. If you both will excuse me?"

Without waiting for their responses, she hastened from the sitting room, leaving the two bickering men and the cooling tea behind her. The time had come for her to put an end to her folly before it was too late.

CHAPTER 20

*R*hys stared at the crumpled missive on his desk, the words standing in stark relief to mock him, still scarcely able to believe what he was reading two hours after it had been delivered that morning before he'd even broken his fast.

As our time together has reached its inevitable conclusion, I must look to the safeguarding of my reputation...

I will never forget the weeks we had together...
I cannot help but to think that, in the best interest of my school, our association must conclude now before it is too late...

"A fucking note," he growled at the offending letter, which he had crushed in a fit of rage upon his first reading.

He had nearly thrown it into the fire just to watch the

hateful thing catch flame and burn to ash. But at the last moment, he had changed his mind, opening the missive once more and flattening it on the desk in his study.

All they had shared.

Five weeks of unparalleled ecstasy.

And Miranda had ended it between them with a bloody letter, as if he were a stranger who had requested an audience with her and she was politely denying him. As if what had been between them had meant nothing to her.

With every woman in his past, Rhys had always been the first to sever their ties. He was first to grow weary of their arrangement. First to offer jewels as a conciliatory gesture for a woman who inevitably was distressed by the completion of their affair. He was the one who walked away. Who took a new lover. Who sought pleasure in another's arms.

But now, Miranda—*his Miranda*, who knew how to bring him to his knees with a mere laugh or smile—had thrown him over. There was no doubt in his mind as to the reason either. Her lover, the insufferably smug Marquess of Waring, had returned from America.

And she had gone straight back into that bastard's arms. He should have known yesterday when he had arrived at her house and found them together and then later, when she had sent round a note crying off their customary tryst for the night. At the time, Rhys had put it down to her ire with him, which had been evident when she had dismissed him at tea after he had traded barbs with Waring. He had expected it would fade by today. How wrong he had been.

Such a cozy vignette Miranda and Waring had made, he thought bitterly now, enjoying tea together. He had known, of course, that Waring was the lover who had enabled her to achieve her divorce from Ammondale. But what he hadn't expected was that the bastard would return unannounced from America and lay claim to Rhys's woman.

The realization was akin to a knife to the gut, the betrayal so bitter and vicious that he could taste it on his tongue along with the whisky he'd been pouring down his throat. He wanted to tear the Marquess of bloody Waring limb from limb. To pull down the walls of this blasted study. To smash everything in his sight that was glass. To go directly to Miranda's tiny rooms and demand that she look him in the eye and tell him she truly wanted to end their affair instead of sending him some cowardly goddamned note.

With a roar, he picked up a crystal inkwell and hurled it into the fireplace, the resulting crash failing to feed the blood lust raging within him.

A knock sounded at his study door.

"Rhys?"

His sister's voice.

With a heavy sigh, he passed a hand over his face. "Come."

The door opened, and Rhiannon peered around the edge. "Is it safe?"

"I suppose you heard that."

She nodded, somber. "What did you break?"

He gestured to the silver writing set on his desk, now bereft of half its contents. "An inkwell."

Cautiously, she stepped inside, closing the door behind her. "Something has you overset?"

An understatement of vast proportions, that.

He grimaced. "One could say so."

Belatedly, he realized he ought to stand in deference and shot to his feet, prowling around his desk with the energy of a caged lion as he began to pace the Axminster. His sister watched him in the manner he imagined she might observe a poisonous snake, wondering if it would strike.

"What do you want, Rhiannon?" he asked curtly, his mood hardly improved by her presence.

It still nettled that he had yet to ferret out what had

happened during her supposed trip to Great-Aunt Bitsy. Thus far, that august woman had yet to respond to his letter of inquiry. And short of venturing to her himself, he wasn't likely to have his answer.

"I intended to speak with you about something," Rhiannon said hesitantly, "but perhaps it can wait for a more opportune time."

He sighed again. "Has it anything to do with your visit to Great-Aunt Bitsy?"

She looked hastily away, but he didn't miss the guilt in her countenance. "No, of course not. Why would you ask?"

"Because I know you're lying about your supposed stay with her."

Whisky and frayed emotions had loosened his tongue.

Rhiannon's head swiveled back in his direction, her look startled. "I'm not lying. We have been over this before."

"Yes, we have. And I'm not any more inclined to believe you now than I was nearly a month ago." He raked a hand through his hair, frustrated and furious and all but crawling out of his bloody skin. "Just so you are aware, when I find out who he is, I'm going to take great pleasure in killing him. Slowly."

Rhiannon blanched. "Rhys."

Rhys was being beastly and he knew it, but damn it, Miranda had thrown him over. He was furious with himself. With her. With Waring. He wanted to burn the world to the ground. To claw the sun from the sky. To blot out the stars and the fucking moon.

"Sister," he countered grimly. "I warn you, I'm in no mood to speak gently. But my response remains the same. If I should discover some scurrilous rogue had the temerity to ruin you, I'll flay him alive."

He meant those words to his soul. By God, he was meant to protect his sister. He hated that he had failed her. Hated that Mater had been so absorbed in her own diversions that she had failed to notice Rhiannon was missing until it had been far too late.

He also hated the Marquess of Waring.

But that was a matter that would need to be settled later. With his fists.

"No one ruined me," Rhiannon said, frowning at him. "I am a woman grown, and I make my own choices."

He didn't like the sound of that.

"Apparently, poor ones."

She jolted as if he had slapped her, and he regretted the harshness of his words, though not the emotion behind them.

"You are being cruel."

"I am being pragmatic. The world is a vile swamp rife with betrayals and disappointments, and there is nothing polite society loves better than the downfall of one of its own." He thought of Miranda again, and something inside him seized.

Was it fear that had made her turn away from him? Did she fret over her reputation? Was there something Waring could offer her that Rhys had not? Worse—his gut clenched —did she love Waring?

"Speaking of such matters," Rhiannon interrupted gently, moving toward him and holding out what appeared to be a copy of a gossip rag. "There is something that I thought perhaps you would wish to see."

He had eschewed the morning's paper and breakfast after receiving Miranda's note. Instead, he had retreated to the haven of his study, where, curtains tightly closed from the outside world, he had drowned himself in the paltry comfort of a bottle of spirits. The last thing he wanted was to sit and read the goddamned scandal broth in the mood he was in.

"I can assure you that there is presently nothing I would

like to see at all," he snarled. "If you've naught to offer other than mawkish nonsense, you may as well go. I'm not fit company for anyone at the moment."

His bloody stubborn sister would not be deterred. She followed him across the room to the mantel over the fireplace, which currently possessed several items that seemed to call for a fate similar to the inkwell. Smashing things didn't solve any problems, but ye gods, it felt satisfying.

Not nearly as satisfying as smashing the Marquess of Waring's self-righteous face. But that would be remedied soon enough.

"I do think you may wish to read a certain article, brother," Rhiannon told him gently, thrusting the newspaper toward him. "It appears to concern you and someone referred to as the Fallen Countess."

The blood felt as if it leached from him.

"I beg your pardon?"

"I do believe you are the Duke of W. in question," his sister said, giving him a look of tender sympathy.

He snatched the paper from her. "Where?"

"Page three," Rhiannon told him.

Rhys practically tore the newspaper in half as he turned to the page, his eyes instantly falling upon the article in question. He read hastily, stopping before he had even finished, having seen quite enough.

"Bloody hell," he swore viciously, tossing the filth into the fireplace where it belonged.

"Just so." Rhiannon patted him on the back. "You're in love with her, aren't you?"

He stiffened in shock. "In love?"

Rhys wasn't in love.

He didn't fall in love.

He was the Duke of Whitby, conscienceless rakehell, careless rogue, unrepentant voluptuary. He damn well didn't *have* a fucking heart. Such maudlin tripe was for females. It only existed in fanciful books that were written for wide-eyed virgins who weren't yet jaded enough to realize that love was naught but a fiction.

"Yes." His sister was solemn as she looked up at him, her blue eyes so like his, far too knowing for a young woman of her tender years. "You've fallen in love with her, haven't you?"

He stared at Rhiannon, aghast, unable to speak.

Because she was right, curse her. He *had* fallen in love with Miranda Lenox. That was this feeling, this weight in his chest, this deep and abiding rightness he felt whenever she was in his arms.

Love was real, and he was an idiot.

"What are you going to do about it?" Rhiannon asked.

"I'm going to marry her," he said hoarsely, knowing it was what he had to do.

What he wanted to do. Nothing less than a lifetime with Miranda would suffice. All he had to do was persuade her.

"Good." Rhiannon smiled, but he swore that there remained a touch of sadness in her countenance. "I have always wished for a sister, and I have a feeling I will like this Fallen Countess of yours very much."

"You will." Impulsively, he drew his sister into an embrace, hugging her tightly. "Thank you, Rhi."

She hugged him back. "You are most welcome, dearest brother."

MIRANDA SAT in her quiet classroom where the ingredients had been dutifully assembled for the hot *entrée* class she was meant to be teaching this morning. Two long tables with empty chairs faced her, mocking as the silence. Not a single pupil had arrived.

She had dressed herself with care that morning, pressing a cold cloth to her tear-swollen eyes after dashing off the letter to Rhys ending their arrangement. With a judicious—if trembling—hand, she had applied pearl powder to her reddened nose and cheeks. Her hope had been that no one would take note of her altered appearance or inquire after the reason for her sorrow.

Now, however, it would seem that all her efforts had been for naught.

Because there were no eager young ladies awaiting her instruction. No cooks desiring to hone their skills. The Lenox School of Cookery was as empty as Miranda's heart.

As she stared at the fresh herbs and neatly chopped vegetables before her, tears began to blur her vision. Tears she had done her utmost to keep at bay since she had first settled upon what she must do. Tears she had failed miserably in banishing. Instead, they had fallen, becoming full-bodied sobs that had echoed in the stillness of her little bedchamber.

By dawn, her decision had not been any more impossible than it had felt the night before. She'd scarcely slept at all, dread and agony keeping her in a tight, unmerciful grip throughout. But she had done what she did best. She had faced her obligations. Miranda had always known her divorce from Ammondale would irrevocably change her life. What she never could have known, however, was how it would taint every action that followed, the one rotten apple that turned a bushel.

She had told herself sternly that her choice had been made. That severing all ties with Rhys was for the best. That all good things must come to an end.

And so they all had.

It was over. Her arrangement with Rhys. Her school. What had remained of her reputation.

She had lost it all.

She had nothing aside from her molds and ice caves and the ingredients before her. It wouldn't surprise Miranda to find that even White had abandoned her when she returned home. And what could she expect? The tainted divorcée, the scandalous Fallen Countess, had proven everyone right in the end.

She was an immoral woman. The Duke of Whitby's mistress.

Society's most notorious scandal rag had published the announcement for all London just that morning.

Mrs. Kirkeland had reluctantly shown Miranda the article after the young lad who helped with carrying about and storing their ingredients had given it to her. Miranda had been shocked to read a salacious account of her affair with Rhys, from the wicked country house party in Hertfordshire to their time in London, complete with reports of her late-night jaunts to a certain house in St John's Wood.

Most particularly proven correct about Miranda had been her former husband, the horrified Earl of A. who, by all accounts, had feared the former Lady A. would find an ignoble end. She didn't doubt that Ammondale was somehow behind the article. It was not without irony, of course, that he would prove the architect of her downfall.

Had she not been so desolate, Miranda might have laughed.

As it was, a hysterical bubble of something worked its way up, from deep inside her, and emerged as something that rather resembled the bleat of a sheep.

"Ran."

She looked up, blinking furiously to clear her vision.

Waring stood at the threshold of her barren classroom. How she wished it were Rhys in his place.

"Waring," she managed. "What are you doing here?"

"That infernal gossip rag," he explained, striding toward her, pity in his voice. "I heard about it this morning, and I knew I had to find you."

Good heavens, did all London know about her ignominy already? It would certainly seem that way, particularly given her lack of pupils.

A sob went through her at the reminder of all she'd lost. "You shouldn't have come. I'll only sully your reputation. Have you not heard? I am a fallen woman in all ways now. So immoral that no lady of good breeding would dare to attend one of my classes."

He reached her, dropping to his knees at her side. "I don't care about any of that. The gossips can be damned. Marry me, Ran."

Miranda stared at him, shocked. "Did you not read the article?"

"Of course not. I don't care about such drivel. All I care about is you. I'm in love with you, Ran. I always have been."

Her mouth fell open. "In love? With me?"

He searched her gaze. "Did you not know?"

"No," she admitted. "I had no notion."

"Why do you think I allowed my good name to be dragged through the mud in the divorce from Ammondale?" he asked softly, taking her hand in his.

"Because you knew how miserable I was, and you vowed to help me."

"And because I am selfish. I wanted you as my wife, Ran. But I was willing to wait until you were ready to marry again. That is why I went to America. I wanted to give you the chance to restore your reputation on your own terms and pursue your school." He paused, shaking his head. "I can see now that it was a mistake to go. I should have stayed here, where you needed me."

"I thought you wanted to go to America," she said weakly, feeling suddenly drained of all emotion.

"I wanted what was best for you. I feared that if I would remain, the scandal would only grow worse, but that if I left, it would die down."

"You… I cannot… I don't understand."

"I want to marry you," he said again. "It's why I returned. It's why I helped you to obtain the divorce from Ammondale."

"Oh dear God." She pressed a hand over her mouth, stifling another sob.

How wretched she felt. Waring had claimed he was selfish, but surely it was she who was far more so. She had accepted his aid, thinking them friends, never seeing what seemed plain to her now—that Waring had feelings for her that were decidedly more than merely friendly in nature.

"Marry me, Ran," he said, his expression hopeful. "Please."

"The scandal, Waring. You're not thinking properly."

"I don't care what happened with Whitby. It doesn't matter to me. All that does matter is that you agree to be my wife."

How easy it would be to accept his offer. Marrying Waring might even ameliorate some of the damage done to her reputation by the scandal rag. She cared for the marquess. He had saved her from misery, regardless of the reason, and she would forever be grateful to him for that.

But she didn't love him.

She swallowed hard against a rush of searing misery so acute that it nearly choked her. "I'm in love with someone else."

He rocked back as if she had struck him. "You're in love with him?"

"With Whitby," she clarified, sniffling. "Almost everything printed in that wretched article is true. So, you see, I cannot accept your proposal of marriage, but I do thank you for it. Just as I thank you for caring for me as you have. For saving me from my marriage to Ammondale. For your friendship."

Her voice broke on the last word.

Friends was all that they could ever be. And she hated seeing the hurt on his face now, the disillusionment in his eyes.

"You can be in love with another and marry me," he said quietly. "My love for you has not changed, nor has my offer. Be my wife. We can journey to America together. Start a new life."

She closed her eyes tightly, shaking her head as fresh tears squeezed free and ran hotly down her cheeks. "No, I cannot. I'm sorry, Waring. So sorry."

His hand tightened on hers. "I'm sorry too. I hope he makes you happy. If he doesn't, he'll answer to me."

Miranda opened her eyes, frowning. "You misunderstand. I'm not marrying Whitby either. He hasn't asked, nor do I expect that he will. Our arrangement is at an end."

"Then he's a damned fool, Ran."

In that moment, Miranda was rather certain that she was the fool, for falling in love with a man who would never love her in return. A dashing, beautiful rake who had shown her the depths of pleasure and stolen her heart in the process.

By the time Rhys reached Miranda's narrow house, he was nearly mad. He had gone directly to her school, dismayed to find it deserted. Although he knew she was meant to be teaching a class today, there appeared to be neither pupils nor anyone else about, the front door solidly barred. He had returned to his carriage and given his coachman her direction, not knowing where else she could possibly be.

His overactive mind tormented him with hideous scenarios the whole bloody way there. There were thoughts of Miranda running away with the Marquess of Waring. Her in Waring's arms. Waring daring to kiss her, to touch her. Worst, Miranda telling Waring that she loved him and that she had been awaiting his return so she could confess her feelings.

The carriage had not even come to a complete halt before he vaulted from it, rushing along the pavements until he reached the front door. He didn't even bother to catch his breath before knocking.

No answer.

He rapped again, his knuckles smarting from the effort he put into it.

Where was she? He had to find her. To tell her that he loved her. To ask her to marry him before it was too late and she eloped with that milksop marquess.

"Miranda," he called out, not caring if he made a scene for her neighbors to overhear.

Let them. Likely all London knew by now that she had been sharing his bed for the last five weeks. The damage had already been done.

The door jerked open suddenly, and there she stood, heartachingly beautiful but pale, her cheeks tearstained, her green eyes rendered even more vibrant by her bloodshot eyes. He hated the evidence of her sadness. Hated knowing he was likely the cause of it.

"Miranda," he breathed, reaching for her. "You've been weeping."

"Rhys." She frowned, taking a step in retreat. "What are you doing here?"

"I'm hoping I might explain inside rather than out in the street," he said wryly, his gaze devouring her.

How had it only been a day since he had seen her last? It felt more like a year.

Her frown deepened. "I cannot think it wise. I've already told you, our arrangement is over."

"I would like a new arrangement with you," he told her.

She shook her head. "I do not dare after all the damage that has been done to my reputation. Have you not heard about the gossip rag?"

"I have." He ground his jaw against a rush of righteous anger. "And I'm sorry for it. I promise you that I'll find whoever was responsible and make the bastard pay."

"You should go." She began to close the door on him.

He wedged his booted foot solidly in the jamb. "Not until you let me in."

"Rhys," she hissed, her nostrils flaring. "You are causing a scene."

He held her gaze, determined. "Only think of the scene I'll cause when I'm forced to climb your house and break in to one of your windows."

"You wouldn't dare."

He raised a brow, unflinching. "Oh, but I would, darling."

He would do anything he had to do. Anything to rectify the wrong he had done, the damage he had caused her reputation. Anything to make amends for his colossal stupidity.

At last, and with a huffed sigh of irritation, she pulled the door back open and moved to allow him entrée. "Very well. If you insist."

"I do." He strode over the threshold and kicked the door shut, all the courtly charm completely gone from him now. He was nothing but raw, burning emotion as he took her cool hands in his. "The new arrangement I want with you is marriage."

Her lips parted. "What?"

"I want to marry you, Miranda. I want to be your husband, and I want you as my wife."

The words felt so thoroughly right as they left him.

"You're only saying this because of that dreadful article and the scandal," she said, tearing her hands from his and moving away. "I'll not have your pity, Rhys. It is worse than your disdain."

How wrong she was. He would show her. Prove it to her.

Rhys followed, reaching for her again, this time taking her waist in his hands and pulling her against him. "I'm not saying it because I pity you or because of that bloody gossip rag. I'm saying it because I love you, Miranda Lenox. I love your stubborn determination to succeed, your dauntless fearlessness, your passion, and your talent. I love your courage and your compassion, your laughter and your smile. I love your hair and your nose and your emerald eyes, and I love your sinful mouth and your delicious breasts and your perfectly formed bottom and your—"

"Madam?"

The shrill voice of Miranda's maid of all work intruded quite rudely on Rhys's declaration. He turned to the unsmiling woman with a frown of his own.

"That will be all," he said with a grin. "If your mistress needs you, she will ring the bellpull."

Miranda nodded, her eyes never leaving his. "Yes, White. Please do go. All is well."

The older woman bobbed in a curtsy, her expression made of stone, and fled in a flap of dun skirts.

"Do you mean it?" Miranda asked when the servant had once more disappeared.

He cupped her cheek. "Well, I wasn't nearly finished when I was interrupted. There was more."

"There was?"

"Yes, but I've forgotten it," he admitted. "I feel reasonably certain it had something to do with your responsive nipples."

"Rhys," she scolded, smiling through the chastisement. "You are positively scandalous."

"And so are you. We are well matched, you and I. So you see, that is why we should wed." He caressed the elegant sweep of her cheekbone with his thumb. "That and the fact that I love you. Have I mentioned it?"

Her eyes glistened with unshed tears. "You love me? How? Do you mean it?"

"Of course I mean it. I'm sorry I was too bloody stupid to realize it until it was too late and I caused you to be the subject of gossip yet again." Guilt lodged in his throat, making his voice go thick. "I would do anything to undo the damage I've caused."

She shook her head. "The damage is every bit as much my fault as yours. I knew the risks and decided the reward was worth it."

"Why?" he asked softly, needing to know.

Needing to hear her say the words. Praying he wasn't wrong and that she loved him, not anyone else.

"Because I love you," she said.

"Not Warting?" he asked.

"Rhys, you know that isn't his name."

"Yes," he countered determinedly. "It is and forever shall be. I don't like him."

"He has been a good friend to me, helping me to obtain the divorce from Ammondale through great harm to his own reputation. All the world believes him an adulterer when he's not. The two of us were never lovers."

"And so he can continue to be a good friend," he growled.

"From another bloody continent. Now, say it again, if you please."

She smiled. "I love you."

"And?"

"And I'll marry you."

"Thank God." He kissed her then, tasting the salt of her tears and the sweetness that was simply Miranda before breaking away again to gaze down at her. "I am going to make this right, my love. I swear it to you."

"We will be together," she said softly. "Nothing else matters."

"But your school. I know how important it is to you, how hard you've worked to grow it."

Her smile turned a bit wistful. "Perhaps I can rebuild it one day. Perhaps not."

"But you've been crying over it."

"Silly." She sniffed. "It was you I was crying about. Throwing you over was the most difficult decision I've ever made."

He thought of the hated letter he had abandoned in his study and how he would enjoy finally pitching it into the flames later.

"Why did you?" Rhys asked.

"Because you said you never wanted to marry. I thought there was no hope of a future for the two of us."

To think how close he had come to almost losing her. *Never again*, he vowed.

"I'm an arse," he said. "Do you forgive me?"

"Only if you forgive me."

"Done." He kissed her swiftly before withdrawing and taking her hand in his. "Now, come with me, if you please."

"Where are we going?" she asked as he led her to the stairs.

Rhys grinned at her. "To your bedroom. Since we've

already scandalized all of London, we may as well do what we wish, and right now, there isn't a thing in the world that this wicked duke would like to do more than ravish his wicked duchess-to-be."

Hand in hand, they ascended the narrow staircase to her waiting bedroom.

And some time shortly thereafter, the ravishing commenced.

EPILOGUE

ONE YEAR LATER

"**G**entle reader, it is the humble opinion of this scribe that the scandal concerning the Duchess of W. was, in truth, naught but lies perpetuated by a bitter Lord A.," Miranda read triumphantly as she pored over the latest edition of the gossip rag that had, a mere year ago, nearly proven her ruin.

A gossip rag that had, instead of destroying her happiness, been inadvertently responsible for helping her to secure it. She very much doubted Ammondale would appreciate the role he had played in her marriage to Rhys. But she couldn't lie—there was a certain, profound pleasure to be had in knowing she had triumphed in the end.

Rhys kissed her nape. "Do continue, kitten. I can see there's quite a bit more to it, and I rather like the sound of this. There's nothing I can appreciate more than the Earl of Ammondale getting his comeuppance and my beautiful wife receiving the adulation she so rightly deserves."

She sighed contentedly and leaned into his tall, muscled form, the undeniable ridge of his cock against her bottom a potent lure. "Meanwhile, the new school of cookery recently opened by the Duchess of W. continues to attract far more pupils than it can reasonably hold."

Rhys nuzzled her throat as she paused to once again savor his attentions.

"The Duchess's School of Cookery is going to need to expand to the neighboring property soon," he murmured before nibbling at her ear.

"Do you truly think so?" she asked, delighted by the notion, even as desire shimmered through her.

The sinful man knew her ears were indecently sensitive. A bit of licking and nipping on his part was all it took to make molten heat pool between her thighs.

"I know so," he said.

Miranda had closed the Lenox School of Cookery following the scandal that had robbed her of pupils. But with Rhys's help, she had found a far more convenient location in a larger and newer building. The new school, complete with a fresh name, had a massive room that could be used for lectures or cooking demonstrations, complete with multiple stoves and four immense tables that stretched its length, allowing plenty of room for the pupils who had slowly begun filling the benches. It had taken effort and time, but they had turned opinion in her favor, thanks to their marriage and the support of those closest to them.

"Thank you for believing in me," she told her husband.

"You know you needn't thank me for that. Your skill is unparalleled, my love. You've more than earned your sobriquet the Queen of Cookery." He kissed the hollow behind her ear now, his hands gliding to cup her breasts through the gossamer fabric of her French peignoir.

How she adored lazy mornings when they stayed in their bedchamber and spent hours taking their breakfast in private, talking, bathing, making love, or, as was the case today, reading the scandal rags and newspapers. The rain was pattering lightly on the windows, and all was right in their little world.

"I suppose you were right to call me your queen," she said lightly.

"I do know a queen when I see one." He licked the shell of her ear, eliciting a pang of desire.

She smiled. "So modest, husband."

"Modesty was never one of my virtues." He kissed her temple, inhaling deeply. "Mmm. Have I told you that I adore your scent?"

"Perhaps a time or two," she murmured, enjoying his praise, regardless of how many times she was the recipient of it.

Just as he was a very attentive lover, Rhys had proven to be a most devoted husband. Their marriage was so very different from the icy, miserable union she had escaped with Ammondale. She was grateful each day that she had found the husband of her heart, a man who loved her for herself, imperfect as she was.

He rolled his thumbs over the peaks of her breasts. Her nipples were hard, and his touch felt so wonderful that it took her a moment to recall she had been reading the article to him.

"The rest of the article, darling," he reminded her, plucking at her nipples some more.

Clearing her throat, she continued. "Undoubtedly, the Duchess of W.'s coterie of loyal friends, the Duchesses of B. and C., in particular, and their insurmountable support has proven a boon, as has the more recent praise of her newly married sister."

"I am glad that Daisy has broken with your family and spoke up on your behalf," Rhys said, his hands slipping lower now, to where her full belly stretched beneath the transparent cotton and silk.

"I am as well," she agreed.

Miranda had never blamed her sisters for the estrangement between them following her divorce. They had been under the aegis of their mother and father, with no ability to speak for themselves. With Daisy married, she had finally been free to pay a call upon Miranda, and the two of them had taken tea together for the first time in years, sharing girlhood reminiscences and forging their sisterly bond anew.

She hoped that when Elizabeth married, it would be the same between them, but Miranda was firm in her determination to keep the distance between herself, her parents, and her brother. Not all fences could be mended.

A thump on her stomach distracted Miranda momentarily from her thoughts, the miracle of the small life within her still a source of wonder.

"Did you feel that?" she asked Rhys.

"I do believe our child has just kicked me," he said, and she could hear the grin in his voice. "The rest of the article, if you please, whilst I mend my shattered pride."

Miranda smiled, filled with love so strong she had to blink, lest tears of happiness begin to fall. These days, she tended to turn into a watering pot at the slightest provocation.

"However," she carried on reading, "the hundreds of testimonials from loyal pupils and the delicacies which the duchess has shared in her most recent *Book of Cookery*, which is on its third printing as of this writing, are ample proof that the Duchess of W. is indeed the reigning Queen of Cookery."

"*Brava*, my love." Gently, he turned her so that she faced him, his expression full of so much tenderness that she blinked again, clearing a fresh wave of tears. "You're not weeping again, are you? What is wrong? Do you not like the article?"

"I love the article."

"Then why tears?"

"Because I love you," she sniffled. "And because I could not possibly be happier."

"I love you too, kitten."

A tear rolled down her cheek, and he caught it with his lips.

"I even love it when you call me kitten," she said with another sniff, maudlin sentiment threatening to overwhelm her, along with the desire that was never far.

"That is because everything I say and do is irresistible," he informed her.

"Outrageous man," she said without heat. "How did I ever find you?"

"Well, my love," he began in a teasing drawl, "this love affair of ours all began because I wanted to eat your ices. Now, I'm more than happy to eat your—"

Laughing, Miranda devoured his last word, which would have undoubtedly been vulgar, sealing her mouth over his and kissing her wicked duke with all the love overflowing in her heart.

THANK you so very much for reading *Duke with a Secret*! I adored Rhys and Miranda so much, and I hope you did too. To learn a bit about the inspiration behind Miranda, check out my Author's Note. And do read on for a sneak peek of *Duke with a Lie* (Wicked Dukes Society Book 4), featuring the rebellious Lady Rhiannon Northwick and her brother's best friend, the smoldering Duke of Richford. And don't miss my next entry in the Christmas Dukes series, the stand-alone enemies-to-lovers HEA between a proper duke and a wild American heiress in *The Duke Who Ruined Christmas*.

Please stay in touch! The only way to be sure you'll know

what's next from me is to sign up for my newsletter here: http://eepurl.com/dyJSar. Please join my reader group for early excerpts, cover reveals, and more here: https://www. facebook.com/groups/scarlettscottreaders. And if you're in the mood to chat all things steamy historical romance and read a different book together each month, join my book club, Dukes Do It Hotter right here: https://www.facebook. com/groups/hotdukes because we're having a whole lot of fun!

Now, do read on for that sneak peek of *Duke with a Lie* I promised...

Duke with a Lie

As heartless as he is handsome, Aubrey Villiers, the Duke of Richford, has perfected the art of not caring one whit about anything except his pursuit of pleasure. His past is as dark as his moods, and the rumors about his curious carnal needs would make any proper innocent miss swoon.

Lady Rhiannon Northwick, however, is anything but proper. And as for her innocence? She has a plan in mind to rid herself of that rather nettlesome inconvenience. Infiltrating the sinful house party hosted by her older brother is easy. Seducing his good friend, the brooding Duke of Richford, proves far more difficult.

Although Richford may be a conscienceless rake, he isn't about to deflower the stubborn hellion who tempts him at every turn, regardless of how badly he wants to. Rhiannon, who has long harbored a secret *tendre* for the duke, is equally determined to change his mind.

Torn between his demons, his loyalties, and the last woman on earth he should desire, Richford is faced with an impossible choice—sever all ties with Rhiannon for her own sake, or risk the deadly past repeating itself once again.

. . .

Chapter One

AUBREY VILLIERS, seventh Duke of Richford, had committed an untold number of sins in his life, all of which would be responsible for one day sending him to Hades where he belonged. It was glaringly apparent, given the most unfortunate and present state of his cock, that he was about to add one more to the ever-growing compendium—lusting after his close friend's virginal younger sister.

Lady Rhiannon Northwick was a gorgeous, annoying hellion, and one day, some man would have the colossal fortune of bedding her. But that man would not be—could not be—Aubrey. There seemed no better occasion for reminding himself of that than as he dragged the troublesome minx from a game of naughty charades at a country house party where she decidedly had *not* been invited.

"What do you think you are doing, sirrah?" she growled at him *sotto voce*, tugging at her arm in an effort to escape.

She wasn't going to escape him, however. He was stronger than she was. Wiser than she was. Far more jaded than she was. And he was more determined than she was, too.

Aubrey pulled her down the hall in search of an empty private salon. "Rescuing you, little naif."

As much as the villain in him would have dearly loved to continue watching her parade her saucy curves about whilst she pretended to be a wanton shepherdess in desperate need of a sound shag, he knew better.

He very much doubted she even understood what the phrase *in need of a shag* meant. The urge to show her was strong, which was more proof of just how bloody evil he was. Depraved to his core.

Aubrey paused at a closed door and knocked loudly, issuing a stern rap of his knuckles on the paneled mahogany. When no answer came, he turned the latch, only to find a couple within, the woman bent over a settee, skirts and petticoats up to her waist, whilst her gentleman friend rammed his cock into her with furious abandon from behind.

"Damn it," he muttered, slamming the door and turning to scowl at his unwilling companion. "You didn't see that, did you?"

"See what?" she asked, pouting. "This is outrageous. You must unhand me and allow me to return to the games at once. I demand it."

"Oh, you *demand* it, do you?" Chuckling darkly, he found the next room blessedly empty and crossed the threshold, pulling her with him.

"Yes, I do." She tossed her head in defiance, and her unbound golden curls shook with indignation, emphasizing the unparalleled beauty of her hair. "You are treating me as if I'm a piece of furniture, and I do not appreciate it."

"A piece of furniture wouldn't find a way of stealing into a house party for which she received no invite, my lady." He snapped the door closed and locked it, pocketing the key before he turned back to her, releasing his hold on her arm at last.

Which was just as well, for he was far too tempted to jerk her luscious form into his chest and kiss that sulking mouth of hers.

"Of course I was invited," she lied, blue eyes blazing from behind her mask. "Why else would I be here?"

"Because you are a wayward hoyden." He crossed his arms over his chest, unimpressed.

The hellion had found herself in many scrapes over the years since she'd made her debut in society. But sneaking into an impending orgy was rather bold, even by her astounding standards.

"You do not even know me," Rhiannon huffed. "I am masked."

Of course he knew her. God, how well he knew her. And how he wished he knew her better, but that was a damned stupid thought his puerile prick wanted him to entertain. Aubrey's half-cockstand didn't know that touching Lady Rhiannon Northwick was the rough equivalent of consuming a platter of poisonous wild mushrooms. The rest of him, however, was too intelligent for such tomfoolery.

He cocked his head now, considering her, trying to keep his gaze from the lush breasts her scandalously cut gown put on proud display. "How charmingly innocent. You truly supposed that donning a scrap of silk would shield you well enough, didn't you?"

A flush crept over her throat, giving her away. "Everyone else is masked as well."

"The illusion of anonymity pleases some more than it does others," he offered with a careless shrug.

"What does that mean?"

"It means that a mask cannot hide anyone. It means that the members of this club wear masks at gatherings such as this for titillation as much as preserving privacy."

That much was true. Oh, he had no doubt some of the lords and ladies in attendance—all members of the highly secret Wicked Dukes Society, over which he presided with his five friends, the dukes of Brandon, Camden, Whitby, Riverdale, and Kingham—were either too obtuse or too deep in their cups to recognize each other. But for anyone with a discerning eye or ear, a mask provided no barrier at all.

Aubrey was reasonably certain Rhiannon could walk about with a sack over her head and he would still know her. She could hide in another room and the faintest strain of her husky voice would give her away. Even her scent lingering after she had gone would be sufficient—rose and bergamot with a hint of ambergris. He had taken note of everything where she was concerned.

Far too much.

But Aubrey didn't dally with innocents. And he didn't bed his good chum's innocent sister. Not even a golden goddess who put Venus to shame and possessed a tendency to stare at him as if she wanted to devour him. *Especially* not her.

Wilt, cock, he inwardly urged that unruly appendage. *Wilt.*

"For…titillation," she repeated, her eyes narrowing, as if she didn't believe him.

Christ. He should not explain himself to Whit's little sister. And Aubrey most assuredly should not allow his gaze to slip to her decolletage or to wonder if a hasty tug of her pink silk bodice would release her equally pink nipples.

He clenched his jaw, fighting for inner composure for a moment. "Yes, titillation, my lady. You see, some prefer the pretense they do not know their lovers. For them, it heightens the pleasure. Others may fear repercussions with husbands, wives, or polite society should word of their transgressions reach the gossipmongers. They cling to their masks for fear of discovery. Either way, no one is fooling anyone else. Least of all, you."

Rhiannon blinked, her full lips parting, the lower caught by white, even teeth. "Me? Forgive me if I fail to believe your bluster, sir. You claim to know who I am, and yet you have yet to say my name. Perhaps you've mistaken me for another. Either way, I can assure you that you haven't the right to pull me bodily from the drawing room and lock me up inside this room with you."

She had the audacity to punctuate her diatribe by holding out her hand, palm up. "The key, if you please."

Aubrey reached up to his own mask, untying it and

pulling it away from his face. "On that, I fear we must disagree, Lady Rhiannon. I have *every* right to keep you here, safe, in this room. Your brother would expect no less from me, and when I inform him of your presence here, I have no doubt he'll send you back to London and your mama where you belong. The reckoning for you will be harsh, I'm sure."

Her shoulders sagged, and the defeat in her jaw and eyes made something within him clench. "How did you know?"

I would know you anywhere, he thought before tamping down all such ridiculous notions.

Aubrey shrugged again, one shoulder only this time. "As I said, brat. Masks mean nothing. Did you not recognize me?"

"Of course I did."

He raised an imperious brow. "Well, then. Why should the reverse be any different?"

"Because you don't notice me. You never have. You don't even know I'm *alive*, and now you have seized my one and only adventure and seek to ruin it utterly."

How wrong she was. He *did* notice her. From the moment she'd become a woman, making her curtsy, flitting about ballrooms, he had been irritatingly aware of her. Not just her beauty, but her stubborn nature, her ludicrous bravado, her laughter, her smile.

Fucking hell. He had to stop this maudlin nonsense at once.

"I notice what happens here, within these walls," he said smoothly, because lying was far more comfortable than speaking plain truth. "As one of the founding members of the club, doing so is my duty. And as your brother's close and enduring friend, it is also my obligation to take note when his naïve, wayward sister somehow manages to all but ruin herself. To step in before it's too late."

She scowled, the pink mask she wore which matched her

gown so perfectly still in place and obstructing his view of her lovely face.

Which was for the best, really.

The mask was silly.

Lady Rhiannon Northwick was anything but. Therein lay the danger. To him, to her, to everyone who mattered.

"I am not your obligation or anyone else's," she snapped at him, planting her hands on her nipped waist. "And nor am I naïve or wayward. I am simply in search of a future of my own, to experience life as I choose."

A bitter laugh tore from him. "My dear little naif, there is no future at all to be found at these fêtes. Not for you. Nor for anyone else. These house parties are intended for sin the likes of which a virginal miss such as yourself cannot possibly fathom."

It was the wrong thing to say to a stubborn hoyden, as it turned out. Lady Rhiannon Northwick couldn't resist a challenge. He recognized that in her—so much of himself when he had been younger, before darkness had consumed him.

Her irresistible, dented chin went up. "I can fathom a great deal, Your Grace."

"Not what happens within these walls, I can assure you of that."

"I've read books."

"No book could aptly describe pleasure. Not truly."

Renewed color appeared over her pale throat and chest, almost reaching the tempting swells of her breasts. "I do know about it."

He moved toward her, some impulse he could neither define nor deny rising. "You know about what, little naif?"

"Don't call me that."

"It's what you are, is it not?"

"No!"

He stopped before her, and dear God, the headiness of

her scent and nearness was an intoxicating combination that not even opium could rival. "Then tell me. What do you read about in your books?"

It was a question he shouldn't ask.

Just as lingering here with her was a foolish risk he should not take.

And yet Aubrey stayed, awaiting her response. Needing it more than his next breath.

"About…about lovemaking and what happens between a man and a woman," she said breathlessly.

And his stupid cock, which had begun to settle, twitched back to life.

Such words alone were paltry. They meant nothing. Issued in her sultry voice, however? They meant everything.

Aubrey cleared his throat. "You've been reading vulgar books?"

"*Books*, yes," she corrected with a prim air that had no place coupled with what she had just said. "*Not* vulgar, however."

Damn it all, *why*? Why did she have to make such an inappropriate admission, and why did it have to affect him so?

He had to get her out of this bloody house party.

Out of this room.

Out of his reach.

"Ah, yes. Not vulgar at all. Would you care to repeat what you just explained to your brother?" he asked cruelly.

"It is none of Rhys's concern what I read," she snapped.

"Because you know he wouldn't approve."

Her nostrils flared. "Because I am a woman grown."

He raised a brow and raked her over with a wilting gaze. "Are you? Because I do confess, you look rather like a girl playing at being a woman just now."

For a moment, he thought she might slap him.

But instead, she did the opposite.

Lady Rhiannon Northwick took one step forward, her pink evening gown slamming into his trousers, billowing outward, and then she grabbed his necktie and tugged him toward her. In the next second, her lips were on his.

And Aubrey?

He was bloody *lost*.

Lost in her hot, silken lips. Lost in her curves melding into his hard frame, lost in her scent, in her breasts crushing into his chest, in the way she fit against him, as perfectly as if she'd been made to do so. Aubrey had no choice but to kiss her back with all the suppressed desire within him…

Fuck.

This wasn't going to end well.

Want more? Get *Duke with a Lie* now!

AUTHOR'S NOTE

Agnes B. Marshall, who was a successful Victorian entrepreneur, served as my inspiration for Miranda. The fascinating Marshall ran her own culinary school, published books containing her recipes, went on speaking engagements, and even sold branded appliances and products, such as cabinet refrigerators, patented ice caves, ice breakers, syrups, food colors, and more. She built a truly impressive empire. All the ice confections Miranda creates and the dishes referenced can be found in *Fancy Ices* by Mrs. A.B. Marshall and *Mrs. A.B. Marshall's Cookery Book*.

DON'T MISS SCARLETT'S OTHER ROMANCES!

Complete Book List
HISTORICAL ROMANCE

Heart's Temptation
A Mad Passion (Book One)
Rebel Love (Book Two)
Reckless Need (Book Three)
Sweet Scandal (Book Four)
Restless Rake (Book Five)
Darling Duke (Book Six)
The Night Before Scandal (Book Seven)

Wicked Husbands
Her Errant Earl (Book One)
Her Lovestruck Lord (Book Two)
Her Reformed Rake (Book Three)
Her Deceptive Duke (Book Four)
Her Missing Marquess (Book Five)
Her Virtuous Viscount (Book Six)

Wicked Dukes Society
Duke with a Reputation (Book One)
Duke with a Debt (Book Two)
Duke with a Secret (Book Three)
Duke with a Lie (Book Four)

Christmas Dukes
The Duke Who Despised Christmas (Book One)
The Duke Who Ruined Christmas (Book Two)

League of Dukes
Nobody's Duke (Book One)
Heartless Duke (Book Two)
Dangerous Duke (Book Three)
Shameless Duke (Book Four)
Scandalous Duke (Book Five)
Fearless Duke (Book Six)

Notorious Ladies of London
Lady Ruthless (Book One)
Lady Wallflower (Book Two)
Lady Reckless (Book Three)
Lady Wicked (Book Four)
Lady Lawless (Book Five)
Lady Brazen (Book 6)

Unexpected Lords
The Detective Duke (Book One)
The Playboy Peer (Book Two)
The Millionaire Marquess (Book Three)
The Goodbye Governess (Book Four)

Dukes Most Wanted
Forever Her Duke (Book One)

Forever Her Marquess (Book Two)
Forever Her Rake (Book Three)
Forever Her Earl (Book Four)
Forever Her Viscount (Book Five)
Forever Her Scot (Book Six)

The Wicked Winters
Wicked in Winter (Book One)
Wedded in Winter (Book Two)
Wanton in Winter (Book Three)
Wishes in Winter (Book 3.5)
Willful in Winter (Book Four)
Wagered in Winter (Book Five)
Wild in Winter (Book Six)
Wooed in Winter (Book Seven)
Winter's Wallflower (Book Eight)
Winter's Woman (Book Nine)
Winter's Whispers (Book Ten)
Winter's Waltz (Book Eleven)
Winter's Widow (Book Twelve)
Winter's Warrior (Book Thirteen)
A Merry Wicked Winter (Book Fourteen)

The Sinful Suttons
Sutton's Spinster (Book One)
Sutton's Sins (Book Two)
Sutton's Surrender (Book Three)
Sutton's Seduction (Book Four)
Sutton's Scoundrel (Book Five)
Sutton's Scandal (Book Six)
Sutton's Secrets (Book Seven)

Rogue's Guild
Her Ruthless Duke (Book One)

Her Dangerous Beast (Book Two)
Her Wicked Rogue (Book 3)

Royals and Renegades
How to Love a Dangerous Rogue (Book One)
How to Tame a Dissolute Prince (Book Two)

Sins and Scoundrels
Duke of Depravity
Prince of Persuasion
Marquess of Mayhem
Sarah
Earl of Every Sin
Duke of Debauchery
Viscount of Villainy

Sins and Scoundrels Box Set Collections
Volume 1
Volume 2

The Wicked Winters Box Set Collections
Collection 1
Collection 2
Collection 3
Collection 4

Wicked Husbands Box Set Collections
Volume 1
Volume 2

Notorious Ladies of London Box Set Collections
Volume 1
Volume 2

The Sinful Suttons Box Set Collections
Volume 1
Volume 2

Stand-alone Novella
Lord of Pirates

CONTEMPORARY ROMANCE
Love's Second Chance
Reprieve (Book One)
Perfect Persuasion (Book Two)
Win My Love (Book Three)

Coastal Heat
Loved Up (Book One)

ABOUT THE AUTHOR

USA Today and Amazon bestselling author Scarlett Scott™ writes steamy Victorian and Regency romance with strong, intelligent heroines and sexy alpha heroes. She lives in Pennsylvania and Maryland with her Canadian husband, their adorable identical twins, a demanding diva of a dog, and a zany cat who showed up one summer and never left.

A self-professed literary junkie and nerd, she loves reading anything, but especially romance novels and poetry. Catch up with her on her website https://scarlettscottauthor.com. Hearing from readers never fails to make her day.

Scarlett's complete book list and information about upcoming releases can be found at https://scarlettscottauthor.com.

Connect with Scarlett! You can find her here:
    Join Scarlett Scott's reader group on Facebook for early excerpts, giveaways, and a whole lot of fun!
    Sign up for her newsletter here
    https://www.tiktok.com/@authorscarlettscott

facebook.com/AuthorScarlettScott

x.com/scarscoromance

instagram.com/scarlettscottauthor

bookbub.com/authors/scarlett-scott

amazon.com/Scarlett-Scott/e/B004NW8N2I

pinterest.com/scarlettscott

Printed in Dunstable, United Kingdom

67135373R00197